DUEL OF ASSASSINS

Also by Daniel Pollock

Lair of the Fox

DUEL OF ASSASSINS

DANIEL POLLOCK

POCKET BOOKS

New York   London   Toronto   Sydney   Tokyo   Singapore

The line from the *Hagakure* is quoted from *The Way of the Samurai* by Yukio Mishima, translated by Kathryn Sparling, copyright © 1977, Basic Books, Inc., New York.

This book is a work of fiction. Names, characters, places and incidents are either the product of the author's imagination or are used fictitiously. Any resemblance to actual events or locales or persons, living or dead, is entirely coincidental.

POCKET BOOKS, a division of Simon & Schuster
1230 Avenue of the Americas, New York, NY 10020

Pollock, Daniel, 1944–
   Duel of assassins / Daniel Pollock.
     p. cm.
   ISBN 0-671-70578-4 : $18.95
   I. Title.
PS3566.O5346D8   1991
813'.54—dc20

90-47944
CIP

First Pocket Books hardcover printing April 1991

10 9 8 7 6 5 4 3 2 1

POCKET and colophon are registered trademarks of
Simon & Schuster

Printed in the U.S.A.

For Constance, my darling wife

Acknowledgments

This novel and its writer owe a considerable debt to the following:

for making it all possible, Angela Rinaldi;
for making it happen, Jed Mattes and Bill Grose;
for editorial acumen and persistence, Dudley Frasier;
for unflagging collegial support, Douglas Clegg;
for structural insight and tutorial zeal, James Sewell;
for guidance in Soviet matters, Paul Goldberg;
and for invaluable technical assistance, Lieutenant Colonel Harold Barr, USAF (Ret.), Kenneth Goddard, David and Marie-Luise Pal, and Ted Zahorbenski.

"The only tough part is the
finding out what you're good for."

—Owen Wister, *The Virginian*

DUEL OF
ASSASSINS

Prologue

HE WASN'T SURE WHETHER HE WAS IN HIDING, OR EARLY retirement. He'd led an active, Odyssean life. Dropout and hitchhiker at seventeen, carnival roustabout at eighteen, blue-water sailor and international vagabond at nineteen. Then, by dizzying turns in his twenties, he became a political defector, special forces commando, assassin, and fugitive.

Now, in his mid-thirties, youth's roller-coaster ride seemed pretty well over. It had deposited him on a tranquil Alpine lake—a still-young man with an incredible past and no discernible future. And with nothing to do on this cloudless morning but guide a slightly-bigger-than-bathtub-size sailboat across sparkling sapphire water in a sigh of wind.

Or maybe blow his brains out.

Or start all over.

Another possibility was that someone would track him down and blow his brains out for him, or—more exotically—jab him in the buttocks with a poison-tipped umbrella.

A final one was that there would come one last summons from the General. But that possibility was daily diminishing. The General, exiled

1

and apparently under virtual camp arrest, continued to concoct his grand plans and promulgate them along his secret network, but the time to act on those plans was rapidly slipping past. The General was on the point of becoming a relic, ending up very much as had old Chiang Kai-shek on his tiny island, shaking a withered fist at the mainland colossus. Events were passing the old soldier by. The summons must come soon, or not at all.

And if it did not come, the still-young man would have to think seriously and quickly about turning his hand to something new. Or, more likely, set about marketing his hard-won lethal skills, since he didn't fancy being a hired yachtsman again and couldn't imagine working indoors.

In harmony with these mental meanderings, he tacked the tiny boat lazily back and forth across the rippled mirror of Lake Lugano on the Swiss-Italian frontier. Each swing of the little boom and windslap of miniature mainsail carried him a bit nearer the spot from which he'd pushed off an hour before—the steeply terraced, picturebook village of Gandria at the foot of Monte Brè, five kilometers east of the town of Lugano.

The final tack fetched him perilously near the seawall windward of his *albergo,* before he rounded dead into the wind, then backed the main and used the rudder in reverse to drift back slowly under the corrugated tin roof of the ramshackle quay. The hot-dog landing was completely wasted on a pair of muscular, Nordic-looking girls waiting impatiently to take the boat out. One of them grabbed the bow line from him as he stepped off.

"Sie kamen dreizehn Minuten zu spät!" she said, poking her sport-watch. "You are late thirdeen minutes!"

"Sorry, ladies. Ran into some nasty weather out there." He smiled as he trotted past them up the half-dozen steps to the *albergo*'s terrace. He settled at an empty table, extending his long, bare legs to a nearby plastic chair and was presently provided his standard morning fare—cappuccino, roll, and the *International Herald-Tribune* printed in Zürich.

Whatever he was doing in Lugano, he really oughtn't complain. The morning sunlight was a benediction, the onshore breeze fanned him attentively, the terrace was bright with flower boxes, and a sparrow on the railing was eyeing his breakfast cheerfully. The only imperfection was a wet itch under his bathing suit from sitting too long on a waterlogged boat cushion.

He folded the newspaper back to the sports pages. Another baseball season was under way. He hadn't seen a game in nearly twenty years, yet it was still comforting to scan the agate-type hieroglyphs of standings and box scores, old teams with new players, all conjuring the slow summer game.

With less enthusiasm he flipped back to the headlines. The world had changed so drastically in recent years that his long-ago defection now seemed almost quaint. The East-West twain and European powers were getting ready to meet again in mid-July, he saw, at yet another symbolic site—Potsdam, where the Allies had assembled in '45 to divide the defeated Germany. The ongoing wrangle over European realignment was expected to top the agenda, with everyone scrambling for a piece of the big new pie.

He was skimming the tedious story when the breeze riffled several pages and his eye was caught by a by-line on an opinion piece. Charlotte Walsh was a Washington-based columnist specializing in foreign affairs. She was also an attractive lady whom he'd spotted several times on a correspondents' roundup shown on CNN's European feed. He'd paid special attention because his contacts told him she was presently sleeping with an old rival. Small-world department.

She, too, was writing about Potsdam:

WASHINGTON—In the aftermath of yesterday's surprise announcement that Potsdam's Cecilienhof Palace is going to be dusted off for the next round of multinational summitry, perhaps a few random observations and speculations may be indulged. One wonders, for instance, if the Soviet members of the selection committee somehow prevailed over their North American and European counterparts. For Soviet President Alois Rybkin is known to have a certain affinity for style and symbol, and he might have seen in Potsdam the possibility of securing a kind of historic home-court advantage.

It was, after all, a Russian leader—albeit a bloody and infamous one— who made the unlikely choice of the old Prussian capital for the post-World War II conference. And it was over the Cecilienhof's red baize table that the Nazi Reich was subsequently carved up almost precisely along the dotted lines laid down by that leader, Josef Stalin.

Approaching a half-century later, that postwar dismemberment has been pretty well sutured back together. But it will be an equally critical operation that brings the heads of state together over the table at Potsdam—no less than the redefining of Europe, and the Soviet place therein.

Naturally, Rybkin, beleaguered at home and abroad, seeks immediate access to the emergent colossus, as he has made abundantly clear with his own series of somewhat amorphous Greater Europe initiatives. To be left out at this critical nexus of European history could well mean a political death sentence for the Soviet leader—and, more important, an economic one for his country.

Yet, ironically compounding his personal dilemma, Rybkin may face political doom whatever the outcome at Potsdam. For Soviet participation in the expanding Europe would doubtless entail the relinquishing of a goodly measure of national sovereignty—a price exacted with varying degrees of predictable political agony from all signers-on. But the hard-line factions of Mother Russia, having been dragged kicking and screaming so far down westward paths in recent years, seem to have dug in their collective heels very deeply over this issue of sovereignty, and Alois Rybkin well knows it.

Indeed, it will be a very high-stakes game later this summer at Potsdam, and the canny Soviet leader will have three-hundred million kibitzers massed close behind him, second-guessing his every hand—

"Un altro cappuccino, Signore?"

"Nò, Tino, grazie." He put some coins down, folded the paper, and left the terrace. An ornamental but infirm iron staircase led steeply over an arcaded alleyway to his room, affording a brief view of pastel tiers of houses stacked skyward like stone and stucco cliff dwellings. Inside his room, across the tile floor and through the open green-shuttered window, was a grander vista—the shimmering blue surface of Lake Lugano with Cantine di Gandria on the shore opposite. But he was momentarily blind to the luminous beauty. More urgent thoughts were rising rapidly to mind, stimulated by the paragraphs he'd just read.

If anything was going to force the old General finally to act against Rybkin, this Potsdam Conference—with its implied threat to Soviet autonomy—might just be it.

In that hopeful light, perhaps it was also time to end this southern sojourn and move north—a little nearer striking distance—to await that summons. He could stretch his muscles a bit, hone his reflexes, get reaccustomed to taking physical risks. Even if there was no drum-beat along the General's old network, at least he'd be that much readier for free-lance action.

He crossed the room and threw open a tall pine armoire. On the top shelf were three hats—a silver motorcycle helmet, the blue beret of the Soviet special forces, and a black felt cowboy hat.

He reached for the cowboy hat, eased it down over his thatched blond hair. Then he turned slowly to the dresser-top mirror and grinned back at the still-youthful gunfighter.

Chapter

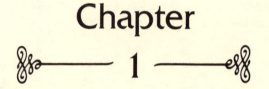 1

FOR TERRIFYING SECONDS THE OLD SOLDIER COULD NOT remember where he was bivouacked—against which army, on what front, in what war. He knew only that he was under attack. Then the approaching brushfire crackle of small arms was obliterated by the close concussion of an exploding grenade, shattering the old man's anesthetic dreams. With a startled cry, Colonel General Rodion Marchenko awoke to danger.

He grabbed for his rifle, cracked his knuckles instead against the birch headboard of the old Swedish sleigh bed—a grandfather's wedding present that had followed the Marchenkos on postings from Havana to southern Sakhalin. The colonel general was, therefore, not on bivouac, but ensconced in his own quarters . . . which were . . . he ransacked his brains . . . yes! in a pine and birch forest southwest of Novosibirsk—a training battalion cantonment in the heart of the Siberian Military District.

But the firefight was no illusion. Outside, machine guns stitched the night, and another grenade blast shook the ground and Marchenko's cabin. *The Chekist sons of bitches were coming for him at last,* he concluded, *and armed with more than an arrest warrant.* The room was pitch black, the bedside digital clock off, the telephone dead against his ear. If power and phone lines were both cut, radio frequencies would be jammed as well. And where in hell was Junior Sergeant Prokhov, his indispensable aide-de-camp? Already dead? Or safely away, as would befit a *stukach,* KGB stooge, a role which Marchenko had more than once suspected the ambitious lad of playing.

The old man's bare feet hit the cold pine floor. He craved his spectacles but dared not take time to grope for them in the dark. He lurched ahead, tripped over his slippers, toppled an ivory Kwan Yin from her candlestand as he plowed into the adjoining office to his campaign desk. It took long, maddening seconds to locate the emergency power switch recessed in the kneehole, but—God be praised!—after a few fitful gulps the seldom-used generator kicked in, feeding juice to the brass desk lamp.

The colonel general's eyes swept once across the scarred mahogany surface, cluttered with the memorabilia of a long, illustrious career. He lingered a moment over two gilt-framed photographs—of the beloved wife now eleven years buried, and the gangly daughter posed in front of her dacha with only the paw of her plump sewing-machine-commissar husband visible after Marchenko's careful scissor-cropping.

Do svidanya, my darlings, he bid them silently as he reached out to the desk's right corner and the meter-high replica of the *Golub I.* The rocket model, with its stylized dove insignia, was tethered to a thin launch rod and sheathed in a gleaming white silo tube. As Deputy Commander of Strategic Rocket Forces back in the early seventies, Marchenko had championed the development of this prototype missile and its subsequent military deployment as the SS-9 Scarp.

The colonel general unscrewed the protruding nose cone, where the SS-9's twenty-five-megaton warhead would have been housed, and set it beside him. From the desk's left double drawer he extracted a bottle of Stolichnaya, uncapped that as well, gulped the ninety-proof liquid fire. Gunfire continued to erupt as the old officer opened the middle drawer, withdrew a sheet of his stationery, a favorite Parker pen, and began outlining in Cyrillic script, now grown palsied, the essential points of his final operational order. He worked quickly against the crescendo of weaponry and a new and ominous sound—the grinding approach of battle vehicles.

7

After the final slashes of his signature—R. I. Marchenko—the colonel general blotted hastily and folded the paper into a tight square, heedless of the smearing of any patches of still-wet ink.

Outside in the dark compound three BTR-70 armored personnel carriers converged on Marchenko's pine-log residence, their 7.62-millimeter turret machine guns trained on his door. From each dark, slab-sided vehicle—through roof hatches and between-wheel hull doors—a stream of smaller shapes emerged against the moonless night to swiftly encircle the structure. These were KGB commandos in black body armor and nonreflective ballistic helmets with headset radios, a dozen from each APC, armed with AKR submachine guns, 9-millimeter pistols, and grenades.

The operation thus far had been as effortless as a practice run-through. The little camp had been stripped of regular army units during the previous weeks. The remaining "shadow battalion," comprising only a few training officers and reservists, had yielded to the attackers with the predictable ease of a regimental whore. The BTR 8 × 8s had encountered no mobile patrols outside the perimeter, and a single concentrated fusillade took out both the undermanned guard posts.

Only a small core of soldiers had fallen back toward their commander's quarters, but these had fought the mechanized advance bravely, if quite futilely. They were cut down, one after another, by the BTR machine gunners with the aid of their laser optics, or were blown up, along with their hiding places, by 30-millimeter grenades from the BTR's roof-mounted launchers. The bullet-riddled corpse of the last of these defenders now lay heaped across the single step to Marchenko's cabin, forming a final pitiful barricade—until it was booted aside by Pavel Starkov, lieutenant colonel, KGB Second Directorate for Counterintelligence.

Starkov paused a moment while a specialist sergeant placed explosive frame charges around the door. The faintly lighted window had surprised Starkov; there had been no mention in the briefing of any auxiliary power unit in the camp. Through the window only a bare anteroom was visible; Marchenko must be in the bedroom or office beyond. Perhaps the old Cossack was preparing a booby trap—or his own suicide. In any case, the decision had come down from KGB chief Biryukov himself, or perhaps from even higher. Starkov was to take his men in without benefit of CS gas or stun grenades, and hold his fire. Biryukov wanted certain questions put to the old man before he was executed.

Starkov started a count into his headset. On five, front and rear doors were blown apart. The lieutenant colonel led the charge through the anteroom and into the office beyond; seconds later the rear assault unit burst in, all half-dozen commandos instantly fanning out and targeting their short-barreled AKRs on the stoop-shouldered old man sitting behind the desk in his nightshirt.

"Who the fuck are you guys supposed to be?" Marchenko addressed the encircling commandos as though he were conducting inspection. To Starkov's considerable relief, the colonel general was unarmed—unless he was planning to chuck that half-empty bottle of vodka at them, or use his desktop rocket model as a bludgeon. Out of uniform, the old man looked frail, almost cadaverous, his sharp Ukrainian features shriveled, the papery skin jaundiced in the lamplight.

Starkov stepped forward and raised his polycarb visor. "Lieutenant Colonel Pavel Starkov, Military Counterintelligence."

"SMERSH!" the old man spat. "What kept you? I've been expecting you vermin for months now."

"Traitors have reason to expect us. Unless you confess your crimes at once, Rodion Igorovich, and tell us everything, you will be shot here and now." As an added insult to the senior officer, Starkov had employed the familiar form of address.

"Confess what? What's my treason?"

"Conspiracy to assassinate President Rybkin."

Marchenko tilted the vodka bottle to his lips. Starkov—along with his men—couldn't help noticing the military honors arrayed on the wall behind the colonel general—Hero of the Soviet Union, orders of Suvorov, Kutuzov, Aleksandr Nevsky, and the Red Star, decorations and flashes for battle wounds in Egypt, Vietnam, Afghanistan.

"If it's treason to want to stop Alois Maksimovich from destroying our homeland, I'm guilty, and so is most of the Red Army—and so should you be, Comrade Chekist. I am a patriot. Rybkin is the traitor. Which is, of course, why he sends thugs in the middle of the night to execute me. He's afraid to put me on trial. He knows he'd have a full-scale army revolt on his hands."

"Is that your whole confession, Rodion Igorovich?"

"All you're going to get, shitface. So why don't you give the order?

9

Come on, you bastards, shoot me!" All eyes were on Starkov, who did not react. The old man snorted. "What are you waiting for? Did Rybkin hand you a list of questions to ask before you can pull the trigger? Like why I've been such a docile fellow, making no protest when he stripped me of my rocket command and exiled me to this shithole? The answer is simple. I *like* teaching *kolkhoz* boys how to dig latrines in the spring mud." Marchenko chuckled, took another pull of vodka, banged the bottle down, wiped his lips. "Either that, or I've got one last ace up my asshole."

"If you've got an ace hidden anywhere, old man, you've waited too long to play it against Rybkin."

"I was waiting for just the right moment. And now it's here. I *will* stop this madman, Comrade Chekist, and you and your stormtroopers cannot stop me."

"We already have, Comrade General. We've been watching you for months, you know, tracing your treasonous little network. We're shutting it down completely tonight. Removing your conspirators in a dozen military districts. And we know from our interrogations that your plans for overthrowing the President are a very long way from complete."

"For overthrowing, yes. Not for killing the bastard. For that I just have to give the word."

"Go ahead. I'd like to see this, Comrade, since we've severed every means of communication from this place."

Marchenko finished the bottle, set it down gently this time. "Alas for your ass-licking career, Comrade Chekist, you have overlooked one means of communication."

"What?"

"Pigeon."

Starkov stared at the old rocketry general without comprehension. Marchenko acted tipsy; was he delusional as well? Yet, despite himself, the KGB officer raked his glance once more over the small office—past books, encased medals and orders, dusty regalia that included a cavalry saber and saddle, photos of rocket launchings, family gatherings, officer academy graduations. There were no carrier pigeons, no birds of any kind.

"Pigeon?" Starkov said, at a loss.

Marchenko smiled for the first time, revealing several stainless-steel teeth. He tapped the rocket tube and repeated the word *Golub*, "dove" or "pigeon." Then he pressed the wireless ignition switch concealed in his palm.

From the base of the *Golub* there came an explosive whoosh, and the projectile, in a compressed-gas cold launch, shot out of its silo tube toward the roof—and a skylight that flew open before it, framing a square of night.

Startled, Starkov and several others swung their AKRs, firing upward bursts at the vanishing missile. It seemed they had hit their target when a gout of flame exploded over their heads. Then his stunned senses registered the diminishing roar and a sudden sulfurous stink in the room, and Starkov realized the explosion must have been the delayed ignition of the first-stage rocket motor. The *Golub* had disappeared into the night.

Yet several of his men continued to direct their machine-gun rounds upward, thudding into the roof timbers and shattering the rapidly retracting Plexiglas skylight. And worse! Starkov whirled and shouted—too late to stop one of his men from opening fire on Marchenko, who crashed backward off his chair. By the time Starkov had rushed around the desk, the colonel general had escaped their grasp like his "pigeon." His nightshirt was a red ruin, and from the scrawny neck arterial blood pooled over the floorboards, dividing around Starkov's boots.

The KGB officer stared down in impotent fury, his right fist clenching and reclenching the AKR's butt-stock. Marchenko's broad skull was thrown back on the floor, his death-glazed eyes staring up at the shattered skylight and blackness beyond. And the old bastard was still grinning his steely smile.

The *Golub* streaked northeastward through the Siberian night like a tiny meteorite, perhaps a straggler from the Eta Aquarid showers of early May, a week previous. Its trajectory was precisely controlled by a tiny Japanese microprocessor, and its solid-fuel propellant burned for a carefully calculated one hundred forty seconds, enough to carry it over twenty kilometers of pine and birch, and well beyond the silent River Ob and the university complex of Akademgorodok sprawled across the *Zolotaya Dolina,* the Golden Valley.

As it passed once again above dense forest, the rocket reached apogee and abruptly cut its motor. A split-second later a recovery ejection charge triggered, the sudden retro-thrust separating the nose cone and deploying a parachute. As the exhausted first stage dropped away into the trees, the polyethylene canopy unfurled and snapped open. The *Golub* payload, swinging slightly in the breeze and now emitting a tiny radio signal, drifted down through the pinetops, its shrouds barely evading entrapment as it slipped past tiers of web-fingered boughs to impact softly into the thick mulch of a small clearing.

An hour passed with only the rustle of pines. Then the wind carried the approaching whine of a truck transmission laboring over the rough ground. Several minutes later twin headlamps lanced back and forth through the night as the vehicle crashed through thickets and slalomed around pine boles. Finally it bounced into the clearing—an old, rebuilt Lend-Lease Studebaker bearing the insignia of the Ministry of Timber—and came to a halt.

Leaving the motor running and the headlamps probing ahead, two men jumped out of the cab—a father swinging an electric torch, and his strapping son with an RDF receiver. It took them less than a minute to home in on the beeper and locate the payload under its collapsed canopy. In another minute the old Studebaker was growling off through the woods, and the clearing was once again empty.

A half hour later, the *Golub*'s nose cone lay hidden beneath the winter woodpile outside the forester's cabin, while inside, Marchenko's final operational order was carefully unfolded, read, encrypted, and sent on its way once more, this time disguised in a stream of meteorological data over the Akademgorodok computer network for distribution throughout the Soviet Union. The last sentence of the colonel general's message was the key one. Decoded, it read simply:

ACTIVATE MARCUS

Chapter

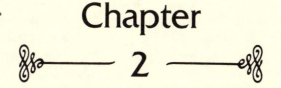

2

ORLANDO, A SWARTHY PARTY ANIMAL UP FOR THE WEEK FROM
Brescia, thought up the stunt around midnight in an ersatz London
pub in Kitzbühel, after considerable quantities of dark pilsner. He
tried to explain it to the two Austrian girls at the table, but they were
unable to hear over indefatigable choruses of *"Fräulein, Fräulein,
Fräulein"* led by the resident zither and accordion duo. Finally the
Italian shouted out his tipsy idea.

"Zu-pa!" answered the girl on his left, Lise—straw blonde, nicely
freckled, smiling while licking off a foam mustache.

"With you everything is 'super.' What do you say, Silvie?"

The dark-haired, slightly more serious girl on his right shook her
head: "Orlo, you want to kill yourself, I don't care. But think of little
Lise. She will be sad forever."

"Ha! Nothing makes Lise sad."

"Okay, maybe not sad forever—"

"Maybe only till I find a new big love," giggled Lise. "Maybe a
week."

"You lovely ladies don't understand. It's not for me to do such a
crazy thing. I must think always of my big future, and of Papa's

13

business. No, this is for our brave and crazy American to do. Wake him up, one of you, so I can tell him."

The three turned to the young man across the table, just now lounging back precariously in his café chair. Only a long, dimpled jaw and muscular smile were visible below a black felt cowboy hat, tipped comically far forward. Silvie reached and lifted the hat.

"Okay, I'm awake," he said, grinning at them out of his long, handsome, adolescent mask of a face. The voice was husky and melodious, the mouth frankly sensual, the light blue eyes playful against a deep Alpine tan. Despite the boyish appeal, he looked to be past thirty, clearly older and more experienced than his companions, none of whom knew his real identity.

"But you don't listen to us, Jack. We are boring you?"

"I heard every damned drunken word, Orlo. I'll try your little stunt tomorrow, as soon as the chair lift starts running up to Hohe Salve. If the weather isn't too shitty."

"But Jack! Orlo was only making a joke."

"Jack"—known to Soviet intelligence as Marcus Jolly—righted his chair, reached into a jeans pocket, and fished out a wad of Austrian banknotes, peeled off a dozen and tossed them onto the beer-puddled table. "Orlando may be joking, but twelve thousand schillings says I'm serious. What do you say, *amico?*"

The Italian grabbed up the notes, shook them dry, and handed them to Lise. "Keep these. It's not much, but I'm afraid our crazy friend will need them for the hospital." He turned to "Jack." "Okay, fifteen thousand. But you wake up tomorrow, you want to change your mind, it's plenty okay with me."

Marcus shook his head and reached for a fresh half liter of beer. "What do you mean 'wake up'? Who's going to sleep?"

Orlo's stunt didn't scare Marcus, it excited him. He'd been getting stale down in Lugano waiting for something to happen. *Not* trying something truly balls-out demented once in a while, going for the blood rush, now, *that* was frightening. If he ever reached the time of his life that he counted all the costs and balked at barriers in his path like a skittish steeplechaser, they might as well just take him out and shoot him.

Oh, there were plenty of crazy and dangerous things beyond Marcus's sphere of daredeviltry—a host of circus stunts, for instance. But only once could he remember being afraid to try something he wanted desperately to do.

He'd been fourteen, showing off for a couple of girls at the local plunge with his self-taught repertoire of forward and backward somersaults. Suddenly a bunch of country club kids, collegiate types, had shown up, and several big, musclebound characters took over the diving boards. Marcus had tried to compete, but was plainly outclassed.

This one bleached-blond guy kept bouncing up and down on the high board, making the fiberglass twang like a bass guitar string. When he had everybody watching, he had bounded straight up and grabbed his knees in a tight backward tuck. There was a collective gasp all around the pool—you could see the big kid was not going to clear the board.

And he didn't. He finished the somersault cleanly and banged both feet right back on the end of the vibrating board. It twanged again as he arced up and out into a graceful forward one-and-a-half pike with hardly a splash. As he broke surface and flung his blond hair out of his eyes, the poolside gasp had turned to applause.

Later, when the college kids had left and the guard was clearing the pool, Marcus had gone out on the low board—the high board was out of the question. He had screwed up his courage to attempt the incredible dive. He had bounced on the end—three, four, five times. But that was all. His knees had turned to jelly, his stomach got oily, cowardice stole his soul. When the guard ordered him out, he slunk away.

Marcus had pretty much given up on diving the rest of that summer. In the amazing run of years since, Lord knows, he'd pulled off many crazier and incomparably more dangerous stunts, while today that country-club showoff was probably pushing insurance and turning into one more lard-ass. But Marcus could never forget that dive. Someday, before it was all over, he'd get up there and do the damned thing.

Now he hung suspended beneath a rainbow-striped hang glider. Increasing his exhilaration, and in violation of all the rules of the Hopfgarten Hang Gliding School from which he had hired his Rogallo wing, Marcus was unencumbered by helmet, goggles, flight suit, or cocoon harness. Except for swimming briefs, Rolex, and running shoes, his sleekly muscled body was bare, stretched prone, and prismed by sunlight through the multihued sailcloth.

Directly above, a tiny, drifting circumflex against the vaulted blue, a golden eagle worked the same thermal that held Marcus. It was a perfect morning for soaring. He had gained a thousand meters in ridge lift from the grassy summit of Hohe Salve, his launch site. That put him something like twenty-two hundred meters above the emerald vales of Brixental and Kelchsau, which joined just beyond Hopfgarten. From here the tumbling Kelchsauer Ache, in a full spring torrent he had kayaked two days before, shone as a fine, golden filament in the sunlight.

Arrayed off to his left were the snow-glossed summits of the Kitzbüheler Alps and the Wilder Kaiser, and beyond them, rising from the Hohe Tauern on the horizon, the bright white saddle of the Grossglockner, at nearly thirty-eight hundred meters Austria's highest peak.

He would have liked to ride the thermal higher, to chase the eagle like Icarus, beyond the limestone crags and the far glistening snowfields, allowing the sense of splendid isolation to overcome him. It was supremely intoxicating, and utterly solitary. Indeed, Marcus prized this feeling precisely because—like all the really extraordinary experiences of his life—it could not be shared.

But a wager was on, and far below, the little trio waited witness. Mundanity, more than gravity, thus summoned him down. Reluctantly he exited the updraft, drew his body toward the control bar, dipped his wings below the horizon and, carefully gaining airspeed, began a slow, spiraling descent to the valley.

Several minutes later he was skimming steep green pastures dotted with butterscotch cows, then banking in a wide turn above the storybook village of Hopfgarten, with its plump, white and wood *gasthofs* cascading red and pink pelargoniums from their balconies. Marcus's wing shadow passed directly over the tidy parish churchyard cemetery, then flashed across the church's steep roof and between its twin baroque spires.

He was steering toward one of the larger structures, a Tyroleanmodern hotel bordering a grassy meadow. He swooped in from the west over a windscreen of dark solar-glass, unbuckling his harness a dozen meters above the sudden sparkle of a swimming pool. He had only an instant to register the trio of familiar upturned faces on the stone-flagged terrace. Then he let go of the control bar, grabbed his knees, and executed a forward two-and-a-half into the deep end.

He surfaced to cheers from the poolside table, in time to see his glider vanish serenely over the windscreen. The dive had been fairly ragged, but Orlo had stipulated only a successful splashdown, not a thing of beauty. And Marcus had by God pulled it off. He stroked to the side, lifted himself out in one fluid motion, and walked toward the group, grinning and dripping. They continued to applaud, all three in tennis whites, shoes and socks powdered with red clay from the nearby courts.

"Bravo, Jack!" Orlando said.

"The name's Bond. James Bond. Just dropped in for a swim, old chap." He caught the towel tossed by Silvie, bent to her kiss, and sank into an empty chair. "It wasn't half bad, was it?"

"It was *zu-pa!*" Lise said.

"But we should have made a video," Silvie complained. "Jack, could you do it again?"

"*Sì,*" Orlando laughed. "*Encore, encore!*"

"No problemo. As soon as *il grosso Italiano* here pays up."

"*Ecco!*" Orlando tossed some bills across the table. "For you, my crazy friend, you earn it."

"Why crazy?"

"Because, to win only fifteen thousand schillings, you just destroy a beautiful glider for which you are going to have to pay, I don't know, maybe forty, fifty thousand?"

"I didn't hear a crash, did you? I'll bet you another ten thousand the glider's hardly got a scratch."

Orlando shrugged in apparent defeat.

"So, what is it like up there, Jack?" Lise asked.

"It's fucking *zu-pa*, Lise! I was playing sky tag with an eagle. You ought to try it."

"*Scheisse!* Too much of danger."

"Naw! The only really nasty part is catching all the damn bugs in your teeth." Marcus spat over his shoulder. "Seriously, you know what it's like?"

"Sex?" asked Silvie.

"Better."

"Nothing is better!" Orlando protested.

17

"How do you know until you've tried everything else? Okay, I'll agree, great sex is the best thing going. But the kind of high you get from risking your buns hang-gliding, say, or sky-diving or helicopter skiing—I'm talking about really nifty, gung-ho, semi-life-threatening activities—let me tell you, it's usually a whole lot better than your ordinary, everyday, run-of-the-mill fuck—"

"Hey, you bastard!"

"Silvie, take it easy. I'm not talking about you and me here. This is a purely philosophical discussion, okay? All I'm saying is, good danger beats bad sex, or even average sex, okay?" He fished a *Süddeutsche Zeitung* off the next table and began idly leafing through the pages. "As a matter of fact, it's almost the same sensation for a guy, gets you right down in the nuts, *verstehe?* Obviously, I don't know what it's like for you *Fräulein*—hey, Silvie, what's your problem?"

"You! Why you talk so dirty? And you think you are such a smart guy. What are you doing back there?" She slapped the newspaper down. "You can't read German."

"I can read the *Fussball* scores, okay, and today's *Wetter.*" He readjusted the paper. "Anyway, how do you know what I'm looking for?"

Several minutes later, while the others were debating the relative merits of afternoon water-skiing on the Schwarzee or more tennis, Marcus finally took his nose out of the newspaper.

"Sorry," he said, getting to his feet, "you folks will have to excuse me."

"Where are you going?"

"For starters, München."

"München? Now? What about tennis?"

"Well, I'm afraid doubles is definitely out."

"Jack! Stop making jokes!"

"Silvie, I'm being serious now. Something just came up. In fact, my whole damn holiday might have just gone *kaput.* Orlo, can you take care of getting that glider back to Gunther for me at the school? I've got to leave right now."

"But you *are* a madman!" Silvie said.

"I know. I'll telephone you later, I promise, and explain."

Before they could muster further protest, Marcus had collected his morning winnings from the table, folded the newspaper under his arm, and was striding off the terrace, leaving the confounded trio almost as abruptly as he had joined them. They could not see the intense excitement that now blazed in his eyes.

So, he thought, hurrying down the outside hotel stairs toward the car park, *Marchenko is gone*. And how many of his highly placed people had been taken out with him? But the skeleton of the General's network was obviously still intact—at least enough had remained to get the old man's last command relayed to Marcus.

The small, carefully worded display ad—for a nonexistent package tour to the Canary Islands—was the one Marcus had been told to look for, the green light for the biggest assignment of his life. But he had not expected the code words signaling the General's death. It made this morning's foolishness recede' into split-second oblivion, along with the trio of his most recent playmates—fatuous Orlo, silly Lise, sullen and sultry Silvie. (How long would she wait for his call, he wondered, before she gave up?) No matter what happened, none of them would ever see or hear from him again.

As Marcus had predicted, the hang glider had landed safely in the grassy meadow, a giant, exotic butterfly nestled among the Alpine wildflowers. He gave it only a glance before opening the saddlebags of the Moto Guzzi sportbike he had parked earlier, pulling out and zipping into his cycle leathers. Then he helmeted, straddled the saddle, fired up the 1000cc engine, and, spitting gravel, snarled off down motorway 170 through the shining mountains toward Kufstein and the German border.

Chapter

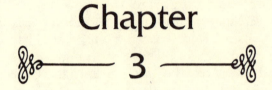

3

THE IDEA WAS PREPOSTEROUS. HOW COULD THE UNLEASHING OF one potential assassin threaten the most protected man on earth—an assassin whose identity, if not his present whereabouts, was known in advance, and on whom both the KGB and GRU had voluminous dossiers?

For—though his frequent foreign visits and television appearances created an image of accessibility—Soviet President Alois Rybkin, like most of his prudent predecessors, worked and lived mainly behind the impregnable Kremlin walls or in his well-protected quarters in suburban Kuntsevo. When he traveled through the streets of Moscow, it was in a caravan of identical, curtained, armor-plated ZILs, heavily convoyed by militiamen. And wherever he went, home or abroad— and especially when, for the benefit of news cameras, he seemed to mingle with crowds—he was enveloped at every instant by an elite cohort of KGB guards.

Yet, quite apparently, Rybkin *was* concerned. Instead of dismissing Kuzin and Biryukov after their briefing in his private office in the Presidium building near the Spassky Tower, he had bidden them both remain while the pretty blonde from Soviet TV came waltzing in with her makeup kit. The two senior Politburo members waited now, slipping farther behind in their own heavy schedules, while Rybkin joked with the girl as she touched up the famous face with Pan Cake stick.

Foreign Minister Ivo Fyodorovich Kuzin, older of the two, consulted his watch once again. The blonde had been in nearly fifteen minutes; in another ten Rybkin was due downstairs in the Kremlin video studio for yet another address on national unity. Kuzin would have to stay for the taping, so his entire evening calendar was now by the boards. He sighed as the girl finally whisked off the shoulder cloth, buttoned up her case, and, squealing at a farewell pat on the rear, sashayed out, leaving Rybkin alone at the other end of the room.

The President stood up from his favorite armchair, which, like most of the furniture in his office and private apartments, was in the ornate Empire style (in marked contrast to the utilitarian tastes of his predecessor). For the moment his blocky peasant figure was silhouetted in the tall windows against the Ivan the Great Bell Tower, its gilded dome afire now from the lingering sun of a Moscow spring evening.

"Well, Ivo, Volodya, what are you wizards going to do?"

Kuzin, after a glance at his younger colleague, KGB chief Vladimir Biryukov, addressed the question in his usual perambulatory style: "It is not worth even a moment's worry on your part, Alois Maksimovich. We will handle it, if I may say, in a routine fashion. That is to say, a perfectly thorough fashion. Permit me to enumerate some obvious things. In an average month there are—how many threats, Volodya?"

"Thousands." Biryukov shrugged.

"Thousands of threats on your life—each *month*. I'm speaking of those we are aware of—most of them, incredibly, contained in actual letters addressed to you by lunatics—every one of which, of course, the KGB Ninth Directorate must investigate. Others are mere drunken ravings or deranged outbursts overheard and reported to us. Of course, these, too, must be followed up. This is the average."

"The White House Secret Service get even more than this," Biryukov added with a nonchalant wave of a plump hand. "Their chief of detail has told me this."

"Unfortunately, that figure has recently escalated," Kuzin continued. "And rather steadily so, since the announcement of the Potsdam Conference and your own Greater Europe initiatives, with the predictable howls from the old wolves that we are proceeding down a path toward surrender of national sovereignty. Volodya has, I daresay, lost count of the threats. Isn't that correct?"

"Unfortunately, that is so."

Rybkin shrugged. "The point, Ivo?"

"The point is, Alois Maksimovich, what is one more potential assassin, more or less?"

"When none has the slightest chance of success," added Biryukov.

Rybkin came closer, his blunt, flat features bronzed and softened by the studio makeup. He searched the faces of his two principal advisers, then turned on his heel and walked heavily back across the Turkestan carpet to his massive rosewood desk, a gift from Queen Victoria to the Tsarevich Sasha, later Alexander III. Rybkin sank back into the red leather upholstery of his oversized chair and pondered the coffered ceiling while the digital clock on his blotter blinked off two minutes.

Finally Kuzin spoke: "Alois, please excuse me. I know you are thinking, but you must be downstairs in five minutes."

"And so I will be. All right, listen carefully, both of you. You are forgetting one essential element. This is *Marchenko*'s hand-picked assassin. And Marchenko was a perfectionist, and an excellent judge of men. This man Marcus is, therefore, not one out of a thousand or a million dangerous lunatics. He is not a statistic of any kind, but rather a special case. And he has my full attention, as he should have yours—because of Marchenko, and because of what this mountain of paper you have brought says about him."

Rybkin gestured toward a console table, on which they had deposited Marcus's KGB dossier, which ran to three hundred pages, and his smaller, but more impressive *Spetsnaz* military file. "According to what I read, and you have confirmed, this man has apparently never failed a 'wet affair.' So yes, I worry a little, perhaps because I am superstitious. Not because I am afraid for my own paltry life, but because I am on the verge of some very important business which I don't wish interrupted."

Kuzin read the half-mocking, half-defiant look in the President's eyes. In recent conversations Rybkin had made more than a few references to certain heroic individuals who, at various times in history, had stood poised on the threshold of greatness—Alexander on the banks of the Oxus; Napoleon in Egypt, casting his conqueror's eye eastward upon British India, and perhaps the Ottoman Empire as well; Lenin secreted on the train back from exile in 1917 to Russia, with the fire of Bolshevism in his heart. The clear inference, for Kuzin, was that, with this latest series of Greater Europe initiatives and a startling new Middle East strategy to back it up, Alois Maksimovich Rybkin was beginning to measure himself in such exalted company. That Rybkin's dreams were of this stature Kuzin no longer doubted. But would their charismatic *vozhd*, leader, bring them off, as had Alexander and Lenin, or would he stumble, as had Napoleon at the battle of the Nile—and again in Moscow and Waterloo? Kuzin, the wily statesman, remained skeptical.

"Alois, as you have already heard," he reassured the President, "Volodya's report on security at Potsdam is very impressive. He has gone far beyond the steps that were taken, or that were even conceivable, at the original conference back in Comrade Stalin's day."

"You misunderstand me. I don't fault the efforts of the Committee for State Security. I leave all these matters in your capable hands, Volodya." Rybkin pivoted the big chair and waved again at the dossiers. "But there must be somebody else."

"What do you mean?"

"No matter how good this assassin is at his business, somebody must be as good—or better. I want you to ransack your files for such a man—whether he's KGB, or another *Spetsnaz* superman like Marcus here. I don't care. He can be a Kazakh, an Irkut, or a Chukcha, for that matter. One who shoots better scores, does better on field examinations, who also has never failed an assignment. I want that person located."

"But Alois, that is exactly how we pick your bodyguards! You already have the elite of the elite."

"I don't want him to guard me, Ivo Feodorovich. I want him employed offensively, not defensively. Locate this man, and give him the assignment of finding and killing this Marcus. At once, do you hear me, gentlemen?" Rybkin stood up and smiled. "Now, if you'll excuse me, the country is waiting."

Taras Arensky was bent over the keyboard, attempting to play "Sabre Dance"—at least some impressive bits and pieces, trademark passages he had memorized laboriously in his youth. It wasn't going well. Taras was only foolhardy enough to let the warhorse out of its stable on those infrequent occasions when, as now, he was more than a little tipsy; but unfortunately, the alcohol, while lending courage, invariably took away dexterity.

Finally he threw up his hands in defeat and found himself grinning sheepishly at a showy, thirtyish blonde who had inserted herself into the curve of the closed grand. She had a high-gloss smile, a black strapless with estimable cleavage, and was regarding him as though he were an hors d'oeuvre.

Taras quelled the twinges of panic he often experienced around predatory females, a breed he somehow seemed to attract, especially in the jungly habitat of the Washington party circuit. *Relax*, he told himself, *learn to enjoy it. It's all part of your new career*. Tonight's glittery occasion would certainly afford a good chance to polish his conversational skills.

Though a relative newcomer to the local scene, Taras had recognized dozens of national and D.C. celebrities eddying in and out of the elegant rooms of the Georgetown mansion—senators, a couple of network anchormen, columnists, TV and print reporters, an activist actress, even the mayor of New York. They were gathered ostensibly to celebrate the brave and inexplicable launching of yet another foredoomed, alternative Washington daily. Moving among them, indeed towering over all but one ex-NBA center turned congressman, was their gangly host, E. Lawrence Hornaday, whose Midwestern-based newspaper group had, for unfathomable corporate reasons, decided upon unequal contest with the mighty *Post*.

"So," the blonde wanted to know, widening her smile, "what *exactly* do you do?"

"Well . . . I'm not a concert pianist."

"Mmm, I guessed that. You *should* be, though."

"The way I play? God save us!"

"No, the way you *look*—and *talk*. *Très romantique*. Like Omar Sharif. Are you a *Slav?*"

"*I* am. But Sharif's an Egyptian, I think."

"Mmm, well, *I* always think of him as Zhivago. So, tell me about *you*."

"Not much to tell, I'm afraid," Taras said, shifting into standard deflection mode. "I consult. Your face is very familiar, you know. Are you on television?"

"Mmm. Every Saturday morning. *Washington Wives*."

"I've seen it. You interview, uh—"

"Washington wives. *Exactly!*"

She found this enormously funny, and Taras laughed along with her, though he suspected his own inept response had set her off. At the height of the silliness he glanced over the blonde's bare shoulder and saw, across the large room, his fiancée. Charlotte Walsh was a showy and elegant woman in her own right—tall and vivid, dark-haired and slim, her sharpish features redeemed by a flashing smile and contralto-rich laugh. She was talking and gesturing theatrically to an all-male group, one of whom he recognized as the French ambassador. She was also watching Taras like a hawk. *I trust you,* her expression said, *but I'm not letting you out of my sight.*

"Heatherly Smith." The blonde was extending her hand with a soft jingle of antique-gold bracelets. *"Et tu—"*

"His name is Taras Arensky." Lawrence Hornaday eased his considerable frame between them. "Sorry, Smitty, but I need to borrow him for a moment."

The blonde's eyebrows went up in mock distress. "Only if you *promise* to bring him back, Larry!"

But Hornaday was already steering him away. "Taras, there's somebody I want you to meet," he said as they serpentined purposefully together out of the room, down a long corridor, and through sliding, double mahogany doors into a paneled library.

Two men got up from a tapestry-covered settee under a framed Audubon print. Taras went through the handshakes and was immediately alert. Despite their easygoing manner, the two were obviously high-powered errand boys. "They're from the White House," Hornaday said with a nod to the men. "I'll leave you to it." He backed out of the room as he drew the mahogany doors silently together.

"You carry a gun," Taras said to the man on the left.

"Very good. It's not supposed to show."

"So what's this about?"

"The President wants to talk to you, Mr. Arensky."

"Why does he want to see *me?*"

"He'd like to tell you that himself."

"When?"

"Tonight."

"You mean now, don't you?"

"That's correct. We have a car waiting in back."

"I'm sorry, but my fiancée is also waiting for me. And, for me anyhow, she outranks even your boss. I'll have to talk with her first."

"Mr. Hornaday assured us he will explain your departure to Ms. Walsh. This is an urgent matter, Mr. Arensky. Please." They gestured at the French doors which opened onto a garden.

Taras glanced at their Treasury Department credentials—five-pointed silver stars with engraved Secret Service photo IDs—before following them outside into the warm night, down a gravel path, across a dark tennis court, and out a chain-link back gate into an alley where an unmarked black sedan waited.

A little stagy, he thought, but then, the street in front was thick with paparazzi and stretch limos. He decided to ask no more questions, and no further explanations were offered. He sat back and watched as the Secret Service driver skillfully skirted the hellish traffic around Wisconsin and M on his way to Pennsylvania Avenue. In less than ten minutes they were waved through the White House northwest gate.

A few minutes later, having entered the West Wing through the basement and by now nearly sober, Taras was ushered into the Oval Office.

Chapter

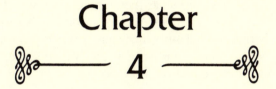

4

As he often did after a grueling day, President William Ackerman was relaxing by watching a videotaped sporting event—in this case a hockey playoff game. But when his intercom light flashed, Ackerman hastily switched off the gizmo, which recessed into a Federal mahogany sideboard behind a potted palm. It was damn silly to hide an innocent pastime, Ackerman thought, but considering the gravity of the interview ahead, with a man he'd never met, he didn't want to risk diluting the impression of his seriousness.

When the three men entered, he rose and came around the big, carved oak Rutherford Hayes desk, which had been fashioned from British ship timbers. The President's shirt-sleeves were rolled up, his hand extended, his smiling gaze locked on Arensky.

"Thanks for coming along. I apologize for the lateness of the hour and, uh, shall we say, abducting you from Larry Hornaday's little soirée. I think you'll see the reason for it." With his bull neck, ruddy complexion, and bluff, engaging manner, Ackerman reminded Taras of a tough, likable military man or sport coach, neither of which fitted the facts. This President, Taras knew, was entirely a political creature.

The group moved, at Ackerman's expansive gesture, across the pale gold oval carpet to twin white sofas by the marble fireplace. Outside, in the West Wing Reception Room, Taras had been shed of his errand boys while being introduced to the other two men—Buck Jones, a crewcut former aerospace executive who served as White House chief of staff; and Dr. Eugene Ledbetter, a rotund, wheelchair-bound Vietnam vet whose subsequent career path included a master's in physics, a doctorate in European history, a term in Congress, and a short stint as a distinguished Defense Department analyst followed by a Defense undersecretaryship. Now, under Ackerman, he was National Security Adviser. Ledbetter parked his wheelchair between the facing sofas; Arensky sat beside Jones, with the President opposite. Coffee was brought in, and they helped themselves.

"All right, let's get right to it, shall we, gentlemen?" Ackerman said.

Jones turned to Arensky. "Earlier Gene and I were briefing Scotty about your work with the CIA, and he's very impressed."

Taras nodded. He was still, frankly, a little boggled at not only finding himself in the White House, but seated across a coffee table from an affable, accessible President of the United States. It took a moment to recall that among Washington insiders, "Scotty," for some obscure reason, referred to Ackerman; Taras had heard Charlotte use the nickname.

Ackerman assented: "It seems, Taras—may I call you that?—your old bosses in the KGB want to hire your services."

"I never worked for the KGB, sir. I was in GRU, military intelligence, and special operations, *Spetsnaz*."

"Forgive me," Ackerman said.

"In any case," Jones resumed, "it's actually the Politburo who want to hire you. But if you accept, you'll be working with the KGB."

"And that's precisely the point," Ledbetter said, hunched in his wheelchair and sipping coffee. "That division defines one of so many volatile situations in the USSR, of which you are doubtless aware. The KGB is mounting this operation against a renegade *Spetsnaz* assassin, who is apparently directed by a conspiracy of high-ranking Red Army officers, led by—"

"Rodion Marchenko," Taras said. "I worked with him. But he's been exiled, to Novosibirsk."

"A little farther than that, I'd say," Ackerman said.

Buck Jones turned to Arensky: "The Politburo notified us earlier today that General Marchenko has been executed as a traitor—"

"*Svolochi,*" Arensky swore in Russian. "Bastards."

"—but not before he unleashed his best assassin."

"To kill Rybkin?"

"That's the general idea."

Ledbetter sketched in the few other details that were known of the conspiracy. The attempt, clearly, was to eliminate President Rybkin before he could go any further with his overtures to the West, and specifically surrender any measure of Soviet sovereignty in order to secure his country's place in the new European order—things the conspirators obviously feared might occur at the Potsdam Conference.

"But this is nothing new, gentlemen," Arensky said. "It is a very long-running Mussorgsky opera we are seeing over there again, an endless Time of Troubles. Why shouldn't everyone want to kill him?"

"You're being facetious," Ledbetter said.

"Perhaps a little."

Jones chuckled. "So what do *you* think Rybkin's game will be at Potsdam?"

"His 'Greater Europe' initiative? Personally, I think it is a desperate PR measure. The man is running out of cards to play."

"Exactly," said Ledbetter. "One would have thought, for instance, that more could have been gotten in exchange for all of Eastern Europe."

"But my opinion is meaningless. There are many varieties of anti-Rybkinism in the Soviet Union. Some, like Marchenko, think the President is simply a traitor, eager to trade the Russian birthright for a mess of European pottage. Others think he is a megalomaniac intent on restoring Russian greatness, and possibly even with Napoleonic designs on being the emperor of this supposed new order from the Atlantic to the Urals. Members of *Pamyat,* on the other hand, are convinced he is contaminated with Jewish blood and is a tool of an international Zionist conspiracy. And there are Orthodox fanatics who are equally convinced Alois Rybkin is the Antichrist, who will turn the Eurasian continent into a Beast with Ten Horns and Ten Crowns. Take your pick."

"I agree with you," Ledbetter said. "Rybkin is not Ivan the Terrible, Rasputin, Napoleon, or the Beast from the Apocalypse. He's really coming to Potsdam with his hand out. Their energy crisis is endemic, and without oil and gas to offer Europe, what have they got?"

"Weaponry," said Jones. "That's his hole card to buy into Europe, and everybody knows it."

"Amen to that," Ledbetter said. "The trouble is—"

"The trouble is," Ackerman cut in, banging down his coffee cup, "whatever Rybkin's play, we're committed to going along with it—to a point. He can stretch his 'Greater Europe' to the Urals and all the way east to Siberia if it makes him happy, so long as it also stretches west across the Atlantic to include us. But Christ, the man knows this. I went cross country skiing with him in Finland, for God's sake. Alois Rybkin is one tough, shrewd bastard."

"What Scotty's saying—" Ledbetter began.

"I think I can speak for myself, Gene, without you interpreting. What I'm saying is, we didn't bring Taras here for a pointless debate on geopolitics. We're going forward as full partners with Rybkin on Potsdam. Our technical team is already sitting down with their side in Vienna to work out a draft agreement, and, so far as I've heard, there's nothing that's come up yet that looks like the end of civilization as we know it—"

"That depends, Scotty."

"For Christ sake, Buck, it depends on what?"

"On whether you keep the keys to the ammo dump."

"Gene, make a note of that."

"Right. Keep-keys-ammo-dump. Got it."

"Satisfied now, Buck?"

"I feel much better."

"So where the hell was I? Okay, what scares me—one hell of a lot more than Russian participation in a new European security arrangement—is what happens if we lose Rybkin to an assassin's bullet, and have to deal with a bunch of neo-Stalinists again—trigger-happy generals like this old bastard Marchenko."

"I think that's where you come in," Buck Jones said.

Arensky looked surprised. "Oh? I'm supposed to save the world from the Kremlin hard-liners? Why me?"

"Because the KGB picked you."

"To do what? Protect Rybkin from assassins?"

"Partly."

"Look, I don't know how many Secret Service and White House police you have here on Pennsylvania Avenue and around the grounds and so forth. I'm sure it's more than adequate. But Rybkin has an entire *regiment* of KGB guards, right in the Kremlin, in their own four-story barracks. Why do they ask for me?"

"Simple. They want you to assassinate this assassin—before he can get to Rybkin." Jones pointed his finger at Arensky's chest.

"Wait, Mr. Jones. Let's get something straight here. I'm not an assassin, I never was, I never will be—no matter what the KGB tells you. Yes, I did special operations for the GRU, but there are things I refused to do for my country. And gentlemen, that is why I left it. They are the same things I will refuse to do for my new country."

"Okay, calm down, Taras. I apologize for the . . . uh, unfortunate implication. Anyway, that's not the issue here. Really, all the KGB is saying is that you were very close to this guy, and the only one, apparently, who ever outscored him in *Spetsnaz* training exercises and outperformed him in Afghanistan on special ops."

Taras asked quietly: "Marcus Jolly?"

"Yeah. Funny name for a Russian killer."

"He was born in America," Arensky said.

"Yeah, that's about all we do know about him. A teenaged defector back in 1977. I understand even the Agency's file on him is pretty sparse. They're hoping you can add to it."

Taras sat back, absorbing the blow. Marcus, as the hit man in an attempt on Rybkin. It was lunacy. Yet, if anyone could pull it off, it would be Marcus.

"You did know him?"

"He was my best friend for almost ten years. I begged him to defect with me, in Afghanistan. He said once was enough. Besides, he did not object to the same things I objected to."

"Destroying villages?"

"Among other things."

"Is he as good as they say?" Jones asked.

"At killing? It's been eight years since we worked together. Certainly he was very good with weapons, in combat situations, clandestine operations, survival techniques, taking risks. At certain things perhaps he was the best. It's hard to imagine anyone getting close to Rybkin in Moscow, though."

"What about one of his own people? Didn't some Russian officer almost get Brezhnev?"

"Fairly close. A young army lieutenant pulled out two pistols and shot up his motorcade near one of the Kremlin gates. He killed a driver and wounded a cosmonaut. Brezhnev was in another car, and the man was captured at once. And Lenin was nearly killed in 1918. So yes, under certain circumstances, it could be done. And Marcus is very good at impersonations. But he is a professional, not a lunatic or kamikaze; he would wish to escape after."

"That attempt on Brezhnev would make a hell of a chase scene, wouldn't it?" Jones said. "Fleeing Red Square with a few thousand KGB on your tail?"

"Let's move along, Buck," the President said. "It's getting damn late, and Taras may have a long night ahead of him."

Jones nodded. "Taras, here's the deal. They want you to fly to Moscow immediately, to work with their people on the security details for the Potsdam trip, and then basically to follow your own hunches in tracking down Jolly. They'll provide manpower—whatever resources you want." The chief of staff paused. "I don't have to tell you, this is a big one. Your cooperation here would mean a lot."

Arensky smiled ruefully. "I'm sorry. I can't accept the assignment."

There was sudden silence in the room, broken by Jones:

"We understand your reluctance to return to Moscow. But your freedom has been absolutely guaranteed."

Taras chuckled.

"You find that amusing?"

"You could say that. When the KGB found out I was working for the CIA, they had a military tribunal sentence me to death in absentia. Despite all the reforms, that sentence has never been lifted." Taras poured himself more coffee. "Anyway, I have other reasons for saying no."

"Tell us what they are," Ackerman prompted.

"Several things, Mr. President. I still dare not trust the Soviets as far as my safety or their promises. And that includes Rybkin. Obviously, I am in sympathy with continuing reforms. And I admire his skill as a diplomat, but I don't trust the man or his visions. As someone said about Andropov, he's not exactly a product of a young lady's finishing school."

"We take your point," Ledbetter said. "Go on."

"There's also a personal reason. I'm engaged to be married."

"I didn't know that," Ackerman said. "Congratulations. We're all admirers of Charlotte. She's the one, I take it?"

"If she forgives me for disappearing tonight without telling her. She's got a temper."

Buck Jones grinned. "Maybe Scotty can write you an excuse."

"That won't help—if I accept your assignment. Then it's all over between us. I promised Charlotte I'd turn in my cloak and dagger, as she says. My current CIA assignment will finish early this summer. Starting next fall I've accepted a post in Soviet studies with the Chalmers Institute."

"Is that what you really want to do?" Jones asked. "Retire to a think tank, at your age?"

"I'm thirty-four. Time to slow down, I think. But, okay, maybe it's more what she wants. It is, for her, a necessary condition of our marriage."

"A forceful lady," Ackerman said. "And after all, I'm only the President."

"She wishes children, Mr. President, and a husband who doesn't carry a gun and disappear from time to time. And at her age—I'm being indiscreet, and I must apologize—there's a certain urgency in these matters."

Ackerman nodded. "The ticking clock, yes, I think we all know what you're up against." He looked around. "Anybody have any brilliant ideas for reassuring Charlie?"

"Wait. There is one last reason."

"By all means."

"The last reason is also the first one I gave you. I am not an assassin."

"Hold on, Taras," Buck Jones said. "I thought we pretty much defused that one. This is just semantics. Why not just call it 'chief of security'?"

"But that is not a very accurate job description, Mr. Jones. You told me the KGB wants me to hunt Marcus down, to 'assassinate the assassin.' Is that not so?"

Jones hesitated. Ackerman spoke: "Answer him, Buck."

"Okay, yes. Hell, I should have paraphrased, but those were the words they chose. They'd like you to stop him—before he gets to Rybkin. This Marcus is a killer, you said so. But if you do find him, if it's a matter of conscience, I'm sure you can detail some of their people to pull the trigger."

Arensky shook his head. "Practically speaking, Mr. Jones, I don't think Marcus Jolly can do this thing, nor do I think I can stop him from doing it. The odds are against on both counts. But that is beside the point. The point is, whatever Marcus may have done, or may have become, he was for many years my closest friend. And I do not wish to be appointed his executioner, no matter the cause."

After a moment the President turned to Dr. Ledbetter. "Gene, what was their other inducement?"

"Immediate exit visas for Taras's sister, her husband and children." Ledbetter turned to Arensky. "If you agree, no matter the outcome, they will all be heading west."

Taras swore violently. His sister Luiza, her husband, and their two little boys had been petitioning to emigrate for years. And year after year Taras had been filing State Department "Invitation for Relatives" forms on their behalf. All to no avail.

"I'm sorry, I don't believe these fucking promises."

"They'll be put on a plane—in the custody of our embassy people— before you take off for Moscow."

"Bastards!" Taras pounded his fist into his open palm. "Excuse me, Mr. President. May I stand up?"

"Christ, yes. Pace the floor, swear all you like. God knows, I do. Would you like a drink?"

"No, thank you." Taras stood. Walked to the French doors. Stared out through the colonnade at the lighted Rose Garden. The President's voice came from behind him.

"Taras, I understand your reluctance to accede to any kind of blackmail from the Kremlin. So let me offer you an alternative reason. You're now a U.S. citizen. As your President, I'm asking you to take this assignment. Consider it in that light, in any case."

Taras did not react. He was seeing faces out there in the night. Faces of people he loved. Charlotte. Marcus. But the faces that lingered were those of Luiza, Anatoly, and their boys, Vladik and Sashka—as he'd last seen them eight years ago on a wintry Moscow morning. How much had they suffered, especially the boys, for his sake; how much had been denied them? Luiza had told him once on the phone how terribly they were ostracized at school, how they had been forced to write compositions denouncing him. What diminished prospects remained for them in young manhood as nephews of a traitor to the Motherland?

Couldn't he, for their sakes, compromise his self-image a little, at least go through the motions of a morally repugnant assignment? Even if it cost him his integrity as a man—*dammit, even if it cost him his soul*—wouldn't it be worth it?

As his conjurings faded, Taras found himself looking, through the trees of the sloping south grounds and the Ellipse, at the floodlit spire of the Washington Monument on the Mall. A shining symbol of his new homeland, like this oval room in which he stood. He turned around.

"I accept, Mr. President."

Ackerman offered his hand, then placed the other on Arensky's shoulder. "I won't ask you which argument prevailed."

"Thank you. When does all this start?"

It was Buck Jones who answered: "There's an Air Force jet at Andrews gassed up and ready to leave for Moscow as soon as we can get you on it. Your temporary reassignment is all cleared with Langley, but, for obvious reasons, we ask that you not tell anyone what you're doing or where you're going."

"Especially, you mean, don't tell my fiancée?"

"I'm sorry," the President said.

Taras shrugged. That was to be expected, considering the nature of the assignment. But even confronting the Kremlin bosses in Moscow was going to seem easy compared to the next part—facing Charlotte.

Chapter

5

TARAS WAS PACKING IN THE BEDROOM OF THE CONDO THEY SHARED in Cleveland Park when he heard her enter the front door. He continued tossing shirts, socks, and underwear into the suitcase as her heels came clicking down the hardwood hallway.

"Taras, what's going on?" her voice called ahead. Then the footsteps stopped. "Oh, God, please tell me this isn't what it looks like."

He turned and saw her in the door frame, square-shouldered in her festive six-hundred-dollar dinner suit. In her eyes naked appeal mingled with deep sadness.

"Charlie, I—"

"Please tell me you weren't really going to sneak out of here in the middle of the night without . . . without . . ."

"President Ackerman asked me to go somewhere, Charlie." He laid in a favorite cotton pullover, a birthday present from her. "Tonight. Right away."

"Scotty asked you?"

"Yes."

"Since when have you two been on speaking terms?"

"Since an hour ago. Though I guess I do work for the man. I told him no. But . . . he bent my arm—"

"Twisted, not bent. He's very good at it. That's how he got where he is."

"—until I said yes."

"Obviously. Is it dangerous?"

"I don't think so."

"So, that's all I get to know? Did Scotty swear you to absolute secrecy, especially in regard to *moi?*" She came slowly forward, dropped her purse on a side chair, took a flat-footed, cross-armed stance regarding him. It was her "tough newswoman" pose, Taras knew, but her vulnerability showed through in the distressed flickerings of her eyes. "Were you going to stick a note on the fridge, or was I to be left totally in the dark?"

"I was going to write a note. Charlie, if I could tell you more, you know I would. We've been all through this."

"Yes, haven't we?" Her voice was low-pitched, jagged with barely controlled emotion. "I tell you everything I do, make a mockery of journalistic ethics, and you tell me nothing. For God's sake, do you think I'm probing for a White House leak? I've got gobs of material for columns. I'm asking as the woman you share your bed with, the woman who wants to share your life. Please don't shut me out, Taras. At least tell me how long you'll be gone."

"I don't really know. I swear I'll come back as soon as . . . well, as soon as I can."

She took his wrists. "Taras, I'm sure Scotty made it all sound earth-shaking. But what about me, and what about us? How long is this going to go on? I need a full-time man in my life. We talked this all out, you agreed, dammit! I don't want to turn around at a party and find out you've vanished under mysterious circumstances—"

"I'm sorry. I tried to get back to you, but they said there wasn't time, that Larry Hornaday would explain where I went."

"I don't care what *they* said, or what Larry was supposed to tell me. *You* didn't say a word. I don't like it, and I won't accept it. I need a man who is *there* for me, don't you understand?"

"I know that. And I promise—"

"Oh, please don't promise anymore." She shook her head hopelessly, then leaned against him and grabbed a fistful of his shirt. "I'm crazy about you, Tarushka. You know I have been since I first looked into those damn soulful eyes of yours. But I haven't got forever. Maybe you're just not good for me. And maybe I have to start thinking about what's good for Charlotte, you know? Maybe I've got to start looking around for some ordinary, domestic-type guy to replace you in my life."

"Charlie, come on now—"

"I'm *serious,* Taras, dammit. It'll tear me apart, but if you walk out of here tonight without—I don't know—without a where or what or how long or a promise to call me, don't bet I won't do something. Do you understand?"

Before he could frame some kind of response, she went pale—and pointed at the open suitcase on the bedspread. Taras cursed his carelessness. Visible under his old belted raincoat was the chromed-steel barrel of his Smith & Wesson .45 automatic.

"You're taking that? You said it wasn't dangerous."

"It isn't. At least I don't think it is. But—"

"You promised me months ago you were going to get rid of that obscene thing."

"I know, Charlie. And I will."

"Oh, Jesus, don't you know what this does to me? Damn you!" Her eyes gathered fury, her fists balled at her sides. Then her face crumpled as the tears broke. She fought them, swiping at them with her knuckles, then took a quick, heart-wrenching step backward as he reached to comfort her.

"No, you don't. Just because I'm crying doesn't mean I don't mean what I said. I mean every damn word, Taras. I always have."

"I know that." Arensky stood there, feeling her eloquent misery along with his own inarticulate pain, yet unable to bridge the chasm suddenly between them. The threat about replacing him struck deep. He couldn't quite dismiss it as being all bluff. Having a child, he knew, had become for Charlotte the most important thing in the world, something she would not—dare not—postpone. They had worked out the critical timetable together: he would quit the Agency; they would quickly marry and start a family. Only his part in that equation was obviously replaceable. He dare not doubt her ultimate resolve to pursue her dream without him.

She put her back against the bedroom wall, pushed a lock of hair out of blotched eyes.

"I'm going to say it one more time, okay? Choose, Taras. Choose between our life together and the dirty little games they want you to go on playing. Because, my darling, if you walk out now, as you did at the party, so help me . . ." Her voice faltered. "I'll care if you come back. I'll always care. But I may not be waiting."

"Charlotte, you know I love you."

"But?"

"But . . ." He shook his head helplessly. Couldn't she see his misery too? Then, thoughtlessly, he stole a glance at his watch.

"You bastard!" she whispered. "Am I keeping you, then, with my histrionics? Is that black car downstairs for you by any chance?"

"Yes."

"So sorry. Well, I think I've said it all anyway. Excuse me." She whirled and, now just sobbing, walked out of the room.

Taras checked the futile impulse to go after her, finished packing instead; latched and locked the single hard-sided suitcase, zippered his carry-on. Dismissed the idea of picking out a paperback; he felt too much like a zombie to read anything.

He hefted the bags down the hall. Charlotte was in the living room, her back turned, standing in a stiff way in front of her mounted collection of miniature Chinese theatrical masks, a Kleenex Boutique box dangling from one hand. Then he noticed the slight movement of her elaborate coiffure and in the Elizabethan puffed sleeves of the riotously printed silk top. She was trembling. He set down the luggage, came up behind her. Tentatively, as though she were breakable, he touched her.

She turned instantly into his arms, dropping the tissue box and clutching him like a child. He held her close, muffling the convulsive noises against his shoulder, stroking her shuddering back through the silk. The tangle of dark curly hair was pungent against his nostrils, her fingers like talons in his biceps, her tears wetting his collar. Then, with the urgent, anguished cry of a small animal, she launched her face at him in a salty kiss surprising in its ferocity, endearing in its vulnerability. Taras told himself to treasure it, knew it might be their last—and that on pain of death he dare not be the one to break it.

Finally she ended it, pushing him off with her palms, yet only a little way, to forearm distance. She stared at him from wet, mascara-bruised eyes, so close she seemed to look first into one of his pupils, then the other, searching for some faint sign that she might have won after all, and that he had capitulated. When she did not find it, hopelessness claimed her again, and she turned away, trying ineffectually to staunch her welling tears.

Arensky moved woodenly back into the hall, picked up his bags. "Good-bye, Charlie."

Her tremulous voice followed him to the door.

"Be careful, Tarushka."

Outside on the dark, deserted street the Secret Service driver came quickly around to take his bags and stow them in the trunk of the sedan, then opened the back door. Taras hesitated a moment before getting in, glancing up a last time to the lighted windows of their living room. She was not there.

When the President's Chief of Staff, Buck Jones, had said an Air Force jet would be waiting at Andrews, Arensky had visualized something on the order of a C-5 or C-141 military transport, and a space-available jumpseat sandwiched among pallets of tank parts. He figured he'd be offloaded at Wiesbaden or, more conveniently, at Frankfurt Rhein-Main onto a commercial flight to Moscow.

But a dramatically more impressive set of wings had been arranged for him by the White House Military Office. He was taken to the 89th Military Airlift Wing at Andrews, home of the Special Air Missions unit and the presidential air fleet. Here he was met by Mike Usher, a freckle-faced, linebacker-sized Secret Service agent from the Washington district, and an amiable, cigar-smoking Air Force officer, Lieutenant Colonel Clyde "Cat" Brunton, who was introduced as chief of security for *Air Force One.*

"But I don't understand," Arensky said.

Brunton chuckled. "You don't have to understand. Just lie back and enjoy it."

Arensky turned to Usher, who nodded and launched into further explanations. Arensky tried to pay close attention, but found himself distracted by the splendid blue, silver, and white fuselage shining under the perimeter lights outside the window. The suspicion of unreality engendered by the midnight Oval Office chat, then temporarily purged by the painful scene with Charlotte, came back stronger than ever. Surely this was part of some elaborate joke, and Usher and Brunton and others were all having their little laugh at his expense. But the big Secret Service man was continuing in his pragmatic monotone, and on a topic that suddenly got Arensky's full attention—his sister

40

Luiza and her family were apparently now boarding a flight scheduled to leave another airport—Sheremetyevo, five-thousand miles to the east.

"But until we're damn sure," Usher said, "we wait."

About an hour later, around four A.M., Usher got final CIA confirmation that the family had indeed left Moscow—on a KLM flight to Amsterdam—and Arensky felt his heart lift as well. How long and vainly he had labored to bring this to pass, and now, unlooked for, it had all happened in the past bizarre few hours. He couldn't be there to greet them, of course, but that could wait. They were all, thank God, free! In a euphoric daze, Arensky was escorted past two ramrod-straight Air Force guards and across the tarmac toward the big gleaming Boeing 707 with the windswept wings and the American flag on its tail.

Arensky found his heart stirred, oddly more than in the White House, as he approached this sleek symbol of his adopted homeland.

"This is incredible," he told Brunton beside him. "I can't believe it—*Air Force One.*"

"Gorgeous bird, isn't she?" Brunton agreed as they ascended the boarding stairs to the forward door. "She's only a backup, now that we've finally got our first presidential 747. But, what the hell, she's seen it all. Right now, of course, she's just SAM 28000, like it says on her tail. A Boeing VC-137C. She's *Air Force One* only when the Boss is aboard."

On the threshold, as he passed the presidential seal on the open door, Taras had an instant of déjà vu. *He had been on this plane before—at a* Spetsnaz *training camp in Mukachevo in the Carpathian Military District!* As a young special forces lieutenant he'd been given a walk-through of an amazingly detailed mock-up of a Boeing 707 hidden away under forest cover. His guide, a grizzled *Spetsnaz* captain, had boasted that the interior duplicated exactly the presidential configuration used by then-U.S. President Jimmy Carter. When Taras had, with appropriate mock naiveté, inquired what the model was used for, the captain had chuckled: "Why, for brigade tea parties, of course!"

Taras had forgotten the incident until this moment; and somehow it had never surfaced in any of his CIA debriefings. He decided he'd better remedy that little oversight; the Secret Service man, Usher, would certainly be interested.

Inside, except for a minimum six-man flight crew and his two chaperons—Brunton and Usher—Arensky was surprised to find he basically had the luxurious jet to himself. The Air Force officer gave him a once-over tour—ironically similar to the *Spetsnaz* captain's, Arensky thought—starting down a narrow aisle on the port side of the plane past a paneled compartment with the presidential seal on the door.

"First Family's quarters—President's office, First Lady's sitting room, family lounge or conference room. Go ahead, look inside if you want."

Next, just aft of the wings, was a staff compartment the width of the fuselage, then an eight-seat suite for guest VIPs. Further aft, behind a bulkhead, was a considerably more plebeian five-across press area, rear galley, and lavatories. The overall color scheme made Arensky think of the American Civil War—blues and grays, muted blue-plaid upholstery, gray overhead luggage bins and leather inlays, blue-gray carpeting throughout.

"For now, we'll stay up front," Brunton said. "Later on, if you get tired, you can come on back to one of the lounges and stretch out."

The 707's four Pratt & Whitney turbo fans were in full-throated chorus as they rejoined Usher, buckled up in the forward crew section and reading *Sports Illustrated*. "This is where Secret Service usually hangs out," Brunton said, "and since I gather we're all more or less in that line of work, it seemed to make sense. Besides, we're closer to the chow here."

He gestured toward the forward galley, where a flight steward—a uniformed staff sergeant—was busy stowing things in cold lockers. Further aft, just behind the door on the left side, a master sergeant with headset was working a communications console that looked designed for two. Then the chief flight engineer emerged from the flight deck, swung the cabin door shut, and locked it down.

Taras glanced out the portside window in time to see the truck-mounted boarding stairs backing away from the left wing. They were rolling forward without benefit of safety lecture or seat-belt check.

"I hope the taxpayers don't hear about this," Taras joked.

"There's lots of stuff happens on these birds nobody knows about, until maybe years later. Like back when Henry the K was conducting top-secret negotiations with the North Vietnamese, he used SAM 26000 and SAM 970 as his private taxis—all over the globe. Officially, they called 'em 'training missions.' "

"Those were pretty important missions," Taras said.

"Hey, all I know is, if you're on here, so is yours."

Brunton outlined the flight plan as they taxied toward takeoff. They would be heading northeast up over Quebec and the Labrador peninsula, making landfall over Belfast. They would stop at the U.S. Air Force base in Tempelhof, West Berlin, just long enough to refuel and get diplomatic clearance for Soviet air space, which would entail taking on a Soviet navigator. They would land at Vnukovo, the VIP airfield, in about eleven hours—midnight Moscow time the next day.

It was about a half hour out that the euphoria induced by his surroundings and his sister's deliverance began to wear off, and Taras found himself overtaken by thoughts first of Marcus, then of Charlotte. He was looking out the window, following the shimmering moonpath on the St. Lawrence far below, when she gradually coalesced out there in the night, usurping his own faint reflection in the Plexiglas.

If only he had been permitted to tell her the whole of it—the deal to free Luiza, Anatoly, and the boys. Surely, then, she would have understood his going.

As it was, she'd have to trust him, dammit. *Don't be too desperate*, he told the astral image in the window. *Don't for God's sake go putting some damn horny stranger in your bed. I'm coming back, no matter what you said, and I still intend to be part of your crazy life.*

And he really did. Despite Charlotte's stubbornness, her rapid, righteous opinions on every topic you could mention, her stormy moods, insane hours, and constant traveling—despite all these things, Taras had always found her wonderfully feminine and vulnerable. And her fierce determination to have a child summoned up his own deepest, most protective instincts.

But perhaps it was her honesty that Taras prized the most. Charlotte's need to reveal herself, and to probe constantly and painfully for his own thoughts and feelings—and not be stopped when he went into what she called "Slavic withdrawal"—had from the first created real intimacy between them.

They had met on an autumn afternoon two years before at a house party in Chevy Chase. After lunch, while the men huddled around the big TV in the den to watch football and the women held forth among the gleaming Chippendale in the living room, Taras had retreated toward the back of the sprawling house with his dessert plate. An elegant, angular, dark-haired woman had followed him onto the back veranda. Taras gauged her perhaps five years his senior (she was actually six), and was intrigued at once, sensing—especially in the challenging brown eyes—both intelligence and appetite for life. She had launched, after the breeziest of introductions ("Call me Charlie"), into a witty commentary on weekly NFL games as essential American male-bonding rituals.

Taras had reacted with appropriate amusement, but she closed the distance quickly between them, fixing him with those dark, probing eyes and placing, ever so lightly, the pads of her long, tapered fingers on his coatsleeve.

"But I'm terribly serious!" In the District, she emphasized, the dearly beloved and incredibly broad-assed Redskins were the only thing in God's vast creation that had ever successfully united all the polarized factions and neighborhoods of the city and its menfolk—liberal and conservative, black and white, blue collar and white collar, ins and outs, even straight and gay.

Charlotte had recently done a column on the subject, and had many of the phrases ready to hand. Taras had been enchanted—not so much by what she said as how she said it. The vivid gestures. The humor that came constantly welling up from some hidden source, crinkling the corners of her eyes and lips, twitching the delicate porcelain nose. Within fifteen minutes the attractive lady journalist had Taras in hilarious disarray, clutching the veranda railing and somehow unable to stop laughing, no matter what inanity she uttered.

"Charlie, please!" he said. "Mercy."

Instead, she had gone for the kill. Without waiting around for halftime and the compulsory gauntlet of good-byes, she spirited her willing catch out a side door and down the graveled driveway. They drove in tandem back to the city and whiled away the rest of the afternoon walking the Mall and matching chapters of their life stories. Nightfall found them in a little Ethiopian eatery in Adams-Morgan, and by morning, wonderfully spent, they lay entwined in her antique bed.

When, several months later, they attended a Super Bowl party near Dupont Circle, it was as a recognized couple. They were jointly entertaining before too much longer—once Charlotte had spruced up her consort's wardrobe and etiquette. Taras wasn't exactly comfortable in the host role, but he did enjoy watching Charlotte function at such occasions—knowing everyone, looking an angel, laughing like a courtesan and debating like a Jesuit. And he particularly relished her wicked post-party comments on the guests and goings-on.

In a way it was Charlotte—far more than his earlier CIA mentors and case supervisors—who had initiated Arensky into many of the mysteries of America, or at least Washington. She taught him more carefully how to interpret the newspapers, evaluate the anchormen and interviewers and columnists, how the city's intricate and inter-locking power structures operated. And she certainly taught him "ad-vanced shopping," and how to properly escort a shopping female. And, to Taras's continual puzzlement, she seemed never to tire of showing him off, especially among her women friends, like a hunting trophy.

When spring came they drove out to what she called her "ancestral Virginia acres"—a modest yellow frame house in nearby Aldie, but set in the exclusive rolling horse-country around Middleburg. Char-lotte's mother, a sprightly sixty, just back from church in white gloves and picture hat, promptly took Taras into the parlor to show him all her daughter's scrapbooks, and then into her old bedroom, where an entire wall was covered with dusty ribbons awarded for both writing and riding.

"Dear God, Mother, spare the poor man!" Charlotte grimaced, and dragged Taras off, out the door, and across the lawn.

"Now where are we going?"

"You'll see."

They squeezed through a hedge and cut across a corner of a neigh-bor's pasture, hiking up a gentle slope into some low, tangled oaks. Charlotte proved quite nimble, leading him through the thicket of boles and branches. After a minute they emerged into a little clearing and hopped up onto a smooth outcrop of granite that afforded a fine lookout down the valley. An afternoon haze overhung the low, spring-green hills, a pickup towing a one-horse trailer vanished and reappeared in an undulation of Highway 50, woodsmoke trailed downwind from a nearby chimney.

"What do you think, Tarushka? Isn't it special?"

"Very."

It was her favorite childhood place. She had gone there often, but had never shown it to another soul—till then. "So you are the very first, darling—not in every way with me, perhaps, but in all the ways that count."

"I'm honored."

Taras had stood there beside her, thinking of that sweet child who had gone there to measure the wide world by her storybook valley, and her innocent dreams against an unknowable future. But he had completely misread her mood. For when Charlotte had turned to him, it was with eyes smoky with lust.

"Tarushka—I want you now."

The shocking imperative carried the full force of her sexuality, and her fingers were already fumbling at his belt buckle. Taras's response was immediate and instinctive—like being sucked into an erotic vortex. Charlotte writhed at his first touch, as if trying to eel out of her own clothes, but actually impeding his efforts to undress her.

"Hurry, darling," she urged, yet made him wrestle her into submission while he struggled to divest her of jacket and blouse and unhammock her lovely breasts. Still she fought against him, laughing to hyperventilation as he peeled off her suede skirt and peach silk panties. But Charlotte had not been totally inept, having managed to bare the essential parts of Taras's anatomy. He stood, slightly foolish, at full point with shirt unbuttoned and trousers about his ankles, but she could wait no longer. With a look of anguish she leaped, girdling herself around him and crying out as they mated in a single thrust.

Charlotte had climaxed right at the start, but hung on willfully for the long gallop, riding Taras till he had bucked and thrust into a final trembling spasm and stood there, breathing mightily and holding her in his arms.

"Oughta put you out to stud right now," she had drawled. "Make us a *heap* of stud fees. 'Ceptin I jes' cain't stand loaning this here big thang out to other fillies."

Taras had chuckled. He did feel a little like one of the stallions they had driven past on the way in. It was, he realized with a shock as he eased her to the ground, the first time in his life he had ever made love out of doors, surrounded by nature. And it had been pretty damn exciting.

By the time they had zipped and buttoned themselves into decency, the sun had slid behind indigo hills. They walked back hand in hand across the twilight fields, their perspiration cooling, but the pungency of lovemaking still in their nostrils.

When they got back, Charlotte's mother had tea waiting on the porch, with shortbread biscuits and olallieberry jam and the smallest spoons Taras had ever seen. They sat three in a row, chatting about trivia, listening to crickets and watching swallows darting across the dark lawn, till the birds—and then their own distinct faces—were lost in the evening gloom. . . .

Taras shook himself free of the seductive reverie, took a breath. It wouldn't do. He had to clear his head. All right, so he couldn't replace Charlie, didn't want to. What was he going to do about it?

Three weeks on this assignment, three weeks to Potsdam. At the end, come what may, Charlotte would be there. As a syndicated columnist specializing in foreign affairs, she routinely covered every economic and diplomatic summit, along with a host of lesser happenings anywhere on the globe. So when the conference was folding its tents in late July, and Taras was finally free of his presidential mission, he would find her and they could come home together.

Unless he had really lost her.

The way it had happened before.

Chapter

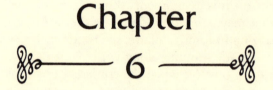

6

IT HAD BEEN SIXTEEN YEARS EARLIER, AND ARENSKY, A FRESH-
faced, not-quite-eighteen-year-old cadet then, as now, was traveling
east with the image of his beloved constantly in mind. But instead of
hopping the Atlantic in a single night, he was crossing the wintry
vastness of Russia, from Moscow to Khabarovsk, in seven and a half
days . . . with the conjured face of another girl keeping pace all that
way, flashing like the low sun through the silver birches. . . .

Uncle Dima had at last grown weary of Taras's unrelenting pleas.
Pulling every string he could reach from his middle-echelon desk in
the Ministry of Defense, he had arranged a special leave for the boy
after the November Bolshevik revolutionary holidays. So, instead of
just a few days off from his second-year studies at the Supreme Soviet
Military Academy outside Moscow, Officer Cadet Arensky would have
a miraculous three weeks—plus a great deal of makeup work when
he returned.

Taras's objective in all this was to spend as much time as possible with his fiancée, a buxom, blond Intourist guide who had thoroughly bewitched him the previous summer at the Odessa seaside. Unfortunately, even Uncle Dima could not alter the fact that Eva Sorokina was currently employed eight thousand five hundred kilometers away in the Soviet Far East.

Taras turned next to his widower father. But hardworking Genrikh, on a factory foreman's salary of three hundred rubles a month, was quite unequal to the demand—was, in fact, richly amused when his son begged two hundred forty-four rubles for an Aeroflot round-trip ticket to Khabarovsk. "Your Eva is a lovely thing, Tarushka," he agreed, "but *that* lovely she is not. Here are fifty-four rubles. Go to her—on the train. Uncle Dima has agreed to pay your return fare."

So, instead of an eight-hour flight on an IL-62, Taras had to face an almost eight-day Trans-Siberian Railroad journey each way in "hard class," squandering more than two-thirds of his precious time and leaving him less than a week with his beloved.

But he could not endure till summer to see Eva. Her letters, one or two every week, had reinforced the spell of Odessa. Especially the letter that contained a fat lock of her tawny hair, tied with a red ribbon into a miniature ponytail. It was so exactly like the original, which had tossed like a palomino's plume in the sea breeze as she fled him over the dunes . . . and was caught and wrestled down and her shrill laughter silenced with kisses—and a blurted out proposal of marriage.

Taras had carried that lock everywhere, even to his classes, buttoned into his tunic pocket and had extracted it again and again from its Pliofilm wrapper when no one was looking in order to savor its heady elixir.

Apparently an old Tungusi woman from Belogorsk had told Eva exactly how much hair to cut and how to tie it, claiming it would exert powerful magic on the object of desire. In her letter Eva had treated the whole thing playfully, but it had worked on Taras exactly as the shaman-woman had decreed.

Of course the love charm came along on his journey, and its magic was meted out carefully—inhaled no more than a dozen, or perhaps two dozen times a day. This ritual offered Taras a fleeting, perfumed escape from the oppressive monotony of those endless, gloomy days and nights; from the wretched hard-class carriage with sixty or seventy benumbed fellow travelers, huddled on wooden benches, sprawled on bunks and in aisles, their pathetic bundles and string-tied boxes heaped in every corner; from the ceaseless, trivial onslaught of piped-in music; and from the pervasive stench of body odor, boiled cabbage, old wool, sardines, beer, and tobacco. Thank God for the old Tungusi woman!

On the eighth and final day, Taras put away his talisman for the last time. He should not need it again. According to the timetable posted by the samovar at the end of the smoky car, they were now less than an hour from Khabarovsk—where the source of the magic would be waiting in the flesh.

Since he could do nothing to quicken the plodding pace of the train—the inaptly named Rossiya (Russia) Express—Taras stared out the window and tried to quiet his clamorous thoughts with the empty landscape—kilometer after kilometer of white waste, with only the barren hills of northern Manchuria to wrinkle the horizon. The trick seemed to work, for all at once the carriage began rumbling over bridge timbers, and steel beams flashed by the window. Below, Taras glimpsed a white expanse of pack ice, perhaps two kilometers wide, here and there sparkling in the low sun like sprinkled rock salt; along its margin, boats and barges were stuck fast. They must be crossing the frozen Amur River—on the outskirts of Khabarovsk.

Across the bridge an oil refinery reared its blackened, industrial tracery against the leaden sky, and a smokestack flamed a ragged red ensign. Beyond, dilapidated bungalows marched away down empty lanes of frozen mud, then were replaced in the train windows by abandoned-looking warehouses of brick and concrete, which gave way in turn to grim blocks of apartment complexes.

Arensky's pulse accelerated as the train slowed, trundling over uneven points into the rail yard, past stooping work crews of women in orange canvas coveralls who scraped at the icy switches with shovels. Then, as the Rossiya's flanged wheels locked and squealed in metallic protest, a roofline fanged with icicles slid into view, followed by the station itself. Taras saw their conductor—the *provodnik*—jump down and trot alongside. Farther down the platform a knot of soldiers sharing a bottle turned and waved at someone as a Mongol-faced family grabbed up its bundles and hurried forward, only to be cut off by a burly woman driving a minitram of hitched wagons full of parcels and mail sacks.

But where was Eva? With a hollow nervousness akin to stage fright, Taras hoisted his duffel bag and flowed with the crowd out of the steam-heated car and into the bitter cold. He stood there on the wide, unevenly paved platform, while a chill north wind knifed through his woolen greatcoat and made his fingers ache inside their thick gloves. But Arensky was not sensible of this, not at this moment. Only the pangs of his anxious heart counted now as he searched the faces of strangers. He told himself to be calm—to be a man, after all. It wouldn't do to appear too eager. Of course, Eva was here somewhere. Perhaps waiting just inside, out of the cold. Or perhaps she'd been detained for some perfectly ordinary and understandable reason. In which case, he would simply have some tea and walk up and down, stretching his train-cramped legs a bit, until she appeared. After seven and a half days, he could certainly stand a few more seconds, or even minutes. But dammit, where was she?

"Tarushka! Tarushka, here!"

He whirled and saw her at the end of the platform, waving as she hurried forward in her heavy coat, her breath pluming in the air. But something was very wrong, something that confirmed the dread that had been stealing over him. A tall young man was striding along close beside her. Even as Eva arrived and launched herself against Taras, and he bent to kiss her flushed, laughing face, he was filled with despair. She was chattering away, but he could not hear her words. His eyes were on those of the stranger, which were slitted, and strikingly light blue, like Eva's.

What was he doing here, this young, cocky-looking foreign bastard—dressed up like a film cowboy in an expensive *dublyonka*, a sheepskin coat, with a black scarf wrapped around his ears, on top of which was a black felt "gunfighter" hat? He even wore a pair of high-heeled tooled-leather boots, which put him noticeable centimeters above Taras.

"Tarushka, what is wrong?"

"Who is he?"

"This is Marcus. He's an American tourist, silly. He came yesterday on the boat train from Yokohama. He's been assigned to me. Oh, Tarushka, really, now don't be jealous! I won't have it!"

She managed to look quite stern for a half second, before a wide grin crinkled her plump, freckled face in its wreath of gold sable. That sunny smile, exposing just the pearly tips of her little teeth, and the girlish, guileless laugh that followed, summed up all the things Arensky adored in Eva Sorokina. Everything was perfectly fine then! Of course, of course. He pressed her small, gloved hand in both of his.

"I'm sorry, Evushka. I'm so stupid. Forgive me!" He turned at once to the American and stuck out his hand. "I'm very pleased to make your acquaintance."

After they had been introduced, with Eva translating each way—and mispronouncing Marcus's surname Jolly as "Zholly"—the young American grabbed Taras's duffel and swung it onto his own shoulder. But Taras seized it back, shaking his head vigorously.

"Nyet, spasibo."

The stranger shrugged, whipping off his cowboy hat in a low bow that exposed flaxen hair—also too much the color of Eva's, Arensky thought. They were two of a kind—sunny, blue-eyed Nordics. Except Eva was round-faced—"moon-faced," she called it—and this Marcus character had a long, horsy skull, with flat cheekbones almost like a Slav and a strong jaw every bit the equal of Arensky's.

"Just come along, you two, and be best friends," Eva said in Russian and then English, linking arms with each and leading them along the slushy platform. "We've got a car, Tarushka, so let's get you a decent meal and talk."

Arensky had traveled to the end of the earth to be alone with his beloved, to unburden the secrets of his heart to her and her alone. Instead, he sat beside her, intoxicated by her nearness, yet unable to touch her or speak to her as he longed to do. Worse, he had to participate in an absurd charade—this polite, inane, interminable conversation, all laboriously translated for the benefit of the insouciant stranger, who lounged across the table, slurping his Siberian fish soup and grinning perpetually back at them.

They'd passed a half hour in the restaurant of the ugly hotel where Marcus was staying not far from the station, the Tsentralnaya on Pushkin Street, and Taras had achieved a perfect, brooding frenzy. In addition to everything else, the restaurant was almost as stuffy as his hard-class train carriage, and the Hungarian wine Eva had ordered was disagreeably sweet. And then there was Eva herself. The moment she had thrown off her coat and fur hat and settled herself on the bench close beside him, Arensky had been overpowered by her femaleness, and rendered giddy by her full, puissant scent which, in fainter replica, lay locked away in his breast pocket.

Just then she was detailing how she and Marcus had gone walking that morning out on the frozen Amur to observe the ice fishermen at their business. She was spreading her arms wide to indicate the thickness of the ice the old men had to chop through to drop their lines—a gesture that stretched her white woolen sweater and emphasized her splendid bosom. Naturally, Taras couldn't take his eyes off her; but he was very aware, peripherally, that neither could the young American.

Finally, the tortured young cadet could endure no more. Quietly, but urgently, he interrupted:

"Does he know about us?"

Eva broke off her story, her lashes blinking rapidly in obvious annoyance. "What about us?"

"That we are going to be married?"

"Don't speak of this now, especially in this tone. This is still a secret. Besides, you know we haven't decided when—"

"But Evushka! What do you think I came all this way to do? To sit here and drink this gooey Magyar shit and talk all this Intourist garbage? No! I came to decide our future—and to be with you, dammit, not him."

"You are being very *nyekulturny,* Taras Genrikhovich. I must attend to my work, and today Marcus is my work. And also perhaps tomorrow, since I delayed to meet your train and both Mariana and Olya are now busy with a coachload of Japanese businessmen."

"So when is he leaving?"

"Perhaps tomorrow, or the day after. It depends on how long it takes me to cover the necessary sights before he goes on to Irkutsk. We are still arranging his itinerary. Is that good enough for you, Comrade General? Now have some patience. And behave!"

She turned angrily and said something in English to Marcus, which Taras, of course, did not understand.

"What did you just tell him?"

"None of your business. If you talk secretly to me, I can talk secretly to Marcus."

Taras darkened. He was now quite furious, yet afraid to say even one more word for fear of losing her. So he sat, making impotent fists under the table. He was at a terrible disadvantage, and knew it. He was being made to feel like a boor, a *nyekulturny* asshole, while the handsome American guy could sit there nonchalantly, pretending to be not only friendly to Taras, but even deferential. It was too much!

He slapped his palm on the table, making their glasses and cutlery jump. When Eva glared at him, he ignored her, signaling to an idle waitress.

Eva took her strongest schoolmistress tone: "If you do not behave, Taras Genrikhovich, I am going to ask you to leave us. And I am serious."

"What's the matter? I'm only ordering some vodka. I'm tired of this junk."

"And I'm asking you for the last time to be civil."

"All right."

"Well then, why do you not speak to Marcus? He has asked several times about you."

"Sure, all right." Taras turned and smiled millimetrically at the American. "So ask him how he comes to be here in the Far East."

"I already told you this. He came on the boat train from Yokohama to Nakhodka."

"Not how, *why*. What is he doing here?"

Eva shrugged, then translated the question. Marcus listened carefully, nodding. Then, when the waitress brought the carafe of iced vodka, he reached for one of the small tumblers.

"Marcus says it is a long story, but if you would like to hear it, and I wouldn't mind translating, he will gladly tell you. But to do this properly, he also will need a little vodka." She smiled faintly.

Arensky filled all three glasses. They toasted in Russian and English, with Arensky demonstrating how to take the vodka in a gulp, leaving the little glass upended on one's nose.

Then the American began to tell of his adventures. It was a tale, recast in the melodious voice of Eva Sorokina, such as Taras Arensky had never before heard, a contemporary odyssey which both inflamed his jealousy and captivated his Russian soul.

Chapter

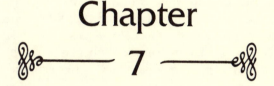

7

THE VODKA, A BRACING, ICY SYRUP ON HIS PALATE, TRANSFORMED itself farther down his throat into molten lava. Marcus gasped for breath, then grinned at the two Russians across the table. His lovely blond guide smiled back, dimpling plump cheeks, plainly eager for the promised story of Marcus's life; her sullen military cadet boyfriend, meanwhile, maintained his inhospitable glare. *I love you too, pal,* Marcus subvocalized, then addressed Eva:

"Don't translate all this stuff, or you'll bore your friend Taras to death. Just hit the high points. It starts with me being born in a log cabin in Illinois, like Abraham Lincoln."

"But this is not correct," Eva said. "Abraham Lincoln was born in Kentucky."

"Are you kidding me? And all these years I thought I was following in the big guy's bootsteps. Anyway, *I* was born in Illinois, so help me, and grew up in a one-gas-station town like some of the hellhole places we passed on the train between here and Nakhodka."

"Why you did leave?"

"Well, I didn't actually leave, Eva. I'd rather not go into all the details, okay? A fire burned my grandparents' house to the ground, killed both of them. My grandmother's damn kiln started it, blew up one afternoon when she was firing some of her china painting. Ted and Cassie were my whole family, you might say, raised me from a little guy."

Eva reached for his hand, but Marcus pulled it away. "Hey, thanks, darlin', but it's past, and I'm not looking for sympathy." Marcus had caught the extra flare of jealousy in Arensky's dark eyes at Eva's sympathetic gesture. And Marcus didn't want to scrape away at the scar tissue of his own feelings. Let it all stay safely buried, with his grandparents.

The Adventures of Marcus Jolly really began in the fire's aftermath anyway. He'd been left, after funeral and other expenses, with about a thousand dollars insurance money and an empty feeling—like he no longer belonged to the town, or himself. He had moved in briefly with school friends to finish his senior year. But one morning he stuffed his backpack with food instead of books and started walking west.

The direction felt right—following the sun. He hitched rides here and there, mostly walked. Days and nights passed. He crossed into Iowa, then Nebraska, slept in fields to save money. Gradually a plan took shape in his mind. It was a scheme at once lazy and ambitious, grand and aimless enough to match his mood. Why not just continue walking toward the sunset—till he'd gone around the world?

He liked seeing what lay around the next bend in the road, but was in no hurry, with no particular destination. Maybe when his footsteps had circled the globe, he'd find his way back to Illinois and decide what to do with the rest of his life. More likely he'd never come back. Probably jump ship somewhere, Tahiti maybe, shack up with some little cocoa-skinned girl.

Eva rolled her eyes at that, then translated very briefly. Marcus suspected censorship. When she signaled him with her eyes to proceed, he did so.

As his adventurous plan took shape, Marcus had begun to feel life flowing through him again. He would become a person nobody knew. A mysterious stranger, like Clint Eastwood, the way he'd ride into a town with that funny squint. He'd do things he'd read about, or seen on television. He remembered them in handfuls. Crazy things. Go hang-gliding. Jump out of a plane. Ride an elephant and maybe Gilley's mechanical bull. Climb the biggest pyramid in Egypt; if there was enough room up there, he'd unroll his sleeping bag and spend the night. He'd run with the bulls in that place in Spain. And survive a knife fight in a waterfront bar . . .

"You are total crazy!" Eva said to him.

"Hey, this was a couple years ago, remember? But yeah, maybe I'm still a little 'rad,' as the surfers say. What the hell do you think I'm doing here in Siberia ten degrees below zero wearing a pair of dumb cowboy boots?"

"This is the Far East, not Siberia, but anyway, that is a good question, about those high-heeled boots you are wearing. Taras thinks they are from Texas."

"You tell Laughing Boy there I got them from Tohei Films, which is outside Tokyo, for two days of stunt work in a Japanese cowboy-samurai movie. This here is genuine armadillo, something like that."

"But how did you come to Japan?"

"I'm going to tell you that too. First I need more vodka." Marcus fished ten rubles from his jeans and semaphored his arm at the waitress. "*Dyevushka!* More vodka! *Bolshe, bolshe!* How's that, teacher?"

"Fantastic!" Eva laughed. "And see, for you she comes quickly!"

"Can't help it if I was born beautiful. Now, where was I?"

"Nyebraska?"

"Somewhere along there. Dreaming up adventures. Like Indiana Jones. And what I figured was"—he tapped his blond head—"if I kept heading west, eventually the continent was going to come to an end and I'd be staring at nothing but ocean. See, I'd studied my geography in school."

Marcus's little joke perished somewhere in translation. Neither Eva nor Taras cracked a smile.

"Anyway, I decided what I really wanted to do was cross the ocean—the whole damn Pacific, preferably in some kind of a sailboat. I decided this somewhere in Kansas, I think, which is pretty much like being out in the middle of the ocean. And I'm thinking, why not? The whole wide world is out there just waiting for me, and absolutely nobody cares what I do. I'm totally free. I can do anything, be anybody, go anywhere. Understand? *Ponimayesh?*"

Like his last joke, this bit of vehemence seemed lost on Eva, who now registered skeptical amusement. But Marcus detected definite glimmerings of interest in Taras's dark eyes. Following one's own star was obviously not a very Russian notion, he decided, but wanderlust certainly ran rampant in the young people Marcus had run into, all the way from Champaign-Urbana to Osaka. He thought of Yuli, a pimply Latvian teenager he'd met on the M/S *Dzerzhinsky,* the steamer from Yokohama, who'd spent most of the rocky two-day voyage listening to John Denver's Greatest Hits on his Walkman.

Anyway, with the Pacific always gentle on his mind, like in the old song, Marcus had begun hitchhiking farther west, stopping for odd jobs here and there to save up passage money—in case he couldn't work or bum a ride across the ocean. Again Eva hesitated in her translation.

"Hitchhiking, right?" he said. "You probably don't do much of it here. Not enough cars. I can just see some poor bastard standing out on a lonely road till he freezes to death, waiting for a truck to come along."

"No. We have many cars, even here in Khabarovsk. On Karl Marx Street you see many, many. And we have a word for hitchhiking. But this is not the way to cross a country like ours. Even driving, it is much too far. Only the Rossiya Express or Aeroflot can cross the entire Soviet Union. Roads and cars are for cities, or between cities and towns, or to drive into the country." She paused. "But 'odd job' is a more difficult word."

He laughed. " 'Odd job'—'strange occupation,' I guess it doesn't make much sense." He tried to clarify but apparently the concept still posed difficulties.

In the Soviet Union, Eva explained, workers could obviously not be allowed to walk away from their jobs without permission, simply in order to work somewhere else. Anarchy would result. But there was one exception. Those were the *shabashniki,* migrant workers or "moonlighters." These itinerant labor gangs, many of them Armenian, were sometimes hired in emergencies, to help with harvests or on construction projects. "Perhaps this is similar to your 'odd jobbers'?"

"Close enough," Marcus said. So, that's what he'd been—a *shabashnik*—more or less from Nebraska to Yokohama, in between the fun and games. He'd spread and tamped asphalt on highway crews in Colorado. Done rough-framing carpentry in Oregon and Washington. Even picked apples up there, real *shabashniki* work. A couple of the sleazier jobs he omitted from the account, like a weekend of dancing bare-ass in a "boylesque" bar outside Reno.

But both Eva's and Taras's eyes lit up when he told about joining up with the traveling carnival. It turned out they thought it was a *tsirk*, a circus, something all Russians apparently adored; they even had one in Khabarovsk.

Marcus hated to disillusion them. There'd been no elephants, no trapeze girls, trained bears, or clowns. Just a bunch of old trucks and trailers that in a day's gut-busting labor could be slammed together into a neon midway, freak show, shooting gallery, three-for-a-buck tosses, tattoo parlor, Ferris wheel, Big Whip, and other lose-your-lunch mechanical rides. Marcus drove a truck, helped with the setup and takedown, hung out with the other roustabouts, did a little barking.

But when the caravan hit Oakland, and Marcus got his first glimpse of San Francisco shining across the Bay, and the vast Pacific through the Golden Gate, he walked away from the sawdust without looking back, just the way he had left his hometown.

The land had finally run out; it was time to go to sea.

But how? He wasn't about to join the Navy or Merchant Marine. He didn't want to spend his hard-earned money on a passenger berth. He wanted to sail. There were sailing schools, he found, but they were for rich hobbyists, too expensive and too slow. Besides, Marcus never played by normal rules. His method was always to jump in and learn by doing.

The next morning he showed up in the Sausalito marina, in the majestic shadow of the Golden Gate. He went sauntering along from one slip to the other, wherever he saw people readying boats to go out, chatting, asking if they could use some extra crew.

"Sorry, not today" was the usual answer, though several inquired if he had any experience.

"Nope. But I work hard and learn quick."

"Some other time maybe."

After an hour he'd found himself standing on the dock, watching longingly as, one after another, the nifty little sloops and ketches and yawls followed one another out of the channel. "I was totally frustrated, like the kid stuck outside the candy store," he told Eva. "So guess what I did."

She couldn't.

"Simple. I got so damn desperate that I took off my jacket, my shirt, my shoes and socks and jeans—everything, right down to my Jockey shorts—and I jumped into the water. Let me tell you, San Francisco Bay is frigging cold, even in the summer, which it wasn't.

59

And I swam out into the channel. So I'm out there treading water, freezing my ass off and a few other parts, and as each boat comes by, I'm waving like this. And people are standing up and grabbing their life rings and shouting, 'Hey, are you okay? Do you need help?' And I'd shake my head and yell back, 'I'm fine. Need any crew?' "

The fourth or fifth boat had picked him up—a fat, bearded ex-Marine Marcus had talked to earlier on the dock. Five minutes later, toweled off and wearing borrowed, giant-size foul weather gear, Marcus was learning how to bring a genoa across the bow and winch it tight in fifteen knots of wind.

"You liked this?" Eva asked.

"I loved it."

Within a year, he told them proudly, he was not only a pretty fair country sailor; he was actually skippering sailboats up and down the Pacific Coast himself, from Vancouver to Acapulco.

As this was all being relayed to Taras, Marcus detected a different kind of envy, almost admiration, in the Russian's eyes. Marcus stood up.

"The moral is—be sure you translate this, Eva—the moral is, find out what you want to do in life, and then jump in feet first, goddammit! And do it!"

"But Marcus, where are you going?"

"Let's take a break here. I'm tired of talking and I'm tired of sitting, and in case you didn't notice, this place is turning into a sauna. Aren't you supposed to be my guide? Let's go see something. Let's go back and watch the old farts fish through the ice, I don't care."

"Of course you are right, Marcus. I am not doing my duties. Taras also is here for the first time, and there is much to be seen in such a fine city as Khabarovsk. But," she added, her blue eyes flashing as Marcus narrowly beat Taras in helping her on with her heavy coat, "we wish to hear more of your adventures."

"That can be arranged."

And so the three bundled up and went out into the brutally cold day, then quickly squeezed into Eva's tiny, apple-green Moskvich.

Chapter

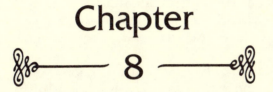

8

Many of the recommended sights of Khabarovsk—those to which Intourist guides invariably drag their helpless victims—are lugubrious in character. And Eva Sorokina did her cheerful utmost to conduct her two young men to as many of these as possible. Reluctantly bypassing the oil refinery, machine-tool factory, and other shining examples of local industry, she drove Marcus and Taras to a succession of war memorials. There was one honoring the fallen Amur sailors; another (erected over a ravine where mass executions had taken place) commemorated civil war victims; and a tower beside the Amur River marked the spot where Hungarian and Austrian prisoners had been shot for refusing to play the imperial Russian anthem. Only the most vocal opposition from her charges dissuaded Eva from driving them fifty kilometers over icy roads to view the wonders of the Volochayevka Battle Museum.

By the time they returned to the Tsentralnaya, on the inevitable Lenin Square with its inevitably monumental statue of V. I. Lenin, both young men were out of sympathy with slaughtered martyrs. And they did not brighten when Eva pointed out the tombstone nearby of four soldiers killed in a long-ago skirmish with the Chinese.

Taras had plainly had enough, and said so in a muttered protest, which Eva translated for Marcus:

"It seems Tarushka is now angry with me. He would rather hear about your trip to South Seas, and also about those bad Tahiti girls."

For the first time since the restaurant, the two men exchanged smiles. Boredom had temporarily allied them, much as vodka had done earlier.

"However, while you are telling us more naughty things you did," Eva said, "let us visit our famous Museum of Local History. It is in the Park of Culture above the Amur. There are no graves, I promise, but two tigers, some sea otters, and other most interesting exhibits."

As they wandered the overheated corridors, peering at stuffed Siberian tigers and the artifacts and handicrafts of various northern tribes, Marcus resumed his narrative. He told how the westward urge had carried him on to Hawaii, and how, for a short time, he had even rowed tourists in a Waikiki outrigger—an unusual job for a haole, or Caucasian. He'd spent part of a summer operating a skip-loader on Maui, helping to rape paradise for a Japanese construction company. Which had in turn paid for a winter of hanging out on Oahu's North Shore, where he'd learned to surf—and been damn fool enough to get himself wiped out on a twenty-foot storm wave at Waimea Bay, and just lucky enough to survive.

"How high in meters this is?"

"Maybe three times higher than that doorway over there. And about a ton of water, which is, shit, a thousand kilos or something, all falling on my head. Pretty stupid, huh?"

Eva agreed vehemently.

They gave short shrift to the dusty upstairs displays dedicated to agrarian and industrial progress achieved in the Far East under socialism. By then both Eva and Taras were caught up in Marcus's adventures on a sixty-foot gaff-rigged ketch he had helped crew all over the South Seas. They followed his long strides over to a Pacific wall map and watched his finger trace a zigzag route across the vast blue expanse. South from Lahaina to the Marquesas, east to Tahiti, Moorea and Bora Bora, northwest to Samoa, then on up through Micronesia and Guam to Yokohama. Nine glorious months.

"You see no Tahiti girls?" Eva teased.

He'd seen his share, but none to play with. No pretty island playmates of any kind, unless he counted a couple of unattached New

Zealand girls he'd met on Ponape, living aboard their uncle's big schooner in Jokaj Harbor. Kiwis were islanders, after all. But Eva didn't want to hear about them.

Finally, two and a half years after leaving home, Marcus had arrived in Japan. He'd spent the past six months mostly in Tokyo, doing more "odd jobs," including teaching English and trying his hand at movie stunt work. He'd also managed to climb Mount Fuji and acquire a brown belt in aikido and Japanese fencing along with a taste for raw fish.

As the trio returned to the museum's ground floor, Marcus brought his story up-to-date. Next, as they knew, he intended to head west on the Trans-Siberian, stopping twice along the way—in Irkutsk to see Lake Baikal, and at Novosibirsk. He'd go on to Moscow and Leningrad. After that, he had no idea.

Then, as they were on the verge of leaving, Marcus paused to look at some old photographs. Eva explained they were actually stills from a recent Soviet film about a famous explorer and ethnographer of eastern Siberia, Vladimir Arsenyev. There was, in fact, a plaque honoring this same Arsenyev on the museum wall.

"I know these pictures," Marcus said. "They're from *Dersu Uzala*. A great movie. I saw it in Tokyo in a Kurosawa film festival, with some of his old samurai movies—like *The Seven Samurai* and *Yojimbo*. Sorry, Eva, but it's Japanese, not Russian."

"*Dersu Uzala,* yes, it is the title. But this is a Soviet film. Mosfilm."

The museum director emerged from his small office to shed light on the matter. His name was Serdyuk, and he was a thin, schoolmasterish fellow with round, rimless eyeglasses that miniaturized his watery gray eyes. "You are both correct," he said in singsong English. The film had been a Russo-Japanese co-production, made in the Far East in the early seventies by the very well-known Japanese director. Indeed, certain of the events depicted had taken place in the vicinity of Khabarovsk. For many years Arsenyev had worked in this very museum, and his house was still standing not far away. And Dersu— the native hunter who was Arsenyev's loyal companion on many expeditions—had been buried just south of the city, near what was now the Korfovskaya Station along the Ussuri River.

Marcus remembered passing this stop on his train up from Nakhodka. He was becoming excited. "This is what they call serendipity," he told Eva.

"What is this?"

"Travel surprises. Stuff that can't happen to you if you never leave home, or don't take a chance. Okay, for instance, I saw this movie *Dersu* only because I went with a guy I met in aikido class, which I took mainly because the teacher, Master Kobayashi, was the brother-in-law of this big Buddha-head I knew in the Islands, the one who also got me the ride on the ketch. And here we are. That's serendipity. You go with the flow."

When Marcus expressed interest in seeing where Kurosawa had filmed, Serdyuk went back to his office and came out with the address of a local trapper, who, he thought, had been a technical adviser on the film. In fact, this man claimed to be a descendant of Arsenyev. Whether or not this was so, he was certainly knowledgeable about the filming, and about the *taiga*, the great Siberian forest.

A half hour later, propelled by Marcus's enthusiasm—and quite against Eva's sober judgment—they found themselves several kilometers outside Khabarovsk along the Ussuri, inside an old peasant cottage, or *izba*. The trapper, whose name was Kostya, turned out to be a big, wild-eyed man with doughy skin and stringy, shoulder-length brown hair. He was apparently unused to company, and rushed about ineffectually, till Eva took charge. In a few minutes, under her supervision, the samovar was heating up, and they were seated on chairs and benches before a large, tiled stove, listening to the trapper describe, in the most agitated and grandiose tones, his obviously insignificant role in the filming.

Rather, Marcus and Eva listened, prompting with further polite questions. But Taras Arensky leaned his wooden chair against the log wall and focused far off through the windows, watching the early winter twilight deepen into darkness. Actually, he was again mired in his frustrations. If only the damn American cowboy would go away, get on the morning train to Irkutsk! As incredible as Marcus's stories had been—and Taras admitted he'd been carried away for a while—he couldn't stand another day of them, watching Eva staring up in doe-eyed admiration. And *two* more days of the bragging, swaggering foreign bastard would definitely call for murder.

Besides, all those adventures couldn't possibly be true, not even half of them. It was impossible. Giant waves! Mountain climbing! Hang-gliding! Lumberjacking! Sailing ships! Japanese sword-fighting and samurai-cowboy movies! And he'd done it all in, what, less than three years? And the crazy kid was only a year older than Taras. Shit on all of it! Either this Marcus Jolly was a superman, or a pathological liar. Or maybe a criminal, a dangerous American hooligan on the run from the police. But Evushka, the silly, gorgeous goose, believed every word.

She might even be in love with the perpetually grinning stranger. Taras thought about that—and of how he might distract her from Marcus and tell her about all the fencing medals *he*, Taras, had won at his sports club—as he fingered the pocket that imprisoned the sacred lock of her hair, that hair which he beheld across the cabin, gleaming buttery gold in the light from a single overhead bulb. How raptly she was listening to Marcus telling another of his Sinbad stories. Beside her the wild-eyed trapper was also listening, waiting for her translation as Taras had done all day.

Fuck you all, he thought. His gaze wandered to the overmantel trophy. A double set of antlers, locked together. Two red deer, Kostya had explained, wapiti bucks, had fought so violently over a doe they'd become entangled and unable to wrench apart, and were thus linked forever in death. A perfect symbol, Taras thought. It could be Marcus and himself, fighting for Eva. Like the American, Taras had come nearly half around the world to be here tonight, in this smoky little room. And he hadn't come all that way to back off and lose Eva to any rival.

The excitable Kostya hurried off to an adjoining pantry, returning with four chipped mugs and a liter of local vodka. Then there were toasts, and, at Eva's insistence, Taras joined in. To America. To Russia. To health, freedom, peace, and international fraternity! To Abraham Lincoln and John F. Kennedy, Arsenyev and Dersu! Down the hatch and bottoms up!

Food was brought out, unwrapped, passed around. Salted herring, black bread, sausages. The trapper began telling how a caged tiger had been carried into the taiga for the movie, although there were many Siberian tigers still lurking in the area. He found this enormously funny for some reason. The food and talk made them all thirsty, and the grinning trapper triumphantly produced another bottle.

Soon they were singing Russian songs. Marcus, who, of course, didn't know the words, fished a small harmonica from under his sheep-skin jacket and began to accompany them—with a skill that impressed both Eva and Kostya and aggravated Taras.

"But this is a toy; anyone can play it," he said.

Marcus tossed him the instrument. Taras blew into it with all his force, producing an ear-splitting squeal, till Eva snatched it away.

Taras protested: "But that was Shostakovich!"

When they all laughed, Taras was swept into the party despite himself. Another bottle materialized. It became somehow obvious that there was to be no trekking back to Khabarovsk this night. Snowflakes were sifting silently against the windowpanes, and Taras saw, pushing back filthy lace curtains, a powdery mantle covering the little Moskvich coupe.

Eva's protests were strongly worded, but only halfhearted. Intourist at the Tsentralnaya would be worried over Marcus's absence. Not to return would be an itinerary violation, and she would be held accountable. If only there were a telephone . . . But Kostya sloshed more vodka into her mug, which made her lose her train of thought, which in turn made her quite furious, and then helplessly giggly.

So, Taras thought, cocking his head, his darling Evushka was also tipsy. Tipsy, and so girlishly desirable that it made him ache to look at her yet not be able to touch her, the way he had done last summer.

Outside, wind-whipped snow was now swirling in every direction. Inside, time had begun subtly to alter, speeding up, then slowing down, like a clockworks with slipping gears. Events lost continuity, ran together in a bright blur, then stood forth in a series of sharply etched, bizarre vignettes. Marcus juggling three, then four potatoes, finally dropping them all and collapsing himself in a cackling spasm. Eva, childishly demonstrating some silly upside-down yoga posture, with her head on the floor and woolen legs kicking the air, toppling sideways to resounding male laughter. And Kostya, grinning and pouring, looking more and more like Rasputin with his deranged smile and ragged, greasy hair.

One moment stood out. Marcus had stumbled outside in the snow, leaking vodka. Then Kostya also vanished, either into the pantry for more food, or also outside, to fetch more stovewood. In his sodden state of mind Taras did not immediately grasp the enormity of the moment. Then all at once he realized, and slid off his bench and onto the wooden floor beside his beloved. After the wretched eternity of

66

the day, here he was—suddenly and miraculously—alone with Eva. Yet the others might come back at any second.

He couldn't restrain himself an instant longer. He reached for her, pulled her close, drowned his face in the intoxicating golden mane of her hair, snuggled against her.

"Evushka, Evushka," he had whimpered, all his pain coming out. "How I adore you, Evushka! I think of nothing but you, always. I must have you!"

If she answered, he could not hear it. He began kissing her passionately, demandingly, throwing his arms around her. She cried out as they tumbled over. He remembered kneeling astride her, looking down at her, blind with desire and then confusion, as she had screamed over and over. He had shaken her, simply to make her stop. She had wrenched away from his grip, then scrambled off to the darkest corner of the shadowy room, where she huddled, weeping.

The other two men were suddenly standing in the doorway. Taras had felt stunned. He began to stammer. Eva looked at him as though he had transformed into a monster before her eyes. He got up and stumbled about, apologizing over and over, to Kostya and Marcus, and endlessly to Eva, till she finally yelled at him to stop. Then he had wept.

Incredibly, the party had gone on after that. There was more singing, and at one point Eva even forgave him. But she stayed nearer to Marcus, Taras saw, and had more to say even to the simpleton Kostya than she did to Taras. When she began to drink again, so did Taras, seeking swift oblivion.

The room became a swirling carousel, careening so fast he could no longer attach names to faces or words to voices. Only at the very last, as he slipped into insensibility, did a single, fleeting thought take frightened flight across the fading sky of his mind: By being the first to pass out, he was leaving his beloved alone with two strange men.

Taras awoke in a freezing room with a sledgehammering headache— pain so blindingly intense it felt like a saber being thrust again and again through his brain. When he tried to open his eyes, white light seared into his sockets. He screamed and rolled over. He was aware now that he was uncovered, freezing to death. Yet he could not bring himself to move again.

But there was something else, something even more terrible than the pain. A nightmarish afterimage, something glimpsed in that hideous, flashing knifeblade of daylight, something etched retinally inside his mind. He willed himself to roll over and squint through his eyelashes.

Across the frost-rimed pine floor, protruding from behind a low wooden chest into a slush-stained rectangle of windowed sun, was a bare foot. A small, plump foot with a lovely arch. He had held that foot in his lap and caressed it as they lay tumbled and sandy together on an Odessa beach. Her skin had shone peaches and cream in that southern sun; now in the cold winter luminescence it was ghastly bluish-ivory. Taras felt something precious dying inside his soul as he forced his eyes wide.

Eva's body—naked, as he had only dreamed of it—lay sprawled on the floorboards. Taras sprang up, ignoring his exploding headache, bellowing her beloved name into winter silence. He took three lurching steps toward her and fell to the floor, just close enough to reach and touch her cold breast.

His darling had been strangled by fiendish hands that had left a livid necklace in her flesh. She had been violated as well—Taras knew it, though he wrenched his head aside from her blind stare, unable to look more closely, especially *there,* between her thighs. Instead, he ripped a woolen blanket off the trapper's bed and, weeping and apologizing for its filth, laid it reverently over her. Once more he dropped to the floor, sobbing. He touched the blanket, then a sheaf of tawny hair that had escaped the shroud into a shaft of sunlight. Unable to help himself, Taras drew the long, silken strands through his fingers, then brought them to his lips. The ripe fragrance seduced him, undiminished by death, whispering earthy promises never to be fulfilled.

Taras staggered to his feet, but the name he bellowed now was Kostya's. The wild-eyed cretin had surely committed this atrocity, then vanished with all their clothes. Even their winter underwear had been taken; only Marcus's black cowboy hat was left behind.

Across the cabin floor Marcus himself lay alternately snoring and shivering in sleep, like Taras stripped to his shorts. Taras touched his body; Marcus was alive, but cold.

Taras shook him violently, shouting his name.

It took several minutes to rouse Marcus from the frozen stupor. And when the American was finally able to unglaze his eyes and understand where he was, and what lay lifeless under the blanket, he erupted in fury, grappling Taras to the floor. "You bastard!" he screamed. "Why did you do it?"

An elbow to the jaw stunned Marcus, and a vehement explanation finally convinced him of Taras's innocence. Marcus staggered up again, still freezing, unable to hide his own tears when he lifted a corner of the blanket. The next instant he was ready to charge naked into the snow and wreak vengeance on the trapper. Instead, Taras pushed him toward the wall pegs on which hung some of the murderer's filthy garments. With near-frozen fingers, the two fumbled into dirt-glazed corduroy pants, stained quilted coats, and *valenki,* felt boots, all several sizes too large.

Not only had the trapper made off with their clothes. Also missing, they now discovered, were all their identity papers and Marcus's money belt with nearly five hundred U.S. dollars—a potential fortune on the Soviet black market.

Once bundled up, they had rushed outside. Eva's Moskvich was there, but buried under a mound of snow. It must have snowed steadily since the trapper had made his escape, for no tracks marred the crystalline white carpet surrounding the *izba.*

They had rushed about like madmen, seeking clues, their *valenki* postholing through the soft powder. They had slogged down to the banks of the frozen Ussuri, then up to the main road without finding a trace of Kostya's flight. Exhausted, their breath plumes mingling in the air, they had stood, staring both ways down the empty road. It began to snow again, wet flakes spinning down out of a mother-of-pearl sky.

Then a bus came grinding through the vaporous clouds. Taras flagged it down and talked the driver into dropping them off at militia headquarters. There, still shivering despite the overheated vestibule, Taras blurted out the grim tale to an already mournful-looking duty sergeant, who could not seem to comprehend the need for immediate action.

It wasn't until almost an hour later, when several detectives returned noisily from a nearby cafeteria, that urgency was manifested. Taras and Marcus were driven back to the scene of the crime in a cream-colored van with a red militia stripe. The detective captain apologized for the strong disinfectant smell; a drunken hooligan had been violently ill in the back earlier that morning. Riding along in the van beside them was a tearful Intourist guide, Mariana, Eva's friend, now pressed into service to translate for Marcus.

The detectives combed the area all around the *izba,* flapping about in the snow in their heavy gray greatcoats and communicating by walkie-talkie. But, like Marcus and Taras, they could discover nothing beyond Eva's pitiful corpse, which was photographed extensively, then taken away in a second van by the militia pathologist. The detective captain was phlegmatic as they drove back through thick snow flurries to headquarters. The trapper might have taken to the *taiga,* in which case, he was either holed up in a cave or frozen in a snowdrift. If he didn't come in to confess when he sobered up, they'd probably find his body in the spring. Still, he might have escaped on the train, using Arensky's military papers and clothing. At the terminal it was learned that several soldiers had indeed purchased tickets that morning. A description was flashed along the line—westward to Birobidzhan, Belogorsk, and Skovorodino, and east to Vladivostok and Nakhodka, and to dozens of little stations in between. Unfortunately, the captain pointed out, Kostya might easily have dropped off undetected between stops.

Several more times, that day and the next, Taras and Marcus retold their story, filling out and signing endless carbon forms, contributing a sense of overwhelming futility to their already full measure of grief. Through it all, they sat together, these former rivals, now united in tragedy.

On a leaden afternoon—on what should have been the fourth and final day of Arensky's idyllic visit to his fiancée—he stood beside Marcus at Eva's burial. The gravediggers had set a fire to thaw the frozen ground, and now an icy wind whipped both snow and ashes among the few mourners. Besides Taras and Marcus, there were only two militiamen and three of Eva's Intourist coworkers. As the pine coffin was lowered into the grave, both young men, despite their resolve, had wept openly. Then, unable to bear the sight and sound of earth being shoveled in, they had turned and walked off, hunched over against the wet wind.

Taras could think of nothing but his great loss, and the emptiness of his life ahead. He recalled with new understanding the bitter words of a Lermontov poem he had memorized in school: "And life, when you look around you with cold attention, such an empty and stupid joke." The last phrase especially he repeated to himself as a litany, over and over: *takaya, pustaya i glupaya shutka!*

Yet—how strange!—Marcus, his former, detested rival, was now almost his only comfort, his one living link to Eva. And when Taras made preparations for his immediate return to Moscow, he was not displeased when Marcus asked to come along with him, forgoing stops in Irkutsk and Novosibirsk. In fact, thanks to partial compensation from Intourist for the stolen funds, the American insisted they travel together in soft class, and that he pay for Taras's upgrade.

On that marathon journey the two had forged a friendship. They gave each other nicknames; Marcus became "Cowboy," Taras was "Cossack." By sheer doggedness they found they could communicate almost anything—by gestures, by pictographs, and by endless resort to an English-Russian dictionary. And when these failed, they even found a few common words in French, words Taras recalled from his older sister Luiza's school lessons and which Marcus had picked up in the South Seas.

On the fifth day, as the Rossiya Express wound through the rocky Urals past Sverdlovsk and the trackside obelisk marking the boundary between Europe and Asia, they had pledged lifelong friendship over a shared half liter of vodka. The second oath was for vengeance—on Eva's killer.

"But you go away, Cowboy," Taras had said when the bottle was empty, reluctantly pointing out the obvious flaw in their plan.

"*Nyet!*" Marcus had said, flipping through the dictionary for the Russian words he wanted. "I stay here. Be soldier like you, Cossack. In Soviet army. My new adventure." He grinned, tilting back his cowboy hat, the only remnant of his old costume.

Incredibly, the young American had followed through on what had seemed clearly an empty, alcohol-induced boast. In Moscow, with Taras's help, Marcus had applied for and received political asylum. This decision, astonishing at the time in light of the American's enviable free spirit, continued to perplex Taras for years. Had Marcus some ulterior motive in fleeing his homeland? Fully fifteen years were to pass before Taras would receive a satisfying answer to this puzzle.

Nevertheless, the two managed to remain fast friends while going their separate ways—Arensky pursuing his studies at the Supreme

71

Soviet Military Academy, and Marcus not only entering the Red Army at the somewhat ripe age of twenty-one, but being selected for special forces, or *Spetsnaz*.

And from that time to this, no trace had ever been found of Eva's murderer.

Chapter

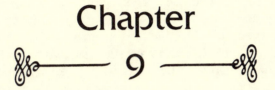

9

MARCUS JOLLY BURST INTO THE SMALL, DIMLY LIT ROOM, PIVOTING and firing the 9mm automatic as targets popped up around him, one after another, at extreme close range. There were eight friend-or-foe silhouettes—four terrorists, four hostages. The idea was to take out only the ones with weapons. He reacted instinctively, pointing and shooting, two head shots for each "bad guy," until only good guys were left standing in the acrid aftermath. He had cleared the room in less than four seconds—actually 03.69 according to the digital readout over the door—with seven bullets still in the clip.

A surprisingly schoolboyish-looking Green Beret instructor hurried in, hit the overhead fluorescents, and whistled appreciatively as he checked the targets.

"Holy shit, sir! You've got four kills, right between the eyes, one-inch groups. If this is your hobby, what the hell do you do for a living?"

"Sank you, *ja,* it is good sport. I sell hardware, software, it is, *ja?*" Marcus tapped his golf cap, which bore the logo of the German electronics giant, Siemens A.G.

"Well, if you ever get bored, the *Bundeswehr* could use you, maybe even GSG-9." The reference was to Germany's famed counter-terrorist warfare unit, *Grenzschutzgruppe* 9, or Border Marksmen Group 9.

"No, only targets I shoot, not people, ha-ha. Other three rooms not open today, *ja?*"

"Sorry about that. I'd like to see what you could do in them myself."

Marcus smiled and took off his ear protectors as he exited into the Bavarian sunshine. Besides the Siemens golf cap, he was wearing trendy Boris Becker–endorsed tennis shorts, shirt, and shoes, and a bushy brown mustache attached with spirit gum, which matched his recently darkened hair. Outside, a stout man, whose resemblance to Teddy Roosevelt included steel spectacles, grizzled mustache, and even a toothy grimace, handed Marcus a can of Coke. The man's uniform identified him as a captain in the *Bundeswehr*'s 1st Mechanized Infantry Division.

"Marcus, I told you to try and miss a few, not cause a damn sensation," the captain said in Bavarian-accented German as they moved off a little ways.

Marcus answered with a fluency that would have astonished his erstwhile Austrian girlfriend: "I did try, Walter. I was shooting weak-handed." He transferred the Coke to his left hand and the matte-black Czech CZ75 pistol to his right. "Want to see me do it faster?"

"Wonderful idea, blow both our covers. Let's get out of here."

The two men walked away from the shooting house, which, the captain had informed Marcus, was modeled after the Delta Force "House of Horrors" in Fort Bragg, North Carolina. Which, in turn, had been inspired by the SAS "Killing House" in England. This one was located in Bad Tölz, forty-five kilometers south of Munich just north of the Austrian border, headquarters of the USAEUR 10th Special Forces Group, 1st Battalion (the balance of the 10th having relocated in 1968 to Fort Devens, Massachusetts). The shooting house had been hastily assembled in 1980, the captain explained, to train a thirteen-man Special Forces unit that had accompanied Delta to Iran as part of the abortive Eagle Claw hostage-rescue mission.

"The Green Beret kid back there mentioned GSG-9," Marcus said. "They're located around here, aren't they?"

"Just across the Rhine from Bonn. In St. Augustin. Why?"

"I heard they've got a fantastic underground shooting range. Maybe you could get me in there. How's your pull with the *Bundesgrenz-*

schutz?" This was the German Border Police, the parent outfit of GSG-9.

"Marcus, just behave yourself." They were approaching the camp's main gate, where the *Bundeswehr* captain's Opel Kadett was parked. "My connections aren't *that* good. And I'm afraid your German is good enough to fool only Americans."

The two men lunched at an outdoor café in Bad Tölz's picturesque Old Town, on the steep and winding Marktstrasse. It was exceedingly pleasant—weisswurst with sweet mustard, sauerkraut, and schooners of beer under a vine-trellised, overhanging Bavarian roof—until a tiny East German Trabant 601 sidled up to the adjacent curb and began spewing lethal hydrocarbons at their table. Walter, though now out of uniform, rushed over and screamed in full military voice, forcing car and driver into flatulent retreat.

"Damn stinkpots," Walter muttered, resuming his chair. "Worst thing about reunification and opening the Wall was all those Trabis and Wartburgs that came farting in from the east with their shitty two-stroke engines. But we must tolerate them, out of a spirit of freedom and unity—*Freiheit und Einheit*. I say shit! *Scheissdreck!*"

"They're real trendy, Walter. Museums buy them. Rich Austrian kids buy them and put Porsche engines in them."

"Degenerates!"

"Now you sound like old man Marchenko, complaining about Soviet youth and their addiction to Western corruption."

"Well, he was right." Walter motioned to a sheet of paper Marcus had been studying. "So, tell me what you think."

Marcus shrugged. The paper purported to list all of President Rybkin's movements for the next three weeks—up until the Potsdam Conference. "This is nothing. I read all this shit in the newspapers already." Marcus crumpled the paper and dropped it on the table.

"That's all we have now. If the man's doing any other traveling between now and Potsdam, he hasn't advertised it—even in the Politburo, believe me, or we'd know about it. In any case, Potsdam is the only place that makes sense, Marcus."

"You're supposed to help me, Walter, not tell me how to do my job."

"I'm just saying you'll never get close to him in Moscow, or anywhere over there. That's like trying to attack your opponent's king when he's castled. You have to draw him out."

"I don't play chess, Walter. I'm not a real Russki, remember? And I like to sneak up on people. It gives me a hard-on."

"Ah, really? Then here's what you should do, Marcus. Go to the library—I suggest the *Bayerisches Staatsbibliothek* in Munich. Ask for detailed floor plans of all the buildings in the Kremlin Palace. Make a big X on Rybkin's office, or, better, his bathroom, and sneak up on him with your hard-on. I wish you good hunting. Now, what else can I do for you? Do you like the Czech pistol?"

"It's okay. I test-fired an Italian clone back in Austria, made by Fratelli Tanfoglio; you couldn't tell the difference. You keep it, Walter. I'll be in touch if I need anything else locally."

"So, Marcus, where are you going from here?"

"It doesn't work that way. Just do your job for the *Bundeswehr* and wait to see if you're contacted."

"You are trying to scare me now, Marcus, is that it?" Walter pointed to the crumpled paper. "Don't leave that lying around, please. I don't care what you think of it."

Marcus made a fist. The captain tensed, swallowed wurst, measuring Marcus's icy squint.

"Relax, Walter, and just watch." Marcus thumbed a thick steel ring on his forefinger. From the side mounting of its black onyx stone a tiny barrel protruded, and a jet of fire shot forth; the paper flamed up, then shriveled into ash.

"God in heaven! What is that, a laser?"

"Miniature flamethrower. Burns nitric acid and kerosene, just like Marchenko's old SS-9 rockets. Five shots, then you throw the damn thing away. From the KGB toy department. Ugliest hunk of jewelry I ever saw. They probably use it for lighting ladies' cigarettes across crowded rooms."

"Seriously, if you don't like it, give it to me."

Marcus eyed the captain a long moment, then slipped the heavy ring off and tossed it across the table. "You want it, Walter, it's yours. It's got four shots left. Wear it in health. And forgive me for being such a degenerate asshole. But hey, that's the way I am."

As Walter screwed the ring onto his own stubby index finger, Marcus hoisted his schooner. "A toast, Walter."

The captain looked up from his new toy in ill-concealed delight. "Yes, yes?"

"Confusion to the enemy!"

"Confusion to the enemy!" Walter echoed.

"Whoever the fuck he may be," Marcus added.

In return for the gift, the *Bundeswehr* captain had offered to take Marcus on a discreet tour of some of Munich's more interesting nocturnal habitats. There were certain private shows, for instance, which catered to a variety of esoteric tastes and which were said to rival anything available on the Continent. Among the specific enticements Walter offered were leather-clad Aryan goddesses with superb physiques and wonderfully sadistic temperaments.

Marcus declined.

"But you are not squeamish?"

"Some other time, Walter."

Instead, Marcus went early to bed—or early to camp. He had parked his Moto Guzzi and pitched his sleeping tent on the outskirts of Bad Tölz among holiday caravans on the banks of the Isar.

After several weeks of the considerable pleasures of Silvie, Marcus wasn't in need of sex, and certainly not any voyeuristic excursions into Teutonic kink. What he did need was to think clearly about his next step. And to do that, he had first to subdue his swirling thoughts and find his spiritual center, his source of power—his *ki*, to use the martial arts term—and unleash its transforming energy.

He unrolled his down bag inside the little tent, knelt Japanese-fashion on his pillow, and, positioning his flashlight, opened his *Hagakure* at random. He read: *"Instead of victory, concentrate on dying."*

Having found his samurai text, Marcus closed the slim book and meditated, shutting out the pulsing sound of the latest Eurorock from a nearby caravan. His grandparents' death had indeed sent him forth as a young man, and death had intersected his adventurous wanderings again and again. The death of Eva Sorokina had forged his friendship with Taras Arensky, and countless deaths in Afghanistan had severed that friendship—as it drew Marcus deeper into his Russian destiny.

He could not desire death in the samurai way; he had inflicted and witnessed its careless handiwork too often. But neither did he fear or flee it, for death and danger had long been his intimate companions.

The only life he craved was life lived on the flirtatious edge of death.

Perhaps constant courting of danger was his way of seeking death, as the samurai code instructed. But Marcus now contemplated a further step. Marchenko—his samurai "lord," his *daimyo*—had been slain. Marcus was charged with avenging that murder—killing Rybkin—the "shōgun"—as the Forty-Seven Ronin (whose sacred graves Marcus had visited in the Sengaku-ji Temple outside Tokyo) had avenged their Lord Asano. According to *Hagakure,* Marcus's own death must result from the successful completion of that task.

Marcus shook his head, imagining what the old rocketry general would have made of this Eastern nonsense—equating Marchenko's network of loyal *Spetsnaz* fighters with homeless samurai after their leader's death. But how else could Marcus anchor his life against the hurricane winds of change shrieking once more across Russia? What was a defector to do when his adopted homeland betrayed *him?* When its leader was busily dismantling its borders and defenses, exiling or assassinating its greatest patriots, and only smiled enigmatically as civil protest boiled over into armed insurrection all across the Eurasian land mass? Marchenko's simple solution—kill Rybkin!—seemed more and more the only way out of bloody chaos.

But today's meeting had posed a further problem. Walter had faithfully passed along Marchenko's final command; beyond that, Marcus remained skeptical of the captain's *gemütlich* manner. Marcus chuckled as he recalled how avidly the German had swallowed the preposterous story about the KGB flamethrower ring having five shots and being rocket-fueled. The truth was, its one-shot chamber had to be reloaded after each firing with a new gel-flame capsule. Since Marcus had no more of these, the ring was now useless—which Walter would discover if he ever tried to fire it.

The man was not to be trusted, Marcus decided. Hereafter Marcus must seek help only from the inner core of old *Spetsnaz* comrades, and even there be wary.

"Instead of victory, concentrate on dying."

The task ahead of Marcus was indeed formidable. Only by embracing his own death, *Hagakure* counseled, could Marcus achieve that impossible victory—Rybkin's death.

So be it.

Marcus switched off the flashlight, but was denied darkness. Faint light from a neighboring caravan seeped through the red nylon tent fabric. That was all right. Marcus did not intend to sleep yet. He was energized, ready to conjure his own death—a daily samurai exercise. He began to visualize it—and imagine its mental, emotional, and visceral impact—in different forms. Being torn apart by explosives. Dying by his own hand—slashing his own jugular; disemboweling himself samurai style, with a sword-wielding second standing by. Being riddled with bullets. Having a hang glider capsize in sudden, violent air, plummeting earthward with no chute. Drowning at sea. Being crushed in an earthquake, trapped in a burning building. All sudden, violent ends. Marcus did not bother imagining a slow, debilitating death.

The exercise worked, separating his upwelling *ki* from his motionless body. He became for a second a nameless being, a hovering force field with eyes. Yet the old familiar Marcus remained below, kneeling on his pillow, occupied by pangs of hunger and incessant trivial thoughts, tethering him like a kite's tail to the earth.

Inevitably the free-floating spell was broken, and Marcus was plunged back into his familiar self. The body needed sleep. And Marcus was still not ready to embrace the samurai way of death.

As he reached out to unzip the sleeping bag, he saw an approaching figure silhouetted against the backlit tent fabric. Someone from the next caravan, coming over to invite him to a party? For heavy-metal sounds continued to thud into the night from that direction.

Then an arm separated from the man-shape, revealing the stark outline of a large knife.

Electricity surged through Marcus, raising the hairs on his scalp, the back of his neck and forearms. This was no apparition of death. Somebody was out there, coming to kill him!

He watched, barely breathing, as the thrown shadow loomed larger and blacker against the red fabric. The hard-rock din provided pounding syncopation to Marcus's hammering heartbeat. The dark figure flowed onward, sliding like a black tide across the tent, stopping directly above him, the huge knife poised to strike.

Marcus held his breath.

The man grunted and the tent ripped open, the blade slicing down and burying itself in the sleeping bag and earth below—right where Marcus's torso should have been. Then the tent collapsed as the figure fell into it.

Now! Marcus sprang forward and grappled his assailant through the nylon fabric. The man grunted again, this time in shock, trying to writhe away. But Marcus was on him, with surprise and position, sliding behind the torso and pinning both arms, then cocooning the struggling body in tent fabric. There was an instant when the other could have cried out for help, and did not. Marcus exulted. A lone assassin, then, and surely doomed as Marcus tightened the nylon noose, constricting the head, throttling the neck.

The body began to wrench violently under him, emitting the glottal stops of suffocation. Marcus held on fiercely, yanking the fabric tighter, then vising his own hands to crush the windpipe as they thrashed together across the ground.

All at once his opponent's struggles ceased, the muscles going slack. The body collapsed beneath him, vented an abrupt foulness of trapped gases.

Marcus sat back, reared his head, and gorged on oxygen, blinking up at the faint smear of light that was the Milky Way. Music continued to thud nearby, as though nothing had happened. Marcus recognized an Abba oldie, "Gimme! Gimme! Gimme!" Slowly he unwound the corpse from its nylon shroud, fumbled and found his flashlight, knew even before its beam played over the grizzled mustache who the assassin was.

So, Walter had decided to pass up Munich's fleshpots tonight. *Surprise, old man. You were not my death after all. I was yours.*

Marcus moved the beam of light down to the lifeless hand, toward a pale gleam of metal. Marcus tugged, but the steel ring was stuck tight on the fleshy forefinger. But there was more than one way to skin a traitor. Marcus felt around under snarled fabric till he located the captain's weapon, brought it into the light—and swore in two languages:

"*Yob tvoyu mat!* I'll be damned!"

Only Crocodile Dundee or John Rambo would carry such a monster survival knife, Marcus thought. Damn near a foot-long blade, with a chisel-tooth saw. A regular Arkansas toothpick. He feathered his finger along the edge, drew blood. Very keen. Would have filleted Marcus nicely.

He swung the flashlight back to the ring. Then with one hand he gripped the huge knife while the other prepared for surgery by carefully exposing and isolating Walter's beringed forefinger.

Wear it in health, Marcus had said. And so the captain had, for most of a day.

80

Chapter

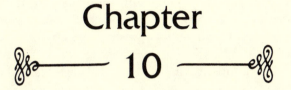 10

EIGHT YEARS BEFORE, AS A YOUNG GRU OFFICER ON BRIEF AS-
signment to England (gathering intelligence on the activities of supposedly retired Special Air Service—SAS—commandos), Taras
Arensky had visited the Tower of London and heard the story of Sir
Walter Raleigh. The part that had both fascinated and perplexed him
was why Raleigh, finally escaping thirteen years imprisonment in the
White Tower by undertaking a last voyage to the New World, would
voluntarily return afterward to his homeland to face a capital charge—
and then stretch his neck meekly upon the infamous Tower Green
chopping block.

As the Boeing 707 touched down in darkness at Vnukovo Airport
thirty kilometers southwest of Moscow, Taras thought again of Raleigh, with a sort of kinship. For Taras was also returning under
sentence of death (though now supposedly withdrawn by the Soviet
Supreme Court), in obedience to an imperial summons. And undoubtedly like Raleigh, he was prey to conflicting emotions, one of
which was a profound and sudden homesickness. But wariness and
distrust were also present in healthy proportions, backed by undis-
missible fears for his own safety—and, though it sounded trite, for

his soul. He was, after all, returning at the behest of tyrants, to stalk and murder an old friend.

And yes, there was guilt. Taras had justified his defection to himself countless times and knew in his heart he had not betrayed Mother Russia, only the parasitic Soviet system. Yet the Russian language had no word for "defector"—only for emigrant or traitor. And as the big Boeing taxied toward the terminal lights, Taras could not escape the sense of returning to face judgment—not God's, certainly not the Party's, more like the collective judgment of three hundred million souls across this vast land—which was really a way of saying his own self-imposed judgment. For no matter what his passport said, Taras would always feel himself Russian, would always wish other Russians to understand why he had left. How would his homeland greet its prodigal after all these years and so many radical reforms? And how would *he* react to *it*?

Of course, no fanfare accompanied Arensky's first footsteps back on his native soil; quite the opposite. He deplaned into the surprising heat of a summer night and was whisked away at once, giving him no opportunity to savor his emergence from a U.S. presidential jet at what was, after all, Moscow's VIP airfield—exactly like all those foreign dignitaries he used to watch on the nightly *Vremya* news program being greeted by Comrade Brezhnev. Only a couple of plainclothes KGB security types were waiting at the foot of the boarding stairs, along with Hank Kelleher, the distinguished-looking, white-haired political attaché—and CIA station chief—at the American Embassy, who hustled Taras and Mike Usher into the back of a black Lada. Within minutes they were following the taillights of a KGB Chaika onto the Kiev highway and through the darkness of the city's suburban forest belt.

"We're not exactly advertising your visit," Kelleher explained when they crossed Moscow's outer ring road. The highway now became Lenin Prospekt, one of the central approaches to the city, and one which happened to trace the route of Napoleon's disastrous retreat. "Which is why we're putting you up at the Metropole for tonight instead of the embassy compound. Hope you don't mind."

"Why should I?" Taras said. "If anyone bugs my room, all he'll hear is snoring. I'm about done in."

"So how does the Big Village look to you after all these years?"

"Bigger," Taras said, recognizing the high-rise complex of the Central Tourist House on their left. A lot of cement had indeed been poured since he'd left, the city solidifying to the southwest beyond the old prefab housing blocks—*Khrushchoby,* or Khrushchevian slums—filling in all the way out to the ring road from Gagarin Square, where the spotlighted titanium cosmonaut atop his forty-meter-high rocket column still looked to Arensky as they passed below like a comic-book superhero blasting skyward. Yet unchanged was the city's air of brooding, provincial gloom—something especially palpable at this late hour, with the streets almost entirely deserted and, despite all the *perestroika* and market-oriented economic reforms, still deficient in the random neon flickerings taken for granted in the West.

"Ugliness on the march," Kelleher said. "Most of the old suburban villages are gone now. And unfortunately a lot of lovely neighborhoods farther in were also razed by Grishin's bulldozers and replaced with more dreary office blocks and 'housing estates,' before the bastard was booted upstairs."

Moments later, as they passed Oktyabrskaya Square on the Garden Ring and doglegged left toward the city center, Taras got his first glimpse of the giant, electrified red stars atop the Kremlin towers, where once the Tsar's double-headed eagles had perched. Moments later, as they crossed over the reflection-streaked Moskva on the Bolshoi Kamenny Bridge, the great citadel itself shouldered into view with its floodlit facades and golden domes and turrets. The Thameside Tower of London was a quaint medieval toy compared to this immense stronghold, whose red brick walls rose twenty meters and enclosed seventy thousand square meters of cathedrals, palaces, and monumental government buildings. Even though the Soviet empire was raveling away at its edges, this medieval fortress still remained the seat of power of a vast region—a sixth continent, as it had often been described.

They came off the bridge into Borovitskaya Square and turned right on Marx Prospekt, alongside the Kremlin's west wall and the Alexandrovsky Gardens. Unlike other monuments to repression—the Bastille and the Berlin Wall came to mind—these great crenellated ramparts might never come tumbling down, but the winds of *glasnost* had rendered them far less menacing. Still, Arensky's jet-lagged nervous system was slightly overwhelmed by the Kremlin's massive reality. He needed a shot of vodka, and a good mattress.

The Chaika now preceded them past Gorky Street (recently rechristened "Tverskaya Street," its pre-Stalinist name) and the gray granite-and-marble bulk of the Moskva Hotel on Revolution Square, then swung round Sverdlov Square on the side opposite the illuminated Greek temple front of the Bolshoi. They pulled up behind the Chaika in front of the five-storied, glass-domed edifice of the Metropole Hotel. Not exactly four stars, but at least atmospheric, with a facade decorated with mosaic panels. Better than the Ukraina or the Leningradskaya, for instance, or the awful Rossiya down by the river, known as the "Big Box" for its gargantuan size and general resemblance to a packing crate. And the Metropole was certainly preferable to Lefortovo Prison, where, as a convicted traitor, Arensky might reasonably have expected to spend his first night back on Soviet soil.

As had been the case at Vnukovo with the formalities of customs and immigration, the red tape of hotel registration was sliced through on his behalf. Arensky kept passport and visa, and was given his key directly at the desk. As he came off the elevator, his KGB escort waved off the sour-faced *dezhurnaya*, the floor lady, whose usual function, besides snooping, was to issue passkeys in exchange for chits. After a brief good night to Kelleher, Taras was left alone. He threw open the windows to let in a warm, humid breeze, decided against vodka, and instead downed a small bottle of Borzhomi mineral water from the minibar, threw his sticky clothes in the general direction of a poisonous-green plush armchair and collapsed into bed.

Welcome home.

At No. 2 Dzerzhinsky Square—only a few long blocks and one Metro stop north of Red Square—stands a massive red-granite and ocher-stucco structure. Actually this monstrosity, which fills the square's entire northeastern side, is composed of two buildings haphazardly matched—a seven-story turn-of-the-century Italianate building (pre-revolutionary headquarters of the All-Russia Insurance Company) and a nine-story extension (built by German prisoners during, and after, the Great Patriotic War).

The site is commonly passed over in guidebooks and Intourist spiels, while attention is directed to the large Children's World department store opposite at No. 2, Marx Prospekt. But the two-building structure requires no identification for Muscovites. It is infamous as KGB headquarters, and still known by its former function as the Lubyanka Internal Prison. Since December of 1920 *dom dva* (house number two) has been the stronghold of the Soviet secret police, the organ of state security founded by the man whose bronze statue stands in the center of this square, which also bears his name, "Iron Feliks" Dzerzhinsky.

During the long nightmare of Stalinist terror, the building's vehicle courtyards were kept busy with NKVD "bread vans" and Black Marias making their ceaseless deliveries of enemies of the state for the Lubyanka's dog kennel cells, or *sobachniki*. During those dark decades, the rococo structure on Dzerzhinsky Square served as combined interrogation center, torture-and-execution chamber, and crematorium.

But those were the bad old days. With the advent of *glasnost* and *perestroika*, the Committee for State Security had changed its spots and considerably polished its public relations, going so far as to institute citizen hotlines and permit a degree of legislative oversight by the Congress of People's Deputies. The current KGB chief Vladimir Biryukov now allowed anti-KGB demonstrations in Dzerzhinsky Square to become quite boisterous without sending in the riot police. "We bow our heads in memory of the innocent victims," one of Biryukov's predecessors, Vladimir Kryuchkov, had said of secret-police brutality under Stalin. "It will never happen again. Never."

Taras very much hoped that that was true as he and Hank Kelleher approached the bas relief of Karl Marx at the entrance of the original Lubyanka building the next morning. Most guests and KGB subordinates, he knew, were required to use one of the headquarters' six side entrances, but the two Americans were conducted past the sentry with no credential check, and without being issued the usual time-stamped pass for verifying the movements of all visitors.

Taras had never before set foot in this vast sanctum sanctorum, but, with the exception of uniformed sentries and frequent security checkpoints, he found it exactly like other state ministries—cavernous, dingily carpeted corridors, with high ceilings and oversized doors, steadily trafficked by mostly civilian personnel. Except here, undoubtedly, the faces were more impassive and the eyes more knowing.

An ancient elevator took them to the fourth floor of the old building, where thick carpeting muffled their steps and polished walnut paneling darkly mirrored their passage. After a considerable trek they were ushered into a large office with a mahogany and tooled-leather conference table at one side, positioned before tall windows opening onto the square; opposite was a large, red-leather-paneled desk. At their entrance, three men—two in uniform, the other in business suit—got quickly up from the table; and a fourth man—squat, long-armed and bow-legged—emerged from behind the desk.

This man, smiling and extending his hand, was also in civilian attire. But the portrait behind his desk showed him in uniform, visored cap under arm, with a colonel general's stars on his red shoulder boards and a chestful of medals—including the Order of Lenin and Hero of Socialist Labor. This was, then, Vladimir Biryukov, current chairman of the Committee for State Security.

Besides being short and simian, Biryukov was pockmarked, with oily, thinning black hair and bushy Brezhnevian eyebrows. The portraitist had done his best to flatter his unprepossessing subject, strengthening the rudimentary features, thickening the hair and smoothing the cratered complexion. But darting black eyes, which Taras thought could almost be described as merry, were more impressive in the original.

Biryukov and Kelleher were already "Volodya" and "Genrikh" to each other. The rest of the introductions were quickly made by the KGB chairman. The two in uniform were Biryukov's sturdy-looking deputy, Lieutenant General Anatoliy Borovik, and a blond, crew-cut, square-jawed lieutenant colonel, Pavel Starkov, who looked to Arensky like a Volga German. It was Starkov, the KGB chairman explained, who had conducted the arrest of Marchenko for treason—an arrest the old general had resisted, violently and futilely, leading, unfortunately, to his death. Starkov was on temporary reassignment from the Second Chief Directorate for internal security to the Ninth Directorate, responsible for guarding the Politburo members—specifically in this case President Rybkin. The fourth man in the room, also in civilian clothes, was a Major General Pyotr Rogovoy, a bald and humorless-seeming fellow with a limp handshake; his reason for being present was not given.

They took seats around the big table, Biryukov in an armchair beside the window—a place from which, Taras thought, he could easily look down on any protests, or commune with Iron Feliks, whose brooding bronze statue outside was circled endlessly and noisily by the square's vehicle traffic. An air-conditioning unit hanging outside one window was out of commission, and a small electric fan atop a file case had been pressed into service to stir a lethargic breeze across the table.

Biryukov laced plump fingers together and leaned forward. "Well, gentlemen, shall we start? My friend Genrikh has been up here before, of course. But Taras Genrikhovich, may I be the first to say 'welcome home'?"

Arensky acknowledged with a slight nod. He wasn't about to express gratitude for the atavistic, Cold War–vintage coercion that had brought him here.

Hank Kelleher stepped in: "This is very genial of you, Volodya, but let us not pretend that Taras is here on a sentimental journey to the Motherland. He has come to cooperate with you, as you know, at the request of President Ackerman, and as quid pro quo for the issuance of long-delayed exit visas for his sister and her family."

"Of course," the chairman continued in a slightly subdued vein, "we are aware of these details. And we are not here to discuss the past. The problems which face us now are common problems, far too critical to permit divisiveness. Let me say, Taras, we all of us here appreciate your cooperation, and the alacrity with which you have offered it. And I very much include in these appreciative words the sentiments of our President."

The others nodded in solemn accord. *Now I'm supposed to feel all warm and fuzzy,* Taras thought as a female KGB sergeant carried in a samovar and a tray of tortes. Since he had breakfasted at the Metropole, Taras restricted himself to a glass of tea.

"Mr. Chairman," Taras said, avoiding the term "comrade," which, in any case, nobody seemed to use anymore, "regardless of *why* I am here, here I am, and I intend to do my best. You know my record. But I must tell you, I seriously doubt that I can do anything to increase the physical safety of Alois Rybkin."

"You're saying we really don't need you to protect the President, or to stop Major Jolly?"

"That is my opinion."

"Well, as a matter of fact, I share your view, and, so, I believe, does everyone else in this room. Are you shocked? It is true. And I've told Alois Maksimovich as much. We can and will protect our *vozhd*. That is our duty. But the stakes at Potsdam are high, and the President can be forgiven for wanting to have an extra card up his sleeve, and that extra card seems to be you."

"If nothing else," Rogovoy said, "bringing Major Arensky here keeps him from performing his normal CIA espionage duties."

"If you're going to make jokes, General," Kelleher said to Rogovoy, "I suggest you learn to smile first."

"*Touché,* Genrikh," Biryukov said. "The fact is, despite the reservations we have both just expressed, we are not so foolish as to think we are invulnerable, or that we cannot learn from a man of your caliber, Taras Genrikhovich. The President was more impressed by your dossier than the assassin's, Jolly's, and remarked that you were certainly worthy of bearing the name of Gogol's old Cossack hero, Taras Bulba. . . ."

Arensky had, in fact, been named for the nineteenth-century Ukrainian poet and patriot, Taras Shevchenko, but he let Biryukov continue without interruption: "We have trained you well. And it is only natural that we would prefer that you use that training on behalf of your homeland. You see, I have come full circle. For this is precisely the opportunity before us. The question is, how can we best use you?"

Taras smiled. "I await your answer."

"And we await yours. The question was not rhetorical. We are granting you a free hand, Taras. Tell us your thinking."

"Well, if I'm supposed to track Marcus down, I obviously want to know where you think he is, or where you last saw him."

"We don't know where he is. No one does. As the English say, we're just beating the bushes and following the hounds. Major Jolly was assigned to Novosibirsk with Marchenko, but never arrived there. Instead, he disappeared. All we can get from GRU is that there was a confusion in orders and he was dispatched to Vienna on a deep-cover assignment—deliberately out of touch. So, no matter our demands, they say they cannot bring him in until he contacts them. Do we believe that? No, we don't. We have been uprooting Marchenko's network, link by link, much of it *Spetsnaz* connected. If the assassin tries to contact it anywhere along the line, we will probably have him."

"Good luck." Taras squeezed more lemon into his tea.

"So, Volodya, you are telling us that you have no specific assignment for Taras?" Kelleher asked, sounding incredulous.

"Don't misunderstand. There are many things I can suggest. For instance, Colonel Starkov is ready to detail our security arrangements for Potsdam, since that is where President Rybkin will be most vulnerable. Or—"

"Or," Starkov addressed Taras, "you might also wish to review the interrogations of some of Major Jolly's *Spetsnaz* collaborators, whom we are detaining in Lefortovo, or conduct your own interrogations."

"I don't think that's a good idea," Kelleher said. "I think we can rely on your skill in that area."

Starkov shrugged. "It was just a suggestion."

"To reiterate," Biryukov picked up, "Taras Genrikhovich, you can have anything you want. Name it, and Colonel Starkov will see that you get it."

"Absolutely," Starkov said. He looked very competent, Taras thought.

"Well," Kelleher said to Taras, "looks like the ball's in your court. What do you want to do?"

"How about going home?"

"Try again."

"All right." Taras turned to Biryukov and began ticking points off on his fingers. "I'd like several things. Marcus's file. An office. A cubicle will do, so long as it's private and has a good reading light and ventilation. An electric fan, like that one, would be nice. And I'd like a pot of coffee—the real stuff if you have it, not the instant shit."

Biryukov's considerable eyebrows arched like twin caterpillars getting ready to march. "That is all?"

"For now. I imagine it will take me most of the day to work through the file, so in a couple of hours, maybe somebody could bring me a cold collation—ham, cheese, black bread. Maybe a bowl of *okroshka* and—what? A Pepsi?"

"We have an excellent restaurant."

"I'd rather not have the interruption."

"As you wish. Anything else?"

"There's something *I'd* like, Volodya," the CIA station chief said. "While Taras is studying, what about granting me afternoon reading privileges in your archives?"

"Sorry, Henry, even *glasnost* has its limits. Unless you're offering reciprocal privileges at Langley."

Chapter

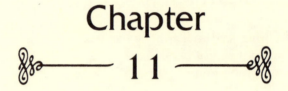

11

THE OFFICE WAS PRIVATE, IF NOT SPACIOUS, A FLOOR BELOW BIR-yukov's, with a view of the square. Some Chekist functionary had undoubtedly been chased out of it. There was ersatz coffee—barely drinkable—and a fan—tiny, shrill and, oddly, made in the PRC—with a jetlike airstream that scattered any unanchored papers in its swath. Discovering no low-speed setting, Taras switched it off and prepared to swelter it out.

On a low, fiddle-shaped table by a settee were the morning *Pravda, Argumenty I Fakty, Literaturnaya Gazeta, Novoye Vremya;* but also European *Newsweek*, the *International Herald-Tribune, USA Today, Bunte,* and the magazine section from the previous Sunday's *Die Zeit.* Behind him was a large walnut-veneer cabinet with built-in minibar and, behind a sliding panel, a Grundig shortwave radio—tuned, he noticed, to the bandwidth of the daily BBC Russian-language broadcast. Within distracting peripheral glance a wall calendar featured a bulky, bikinied blonde dipping a toe into the fantail pool of a Soviet cruise ship off some unspecified sun-splashed coast.

And on the green-baize-covered desk before him were several voluminous folders, laced together, which had been wheeled into the office inside a lockable metal trolley. The brown pasteboard cover bore several grease stains and the concise title: "Dossier on Markus Dzholly."

Taras was near the beginning, working his way through the thicket of MVD reports on the murder of Eva Sorokina, a case which, Taras well knew, had never been solved. Kostya, the big trapper, whose full name was listed as Konstantin Igorivich Yakushkin, had not been seen, alive or dead, after disappearing from his cabin that snowy night in Khabarovsk more than fifteen years before. Nor had any of the stolen money or clothing been recovered.

Though all this was familiar to Taras, it was still painful, summoning up the frozen horror of that morning and unburying old griefs. He passed quickly to the next section, which consisted of background checks on Marcus's youth in the United States.

Here was reason to pause. The information now before Taras did not square with what Marcus had told him—about being reared in Illinois by grandparents and leaving home after a fire took their lives. According to the dossier, assembled mainly, it would seem, from public records, Marcus Jolly was born in 1957 in Wichita, Kansas, and left home after his mother's death from a barbiturate overdose in 1974. His father had been killed ten years earlier when his gravel truck skidded off any icy road into a culvert; there was a microfilm print of a news story on the accident from the *Wichita Eagle*. There was no mention of Illinois grandparents.

And there was no documentation of Marcus's activities between 1974 and his arrival in Khabarovsk in the winter of '77; but this was entirely consistent with Marcus's story of becoming a drifter and working odd jobs as he moved across the western states and the Pacific.

The only early photograph of Marcus in the file was an enlargement from a sixth-grade class picture. Blazing sunlight and high-contrast shadows made it impossible to recognize the boy's features. In an attached memorandum, the KGB case officer requested further corroborative information and photographs, but the dossier yielded no response to this request. Had the indefatigable KGB First Chief Directorate decided, uncharacteristically, not to pursue the matter and to accept the defector's American background as given?

Taras stared at the hazy photo of a squinting, crew-cut Kansas schoolboy and shook his head. What was going on here? Had the Cowboy lied to Taras all these years, lied even during all-night, vodka-fueled truth sessions? And if so, what possible motive could there have been? Taras might well demand clarification from Biryukov, but decided instead to have Hank Kelleher fax Langley for some quick answers.

In the meantime Taras no longer knew what he was searching for in the file before him—clues as to what his old comrade was up to these days, or clues as to who Marcus really was, these days and those. Had there always been a stranger's eyes behind the familiar, grinning face? Taras could not accept that, yet the discrepancy in Marcus's background was puzzling. No, it was worse than that. It left Taras feeling extremely queasy as he turned to the section of the dossier that detailed the American's arrival in Moscow in the winter of 1977 and his application for political asylum. . . .

The grief-and-vodka-soaked comradeship of Taras's and Marcus's westward rail journey from Khabarovsk extended to their first few days in Moscow. They were given adjoining rooms in the Berlin Hotel, just off Dzerzhinsky Square behind the Children's World department store. From here, Taras was able to show his Western friend some of the architectural wonders of central Moscow. They braved the winter winds that scoured the cobblestoned vastness of Red Square, queued with the bundled throngs for Lenin's Mausoleum and the Kremlin tours, tramped the icy sidewalks of the broad, radial avenues and the embankments of the frozen Moskva. But their first foray each morning was across Dzerzhinsky Square for several hours of questioning by KGB and MVD investigators about Eva's death, Kostya's disappearance, and Marcus's reasons for wanting to leave the United States.

Apparently after three days the internal affairs directorate had run out of questions for Taras, and he was told to report back to his class at the military academy. Marcus's future was still uncertain. He was being temporarily assigned to the Moscow flat of two American defectors—a middle-aged dental surgeon and his wife from Cincinnati—while his application for Soviet citizenship was being considered.

The two comrades said their farewells outside the Berlin. Taras then got into one of the Finnair vans that served hotel guests, to be shuttled to the Byelorussian Railway station and a train for Smolensk, where his academy class was witnessing bridging maneuvers on the Dnieper. He had a last glimpse of his friend through the van's rear window. Marcus was standing on the slushy sidewalk between two gray-coated militiamen, waving his old cowboy hat in one hand and holding his new cardboard suitcase with the other. Then the van turned off Zhdanov Street onto Pushechnaya, and the Cowboy was gone.

Five months were to pass before the two friends saw each other again—five months with only a few exchanges of notes to apprise each other of current events and whereabouts. And even this was a feat, for each essayed—courteously but clumsily—to write in the other's language, and by then both were caught up in training regimens that left them exhausted in their bunks only moments before lights-out.

But they arranged a meeting by the Ferris wheel in Gorky Park on a May afternoon the following year, when Taras would be on leave and Marcus was scheduled to be in Moscow briefly between trains. Taras arrived early, searching the crowds that flowed by, even checking the gondolas rising into the warm, golden haze and the boats rowing slowly past on the pond. The hour came, and still no Marcus. Perhaps plans had changed, too late to notify Taras. It was an unthinkably huge country; he might never see or hear from Marcus again. Then there was a tap on Taras's shoulder.

He whirled, faced a tall, grinning young man in a special forces light-blue beret and blue-and-white-striped jersey, holding two ice cream cones. He thrust one toward Taras, kept the other for himself. It was, of course, Marcus.

The two embraced, laughed, embraced again, talking at once and in different languages. They settled quickly on Russian, at which Marcus had made obvious and impressive progress.

"You are *Spetsnaz!*" Taras said. "I can't believe it. Why didn't you tell me?"

"You know how it is, Cossack. Most of what I wrote you was just *govno,* bullshit."

"But how did this happen so fast? I was afraid you'd be working for the KGB forever."

"I got real lucky," Marcus said. "Apparently the KGB didn't know what to do with me. I'm not like some high-level defector they want to put on TV. Like I told them, the only expertise I got is talking American, sailing, martial arts—aikido, kendo. And I wanted to join the army. Special forces, rangers, whatever they call 'em over here. So they let me talk to this old hot-shit major general in the GRU Second Chief Directorate. Marchenko. Ukrainian. Face like one of those old battle-axes they got in the Kremlin armory. Used to run the rocket program, helped bring it back after the disgrace of the Cuban missile withdrawal. Had on every fucking medal you can get. I heard he was well connected with the Central Committee. Spoke pretty good English. Old guy took a liking to me. Told me I was a cocky bastard, just the kind they like in *Spetsnaz*. They also like foreigners, for foreign ops. Especially Americans, you can figure maybe why. Who knows? They'll probably send me back to America to assassinate the president."

"You're really full of it! But the beret looks good." Taras snatched it and placed it rakishly on his own head. "Even better on me."

"Oh, shit! I wish you hadn't done that, Cossack. According to the *Spetsnaz* oath, I've got to kill you now."

The two friends strolled south along the river embankment, from the Krymsky Bridge to the Andreyevsky, and then slowly worked their way back through the park grounds. They talked a great deal, at first profanely and lustily, matching boast for boast. But their tones softened when they spoke of their lost Eva, whose bounties and virtues had only multiplied after her death, till she had assumed, in idealized recollection, the dual aspect of a martyred and sensuous saint. The two were full of themselves, their shared past, their veiled but unquestionably heroic destinies. The people and tableaux they passed seemed slightly out of focus, positioned like so many props or film extras around the park to provide background for their traveling encounter. The spring sunshine felt good on their shoulders, and the plane trees and linden and horse chestnut were in full, refulgent foliage. But these things only floated by on the periphery of consciousness, like the silent lovers holding hands on park benches. Or the people drinking tea and eating sweets in an outdoor café; the family groups picnicking on parceled cold cuts, black bread, pickled fish, smoked herring; the children queuing for the rocket-sled ride or squealing before an outdoor puppet theater; or the older boys playing soccer and hurling Frisbees.

A rock concert at the big outdoor Zelyony Theater did engage them for a time, while it obliterated their dialogue with the amplified shriek of acid rock. But they stayed critically back, behind the swaying, arm-thrusting, stage-circling throng of teenage faithful in their Western motley. The focus of all the enthusiasm was two emaciated guitarists and a pudgy drummer, all in regulation studded, skin-tight leathers, tattooed, mascaraed, and spiky-haired. But costume and makeup meant nothing to Taras and Marcus; could the group really play? After a moment they both decided in the negative and ambled on, into a pavilion where old men sat hunched over rows of chessboards. While they paused again to kibitz, a foul-smelling drunk in grease-stained work shirt lurched into them, offering a half-liter vodka *troika*. When the drunk refused to step back, Marcus gave him a shove. The man went sprawling on his ass, got up threatening to smash Marcus's face, took a second look at the smiling young man in the blue beret, and wisely staggered off, with only an obligatory fuck-your-mother.

Altogether a glorious day, Taras thought. His amazing friend had done it again, diving recklessly into the vast sea of the Russian continent exactly as he had into the Pacific, and coming up a winner—a member of the elite *Spetsnaz* fighting forces! And he seemed taller and fitter in his new trappings—his shoulders broader, his jaw more salient, his squinty blue eyes more glittery. Only the flaxen hair had suffered; under his blue beret Marcus was shorn to the scalp just like all the twice-yearly crop of baby-faced *prizyvniki,* army conscripts. But Marcus obviously didn't care; he was, as that old general had said, a cocky bastard.

And try though he might, Taras could not convince himself that the many sidelong female glances he'd noticed in the last hour were intended for him. No, it was exactly as it had been in Khabarovsk the winter before, when the Cowboy had cast his spell upon Eva—and, eventually, on Taras himself. Marcus always came out on top. Taras had ridden a crowded train across Russia to reach Eva; but Marcus had sailed clear across the Pacific. Now Taras tried to brag about the rigors of his second year at the military academy; but Marcus was already in special forces.

You couldn't hate him for it. The swagger went with the grin, and the daredevil spirit, and the cowboy boots, or the shiny paratroop boots he wore now. At twenty-one Marcus Jolly was a seasoned adventurer who bore the stamp of the self-made man and the indefinable aura of the heroic. Taras not only admired and envied him. He wanted to *be* Marcus.

But they were rapidly running out of afternoon. They made their way to the Oktyabrskaya Metro station and took the circular line to the Kievskaya station, where Marcus collected his gear from a locker and rushed aboard a train for Odessa to report to a *Spetsnaz* brigade at the Higher Infantry School.

Taras remained on the platform for several minutes after the train had pulled out. He was feeling somehow left behind as he replayed in his mind Marcus's last jaunty wave while leaning precariously out the carriage window. Taras sensed himself at a crisis point in his life. When he finally pivoted and headed back toward the station concourse, it was with a sudden and grim resolve that he, too, would join the *Spetsnaz*. And by the time the Metro had tunneled him all the way back to his father's flat in the Nagatino district in southeast Moscow, Taras Arensky felt his destiny thick around him.

Chapter

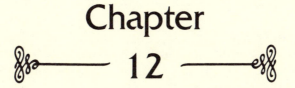

12

BOLVAN!

Blockhead! That was how Taras's father had erupted when he heard of his son's desire to apply for immediate transfer to the *Spetsialnoye Naznacheniye—Spetsnaz,* or Special Designation forces. Among other things, Genrikh Arensky knew, if Taras's application were accepted, it would mean the abandonment of his studies at the Supreme Soviet Military Academy, where the young man was finishing his second year with honors.

"Listen very carefully to me, Tarushka," the older Arensky said after the initial explosion had subsided and he was able to sit down and shakily fill two small tulip-shaped glasses with *pertsovka,* pepper vodka. "You know we have planned this for years, Uncle Dima and I. Getting you into Suvorov Academy was no easy matter, believe me. We are not big shots. And then into the Supreme Soviet Military Academy— every bit as good as Frunze—where, in two more years, you will come out a lieutenant of motorized infantry. Think, in ten years, if you continue your fine record, you will be a regimental commander. In *Spetsnaz* you may be dead from parachute jumping in a month. Is this what you want?"

"More than anything."

"Why? Because of that arrogant American bastard, Marcus? Why do you ape him, a traitor to his homeland? Where are your brains, Tarushka? What are you guys, pansies?"

"Marcus is my friend, Papa. Call me any names you like, but not him. I won't permit it."

"Won't permit it? You think you are running my life now, telling me what I can say and cannot say? Be damn careful, Tarushka. I can still lick you."

"I don't think so, Papa."

"Oh, no? You watch out, then, boy, and be ready for me. Maybe you can beat me when it's all over, but I promise you, those first two minutes will be hell on earth!"

"Calm down, Papa. You know I'm not going to fight you. And I don't want to run your life. I just want to run my own. And this is my decision, not Marcus's. I'm only asking you to respect it."

"Respect a crazy thing like that? When my son says he wants to join a band of assassins?"

"Papa, *Spetsnaz* fighters are heroes, they perform special missions—intelligence, reconnaissance, operating behind enemy lines—"

"Like in Prague in 'sixty-eight? Sure, I know. Big heroes! Nazi stormtroopers! Bullshit, Tarushka! Just be a good soldier, like I was, and your uncle Dima. Not a killing machine."

They faced each other across the kitchen table far into the night, polishing off a liter of vodka between them. In the end it was old Genrikh whose slumping head hit the oilcloth first, and who had to be wrestled to his bed by his dark-eyed son.

"You're a stubborn bastard, Tarushka, just like your crazy, beautiful Georgian mother" was the last volley the old man managed to fire off before collapsing unconscious onto his mattress. It was an admission of defeat, if not consent.

But Genrikh's trump card, which he had been content not to play in the debate, was a surety that his consent mattered little in the final issue. Taras needed his permission, he thought, as much as a cunt needs an alarm clock. His obdurate, moody son would do exactly as he wished—*but it would not matter*.

The Soviet system was not geared for change, for career-switching. It was always and everywhere a one-way maze of choices leading to mostly dead-ends. The great socialist engine of the State funneled its citizens irresistibly through that maze, providing the ever-onward peristaltic impetus—through mandated levels of education, housing, and employment, with diminishing downstream choices—but there was no system for backtracking to a main branch, or even lateral switching from one tributary to another.

And Taras's course through that maze had been pretty well ordained since the age of fourteen, when Genrikh and Dima had proudly enrolled him in the DOSAFF, a civilian support group for future military recruits. If the local draft board, the *voyenkomat,* had certified the young Arensky as a superior physical specimen—suitable for the elite KGB Kremlin guard or security forces, or the GRU special forces—then he would already have been directed there.

But this had *not* occurred. At age fifteen Taras, perhaps slightly tardy in reaching his full physical growth, had gone instead—with his uncle's considerable connivance—into Moscow's Suvorov Military Academy, a direct career path for future commanders. Two years later, as one of the top cadets in his class, he had moved on to his present four-year officers' training academy in a forest outside Moscow.

Now, with a little more than two years remaining till he received his commission, was Cadet Arensky, on an afternoon's whim, ready to scrap the whole business and tell the Soviet military apparatus that he should be reclassified forthwith? Well, such an anarchic thing could not happen! A son might well defy his father's wishes, but Genrikh imagined Tarushka would have rather a more difficult time with the academy commandant, Lieutenant General Gennadiy Buslakov!

Beyond that, even were permission given for Taras to volunteer, Genrikh knew that the *Spetsnaz,* like all Soviet elite forces, ran incredibly tough selection courses. Few made the grade. And Genrikh had heard the rumors that most who did were either Olympic-caliber athletes, genetic supermen, or total criminal degenerates prized for their ruthlessness. But certainly not good souls like his boy.

At least these were the consoling thoughts that had enabled Genrikh Arensky to smile at his bullheaded son—who so foolishly imagined he had bested his old man!—and let himself succumb, with some sense of decorum, to alcoholic stupor.

Genrikh knew ultimately he would be proven right.

And that was precisely what Taras discovered. To a man, his faculty advisers told him to forget the entire matter. All he would get for his trouble, one said, were unfavorable notations on his record. Another professor, a myopic martinet who still taught Prussian cavalry tactics and quoted Frederick the Great, even denied the existence of any peacetime commando force. Was Cadet Arensky perhaps thinking of the sappers and partisans who had operated so effectively behind German lines in the Great Patriotic War?

The only positive suggestion came, surprisingly, from one of the school's ideological instructors, who suggested Taras ask the secretary of his Komsomol cell to submit a letter of recommendation to the GRU, the Chief Intelligence Directorate of the Soviet General Staff, which was responsible for special operations forces. Taras thanked him politely.

But most of those he consulted were factually pessimistic, very much as Genrikh had predicted. It was useless to make such an application now. Taras should have been earmarked for special forces *before* conscription. Oh, occasionally members of regular military units were creamed off during basic training, he was told, but never plucked from officer training academies. He should buckle down to his studies and forget all this *Spetsnaz* nonsense.

Instead, Taras came up with the idea of locating a *Spetsnaz* officer and approaching him directly. But his only link was Marcus, who had gone off to Odessa without leaving his new military address. So Taras turned to the academy library, but his researches yielded no published roster of officers. He did find the official biography of Rodion Igorovich Marchenko, the major general who had invited Marcus into *Spetsnaz,* but among the many illustrious citations there were no mentions of special forces or a present command. The GRU obviously had no desire to publicize the strength, deployment, organization, or very existence of their special forces.

Spetsnaz brigades were contained within each military district, Taras had heard, but usually concealed among airborne or air-assault troops, adopting the uniforms and designations of those units. They also assumed special names depending on the regions in which they operated. For instance, *Spetsnaz* in the Siberian Military District might go by the name of *okhotniki,* hunters, yet call themselves *reydoviki,* raiders, in the GFSG, the Group of Soviet Forces in Germany.

Finally Taras turned to Uncle Dima. And as in the case of his nephew's impassioned pleadings the previous year for special leave to visit his fiancée in Siberia, the Defense Ministry *apparatchik* eventually gave in. A gruff "I'll see what I can do" was all Taras got, but from Dima that was usually enough, and so it proved. A week later his uncle phoned him to report the following Saturday morning at eight sharp to the GRU officers training building on Peoples' Militia Street near the Mnevniki Bend of the Moscow River. Taras was to be in uniform and ask for a Major Kornelyuk.

Recalling Marcus's interview with Marchenko, Taras worked an extra hour perfecting his military appearance and went to the appointment with soaring expectations. Alas, these were brought crashing down in five deadly minutes with a bullet-domed, inhospitable officer who sat with clasped hands and tight lips under twin portraits—of Lenin, of course, and a smaller one of a Marshal Viktor Kondratevich Kharchenko, who, Taras had heard, was considered the father of modern *Spetsnaz*. The major asked only two or three perfunctory questions, waited out each of Taras's answers without giving a flicker of acknowledgment, then announced there were no openings.

"Comrade Major, may I inquire if my answers were unsatisfactory, and if so, in what way?"

"Your answers were perfectly fine. I can only repeat, we are not accepting applications." To emphasize the point, the major closed the folder before him—presumably Taras's—and placed it in his out basket. "Now, I'm afraid I have a rather busy schedule this morning."

Taras, hat under arm, paused before turning to go. "Sir, may I also ask why you agreed to see me?"

"I was ordered to do so. I'm sorry. Your ambition is laudable, but in the future I suggest you keep it in strict harness to the curriculum of your fine academy. Good day, Cadet Arensky."

Taras left, deciding that if Major Kornelyuk was a typical *Spetsnaz* officer, he wanted no part of that organization. In any case, the young man was finally ready to abandon pursuit of the dream.

The dream, however, had not quite finished pursuing him.

For the following year it came true by accident—or, more accurately, because of a perfectly executed *balestra*, a fencing maneuver. Taras had taken up the sport at the Suvorov Academy at fifteen, doing well enough with foil and épée, but finding the saber, with its more athletic cut-and-thrust techniques, considerably more to his liking. By the time he had moved on to the Supreme Soviet Military Academy two years later, his skill with this highly flexible, edged weapon was such that he was given permission to practice in Moscow on weekends and during leave at the Central Army Sports Club (ZSKA) complex on Leningrad Prospekt.

One afternoon in the autumn of 1979 a group of fencers from the rival KGB club, *Dinamo,* dropped by the competition hall for some extramural competition. Taras won several bouts, and rather easily. He was approached afterward by one of the ZSKA's senior sabermen, a very tall fellow with a long face and elegant, Leninesque mustache and goatee, who asked if he would mind one more duel.

Taras agreed, and found himself pressed very hard by the much more experienced swordsman. Still, by sheer speed of reflexes, Arensky hung on, only a touch behind; then, on a stop cut that could have been judged either way, he drew even at four all. With the shout to resume play, Taras sprang into the *balestra*—a forward hop followed by an immediate lunge—and scored again. He was now a point ahead. His older opponent attacked furiously during the final minute, pushing Taras back to the end line, but was unable to score a hit.

When Taras was declared the winner at five–four, the other man unhelmeted and, with the sweat pouring off his face, drew Taras aside. "Damn good fencing," he said, grinning as if genuinely delighted by the outcome.

"Thanks. I was pretty lucky."

"Perhaps a little. Do you know who I am?"

"No, I'm sorry. I don't get here very often."

"My name is Dokuchayev."

"Taras Arensky. I'm still sorry. I should know but—"

"*Osip* Dokuchayev."

A bell rang, faintly. The Olympics? Had Dokuchayev perhaps been a member of the Soviet fencing team at Montreal? Taras inquired.

"Yes, I was. But what is much more to the point, I am also a candidate for next summer's Moscow Games. Only you, my little student, just might keep me off our team."

Taras shook his head and smiled. "I'm not that good."

"You damn well better be—if you beat me!" Dokuchayev knew talent when he saw it. He had, he explained, these past few weeks been scouring the city's sporting clubs—ZSKA, *Trud* (*Trudoviye reservy*), *Spartak, Burevestnik,* even *Dinamo*—for promising fencers, specifically sabermen.

"In fact, I was pretty enthusiastic about a couple of those *Dinamo* guys, until you cleaned their clocks."

"I guess we army lads have to stick together. Who wants a KGB champion? *Spetsnaz,* sure, but not Committeemen."

"Why do you mention *Spetsnaz?*"

"Well, it happens I know someone who just joined, or got selected. A good friend. And everyone has heard that some of the best ZSKA athletes are actually special forces officers. But you never know which ones."

"The *best* ones are," Dokuchayev said. "And you could be one of them. Why are you laughing?"

"Because it's funny, that's why. Last year I tried every way I could think of to get into *Spetsnaz,* or even apply, and I was told to stop making a nuisance of myself."

"Whom did you talk to?"

"Major Kornelyuk."

"Who's he? Never heard of him."

"Some officer over on Peoples' Militia Street. He gave me two minutes, then told me to forget the whole thing."

"*Govnyuk!* You were sticking it up the wrong hole, that's all. Believe me, Taras, I can get you an appointment with somebody much higher than that."

"Who?"

"Me. I'm a lieutenant colonel in *Spetsnaz.* And last time I checked, that outranked a major. You want to talk, go ahead, I'm listening."

"This is a joke—sir?"

"Forget the 'sir,' since you just whipped my ass. And no joke, Taras. Do you still want to join *Spetsnaz?*"

"Sure I do, unless everybody's like that major."

"Forget that prick-twister. If you want in, you're in. It'll take a couple weeks to clear away all the *mudistika*—bureaucratic bullshit—between the sports club and your school, but I'll start shoveling the manure tomorrow. And before those two weeks are past, I promise, you'll be training here full-time."

Taras shook his head in disbelief. "How can you do this? Nothing moves that fast."

"Hey, where have you been all your life? The Olympics are coming, my young friend, maybe you heard of them? The biggest invasion of

Moscow since the *Wehrmacht* or Napoleon's *Grande Armée?* Comrade Brezhnev is spending a billion and a half rubles on construction in Moscow alone. You've seen the Olympic Village they're building off Vernadsky Prospekt." It was hard to miss—eighteen high-rise housing blocks sprawling over nearly three hundred acres of southwest Moscow. "I understand they're already in a panic down there. They've got army battalions and Komsomol 'volunteers' working around the clock just to be ready by next July."

The fencing competition would be held right at the ZSKA complex, Dokuchayev went on, at a five-thousand-seat hall under current renovation. "You're good enough to be there, Taras. And with the right training, you could not only make the team. You could medal."

"What am I supposed to say?" Taras had always known he had talent, but knew as well he would never have the time or proper coaching to develop his potential. Now he was being told it could all be arranged—in time for next summer's Olympics!

"What you say, my little idiot, is yes!"

And so he did.

Lieutenant Colonel Dokuchayev was true to his word. Within two weeks Cadet Arensky of the Supreme Soviet Military Academy had become Sergeant Arensky of the Central Army Sports Club, with a full sergeant's pay and special allowances for sports clothing, equipment, and diet.

And Genrikh performed his own stunning about-face. Far from being upset at this peremptory and unauthorized career change, his father couldn't have been more proud. He spent a good deal of his daily shift on the factory floor keeping his workers apprised of the latest developments in his son's life, even telephoned members of his wife's family he hadn't spoken to in years. As more than one captive listener was told, the demands of fatherhood had kept him from fulfilling his own potential as a football midfielder. So it was only fitting that the Arensky prowess would shine through in his boy. And who knew what glories lay ahead? An Olympic medal—even gold—was not out of the question. Sportsmen were, after all, national heroes, like cosmonauts.

The older Arensky even spruced up his son's old room and offered to let him move back in, for a nominal rent. But young Sergeant Arensky was now billeted with two other ZSKA fencers—both lured away by Dokuchayev from other local clubs—in a four-room flat in a refurbished pre-revolutionary building just off Leningrad Prospekt near the Aeroflot Hotel. He was given full access to all the ZSKA facilities, including trainer, sports-medicine clinic and fitness coaches, plus entrée into the master classes of Dokuchayev's own teacher, the Hungarian Takacs, twice world champion.

Also as promised, Taras was made a member of the *Spetsnaz*. But, Dokuchayev stressed, he was to divulge this to no one—not even to his roommates, neither of whom had been accorded the same distinction. And in practice, the *Spetsnaz* connection meant little, for Sergeant Arensky's military training was, for the time being, almost nonexistent, so as not to interfere with an intensive athletic regimen. A third of his day was spent on overall conditioning—increasing stamina, speed, strength, and flexibility, by squatting, stair-climbing, sprinting, jogging backward, stretching, and high-repetition abdominal exercises; another third was devoted to specific fencing movements—barbell lunges, endless blade and footwork drills; and the final third was actual combat practice.

Only three times in the first two months was he spirited away for weekend *Spetsnaz* training, at a GRU complex near the village of Sezhodnya twenty-five miles northwest of Moscow. And this was not intensive—some paramilitary sports (competitive shooting and martial arts), topography, radio communications, and, most of all, language work. For Taras was expected to perfect a foreign language—he chose English—as rapidly as possible to colloquial level. After one year he would receive his commission as a lieutenant—or higher, depending on his placement in the Olympics and subsequent international competition.

He was, it turned out, in a special branch of *Spetsnaz* constituted entirely of professional sportsmen (though, for the purposes of international athletic competition, they were all considered "amateurs"). There were two other parts of *Spetsnaz:* networks of intelligence agents and actual fighting units—the elite cadre which Marcus had joined and in which Taras imagined him by now totally immersed. But Taras did not really know; he had heard nothing from his friend in nearly ten months.

The Cowboy's last letter had been from Odessa, just before he was set to leave for jump school in Ryazan, a hundred and seventy-five kilometers southeast of Moscow on the Oka River. Taras could only hope Marcus was still alive, for Taras had heard from his military instructors that *Spetsnaz* combat training was the most rigorous in the world, involving such character-building stunts as swimming icy rivers and parachuting onto mountaintops or into craters.

But if anyone could survive such gung-ho fanaticism, even thrive on it, surely Marcus Jolly was the man. Probably he was just too swamped with Ryazan's superhuman curriculum—and actual combat exercises—to put pen to paper. Certainly there was no point in worrying about the intrepid American, or in envying him. Besides, Taras was totally immersed in his own regimen—and Olympic dream.

And he was making substantial progress. There was no question about his ability to hold his own with his teammates, and he was winning more and more matches. His most dramatic improvement had been in the crucial area of tactics—in feeling out, and then deceiving, his opponent; in staying always a move ahead in the constant mental chess of competition; in varying his foot- and handwork patterns, his tempo and rhythm and attack combinations. In the process he had become tremendously fit. As hard as *Spetsnaz* officers pushed their combat units, it was difficult to imagine them equaling the standards of Olympic fitness reached by Taras and his clubmates.

In late December of 1979 Taras and selected members of his ZSKA fencing squad—specifically the *Spetsnaz* contingent—were told by Lieutenant Colonel Dokuchayev they would be visiting the Olympic Village the next day. This puzzled them, as the training facilities were still being laid out at the huge athlete-housing complex a dozen kilometers to the south, and even when completed would not be on a par with those available at their own club. Dokuchayev smiled. This "Village," he explained, was not in Moscow, or even in the RSFSR, the Russian Republic, but in the Ukraine. "Olympic Village" was the nickname for the principal *Spetsnaz* training center in Kirovograd, southeast of Kiev.

It seemed an irregular outing—half a day by An-26 turboprop, troop train, and ZIL 8x8 army trucks, to be deposited in the middle of a godforsaken compound somewhere on the southern steppe, then marching through the slush toward a dismal, cement-block recreation hall—all just to match blades with some intermediate-grade fencers. But Taras and his mates were soldiers, after all, and Dokuchayev definitely hadn't asked their opinions.

Taras had hoped perhaps to glimpse some real *Spetsnaz* combat training in the process, but all he saw was the dark tracery of parachute towers against the early winter twilight. Then they were inside the big, bright-as-day, overheated sport hall, surrounded by the echoing cacophony of half-court basketball, box-and-kick martial arts, and several fencing bouts all proceeding at once.

Taras was directed toward the saber strip, where a tall, undisciplined left-hander was leaping to and fro, swinging wildly, immediately confirming Taras's suspicions about the level of skill he should expect. He passed a glance to Dokuchayev.

"Are we supposed to critique them?" he asked.

"No, just fight. That's what they asked for, and that's what they'll get. I've put you in the next round."

Taras moved off to begin his warmups, but kept an eye on the saber strip. He was fascinated by the southpaw, who, despite his excessive movements and being assessed a point for hard slashing, was scoring repeatedly. Of course, his more orthodox opponent wasn't showing much aggression.

The six-minute bout ended with the left-hander winning five–two. They saluted—the left-hander excessively, according to strict saber etiquette—and came away together as they stripped off their mesh masks and shook hands.

Taras gasped. The victor, now twenty meters away and striding directly toward him with a wide grin of recognition, was none other than Marcus Jolly.

Chapter

13

"WHAT THE HELL ARE YOU DOING HERE, COSSACK?" MARCUS ASKED after releasing Taras from a bear hug.

"What does it look like? I joined special forces to track you down, Cowboy. I had to. You never write."

"I was going to get around to it. Trouble is, I've been doing all this classified shit. I'm not even supposed to tell myself what I've been up to. But hey, are you really in *Spetsnaz,* or just fencing with the Central Army club?"

"Both. By the way, your Russian is very good, Marcus. You need to work on your *zh*'s, though. They should be more guttural, almost from the chest."

"*Idi v'zhopu!*—Kiss my ass!"

"That's a little better."

"And fuck your mother. Come on, Cossack, you can answer all my dumb questions later. Right now I want to show you off."

Marcus put his arm around Taras and escorted him to every part of the large hall, even walking through the middle of a basketball game to introduce him around and interrupting a kick-boxing match so Taras could shake hands with the referee. There were some young women as well, a quartet of moderately attractive foilists doing their intensive pre-bout stretching.

"I got to warn you about this guy," Marcus said after introducing Taras as his best buddy. "A good-looking devil and a real swordsman, if you know what I mean, but he's got a twisted mind."

Taras laughed along with the girls, but wondered at the odd joke. Could the Cowboy, whose rugged handsomeness Taras had always envied, possibly feel jealousy toward him?

Finally they worked their way back to the fencing strip, where Taras met Marcus's coach, Captain Merab Balavadze, a stocky Georgian with a grisly scar furrowing his right cheek from ear to corner of mouth. A saber slash, undoubtedly. Balavadze put out a big paw and grinned—or tried to, but, with severed facial muscles on one side, the result was a lopsided grimace. Dark, heavily lashed Georgian eyes, however, retained their good humor.

"In case you're wondering," Marcus joked, "Merab is not a graduate of Heidelberg University. Says his fencing teacher used to make him practice saber without a mask. Says he's going to make all of us try it one of these days."

The captain's eyes sparkled. "You'd be surprised how it encourages students to pay close attention to their parries."

"I bet it does, sir. Pleased to meet you."

"Likewise. My old friend Osip has been telling me very good things about you, lad. Olympic material, certainly in team saber, maybe even individual."

"No bullshit, Cossack?" Marcus said. "Are you that good?"

"Win your next match," said Captain Balavadze, "and maybe you will find out just how good Sergeant Arensky is."

Until that moment neither Taras nor Marcus had bothered to check the pairings. A glance at the chalkboard showed them that Balavadze was correct. If Marcus won another bout, and Taras his first two, they would meet in the semifinal round.

"I've never actually seen you fight, Taras. But you've just seen me. Do I stand a chance against you, or are you going to kick my butt?"

"It's hard to say. You're pretty . . . damn unorthodox, Marcus. What are you doing fencing anyway? You're supposed to be jumping out of airplanes."

"I do plenty of that. I don't even bother wearing a parachute anymore, I'm that good. Fencing is just a hobby."

"Why saber? It's not a beginner's weapon."

"Who you calling a fucking beginner? I've been doing this six months, Cossack, and so far I'm beating everybody here, including Merab once or twice. You forget, I studied Japanese-style sword-fighting—*kendo, kenjutsu, bojutsu,* all that shit. Saber isn't so different."

"I'm sorry, Marcus. I didn't mean—"

"Forget it. There's another reason, if you want to know the truth. You mentioned your skill at saber to Eva way back, and it kind of stuck in my mind. What do you think? Maybe I secretly want to be like you, huh, Cossack?"

"Very funny."

"I might be serious."

"You might be full of crap. If anyone has been a copycat, it's me. And I *am* serious. Why do you think I tried to get into *Spetsnaz?*"

"I was wondering. You seemed pretty well grooved in out there at that officer factory."

Taras put his hand lightly on Marcus's knee. "Oh, I *was,* Cowboy—till I saw that absolutely *adorable* little powder-blue beret you had on that day in the park. And suddenly I just wanted one—so *much!*"

Marcus flicked Taras's hand away. "*Zhopnik!* Did I pronounce that right?"

"Not bad. Anyway, it turned out *Spetsnaz* had no interest in me as a real soldier, only as a fencer. And if I don't make the Olympics, who knows? I may be out on my ass."

"No, my friend, once you're in the brotherhood—sportsman, commando, makes no difference—it's for life. We stay in touch now, Cossack, no matter what. One for all, all for one, all that musketeer shit. But we'll talk later, or what do they say—'converse in steel'? Right now you got a bout coming up."

Taras, in fact, had left it a bit late, and didn't have time to properly warm up. It didn't matter. His first contest, with a brawny and energetic young soldier, took less than half the allotted six minutes. Taras scored a clean sweep, five–zero, scarcely breaking a sweat. In fact, it might have been quicker yet, had Taras really wished, for his opponent had no notion of defense. At one point Arensky had scored three consecutive head touches, and won when his opponent was penalized for retreating a second time off the end of the strip.

The young athlete smiled ruefully when it was over, and challenged

Taras playfully to a duel with any other weapon in the entire world, from AK-47s to the Soviet Army's legendary small spade.

"Sure," Taras said. "But I'm betting on you."

After a short tea break he dispatched his second opponent with only slightly more fuss, yielding but two touches. Taras was beginning to suspect that he and his Moscow mates had been transported all this way to administer an object lesson to the local brigade of *Spetsnaz* supermen—a surmise Lieutenant Colonel Dokuchayev stubbornly refused to confirm or deny.

But Taras was surprised to learn, moments after his second victory, that Marcus had just narrowly upset one of their better team members, a man who had almost gone to the last European championships. And Marcus had managed to do it again despite losing a penalty point.

Taras experienced a strange feeling at this startling news—but it wasn't surprise. On the contrary, he was filled with a sense of inevitability, as though it had all happened before. Yet he and Marcus had never competed directly in anything. Oh, there had been the brief rivalry over Eva Sorokina. And the friendly contests they'd staged to break the monotony of their Trans-Siberian rail trip. Like arm wrestling, in which the older Marcus had usually prevailed. And chess, which was strictly no contest, with Taras winning easily even after retracting his best moves. But the two had never seriously measured themselves against each other. And now they were about to match swords. Six minutes, five touches, no draws allowed. Taras turned around.

Marcus was standing right behind him, grinning.

"Looks like we're on."

"Yes, it does, doesn't it?"

"Give me your best, Cossack. Don't do me any fucking favors."

"I won't."

Taras walked away to a far corner of the sport hall, lay back on a tumbling mat, legs elevated against the wall, willed himself to relax. He felt oddly nervous, as though it were suddenly the Olympics.

The truth was, he thought, he really didn't want to fight Marcus. Their friendship seemed poised, all these years, on a knife-edge of rivalry, had been born of rivalry—and the sudden, devastating loss of the dear girl they had both desired. Their camaraderie, then, was Eva's only legacy to them. And it was that precious, intangible thing that Taras felt now in jeopardy.

He tried to tell himself he was making too much of what was, after all, only a simple duel. But it wouldn't work. Fear persisted, fear of loss—of *something,* dammit, something that he prized—enough apprehension, at any rate, to make a shambles of his usual pre-bout preparation. When he tried to visualize the match and moves ahead—which he often was able to do in surprising detail—he drew a complete blank. He could not see himself winning, as was certainly expected of him. Yet neither did he see himself losing to Marcus. There was only an impending void—caused by his mind's refusal to grapple with an insoluble problem.

Suddenly a teammate was calling his name. It was time. Taras returned to the fencing area.

His opponent was bouncing up and down on the end of the strip and grinning as Taras walked up. "Let's boogie," Marcus called out in English, showing no apparent reluctance for the coming duel.

So what's the matter with me, then? Taras thought suddenly. *Let's just go for it—give the cocky bastard a fencing lesson!*

They faced off in the center of the two-meter by fourteen-meter-long strip, lightly tapped each other's chest, then stepped back to salute—a quick flourish, in which weapons were pointed at each other, lifted with guards brought to chin, then whipped downward.

Marcus kept smiling as he slid his mesh mask forward, and Taras smiled right back, for whatever it was worth. Then he helmeted and crouched balletically on-guard—keeping heels light, rear fist on hip, fighting arm forward, blade vertical, inviting *tierce.* Poised on the sidelines, the president of the jury—one of the senior ZSKA members—shouted "Go!"

They engaged blades in *tierce,* and Taras felt his opponent's considerable strength at once, as Marcus attempted to beat Taras's blade outside with sheer force of steel, in order to uncover a larger target. Behind his mask Taras figuratively shook his head. Did the crazy Cowboy really imagine that sort of thing would work against an experienced fencer? Taras simply slid his weapon around Marcus's, gliding metal on metal. But Marcus pressed blades again, and the saber dance continued, like two boxers circling, jabbing, feeling each other out, measuring each other's reach, speed, and power.

Taras suffered the time-wasting rigmarole, mainly because it afforded a moment to assess the peculiar problems of a left-handed opponent. Certain differences were obvious—a narrower opening to

112

the chest, for instance, and reduced effectiveness of point attacks. Dokuchayev had promised to recruit more left-handers—perhaps Marcus was a candidate—but as it was, the top-echelon ZSKA club fencers were mostly righties, and Taras had had to rely on mirror practice to simulate facing an opposite-handed opponent. Marcus, of course, would have fenced almost exclusively right-handers.

Well, Taras thought, the Cowboy would need a larger advantage than that in the next six minutes—if the bout lasted that long.

But Taras decided not to rush matters, to let Marcus make the play. He didn't have long to wait. The Cowboy exploded forward, slashing to head, then to chest. Taras parried, moving smoothly out of range, while mentally inventorying the numerous flaws in Marcus's technique. The footwork, for instance, was more appropriate to a boxer; the Cowboy bounced loosely forward and back on the balls of his feet rather than employing the rapid, floor-skimming steps Taras and his teammates had spent hours perfecting. And Marcus's parries were too large, uneconomical, taking him again and again out of sound defensive position.

But Marcus's recoveries were startlingly fast, and his bladework remarkable. Marcus had already handled dozens of Taras's ripostes. Undoubtedly, Taras thought, the Westerner's very erraticism tended to confuse some opponents. Besides, fencing was a fight, not an exhibition of style; points were awarded for hits, not good form.

The tempo of the duel quickened, the rhythmic cymbal-clash of steel coming in bursts, longer or shorter, with fleeting rests between, accompanied by the stamp and squeal of shoes on the rubberized strip and the incessant gasps and grunts of combat, sibilant, guttural, plosive. The right-of-way flashed back and forth between them several times a second, as each attack was initiated, blocked, and countered, riposted and counter-riposted.

From a parry Marcus made a half-lunge, then *flèched*, sprinting forward with a feint toward the head. As Taras parried in *quinte,* Marcus, with full extension and lightning twist of wrist and forearm, slashed at Taras's open flank.

Taras had seen it coming, but the sheer explosiveness of the move carried the day, and Marcus scored a touch.

"Yes!" cried the referee, throwing up his hand to indicate a successful hit.

It was one–zero as they resumed play.

Taras had seen enough. He lunged, Marcus parried in *tierce,* but Taras whipped his blade over and caught Marcus's arm. Marcus's riposte hit an instant later, and halt was called.

After quick deliberation Marcus's riposte was adjudged delayed and the point was awarded to Taras on the continuation.

One–all.

Taras was beginning to enjoy himself. Marcus was certainly a challenging opponent. And he was seeming suddenly a little less idiosyncratic than in his earlier bouts—maintaining better distance, tightening up his hand- and footwork, making fewer meaningless foot and head feints, using less steel. And, Taras noted, his opponent had also learned the correct lesson from the last point and was now taking care to cover the elbow of his fighting arm.

Was the Cowboy, perhaps, growing a little wary of the Cossack?

The answer came an instant later, as Marcus exploded catlike again, *flèching* forward—making a running attack, which Taras neatly avoided. As Marcus's momentum carried him off the two-meter-wide strip, a halt was called, and Marcus penalized two meters backward.

The play continued, phrases and patterns becoming more intricate, with more deception, composite attacks and secondary intentions. But Taras's superior footwork began to tell, frustrating Marcus again and again as the Cossack floated just out of blade reach. Then, while maintaining long range, Taras scored with a narrow parry and riposte to top cuff.

Two–one.

A moment later Taras, indulging a slight didacticism perhaps, was maneuvering to score in exactly the same way, when Marcus totally surprised him and, by sheer strength, simply overrode Taras's *tierce* parry to score an outside cut to the shoulder.

Taras couldn't recall that ever having happened to him, certainly not since early days. It was suddenly two–all, and Taras felt a twinge of panic. There was no way Marcus Jolly should be fencing even with him. But dammit, he was!

Taras resumed furiously, pressing the attack and letting his own temperament take control; when Marcus feinted the same outside attack, Taras went for it—and lost another quick point to an inside chest cut.

He was down two–three.

The referee gave the warning for the final minute. Taras imagined he could see Marcus grinning through the mesh mask.

Got to give the bastard credit, Taras thought. It was no longer a question of not doing Marcus any "fucking favors"; Taras was fencing as well as he knew, and was on the verge of losing. And Marcus wasted no time, crouching unusually low and attacking with what Taras thought must be samurai-style bladework. This Taras easily parried. Then, as Marcus advanced, Taras, instead of retreating, lunged forward and scored a head touch.

Three–all.

Seconds after resuming, time ran out. By convention, a point was added to each side to bring the score to four–all. The two opponents grabbed a moment's respite. Perspiration now stung their eyes behind the heavy masks, soaked their gantleted hands, and darkened their padded tunics. But it was time to go on. They crouched once more, touched sabers. They were entering unlimited "sudden death" over-time. Whoever scored next would win.

"Go!"

Marcus exploded, feinting and slashing. Watchful for his opening, yet wary of overcommitting, Taras gave ground reluctantly, ratcheting his back foot sideways toward the end of the fourteen-meter strip. He heard clearly now Marcus's every gasping breath, every scrape and clash of edged steel and ringing of guard. These things seemed louder, Taras realized, because he and Marcus were suddenly cocooned in silence and cordoned with people. Activities all around them had been broken off as the participants drifted over, one by one and then in groups, to try to follow the slithering, darting blades that fought like dueling snakes.

But the enveloping hush was suddenly shattered. Across the hall a commotion broke out, excited shouts that caromed high off the gir-dered ceiling. Somebody close by yelled for silence—*"Tishe, pozhaluysta!"*

Taras and Marcus fought on, but the shouting continued. More than once Taras thought he caught the two syllables of *"voy-na!"*—war!

Another door burst open, more running footsteps, voices yelling. Taras battled the distraction, trying to occlude the world and limit his focus to the teasing sword-point before him. . . .

Marcus lunged, Taras barely blocked, avoiding defeat by the tiniest of margins. He dared wait no longer. It was time to make his move. He foot-feinted, hopped into a *balestra,* lunged forward—but Marcus had simply stepped off the strip . . . and was walking away!

Taras yanked off his helmet. There was swarming chaos in the sport hall, people running in and out, clustering, shouting. Taras caught up to Marcus, who was talking to another man, grabbed his shoulder, spun him around.

"What happened? Where are you going?"

"Taras, can't you hear? It's war!"

"War? *Yob tvoyu mat!* With America?" The ultimate nightmare of nuclear holocaust mushroomed in Taras's mind.

"Fuck, no! With Afghanistan. The Chinese have been massing to attack through the Wakhan Corridor, but we beat 'em to the punch. Word just came through. Two Antonovs full of *Spetsnaz* commandos have landed in Kabul, disguised as Afghan Army units. Goddammit, Cossack!" Marcus punched Taras hard in the biceps. "It's what we've been waiting for—time to kick ass!"

Marcus was heading for a large group by the door, and stripping off his tunic and the plastron underneath as though their bout had never happened.

"Are you going, Marcus?"

"Fuck your mother I'm going, Cossack! Aren't you?"

"I . . . I guess so. I don't know."

Lieutenant Colonel Dokuchayev, coming suddenly alongside, supplied the answer: "No, Taras, you *won't* be going. It doesn't affect you. You will continue with your training."

"How can it not affect me?" Taras said. "With a war on, I'm supposed to be playing games?"

Marcus horse-laughed. "Not just *any* games—*Olympic* Games. Mustn't have our future gold medalists facing live fire, right, Colonel? Sorry, Cossack. Damn good contest, though. Maybe we'll finish it one day."

Taras felt Dokuchayev's restraining grip on his arm as Marcus hurried off to join a tide of young men flowing out the doors of the sport hall and into the night, as though eager to reach Afghanistan before the fighting was all over.

Chapter

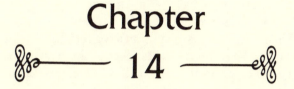 14

TARAS AND THE OTHER ZSKA CLUB FENCERS FLEW BACK TO MOS-
cow the next morning, expecting to find the capital bursting with
news about events in Afghanistan. There was certainly no shortage of
war rumors making the rounds of the Central Army Sports Club—
the main concern being the scale of the deployment and its imminent
impact on each of them. But the government news organs—such as
Pravda, Izvestia, and the nightly *Vremya* TV news—seemed more
preoccupied with the ramifications of a caviar scandal in the Ministry
of Fisheries. *Pravda,* Taras discovered, had several days before denied
the presence of Soviet troops in Afghanistan, calling rumors to the
contrary "pure fabrications" disseminated by the American news media. And *Pravda* reiterated the Soviet Union's long-standing policy of
noninterference in the internal affairs of neighboring countries.

Shortly thereafter, however—just a few days into 1980—*Pravda*
was acknowledging that a limited Soviet military contingent had indeed been dispatched to Kabul—at the impassioned request of the
new socialist leader, Babrak Karmal. The soldiers were there, the story
said, to render "fraternal assistance"—specifically to restore order and
to combat an undeclared war being waged by mercenaries from Pa-

kistan, China, and the United States—and would be withdrawn as soon as possible. *Izvestia* followed with a report that CIA agents were training counter-revolutionary terrorist elements near the Afghan-Pakistani border. And it was said—at least by one GRU officer of Taras's acquaintance—that operatives of the Israeli Mossad were also involved in fomenting the conspiracy against the Kabul regime.

But Taras wondered if there were not other, more compelling reasons for the intervention. The Afghan rebellion, after all, had been simmering for years between Kabul and the countryside. But the recent fall of the Shah of Iran on Afghanistan's western border must certainly have alarmed the Kremlin to the dangers of the Ayatollah's Holy War spreading to the neighboring Islamic Soviet Central Asian republics—Turkmenistan, Uzbekistan, and Tadjikistan.

Whatever the real reasons, Taras was desperate to be involved, like Marcus, in whatever was going on—and, despite *Pravda*'s protestations, there was a great deal. The "limited military contingent" was obviously not in process of early withdrawal, judging by the saber-rattling Taras heard increasingly all about him. Motorized divisions—the 357th, the 360th, the 201st, and others—were fanning out across the countryside, a retired tank officer told him, and Kabul was already in the hands of the 103rd and 104th Airborne Divisions and the 105th Guards Airborne Division.

If further evidence were needed, every day now Taras's fellow ZSKA members were receiving transfer orders. One was sent to the 103rd Airborne's home base in Vitebsk in Byelorussia; several others were going east, either to Kirovabad in the Azerbaidjan SSR, home of the 104th, or to Ashkhabad, capital of the Turkmen Republic. And more than a dozen were headed direct for Tashkent, just four hundred kilometers north of the Afghan border and headquarters of Marshal Sokolov's 40th Army, which had crossed the Amu-Darya on pontoon bridges to spearhead the drive into Afghanistan. All of these troop movements, Taras was assured, were preceded by *Spetsnaz* elements, whose job was to secure airfields, communication centers, and other key points.

Yet through it all, Taras and the other Olympic hopefuls remained untouchables. Among the ranks of full-time *Spetsnaz* sportsmen of his acquaintance, not a single transfer order was received, and no slightest alteration was made in their training regimen. They stretched, they ran, they bouted; they continued to be coached and cosseted like prize livestock. Taras grew desperate.

Marcus had promised Taras to speak with some *Spetsnaz* commanders on his behalf, but weeks passed with no word from the Cowboy, and no change in Taras's status. By then, assuming Marcus to be already out of reach in Afghanistan, Taras redoubled his own petitions to Dokuchayev—to no avail.

"Which would you rather have?" the lieutenant colonel demanded with biting sarcasm. "An Olympic medal round your neck, or an Order of the Red Star on your casket?"

"I choose real life, Osip, over a game."

"The Motherland might endorse your choice, but our sports federation won't. Not this year, Tarushka. This year you'll do just as you're told. Now, go practice your *rémise*."

Taras obeyed, but only disengaging—in the parlance of fencing— to reconsider his tactics. Obviously Dokuchayev and his superiors would do nothing to alter the status of a promising fencer on the runup to the Summer Games. But what if Taras himself did something dramatic to change their opinions?

Several days later Dokuchayev drew him angrily aside.

"It won't work, Tarushka," he said.

"*What* won't work?"

"Your clever little scheme. You're dogging it. Deliberately losing matches."

"But you're joking. I've lost only two or three times in the last dozen bouts. And they were very close."

"Because you *made* them close. A point here and there. You're cutting it very fine, Taras, off—what?—a hundredth of a second in your splendid reflexes? Two of those matches you should have won easily. And I fully expected you to win the third."

"I tried."

Dokuchayev's fist hit the table. "You tried to lose—and you damn well succeeded! Do you take me for an utter fool? I see every move my students make out there. You showed more expertise in being defeated by such a tiny margin than if you had won convincingly."

Arensky smiled fractionally and reached for his glass of tea. "I suppose I should be flattered—"

119

Dokuchayev backhanded the glass off the table, smashing it against the cement wall of his small office. "You should be court-martialed, you little shit! You're throwing away a chance of a lifetime, something that will never come your way again. Can't you see that? No, it's worse than that. By going to Afghanistan, you'll be throwing away your life! And if you ever quote me on that, Tarushka, I'll cut off your fucking balls and send you to the ladies' foil team."

It was very hard for Taras to do what he did next, to look his friend and teacher straight in the eye and say, "I don't know what you're talking about, Osip."

"Then get out of here. I've nothing more to say."

A week later, after Taras had been eliminated in an early round of an important tournament with *Dinamo,* there was another meeting in Dokuchayev's office. In the interim there had been no rapprochement between the two men, rather a day-by-day entrenchment of hostile positions. Now, as Taras stood, mask under crook of arm, dripping perspiration after a hundred practice lunges, the lieutenant colonel idly turned pages, ignoring his student's presence.

But finally Dokuchayev glanced up. "Well, Sergeant Arensky, it seems you're getting your wish. You're out of the program as of today. 'Does not meet norms for Olympic sportsmen,' it says here. 'Reassign to officer training.' "

"Training? I don't want to go back to school, I want to fight."

"Oh? Do you actually imagine the GRU gives a shit what you want? You're lucky they don't ship you out to Afghanistan in a penal battalion and use you as a human mine detector."

When Taras made no response, Dokuchayev continued:

"And let me give you one last piece of advice. Wherever they send you, stick the course for a change. Your washout here makes my judgment look piss-poor." He tossed a packet of papers across the desk. "There's an address listed on top there. You're to report to that office tomorrow morning." Dokuchayev leaned back in his chair, looking straight at Taras, yet focusing well beyond, as though the younger man were quite invisible.

"Is there anything else, sir?"

"Yes. Clean out your stuff here this afternoon. As for your apartment, the club would like you out by the end of the week. You won't be needing it where you're going, and I've got a real saberman I want to get in there."

120

Arensky stood up, saluted smartly. "Good-bye, sir."

Dokuchayev ignored the salute, waved him out.

At the door Arensky paused. "I'm sorry, Osip."

"So am I, Tarushka. So the hell am I."

The reporting address was the GRU building on Peoples' Militia Street, and the officer in charge none other than the bullet-domed Major Kornelyuk. If anything, the interview was even more perfunctory than the previous one had been, with the wooden-faced officer betraying no recognition of the young man whose papers he was perusing a second time. Five minutes, a few rudimentary exchanges and rubber stampings later, Arensky about-faced and exited, having been assigned to the Ryazan Higher Airborne Academy to complete his interrupted officers training.

Two days later, after a four-and-a-half-hour southeasterly train ride from Moscow's Paveletsky Station, he was tossing his gear onto his bunk in the Ryazan barracks, still with no real idea of what he was getting into.

Was he really going to spend the next year and a half out on the prairie, sitting in classrooms and slogging through the Oka River marshes, while a war was going on? From all indications, that was exactly what he would be doing—merging into Ryazan's regular four-year curriculum, which was designed to graduate five hundred airborne officers a year with degrees in military engineering, just as Taras's former school, the Supreme Soviet Military Academy, turned out lieutenants of motorized infantry.

He conveyed his impatience to the first officer who would listen, a perpetually grinning, leather-faced Tatar captain of the Special Faculty. This was a school within a school, whose function was to continuously monitor the progress of all students, looking for those few who met the supreme standards for *Spetsnaz* officers. All the rest would be posted on graduation to regular units of the airborne forces—the VDV, *Vozdushno Desantnye Voyska*. The truth was, Taras told the fellow, he was not so eager to earn his lieutenant's shoulder-straps as he was to get into combat, even if that meant going to Afghanistan as a noncom.

The captain slapped both his fat thighs and bared his bad teeth. "What's your hurry, duckling? We've been fighting those bandits for a hundred and fifty years. Believe me, there'll be plenty of bullets waiting out there for you."

Taras was told to forget all his crazy notions—along with his sportsman's "sergeant" ranking—and to conduct himself like any other Ryazan *kursant,* airborne officer cadet.

He did so, and found himself plunged at once into a carefully coordinated nightmare, flogged by sadistic instructors down a daily gauntlet of pain so unremitting that it erased from his memory the minor tortures Dokuchayev inflicted on his fencing squad. He was given no time to think of Afghanistan—or of anything but surviving the next few hours or minutes; indeed, after Ryazan, Taras was soon convinced, war itself would seem a holiday outing.

And the demands on Taras were especially fiendish because of the extra efforts required to catch up with the third-year officer's class— something he was determined to do rather than lose another year.

For instance, he found himself lagging seriously behind in basic skill-at-arms, and had to spend many extra hours on the firing ranges, training with both Warsaw Pact and NATO weaponry—sidearms, sniper and assault rifles, machine guns and grenade launchers. There were no points awarded here for fencing prowess, nor did the slashing techniques of the saber bear any helpful resemblance to infantry bayonet drill. And he took more than his share of lumps during those early days, from the camp's gung-ho specialists in *rokupashni-boi,* close-quarter battle method, and *sambo—samooborona bez oruzhiya*—unarmed combat, Red Army–style. And these brutal disciplines, he learned, were mere prerequisites to more advanced *Spetsnaz* techniques of silent killing.

And each night on his bunk, exhausted—all but comatose—Officer Cadet Taras labored an extra few minutes to make up his huge classroom deficit. He committed to benumbed memory long lists of current American and British slang, Marxist dialectics, electronic schematics, military theory from Sun-Tzu to Clausewitz and Ho Chi Minh—until lights-out brought blessed oblivion. He also devoted to his studies those precious hours each week meted out to cadets for personal or family matters.

But this was not all. Because of his late transfer, Taras was the only man in his class not qualified in basic airborne operations. To remedy this embarrassing deficiency, while other cadets were enjoying "free Sundays," Cadet Arensky would report to Ryazan's jump school—an extensive parachute-training area in the rear of the academy. He learned to pack his own chutes, both drone-assisted D-5s and UT-15 sport chutes. He spent hours maneuvering on the suspended canopy simulators. And finally he earned his wings, exiting an An-12 at a thousand meters and gentling down smack in the center of a landing zone beside the Oka River.

In two more months he was qualified in HALO (high-altitude low-opening)—which entailed jumping at ten thousand meters and free-falling most of the way before pulling the ripcord—and HAHO techniques. He had landed on top of buildings, in water, and on nearly every kind of terrain, including spruce and birch forest. Now, in addition to his parachute insignia, Taras sported the blue beret and blue-and-white *telnyashka* T-shirt, precisely the jaunty outfit he had admired on Marcus two summers before in Gorky Park. And, like Marcus, Cadet Arensky now tended to walk with a slight swagger.

The month of June 1980 saw the graduation of Ryazan's officer class; but Taras and a select group of his third-year mates, instead of being sent home for a month's holiday, were kept in barracks. Rumors sprang up and spread everywhere, like flames across the summer grasslands—and every one involved Afghanistan. They would be shipping out at once, or within a week at most; they were headed for the southern deserts, to organize and arm Baluchi tribesmen and encourage them to secede from Pakistan; they would be air-dropped into rebel strongholds high in the Hindu Kush; survivors would be rotated back every few weeks to Ryazan to complete their coursework; others were convinced that the battlefield was to be their classroom for the final year, and that commissions would be awarded in the field, based on combat performance. But whatever the ramifications, that they were for Afghanistan, none doubted.

The need seemed plain enough. After the initial successes of the Karmal coup and the shock invasion of Kabul, matters had not gone well. Unlike Hungary in '56 or Czechoslovakia in '68, the operation was not turning out to be a swift surgical strike. The Red Army was rapidly becoming enmeshed in full-scale guerrilla war, with its "limited military contingent" already upwards of a hundred thousand men and still growing—the largest Soviet combat commitment since the defeat of the *Wehrmacht*.

Some of this had been necessitated by wholesale defections on the part of the new Afghan Army. Taras and his fellow cadets heard tales of whole battalions going over to the guerrillas—and taking their rockets and mortars and machine guns with them. Karmal's army was now estimated to have lost at least half its initial strength of eighty thousand.

Even more alarming were stories of desertions and defections among Soviet Muslim troops—Tadjiks, Uzbeks, Kirghiz, Turkmens—who constituted several reserve divisions of Sokolov's 40th Army. The high command was apparently replacing these unreliable Central Asians as rapidly as possible with Slavs—Russians, Ukrainians, Byelorussians— or Balts.

Taras, with the dark hair and southern complexion from his Georgian mother, had even come in for some good-natured kidding on this score from fellow *kursanti.*

One barracks prankster went so far as to present him with a gift-wrapped, dog-eared Koran. Inside, on the flyleaf, had been scrawled some Arabic letters and a single line of Russian: "This Most Holy Book Property of Taraz al-Arenskeem."

Taras laughed heartily, then manhandled the humorist into the adjoining latrine, where he was dangled upside down and head first into a roaring, flushing toilet—and held there until Taras judged the screams of contrition convincingly sincere and any would-be imitators sufficiently deterred.

In late June, after two weeks of rampant speculation, their orders finally came through—and left them dumbfounded.

Taras and his eager mates would not be heading east to hunt bandits under the scorching sun of Afghanistan. Their destination was farther, and even more remote. They were going all the way up to the Arctic Ocean off the northeastern coast of Siberia for two weeks of simulated combat on icebound Wrangel Island.

In the midst of his keen frustration, Taras was just able to appreciate a certain bleak irony in the matter. Whatever epithets Dokuchayev had heaped on him, Taras concluded, had all been abundantly justified by events. After turning his back on the chance of being in the summer Olympics, here he was—on the eve of that glorious event, which all the world would be watching—getting ready to play winter war games, for an Arctic audience of ferrets and foxes.

Had he, perhaps, chosen unwisely?

Chapter

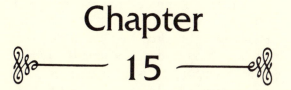 15

YET TARAS WAS TO ENJOY THOSE TWO WEEKS SCRAMBLING OVER barren granite and frozen tundra with his ghostly mates in their white camouflage. They had the godforsaken place to themselves—unless you counted a few Arctic mammals and seabirds, a surprising number of ducks and geese, and somewhere on the eighteen hundred square miles of desolation a tiny colony of Chukchi tribesmen, deposited there by the Soviet government to establish ownership.

The *Spetsnaz* cadets were broken into teams, sent against one another on raids and ambushes; timed in marathon land-navigation exercises whose coordinates took them up and down over the island's moun-tainous interior—and deliberately beyond the limits of physical exhaustion.

Especially did Taras exult in the wild freedom of the long-range survival courses, which afforded total escape from the constraints of barracks life. On his own, with only map, compass, and survival gear, he felt the emergence of a more instinctive self from deep within, a self-reliant being who never came forth under officer scrutiny or coer-cion. It was, Taras thought, the same primitive persona who often possessed him in saber duels, a creature violently and voraciously alive, with atavistic impulses that Taras feared ever to fully unleash. But he enjoyed running and hunting with this other man, stride for stride and hour after hour.

During their second week Wrangel was invaded by an entire *Spetsnaz* brigade. Taras and his companions watched in fascination as five Il-76 transports took turns coming in low over the drop zone, from its four doors each extruding a hundred and twenty "little falcons" in its wake, turning the gray skies white with blossoming airfoil canopies. Within ten minutes all six hundred men had landed and rolled on the hard permafrost, and stood ready as the final Il-76 came in with their supply drop—BMD air-portable combat vehicles, assault guns, and field howitzers—strapped to a dozen padded cargo pallets suspended from parachute clusters and cushioned, just before impact, by retro-rockets. In twenty minutes the drop zone was cleared and the brigade fully operational.

The next morning Taras was delighted to discover a familiar face among the new arrivals in camp when Marcus Jolly slapped him on the back and spun him around. Marcus was a senior sergeant now, with barely enough time to exchange a greeting. He had a full schedule that day, running his privates through what he called *Spetsnaz* "finishing school."

Taras caught up to his old friend the following afternoon. Marcus was standing on a windscoured ridge of Berry Peak, timing his charges at the midpoint of a twenty-five-kilometer run—a run made all the more challenging by the crippling thirty kilos of gear each man carried on his back.

"I thought they needed you in Afghanistan, Cowboy. No wonder the war isn't over."

"Yeah, I thought so too, Cossack. I got as far as Termez, right across the fucking river, when the imperial high wizards of the Defense Ministry changed their collective mind. Sent me and my mates all the way back to Kirovograd." The tactical decision, Marcus said, was to phase out special forces, which had been used so effectively in the coup, and replace them with conventional troops. While at Termez, Marcus had watched construction begin on a mammoth bridge over the Amu Darya, to accommodate tanks and motorized infantry.

"So it's back to playing games," he summed up.

"Well, at least they're dangerous games," Taras said, and detailed

126

for Marcus some of the mock raids they'd conducted the previous week.

"Nursery school," Marcus said. He told of going on nonsimulated training assaults, traversing actual mine fields to attack fortified border installations manned by KGB troops. "They were shooting real bullets at us, Cossack, and nobody warned them it was all in fun."

Taras laughed and shook his head. "You win again, Cowboy. Reminds me of your crazy fencing teacher, what's his name?"

"Balavadze?"

"That's the guy, the one who advocates saber practice without a mask. *Touché!*"

A week later the two friends made their farewells on the frozen airstrip. Taras was to return to Ryazan, Marcus to Kirovograd.

"One of these days we'll get there, Cowboy, you and me," Taras said. "We'll meet somewhere up in the Khyber Pass, wearing turbans and riding camels."

"Sounds just like us, doesn't it? Except if you get your commission, I'll have to obey your fucking orders."

And they laughed, and parted.

Taras was back in time to watch the Olympics on television. Krovopuskov, who had won the gold medal in individual saber at Montreal, repeated handily in Moscow; and the Soviet saber team, with three of the four men who had won at Montreal, did likewise. Taras permitted himself no regrets, but could not altogether stifle the thought that, had he not sabotaged his chances, he might have displaced one of the team medalists.

The Games themselves, which, of course, the Soviets won, were hailed as a monumental triumph in the national press and on TV. But to Taras and his fellow cadets the absence of the Americans tarnished the luster somewhat, especially in such sports as basketball, boxing, swimming, and track and field.

This U.S. boycott over events in Afghanistan had, of course, no effect on Soviet policy. Throughout the rest of 1981 Taras read report after official report that the Kabul regime was steadily pacifying the countryside, and that the counter-revolutionary bandits, lacking all popular support, were propped up only by Pakistani and Israeli mercenaries—and, naturally, CIA agents.

The word reaching Ryazan from returning officers and noncoms was, however, quite different. The Afghan Army was hopeless, Taras was told again and again, the Soviets would have to do all the fighting themselves; conventional tactics, with mixed tank-infantry columns moving into the foothills and high valleys, were proving ineffective—and often disastrous—against the hit-and-run ambushes of the *mujahideen* guerrillas. Something had to be done, and damn fast.

One decision, long overdue, was a switch from motorized infantry to more airmobile operations—using armed helicopters and airborne assault units to patrol for the *mujahideen* and attack their mountain strongholds. And this meant fewer infantry and mechanized units and more special forces. The word came to Ryazan that two brigades of *Spetsnaz* were to be sent at once to Afghanistan, based at Jalalabad in the east and Lashkar Gah in the south. And Marcus was in one of those brigades, Taras was delighted to read several weeks later in the Cowboy's own hand, in a note hand-carried from Kabul.

"Visit the exotic East," Marcus had scrawled on the back of a crude propaganda cartoon torn from the *Kabul New Times*. It showed a sinister *mujahid* about to shoot two praying *mullah*s in the back with a pistol emblazoned with a U.S. dollar sign. "Don't worry, Cossack. I promise to go easy on these filthy beggars till you get here."

Taras thought he would be joining his friend fairly soon. With four thousand *Spetsnaz* out of a total of only twenty-five thousand now involved directly in the war, the odds were good of the net dragging him in—perhaps as soon as he received his commission the following summer.

And in June of 1982 many graduates of the Ryazan Higher Airborne Academy were shipped straight to Afghanistan, especially those who, like Taras, had been earmarked by the Special Faculty for careers in *Spetsnaz*. But "freshly baked" Lieutenant Arensky was somehow not among these.

Instead, two weeks later, wearing brand-new Hungarian shoes and a custom-made suit from a Moscow *atelye,* Taras was standing in the arrivals lounge at London's Heathrow Airport, looking for a man with a sign. Once found, he followed the man outside to a curbside Austin and was driven an hour through sheeting rain and on the wrong side of the road to the Soviet Embassy on Kensington Palace Gardens. Here, sharing a smoky basement cubbyhole with two other GRU officers, he was to spend the next ten months nominally as an attaché—and actually as a junior intelligence officer.

It didn't take him long to decide that he preferred his new posting to Afghanistan, even with the constant drizzle. He was intrigued by his first assignment—investigating the activities of supposedly retired SAS officers, several of whom were suspected of working closely with America's Delta Force in preparing a commando mission to rescue the U.S. Embassy hostages held in Tehran.

And, perhaps not surprisingly, Taras liked the West. It was a totally different world, one he found vastly stimulating, though bewildering. Even after several months he experienced daily shock at seeing so much random activity: so many cars, colors, signs, fashions, choices; so many things to buy and eat and wear and look at. Not that all these choices were available to him necessarily; he could merely window-shop the West, not really partake of it. His own life was carefully sequestered within the walled embassy compound—and carefully surveilled when he left it. Nevertheless, Taras thought wryly, he had undoubtedly been infected, at least mildly, by what one Party dialectician had branded *Veshchism,* or "Thingism"—the virulent fungus of Western consumerism.

If so, he was certainly not alone. Most of the men and women of the Soviet mission managed to contrive frequent shopping forays down into Knightsbridge or along Oxford Street, and some of the minister counselors and first secretaries boasted hand-tailored suits from Bond Street or Savile Row, and their wives couture outfits from Harrods or Liberty.

But it wasn't necessarily glitter and glamour that fascinated Taras about the city and its people. He enjoyed riding the tube, noisy and filthy compared to Moscow's showpiece Metro and almost as crowded, with commuters every bit as ethnically colorful and shabbily dressed, but far more animated. He liked eavesdropping in the midst of this human swarm, and attempting to decode the babel of dialects—public school, cockney, Caribbean, Midlands, Scots, Indian, Pakistani, and heaven only knew what else. After a few weeks, having drastically updated his slang, he discovered he could converse with nearly everybody, after some fashion. He particularly enjoyed engaging in the prolonged civilities and courtesies that might accompany the simple purchase of a bar of chocolate or roll of film. "How are you, dear? Is that all you'll be wanting, then? That's right, 50p for you, dear." But then, why shouldn't he enjoy this? His linguistic expertise was English, after all, not Pushtu or Dari-Persian, the principal languages of Afghanistan. London was a logical posting.

And when he got an evening free, he liked strolling with the tourist swarms between Piccadilly and Leicester Square, through the neon gauntlet of movies and discothèques, video arcades and fast-food emporiums, dining on takeaway as he walked—*döner kebab* or *bratwurst* on a bun, Scotch egg or Cornish pasty.

To maintain his fitness, he jogged every morning through Kensington Gardens and Hyde Park, past the Serpentine, enjoying the equestrians cantering along the bridal paths and the millrace of black cabs swirling around Hyde Park Corner and charging up Park Lane. To keep his hand in, he formed a fencing club and by the end of summer was conducting weekly lessons in foil in the embassy gymnasium.

In December he was promoted to captain and appeared on the 1983 diplomatic list as an assistant military attaché. He had definitely adjusted his career sights when, in early April 1983, the KGB deputy *rezident,* Colonel Oleg Karamzin, called him into his plush fourth-floor corner office and gave him a generous shot of vodka along with the startling news that his request for transfer to Kabul had finally been approved. He should be ready to leave tomorrow.

Karamzin hoisted his glass. "To your health, Captain!"

Chapter

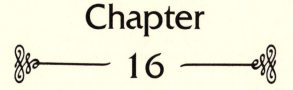

16

THE SUN CAME TARDILY TO THE LITTLE VALLEY, DELAYED BY THE limestone peaks that formed its eastern barrier. But on this first day of June, it came mercilessly, angrily ablaze as it vaulted those jagged summits to blast the rock walls and meandering watercourse below. On the valley floor it was soon above eighty degrees Fahrenheit, on its way to a hundred. Along the ridgelines first struck by the sun's high hammerblows, it was hotter still. And it was there, on a naked spur of rock, that a heap of stones and dust began to stir itself and assume vaguely human shape. A man lying prone, a man who knew his hiding place was now on fire and that he must quickly make his move.

He was wrapped in an earth-colored *patou,* the woolen blanket used by the mountain fighters for both warmth and camouflage. Beneath this, a khaki *kameez partouk,* the baggy Afghan pajama suit, was already encrusted with salt sweat. His feet, blistered and bleeding from a night's scramble over rocks, were shod in cheap Pakistani sneakers, in preference to *chaplis,* the traditional Afghan sandals. Slowly he lifted his head, dark eyes showing first beneath his *lungi,* the rough cotton turban, then a flowing black mustache that tightened over a grim mouth. Binoculars lifted to mask the dark visage, and the concealed man squinted out along the valley, careful not to betray his presence by a blinding sun-flash off the coated lenses. In his every aspect he seemed the epitome of the wild *mujahid,* the ferocious freedom fighter of Afghanistan.

Except this man was Russian.

Major Taras Arensky knuckled the sweat from his eyes, shifted the binoculars, and began to study, meter by square meter, the exfoliated, stratified cliffs that faced him across a narrow ravine. It didn't take long to find what he was looking for. A transverse ledge just wide enough for a single man showed human tracks in several sandy places, and among the limestone strata were several openings that could be caves—shelters hidden from the Antonov reconnaissance planes and protected against even the five-hundred-pound bombs of the Migs and Sukhois.

He was looking at a *mujahideen* hideout; Arensky was sure of it. He had followed a band of them—perhaps as many as twenty—hereabouts the previous night after they'd rained their 60mm mortars and 107mm rockets on a tank and infantry column down the valley near the Chagan Sarai firebase. Had he required further confirmation, less than an hour before and a kilometer away he'd surprised a mountaintop sentry leaning against his Chinese-made Dashika 12.7mm heavy machine gun. Only after pulling his combat knife from the ragged corpse had Taras discovered to his disgust that he'd killed a barely bearded boy. Not that this was an oddity among the Afghan rebels; these days they were going to war at ten.

This busy little cliff-dwelling committee of *muj,* however, was about to be permanently disbanded. Arensky dusted off his R-350M portable radio to call up the Jalalabad airbase thirty kilometers away. In a matter of minutes a couple of Mi-24 Hind helicopter gunships would be hovering right outside the rebels' front door, strafing and rocketing the cliffside into vaporous powder. Taras, meanwhile, would be plucked off the mountain by one of the Mi-9 Hips and evacuated back to Jalalabad, one more mission accomplished.

With any luck, Lieutenant "Markus Dzholly" (for the Cowboy had collected a battlefield commission along with numerous combat medals) would be at the base waiting for him. Or Marcus might yet be working one of those ridges across the narrow valley, where an Mi-9 had dropped him as part of a four-man *Spetsnaz* team, searching for a second *mujahideen* band that had participated in the previous night's raid at Chagan Sarai.

Both groups, Taras was convinced, were key elements of the fierce resistance they had encountered during the preceding week in the Kunar province, resistance that was preventing this Soviet thrust—the second Kunar Valley offensive of 1985—from relieving the Afghan garrison farther up at Barikot on the Pakistani border. As elsewhere in Afghanistan, the tortuous topography here, with its many side valleys and deep defiles, was perfectly tailored to the *mujahideen*'s hit-and-disperse mountain warfare. The steep-walled and narrowing river valley twisted its way a hundred kilometers through the Northwest Frontier with Pakistan, all the way from Jalalabad east of Kabul to the Kunar's headwaters high in the Hindu Kush.

The main combined-arms column was pinned down just beyond Chagan Sarai, unable to move. Taras had flown over it the day before, a long, ocherous, metal-scaled snake basking lazily in the sun—big T-55 and T-62 tanks interspersed with smaller BMDs, and BMP and BTR armored personnel carriers, all strung out along the dusty river road—halted by the threat of grenade and heavy machine-gun fire from the flanking hills.

"Fucking *basmachi!*" the chopper pilot had sworn. It took only a couple of dung-eating bastards hiding in the rocks with a beat-up RPG-7 to stop an army—just like a spoonful of shit in the honey barrel!

And it almost was an army, Taras thought. There were elements of the 9th and 11th Afghan Infantry Divisions down there, reinforced by the 37th and 38th Commando Brigades from Kabul and the 31st and 46th Infantry Regiments. The entire parade, heavily armored and perfectly motionless, was spearheaded by two Soviet units—the 191st Motor-Rifle Regiment and 66th Motor-Rifle Brigade.

Which is why he and Marcus and their special operational teams had been called in, along with a brigade of crack Soviet airborne-assault forces. For the past several days heliborne detachments had been deployed along the ridges to develop flank security; but these units were routinely withdrawn at night, whereupon the *mujahideen* raiders would simply move back in. The *Spetsnaz* teams were more formidable.

He and Marcus had done this before. They had fought from the southern deserts around Kandahar all the way to the mountains of

Nuristan and Badakhshan in the north; had led offensives in the Panshjir, in Paktia province, Paghman, Khost, and now the Kunar. They had been among the first to cast off the traditional paratrooper outfit and disguise themselves as *mujahideen* in turban or pillbox hat, shirt and baggy trousers, concealing their special weaponry. It made eminent sense, and it was no sacrifice to forgo the jaunty blue beret. Lately even motor riflemen with two weeks of air-assault training were permitted them—along with the coveted blue-striped T-shirts under their camouflage overalls. As far as Taras and Marcus were concerned, it took more than a fashion statement to make a man a *Spetsnaz* fighter.

They had employed their climbing skills to scale steep mountain faces at night—and thus to fall upon totally unsuspecting *mujahideen* bands. Taras recalled a dawn attack on a bivouac apparently considered so impregnable that the confident rebels had posted no sentry. After several hours of fairly straightforward class-five climbing, the *Spetsnaz* team had burst into a clifftop camp to find the entire band kneeling in three rows, facing Mecca for dawn prayers, their sandals and rifles stacked neatly to the side. In a hideous, muted fusillade from silenced AKR submachine guns, twenty-three devout warriors had simultaneously acquired the status of *shahids,* martyrs.

Other favorite *Spetsnaz* tactics were to be air-dropped in the rear of a rebel raid, to cut off retreat routes. Or, using night-vision equipment, to ambush night-traveling groups of *mujahideen*, who had come to rely, with proud contempt, on the fearful Russians withdrawing to the safety of their firebases after dark, where officers would souse themselves in imported vodka and conscripts would get stoned on cheap local marijuana or hashish.

It had taken a little while for word of these terrible new enemies—who looked and fought and moved across the land exactly like the *mujahideen* themselves—to spread among the scattered mountain tribes of the resistance. But eventually it had done so, and had now filtered back to the Soviets by way of rebel POWs. They had attested again and again that the foreign *Spetsnaz* devils were the only enemy fighters the *mujahideen* truly feared.

Well, there *were* similarities, Taras thought. Like the *mujahideen*, he had become inured to death, and to life. He no longer asked himself why he did the terrible things he did, took such suicidal risks; or why he'd volunteered to remain in Afghanistan beyond his two years. It wasn't the money, heaven knew—though, at three times normal officer pay, Taras had nearly twenty thousand rubles put by. And it wasn't the damn combat medals. He had a drawerful now—nearly everything but a Hero of the Soviet Union. Only the crazy Cowboy, who'd been there a year longer, was still hoping to get one of those.

No, Taras fought on because he had somehow lost the vision of any other, more normal kind of life. His ten months in London, for instance, now seemed to him an impossibly distant daydream, the vaguely recalled fantasies of another man. How could he ever go back?

On his sunblasted ledge he wiped his brow again. He hadn't really mastered the proper winding of the three-meter-long turban cloth to keep the sweat out of his eyes. He squinted again at the valley below, at the onrushing, silt-clouded Kunar, pearl-gray here in deep cliff shadow, but further downstream flashing and frothing into momentary sunshine, endlessly cutting its fertile swath, a blessed relief in the otherwise barren landscape.

It made for a lovely and tranquil scene—deceptively so, as was proven an instant later, when the morning stillness was shattered by the deafening roar of turbojets. Taras looked up to see four silver streaks across a sky of deep cobalt—a line of Su-25 Frogfoot ground-attack fighters. They went screaming down the valley, probably to shell rebel positions around Asmar before returning to their squadron at Bagram airfield north of Kabul.

Taras chuckled. *Good hunting, comrade pilots, and thank you for rousing a daydreaming* Spetsnaz *and reminding him of his morning business.* He fingered the radio to call for gunships—then froze.

Across the narrow ravine—too close for binoculars, only a few meters below him—a tiny Afghan girl had suddenly appeared on a ledge. She was barefoot, dressed in an embroidered cloth cap and filthy gray smock, and her brown, doll-plump face was canted skyward in the direction of the vanishing thunder. So, there *was* a cave opening here; a whole village might be hidden away in a network of passages in the fissured limestone. And Taras was right on top of it.

Still he hesitated, watching her, his thumb massaging the radio's flex antenna. He became aware of a hammering in his chest, an absurd welling panic that the toddler was much too close to the precipice, might fall to her death before his eyes. His teeth bit down on an obscenity. He told himself there was no reason to delay. His job was to call in the coordinates and get the hell out. What was the alternative? Let her go, spare an entire village, so they could go on killing Russians?

135

It was war. The enemy was woman, too, because mothers made rebel soldiers. A boy was ready to join the *jihad* by twelve or thirteen; maybe seventy thousand of them came of age each year, in isolated villages like this or infiltrated back from the camps in Pakistan. Could the Red Army kill *mujahideen* faster than Afghan women could bear them? Probably not, but that was still their soldierly business, the endless business of war, and Taras had been trained to do it well. Killing the other guy. Or, if need be, the other guy's little girl.

He watched as a breeze ruffled the black bangs under her cloth cap. She was still too tiny to be hidden away forever behind the *chadori*, the tentlike veil worn by Afghan women. She frowned, clenched soiled, chubby cheeks, bent slightly forward.

He swore silently again. The little girl was waddling recklessly toward the brink. She had spotted something just ahead, something that crinkled her eyes and drew her mouth wide in delight. Leaning far out from his own ledge, Taras saw it too. A little green bird-shape was wedged among rocks along the precipice, its plastic surface burnished by a sudden shaft of sunlight through the ravine.

It was a "toy" mine. Low-flying Soviet helicopters had scattered them by tens of thousands over trails, mountain passes, and caravan routes, along with hundreds of thousands of PFM-1 "butterfly" antipersonnel mines. The idea was to interdict rebel supply lines, but the bright plastic objects—diabolically shaped like dolls, trucks, birds, combs, pens, watches—were irresistible to Afghan children, despite incessant warnings. Had this child accidentally stepped on the toy, her foot would have been blown off. If she picked it up, she'd lose a hand, perhaps both, maybe her eyesight. In any case, she was about to be maimed for life—if she didn't die of infection.

The pressure came boiling up from deep within, bursting out of him:

"*Nyet!*"

The tiny figure, across the gap, froze—squinting up at this strange *mujahid* who had suddenly appeared on the opposite ledge and roared so fiercely at her, a frightening sound that was still reverberating off the rocks.

Knowing the echoing cry could summon *mujahideen* any instant from the caves, Taras waved his AK-47 at the motionless child, first menacingly, then frantically.

She was frightened, took a faltering step back. But the shiny toy was too close, almost within reach, and the desire to pick it up too powerful. Taras saw her small body bending, her hand reaching. She had made her decision.

And he made his—one that went against all his *Spetsnaz* training—and hurled himself forward over the ravine.

Through a midair blur of cliffside he saw a turbaned torso shouldering a rifle—someone thought Taras was attacking the child. Too late now! The rocky ledge below, bright green bird, reaching child, all rushed toward him. He was going to land right on the damn thing, detonate it himself! But his body would take the blast, shielding the girl.

Taras never heard the full-auto racketing of the AK-47, nor felt the swarming hail of steel-core slugs that tore through his turban. There was only exquisite, exploding joy as his sneakered feet landed just beyond the hideous toy and his body crashed down on the tiny, terrified child. Joy—and nothingness.

When he dared fire no more for fear of hitting his niece, Nazar Khan also leaped, plunging recklessly ten meters down the sheer cliff face. He landed badly on the narrow ledge, twisting his ankle, but ignoring it in his panic to free the still-screaming child. She lay trapped now under the corpse of the madman who had tried to kill her.

He tore at the body, fingers slithering in the warm, viscid fluid that gouted from the turban. Blood was everywhere, soaking the *patou,* half masking the face of the strange *mujahid* as Nazar struggled to pull the terrified child free. Finally he held her precious weight safely in his arms.

"My little Aziza, yes, you are safe," he whispered, caressing her dust-and-tear-grimed cheeks with his callused fingers. Then, using the toe of his sandal, he prodded the corpse again, studying what he could see—through the gore—of the mustached visage, the bronzed skin now ashen beneath, for a clue as to tribe. The mad fellow had clearly not been a fellow Pushtun. Perhaps a Nuristani, then, or a Tadjik or Kirghiz from even farther north.

Then Nazar saw something else, beneath the man's *kameez*—a sunglint off oxidized metal. It was the radio, dropped by Taras when he'd grabbed for the child. Nazar kicked at the dust again, exposed faded Cyrillic letters, a rubberized antenna, knurled knobs. *Badal*—vengeance—flamed in his heart. Nazar unslung his AK-47, letting the swinging muzzle impact the dead man's jawbone. The *mujahid* prayed there were enough rounds remaining in the clip to shred the despised thing at his feet.

He fitted his finger to the trigger and spat out his curse: *"Mordabad Shuravi!"* Death to the Soviets!

Then Aziza wailed in his eardrum. He cocked his head, took in her stricken gaze, her tearful, wretched pout, her arm pointing imperiously down. She wanted something.

Nazar looked down and saw the bright green plastic object.

And understood at once what had happened. The Russian had risked—and lost—his life to save the child.

Others now came forth from the caves. Nazar waved them back urgently, turned around on the path to protect his niece, then slowly sidestepped along the narrow ledge away from the mine. When he judged that he had retreated far enough, keeping tiny Aziza well behind him, he took careful aim with his assault rifle and detonated the plastic bird.

Chapter

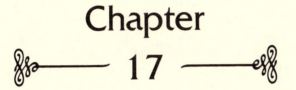 17

It was good to kill Russians, especially one of the feared night raiders. But a Russian with a radio just outside their caves, this was very bad. That meant more of the accursed infidel invaders might be coming soon, and they would surely come in their Village Killers from Jalalabad. These big brown-and-yellow mottled *halikoptars* could hover for an hour, raining death and destruction with all the fires of hell.

They had witnessed such terrible things, all of them, and there were thirty who now dotted the cliff face in the aftermath of the explosion. Fourteen were *mujahideen,* who used the caves as their camp. These intrepid young mountaineers scuttled over bare rock and dropped from ledge to ledge with casual aplomb to look upon the dead Russian disguised as a *mujahid.* The rest were veiled women, children, and old men, equally curious, but clinging gingerly to the narrow footways and reluctantly releasing each handhold. They were the pitiful remnant of a once-thriving village farther up the Kunar, a village whose mud-brick homes now lay in rubble and whose terraced wheat fields and fruit orchards were withered and weed-choked. They eked a bare subsistence from a few sheep and goats, and from collecting the spent casings from Soviet BM-21 rockets, packing them on donkeys fifty kilometers across the mountains to the Pakistani border and selling them for scrap, fifty rupees apiece.

As the warriors crowded around the corpse, Nazar described briefly how he'd shot a strange *mujahid* attacking Aziza, only to discover the man was an enemy soldier trying to stop the child from picking up the toy bomblet. The incredible tale, of course, could not dilute one drop of their cherished hatred of the foreign devils. The Russian, after all, had not come on an errand of mercy, but to destroy them, a fact brought instantly home when a shout from above announced the discovery of Qasim, butchered beside his machine gun.

But there was no time to mourn the martyred boy. The dead Russian must be hidden at once, so he could not be seen from the air. Then they must abandon the caves forever, taking Qasim's body for later burial. The holy warriors would find a new hiding place from which to carry on the fight for their valley, while the villagers must flee across the frontier.

At Nazar's direction, two men bent to lift the Russian. The next instant both yelped and leaped back as if scalded, dropping the corpse onto the ledge, and nearly off the cliff. The thing had groaned—was groaning still!

Nazar knelt in the bloodied dust, found a feeble pulse in the carotid. The Russian lived—but there was no way to determine the extent of his injuries under the red-drenched turban and blood-matted hair. He might be merely stunned, or in deep coma, his brain dead. Either way, they must leave him in the cave. If he had radioed his position, he might be found in time by his comrades. If he hadn't radioed, he'd die, like young Qasim.

The Russian moaned again, a child's plaintive call for comfort. Nazar stood to give his brusque order, heard himself alter the words at the last instant: "We take the *feranghi*—the foreigner—with us."

There came the expected cries of outrage, most passionately from Qasim's cousin, Mirbad, who ached to avenge himself at once with the Russian's own knife. But Nazar calmly invoked his authority as commander. If the *feranghi* died of his wounds, so be it; but as a war prisoner he would not be killed. And this, he reminded them, was not only decreed by Koranic law, but was the express order of the chief of staff of the National Islamic Front of Afghanistan—one of

140

the seven principal resistance groups, and the one that supplied their weapons. If the Russian survived his wounds, he must be turned over to NIFA.

A stretcher was improvised from rifles and blankets, and the refugees moved off single file along the ledge, vanishing one by one into the shadowed ravine.

Fifteen minutes later the cliffside echoed the thunderous vibrato of turbo-driven rotors. Five Mi-24 combat helicopters swept down the valley, their gun blisters flaring in the sun, their huge insectile shadows flitting over the turbid river.

His mother was frying up his favorite supper—potatoes and mushrooms. The savory smell was carried along with the woodsmoke through the stark winter woods to where Taras and his big retarded friend, Ulyan, were gleefully destroying an entire German Panzer division with accurately thrown snowballs. Identifying the cooking aroma, the two boys broke off the engagement and raced homeward through the evening-dark slashes of alder and birch boles. Their snowshoes squeaked over the crusted surface; their breath-clouds vapored in the frosty air, eyes watering, woolen underwear sweat-sopped under their coats and scarves. In sight of the cabin and frantic to be first, Taras surged ahead and burst across the threshold . . .

. . . And was shoved upright by a strong hand. His head was reeling, a sick, bloated throb, but he was too feeble to care. His pain-sealed eyes recoiled from lancing light. His body contained not a gram of strength, tried to fall back, could not. A steaming cup of tea was held under his nostrils, metal scalded his lower lip. He sipped, braced as sweet medicinal fire cauterized the back of his throat and chest. Finally he opened his eyes, saw blue sky filtered through a lattice of palm fronds. Ragged Afghan youths, slung with cartridge belts, hunkered against mud walls, assault rifles propped beside them.

Suddenly a bearded warrior, face thrust close, exhaled hot, sour breath, dark eyes probing his.

Taras flung sideways, tearing at his *kameez* for the cyanide capsule in its pouch. Only the elite battalions had been issued these bite-or-swallow-and-recycle suicide pills, but all Soviet soldiers had been thoroughly dosed with horror stories of what to expect if they were ever captured by, or defected to, the Russian-hating *mujahideen*. They would be chained up in caves, they were assured, ingeniously tortured, finally executed, their corpses dumped for wolves and vultures. Like his comrades, Taras had no wish to authenticate these lurid tales.

But his fingers fumbled uselessly at the blood-crusted *kameez*, then his sinewless arms slid to the ground. Sick with fatigue, Taras slumped back, staring skyward as the rubbled room began slowly to wheel around him. He had nearly slipped through the doorway to the void, when a strong voice snared him and held him back:

"Russki, Russki, muy nye ubivayem vas." In rudimentary Russian he was told he would not be tortured or killed. If he lived, he would be interned in a prisoner-of-war camp run by the National Islamic Front of Afghanistan, visited by the Red Cross. "We are not savage beasts," the voice insisted. "But to live, first you must eat, drink. You are very weak."

Again Taras was propped up, fighting waves of dizziness and pulpy sickness in his head. The room was like an oven. The *mujahideen* leader leaned close, sitting cross-legged. His fierce, twisted face was elongated by a squared-off black beard, which flowed down into a black vest worn over a khaki shirt. Taras tried to assemble his mind, but it was scattered into rubble, strewn all over the vast bombed-out countryside. Then he remembered a girl, a bright plastic bird, a leap across a ravine. Nothing after. What had happened to him?

He must have been shot in the head, the part where memory was. What else was gone? He was still too weak to reach up there and feel around, too afraid he'd find parts of his brain missing.

He was being asked something. "The radio, Russki, did you use this radio?" The *mujahid* was waving the portable transceiver at him; it didn't belong in strange hands. "Did you tell Jalalabad where you were?"

Again Taras tried to remember, but there was nothing there, an empty room. The man shook the radio angrily. "Did you? Tell me!"

"I don't remember," Taras answered listlessly.

Something struck his shoulder. He turned too quickly, triggering excruciating pain through his skull. Close behind him a little girl was squatting on the ground. She wore a dirty smock and embroidered cap. Her tiny hands held a soiled turban cloth. Their eyes met, and Taras felt something touch his heart.

"I told her what you did," said the voice of the *mujahid*, momentarily relinquishing its anger. "Her name is Aziza. She is very grateful. She has been keeping the flies away from you."

142

Taras held the child's luminous gaze. A second later he was rewarded with a cautious, gummy smile. She was missing several baby incisors, top and bottom.

"I also must thank you for saving her from the little bomb," the *mujahid* said, and gave his own name as Nazar. "Aziza is very precious. She is the daughter of my only brother. Ismaiel and his wife and their two sons were all killed by shrapnel when our village was bombed last week."

Taras could not evade the man's eyes. Neither could he answer. He was too weak, and there was nothing to say. Against the wall, one of the young warriors spat and made a low, growling noise. Nazar explained it was the brother of the boy he had killed this morning at the Dashika gun. At once Taras recalled the throttled scream, the bright arterial gush; but again could offer no reply.

The *mujahid* motioned, and a woman, cloaked from head to toe in dark taffeta, came forward, placed a tray of food beside him, then looked at his head. For the first time Taras realized he had been bandaged. He found he was able to sip some sugary green tea, even to swallow bits of goat jerky, but he could not chew the *nan,* the flat, unleavened Afghan bread. It was hard and stale. Nazar apologized for it. He had permitted the women to boil only a little water for tea, he said, but not to bake fresh *nan* for fear the smoke would reveal their presence to the Russians. Taras finished the tea and fainted.

When he woke again, the mountain sky was tinged with evening lilac, and people were moving around. Across the room a teenage warrior was dipping a safety razor into hot tea, then shaving himself while squinting into the tiny metal mirror of his snuffbox. Beside him another *mujahid* was filling AK-47 magazines with bullets.

Nazar appeared suddenly, squatted down, explained that the old men, women, and children were waiting for darkness to leave for the Pakistani frontier. They are the last, he said. Before the war, the Kunar Valley had "many many thousand" people—Nazar did not know the Russian word for such a high number. There were rich farms— "hundreds and hundreds"—on both sides of the river, and along the hillsides. They grew many, many things. Nazar groped for Russian words to name the wonderful crops—wheat and potatoes; many fruits—*abrikos, appelsin, limon*; even *mindal,* almonds.

Then came the war. Many, many thousand Russkis, with Migs, tanks, rockets, helicopters, bombing villages and farms, dropping butterfly mines and yellow gas that burned the eyes and skin. Death was everywhere, whole families and towns full of death—women, babies, old ones. Those who lived ran away, as the tanks rolled over the rubble left by the bombs.

Nazar's eyes were feverish now, inflicting his story on his captive listener just as the ghastly events had been inflicted on his tribesmen. His words, and the nightmare images they conjured, were in bizarre counterpoint to the Soviet version given Taras by his briefing officer on arrival in Kabul. The Kunar Valley, Captain Arensky had been told, had been targeted for one of the first mechanized sweeps of the war, in the spring and summer of 1980. The purpose, crisply pointed out on the pulldown map, was to interdict guerrilla supply lines— here, here, and here—from the northern provinces. As such, it was considered one of the more successful operations of that year.

But the Afghans would never give up, Nazar stressed. Many had dared to return to their devastated valley, rebuilding their homes from rubble, reclaiming their farms from wasteland. And many had survived despite occasional shelling. Now, five years later, it was all happening again. The sky rained death every day from gunships and fighter-bombers, and the tank armies were rolling on the river road.

Taras felt the intense hatred kindled around him. Why didn't they kill him and have done with it? A nod from their leader and they'd all be on him with their knives. If they spared him, he foresaw only a miserable existence. But perhaps he would die soon anyway. His head wounds were probably infected under the filthy bandages. He felt his consciousness ebbing, while the darkness deepened and the *mujahid* leader ranted on in a futile attempt to exorcise the horrors of war.

Blessings of Allah be on you all, he thought, *for all your sufferings. May your people escape to Pakistan and a new life. I can't fucking help you.* Dizziness was closing in. He fell back, no longer hearing Nazar's words, staring at tiny points of starlight through the palm ceiling.

My war is over, he thought, *one way or another. And I don't really care which way it is.* He moaned and rolled sideways, curling up into his pain, waiting for unconsciousness. He shut his eyes, opened them again. He had seen something. Outside, silhouetted against the dusk, the top of a head had protruded for a split-second into the doorway at ground level—precisely the way *Spetsnaz* were trained to look around corners. Then it had vanished.

144

Taras felt an adrenaline surge, but before he could react, the room exploded in a blinding-white flash. A stun grenade, Taras realized in the ear-splitting aftermath. Then, through choking smoke, his name was yelled: *"Taras, stay down!"*

He was too weak to do anything else as the silenced submachine gun stitched a lethal swath across the room, ripping into flesh and bone, spattering the mud walls.

The stuttering gunfire ceased, but continued outside. Taras was plucked off the floor and heaved across somebody's shoulder—a powerful man who ducked low through the doorway and sprinted into the night. Taras, dangling head down, heard Russian shouts, agonized screams, the approaching thrash of rotors. A second later he felt the windblast and sand flurries as a chopper settled near on its retractable landing gear. His carrier rushed toward it, bent low.

He was deposited into the belly of an Mi-24 Hind. Several others crowded in after them, filling the cabin. Then the voice of Marcus Jolly boomed over the banshee whine of twin turboshafts: "Get all the *muj?*"

"Every fucking one!" came the shout.

"How many?"

"Maybe thirty, sleeping in paradise!"

"Allah akbar!" shouted another *Spetsnaz,* mocking the Islamic battle cry, "God is great!"

Then the five-bladed main rotor bit and they were lifting and tilting into the night. Marcus brought his face close. In the faint red glow from the cockpit instruments, Taras could see only the gleam of eyes and teeth in black-mask camouflage. "Hang on, Cossack," he yelled, "we're going home. Hell, you knew I'd come and get you, didn't you?"

Taras looked at his friend, but his mind was filled with the horror below. The still-bleeding bodies of Nazar and his little band of *mujahideen* cut down before they could reach their weapons. The pitiful remnant of Kunar villagers, strewn alongside their meager possessions for the final flight to Pakistan.

And little Aziza, rescued this morning from a cruel fate—but oh, how briefly! If there were a paradise, surely she would be on her way there. But Taras could grapple no more with dreadful things. He slumped against his avenging friend and lapsed into insensibility.

145

Chapter

18

"Did you have to take my damn beret off?" Taras asked.

"Yeah, I couldn't resist it." Marcus horse-laughed and gunned the Soviet UAZ-469 "jeep" through an opening in the frenetic warp and weave of downtown Kabul's afternoon traffic. "Come on, did you see her face when she saw that scar? The señorita damn near choked on her champagne. Up until then I think she was really taking a liking to you, Cossack."

"Mandavoshka!"

"Careful who you're calling a cunt-louse. Remember, I'm the guy who saved your life."

"So you keep reminding me."

The incident had occurred at a striptease joint they'd just left—the Blue Club—where Marcus had taken his friend for a drink directly upon discharge from the sweltering and overcrowded confines of the Soviet military hospital. The "señorita" was a vivacious cocoa-skinned Cuban girl who could kick higher than her head, among other talents. She had been perched in Taras's lap when Marcus had reached over and unceremoniously lifted his friend's blue *Spetsnaz* beret, revealing the freshly unbandaged scar. It was not an edifying sight—a saucer-size circle of angry pink skin cross-hatched with rows of black-threaded sutures, forty-nine in all.

"You know what you look like with all those shoelaces in your scalp, Cossack? An American football. Damn, it's almost as ugly as Balavadze's saber slash."

"I'm so glad it amuses you."

"Well, it does, I'm sorry. I forgot. I'm not supposed to make you laugh, right? With your head stitched tight like that, it must hurt like hell."

"Yeah, it hurts. It hurts to smile, it hurts to talk. It even hurt back there bugging my eyes at all those tits on parade. But you notice I never complained once."

"No, I give you that."

"You know why, Cowboy? Mostly, it's real nice just to be alive. And when my hair grows out, if I part it on the other side, no one will notice. Unless you fucking tell them."

"Hey, I'm glad you're alive too, Cossack. In fact, I'm glad we're both alive, and I aim to get us the hell out of Kabul and safely back to base and keep it that way."

Base was Bagram Airbase, in the Shomali Plain sixty-five kilometers north of Kabul, where they were temporarily stationed. Marcus's ice-blue eyes flicked ceaselessly side to side as he drove, seeking out possible threats in the kaleidoscopic maze that choked the streets—pedestrians, Soviet and Afghan soldiers, bicycles, motorcycles, taxicabs, military trucks, and jeeps like theirs. In five and a half years of war, the population of the Afghan capital had swollen from 750,000 to nearly two million. Some of this influx had come from the Soviet Union and its client states, of course, but most was from internal Afghan refugees. And a high percentage of these, Taras and Marcus were convinced, utterly despised their Slavic "liberators." Despite the four Soviet divisions garrisoned in the city, with frequent military checkpoints and a strict curfew, danger lurked everywhere.

Russian civilians had been stabbed in the back while shopping in bazaars. The Soviet Embassy was shelled regularly, and its first secretary gunned down recently in broad daylight. As a consequence, the Russian colony remained mostly within its heavily guarded, sandbagged enclaves, and diplomats in general were restricted to a ten-kilometer radius in the city center. For further security, all the villages ringing Kabul had been leveled to create a *cordon sanitaire* ten kilometers wide—beyond the range of the *mujahideen*'s 107mm rockets.

So Taras appreciated Marcus's vigilance, and maintained his own as their jeep was waved through a checkpoint by two Afghan soldiers in tan tunics and pillbox hats. When he had arrived in Afghanistan from his London assignment at the tender age of twenty-four, Arensky had been armored in all the invulnerability of youth. But two years had stripped most of it away, and that last day in the Kunar Valley had pretty much finished the job.

Taras had been incredibly lucky to survive, and knew it. Had Nazar been a hairbreadth quicker tracking his AK-47 along the arc of Taras's leap before triggering his fusillade, the steel-core rounds, at a velocity of over seven hundred meters per second, would have burst Taras's skull like a sledgehammered walnut. As it was, only two bullets had struck him, both tangentially, merely furrowing his scalp and peeling a patch back to the bone. He had escaped with a minor concussion, a slight edema, tiny hemorrhages, and a great deal of blood loss.

But the army surgeon—a middle-aged and wonderfully droll Jewish woman from Leningrad—assured him there had been no skull fracture, no infection, no damage to the brain case. It was she who had reassured him about the scar, saying if he was determined to let his hair grow out and hide her lovely needlework, he would be as tediously handsome as ever. She also strongly cautioned him against single-handedly storming any rebel strongholds in the future.

Despite all this good fortune, and his bantering tone with Marcus, Taras knew the experience had not left him unscathed. He was no longer the same soldier, or man, he had been. And the world he saw now, on leaving the hospital and the dingy burlesque club, had also undergone subtle change. As if brightness and contrast knobs had been turned up. Edges were sharper, yet Taras seemed a half-step slow and slightly out of registration, impersonating himself for the benefit of this old friend beside him, but not getting it quite right.

Every once in a while, without warning, his mind would slip its gears, and he'd be back in London, haunting an old bookstore on a drizzly Sunday with black umbrellas passing outside on Charing Cross Road. Or back in Khabarovsk that fateful night, trying to stay sober and awake long enough to save Eva Sorokina from the demented trapper.

And too often in his reveries he'd find himself again the captive of the *mujahideen*. Listening to the ranting of Nazar. Waiting for Aziza to smile at him, or the ragged young warriors to leap and carve him into shashlik. Other times he found himself trying to imagine the kind of mind that had thought up the plastic toy-bomb, or put it into production.

To her credit, Dr. Lazareva had sensed something troubling him, and on her rounds had tried several times to get him to talk about it. But Taras had kept things light, feeding her straight lines, insisting he was fine. As far as he was concerned, she could stitch the outside of his skull, but he didn't want her—or anyone else—poking around on the inside.

But something was indeed going on in there.

It began to coalesce two weeks later. He and Marcus were summoned from Bagram to the 40th Army's Operational Command in Kabul for a special briefing. It had nothing to do with the Kunar Valley offensive. That had been going well without them—though mainly, it had to be said, because the *mujahideen* bands had run out of ammunition, especially 107mm rockets and RPG-7 antitank grenades. In any case, the Soviet mechanized thrust had now reached Barikot on the Pakistani border.

No, the two *Spetsnaz* officers were being recruited for a special operation.

The briefing officer was an overfed, heavy-lidded colonel of KHAD, the Afghan state security force. As he rose to speak, his pudgy hands tugged downward on his neatly pressed gray tunic, in a hopeless attempt to stop it flaring over his matronly hips.

But the attention of Taras and Marcus was drawn elsewhere, to the Soviet officer seated rigidly in the corner. He was a large-boned man of around sixty, with huge, gnarled hands, a lean, craggy face under a bristly crew cut, and the baleful glare of a loitering buzzard.

In singsong, serviceable Russian, the colonel began to introduce him as the recently appointed deputy commander of the LCSFA, the Limited Contingent of Soviet Forces in Afghanistan. But Taras had already recognized the man—by the unique features, shoulder-board stars, and full pectoral of combat ribbons—as Lieutenant General Rodion Marchenko.

And, of course, Marcus already knew the general. Marchenko, Taras recalled, was the GRU officer who had taken a shine to the Cowboy and gotten him into *Spetsnaz*. Marchenko was also the man who, two decades earlier, had helped revive the Strategic Rocket Forces from the ignominy of the Cuban missile withdrawal. And, Taras thought, the old man must certainly be the reason why Marcus and he had been summoned to this briefing.

Taras turned his attention to the lumpish colonel and, somewhere around the second or third sentence of his spiel, knew it was to be a "wet affair"—an assassination. The target, it turned out, was a key Afghan resistance officer who had started a *mujahideen* combat training school outside Peshawar, Pakistan. Taras felt conflicting reactions— revulsion and excitement in almost equal intensity.

"This is Brigadier General Jalil Muhammad Raza," the Afghan colonel said, pointing to an image rear-projected onto a foldout desktop screen. Taras and Marcus moved closer to the ground-glass viewing area and saw a gaunt, bald-headed old man in a gray pajama shirt. His eyes were sunken, his mustache droopy. Around his scrawny neck hung a sign, hand-lettered in Dari-Persian. It was obviously a prison photograph.

"Raza commanded the bodyguard of King Zahir Shah, but when Zahir was overthrown by Mohammed Daoud in 1973, Raza was sent to Pul-i-Charki prison for several years. Unfortunately he was released in 1976. Here is an earlier picture."

The projector now showed a younger, more vigorous Raza. The eyes were piercing, the mustache sleekly groomed. What struck Taras, however, was his uniform, that of a captain in the Soviet VDV. Then, in the background, Taras recognized the familiar barracks of Ryazan Higher Airborne Academy.

"*Yobany v rot!*" exclaimed Marcus beside him. "You're telling us this guy is *Spetsnaz?*"

"No, but he went through a lot of the training." This from Marchenko.

The Afghan colonel went on: "That photograph was taken in the late 1950s. Later, he also trained with British Special Air Service and Green Berets in America, Fort Bragg. We have no pictures from those years."

What the colonel did have, Taras and Marcus learned, was reliable information on the brigadier's current activities, which he regarded as most disturbing. Not only was Raza drilling thousands of young Afghan men from the Pakistani camps in the proper handling of modern weapons and the tactics of mountain warfare. At the same time, according to the colonel, he was attempting to coordinate the various groups of "counter-revolutionary bandits" into a "grand alliance against the DRA"—the Democratic Republic of Afghanistan.

To Taras, this seemed a futile undertaking, with the *mujahideen* factions irrevocably split between Sunni and Shia and along regional and tribal lines. NIFA, Jamiat-i-Islami, Hezb-i-Islami and Harakat, for instance, were often at one another's throats; and each had its own internal rivalries. It was hard to imagine anyone imposing a coordinated command and operational structure on them.

But Raza was undaunted by the challenge, they were assured, and beginning to have some success. Recent rebel offensives in the Helmand Valley and in the Panjshir showed definite evidence of coordinated attacks by several resistance commanders. Altogether a most alarming development.

The colonel turned to Marchenko. "General, do you have something to add?"

Marchenko nodded. "Raza is a hell of a soldier. He says he wants to professionalize the jihad. If anybody can weld that bunch of scrawny bandits and schoolboys into an efficient guerrilla army, he can. He's a serious threat. But if anybody can neutralize that threat, it's you two." Marchenko flashed his stainless-steel grin. "I want you lads to kill the bastard. The colonel will fill you in on the details. Proceed, Colonel."

Marcus punched Taras in the right biceps while the colonel clicked to the next slide. It showed a rough diagram map of the brigadier's training compound thirty-five kilometers west of Peshawar in the Tribal Areas, a region also known for its excellent cannabis and opium crops and many heroin refineries. Raza was well guarded, they were told, and never slept in the same place two nights running.

"Kadafi's technique," Marcus said.

"And he got it from Castro," chuckled Marchenko.

The specifics of the plan were to be left up to them—specifically to Major Arensky, who, if he agreed, would be in charge of the operation. He and Lieutenant Jolly would go in disguise to Peshawar, where they would be joined by a highly qualified grade-six officer of the KHAD, who would serve as liaison.

To Taras, this had sounded as if they would be back in baggy pants and turbans, riding double-humped camels over the Khyber Pass—exactly as he and Marcus had joked about doing years before on Wrangel Island. In fact, they were "disguised" in Western clothing as

Canadian journalists and flew out of Kabul International Airport with a dozen other passengers in a little Yak-40 of Bakhtar Airlines, the Afghan international carrier. Arensky, clean-shaven with a Harris tweed cap covering his scar, was supposedly a recent Ukrainian émigré from Edmonton, Marcus from Vancouver. Both carried passports and supporting credentials forged by the master "shoemakers" in Department D of the KGB's First Chief Directorate.

They checked into Dean's, one of Peshawar's three main tourist hotels, favored by journalists because its gardens and British Colonial–style bungalow rooms permitted unobserved access and egress by *mujahideen* contacts. In their case, it permitted access that evening to a Captain Fareed Qadir, their KHAD adviser and guide, who had been in Peshawar for several months in the guise of a Pakistani taxi driver. "Azib," as they were to call him, boasted of having been involved in several "direct actions" during that time, including the bombing of the Shan Hotel, which had killed several *mujahideen* while wounding a score of others.

This Azib was a disagreeable companion, with a furtive manner, one wandering eye, and the constant habit of giggling to himself. Worse luck, considering Peshawar's hundred-degree heat, his rust-mottled blue Datsun, in which Marcus and Taras were to spend much of the next two days, lacked air-conditioning. Still, it could be worse; they could be back in Afghanistan.

For Peshawar was an absorbing city, crawling with intrigue. If Azib were to be believed, every second person on the swarming streets or chatting over tea in the hotel dining room was some brand of spy. If they were not colleagues—unbeknown to him—from Afghanistan's twenty-thousand-strong security service, then surely they were Pakistani Special Branch, KGB, or CIA.

As for the rest? According to Azib, they were a mixed lot—mercenaries, money-changers, "journalists" like themselves, smugglers, black marketeers, buyers and sellers of weapons and narcotics. He giggled while retailing this shoptalk, all the while engulfed in a vehicular melee that surpassed even Kabul's. He explained how big the heroin business had become in Peshawar, and how in the weapons bazaars of Darra, forty kilometers away, one could purchase anything from .25-caliber pen pistols to Soviet SA-7 Grail surface-to-air missiles.

The neighboring war, of course, was the reason for most of this feverish activity, and the millions of dollars of U.S. aid being funneled through Pakistan—in the form of weapons for the *mujahideen,* and food, clothing, and medical supplies for the millions of Afghans in the refugee camps ringing Peshawar.

"We owe much to the CIA, you see," Azib added after a giggling fit, "for at least seventy percent of these weapons never reach the end of this pipeline, and much food also vanishes. This makes much business for everyone." To illustrate this, he took them to what he called the "U.S. aid bazaar" in the Old City, where they browsed weapons shops offering Vietnam-issue U.S. Army flak vests, jungle boots, and camouflage pants. But other merchants specialized in Soviet military gear, both new and used—and some patently phony, with upside-down hammer-and-sickle shoulder patches.

Afterward they followed a road out to one of the refugee camps, but continued well beyond it, turning onto an unpaved, tread-worn track that wandered off into a void of parched waste and shimmering heatwaves. Twenty minutes of horizon-bouncing, spine-pounding agitation over rocks and ruts brought the groaning Datsun to a merciful halt by a stone-and-mud-brick gatehouse and a rough-timbered barrier across the track. Two turbaned guards emerged from the sentry post with slung binoculars and unslung Kalashnikovs, to which bayonets were fixed. They were both quite young and not particularly friendly-looking. One hung back with his mouth to a hand-held radio, while the other slowly approached the driver's window.

Taras figured these boys had been studying their dust cloud for some time now. Beyond the gate lay what looked like the downsloping mouth of an eroded canyon. Beyond that, presumably, lay Raza's "academy." The brigadier had sited his campus well. It was a hell of an exposed approach from down here, and farther in was probably bristling with Dashikas and Zigroiat heavy machine guns to discourage any predatory visitors from above. The only sensible solution would be to shell the place from across the Afghan border.

Taras, in the taxi's passenger seat, and Marcus in back, remained passive, ostensibly leaving it up to Azib. The "journalists" were festooned with cameras, notebooks, and audiocassette recorders, but Taras had his 9mm Makarov pistol hidden within reach, and Marcus, apparently sipping from an aluminum canteen, was actually holding, behind the metallic false front, a small apple-green RGD-5 hand grenade with the pin out and fingers around the safety lever.

The approaching guard beckoned, and Azib jumped out. There was a quick flurry of Dari-Persian, then the guard thrust his bayonet past Azib's shoulder, pointing back the way they'd come.

Azib overdid the appreciative and explicatory gestures, Taras thought, but at least he wasn't acting furtive or, praise Allah, giggling. The taxi driver *salaam aleikum*ed the guard a final time, climbed into the baking Datsun, backing and filling carefully on the narrow track so as not to raise a particle of dust.

As they were pulling away, Azib kept his wandering eye on the rearview mirror and explained: "I told them we were looking for the Munda refugee camp. He said we had taken a wrong turn."

"And did you thank the man for that?" Marcus asked.

"Oh, my, yes!" Azib giggled.

"Well, if it was an easy job, they wouldn't be needing us, would they, Cossack?"

Taras agreed. It would take time, and he was glad of it. He had things to think about.

But the next day the brigadier all but fell into their laps.

The gardens and public rooms of the hotel served as a clearinghouse for visiting journalists, a place to meet and compare notes. They were either returning from, embarking on, or soliciting *mujahideen*-escorted trips across the border into Afghanistan. To several "colleagues," Marcus complained of his own difficulties in securing contacts among the Afghan resistance groups, let alone arranging a journey "inside," because of his lesser status as a freelancer without expense account or definite assignment.

An English documentary filmmaker spoke up. This man had just returned from the Panjshir Valley under the auspices of the charismatic *Jamiat* guerrilla leader, Commander Ahmad Shah Massoud. For one wildly euphoric moment Marcus had thought he was about to wangle an introduction to Massoud himself, the "Lion of Panjshir"—whose head would be a trophy equaling or surpassing that of Raza. But the documentarian wasn't offering to help directly, only to introduce him to someone else who might—an ex-mercenary who also happened to be a contributing editor to an American monthly called *Deadly Force*. This gung-ho character was supposedly very tight with a key resistance leader, and had just arranged an interview for an Italian woman journalist. Although Signorina DeLuca was admittedly attractive, her journalistic circumstances were similar to Marcus's. She was a stringer for a couple of supplemental European news services.

Perhaps, the English filmmaker went on, this American merc, who was staying at Dean's, might agree to set Marcus up with the same man, perhaps right in Peshawar.

"And who might this leader be?" Marcus had asked.

"A tough old bird, ex-SAS. Used to run the king's bodyguard, but now runs a training camp out in the boondocks. Raza, General Jalil Muhammad Raza."

Marcus let his enthusiasm show. "Thanks for the tip. It's sure worth a shot."

He and Taras discussed it later in their bungalow. There were two ways to play it. Marcus could try for the meeting with Raza, kill the old guy face-to-face, and then shoot his way out, with Taras attacking from outside. Or they could use Azib's taxi to track the Italian woman to her meeting with Raza, which was to take place the next day somewhere in Peshawar, and improvise an assault on the spot.

They decided against Plan A. Marcus's phony journalistic credentials and letters of reference from two Canadian magazine editors might not pass scrutiny. Certainly not if either the ex-merc or Raza went to the trouble of making some phone calls. And that would jeopardize not only the assignment, but their lives.

Plan B would be easier to effect. They'd follow the Italian woman to her rendezvous. The trunk of Azib's Datsun would hold all their equipment—stun and frag grenades, silenced pistols and submachine guns, Dragunov sniper rifles, rappelling ropes and harnesses, bolt cutters, sledgehammers, explosive charges. They were both skilled in urban assault, and would be wearing soft body armor. If the location wasn't a goddamned fortress, they'd hit it. Azib would wait outside for the getaway.

That night Taras went for a walk. He returned a little before midnight, found Marcus cleaning his disassembled Makarov pistol.

"Long walk, Cossack. Been thinking?"

"Quite a bit."

"What about?"

"Migratory genocide. Scorched earth. Whatever you want to call what we've been doing to the Afghans. Destroying their country. Driving people out, fragging kids, burning crops, bulldozing villages."

Marcus gave a puzzled smile. "What's this all about? You don't want to do the old bastard, is that it? Getting cold feet?"

"That's part of it, I guess. But it goes back a ways, even before what

155

happened in the Kunar. I finally made up my mind in the hospital. I'm all through here, Cowboy. I'm dead."

"Oh, fuck, Cossack. What you need is some R and R. I told Marchenko that, but he said the best thing was to send you right out again. Listen, after we pull this job, we'll take off someplace, you and me. Bangkok, Amsterdam, Pago Pago. You name it, I'll get Marchenko to pull the strings."

"That's a great offer, Marcus. Sorry. It's too late."

"I sense you making problems here, Cossack. What are you saying exactly?"

"I'm saying I'm going to do what you did."

"Which is—what?"

"Defect."

Marcus stared at him unblinkingly for long seconds. When he spoke, his voice was deeper, and softer. "When is this going to happen? Or has it? Have you already been sending love notes to the CIA?"

"It hasn't happened yet. I'm ready though."

Marcus had assembled the Makarov and dry-fired it. Now he screwed on the silencer and slapped an eight-round clip into the grip, then chambered a cartridge, flicked the safety to cocked-and-locked. "And what am I supposed to do? Give you my blessing?"

"Come with me, Cowboy. America will take you back. Finish your trip around the world."

"Some things are better unfinished. One defection was enough for me, Cossack. I can't go back. Even if I could, I happen to like it here. And I like what I'm doing."

"Be straight with me, Marcus."

"I am. And you can come down from your moral high ground. You trying to tell me what we're doing here is somehow worse than what America did in Vietnam? Come on, Cossack, the only difference I can see is that Afghanistan is actually on the Soviet border, not the other side of the world. And we've got a good shot at beating these *muj* assholes—unless they come up with a real unifying leader like the Viet Cong had in General Giap. Which is why, Cossack, you should get over this idealistic crap about defecting to the wonderful West and just do your fucking job. Help me take out this Raza bastard."

Taras had heard his friend often speak with equal vehemence, but never with more conviction. There was only one thing left to say:

"I'm sorry, Marcus. You'll have to call off the hit. Get out tonight."

"Now, why will I have to do that? Are you going to tell the CIA everything?"

"An hour ago I passed Signorina DeLuca's door. There was a light under it. I heard her talking inside on the phone. I pushed an anonymous note inside, warning her and Raza of unspecified danger tomorrow, or at any time in the near future in Peshawar. And no, I didn't leave my room number."

Marcus's face contorted. Before Taras could react, his friend pointed the silenced Makarov at him and fired twice.

Taras felt the ballistic shockwaves, heard the suppressed coughs of the pistol and a rending cry behind him. He whirled. A meter away, just inside the French doors, Azib was gaping in surprise and letting fall a thin-bladed boot knife in order to clutch his stomach. Marcus crossed the room in a leap, put two more rounds into the bowing head. Azib—Captain Fareed Qadir of the Afghan security service—completed his mortal obeisance and collapsed facedown on the carpet.

"Little bastard was spying from the garden. Guess he didn't like your drift. Guess he thought I'd be happy to sit here and watch him slit your traitorous throat. Maybe I should have. Better get the hell out of here, Cossack."

Instants before the shot Taras had caught a scent, failed to identify it. He realized now it had been jasmine from the courtyard gardens outside, which should have warned him the door was ajar. Now the fragrance was annihilated by gunsmoke, blood, sphincteral discharge. He looked down at the blood, spreading and sheening like strawberry syrup on the tile around Azib's body.

"Marcus, what will you do?"

"I appreciate the concern, Cossack, I really do. Hell of a friendship we had there for a while."

"Marcus, I'm sorry. You know how I feel."

"I'm all choked up about it. Just don't worry about me, okay? I'll think of something. Probably a couple ways I can sell this to Marchenko, as long as I don't know what you're up to." Marcus forced a grin. "Hey, if I could survive a twenty-foot wipeout in Waimea Bay, I can hack this. What are you waiting for? Like the man said, Go west, young man."

Taras hesitated at the open French door. In his self-absorption it had never occurred to him that Marcus would be hurt and angry at his defection. Now it seemed obvious, but there was nothing he could do about it.

"You saved my life again, Cowboy."

"Guess I did. Makes a couple of 'em, doesn't it? Let's just hope they don't make me even the score by coming after you someday."

Years later Taras was to recall those peculiar parting words, and find them incredibly ironic. But at the moment he only nodded a last time at his friend, then stepped out into the dark garden.

Chapter

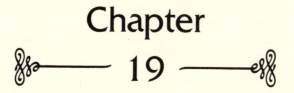

19

TARAS LACED TOGETHER THE PASTEBOARD COVERS OF MARCUS'S dossier, replaced it on the trolley beside the desk. Across the room, droplets chased each other down the window glass in spermatic, quicksilver trails. Outside in Dzerzhinsky Square a slanting drizzle halated the headlights orbiting Iron Feliks's bronze statue. But here and there through the shredding battle smoke of nimbostratus, Taras could see vivid patches of cerulean. At Moscow's northern latitude—nearly the same as Copenhagen's—the early summer twilight had a while yet to linger, though Arensky's watch showed eight-forty. He had worked through dinner. Scattered around him on the baize blotter were the remains of his lunch—a rind of black bread on a plate, an empty bowl slivered with cucumber from the cold *okroshka,* a well-crumpled Pepsi can—victim of a visceral spasm during the Afghan section of his reading.

He leaned back in the chair, rubbed his eyes, let out a deep sigh of deskbound weariness. What had he gleaned? Probably nothing affecting this assignment. But in the past hours of page-turning it seemed his entire adult existence as well as Marcus's had trooped before the reviewing stand of his mind's eye, in all its disarray. It was a disquieting experience, witnessing—and judging—one's life as parade rather than as cross-sectional experience, as lived. There was the added dimension of direction. Where the hell was he going? Or Marcus?

One thing at least was clear. Marcus Jolly's erratic course was intricately interwoven with his own, crossing it again and again, always fatefully. Even eight years after their farewell in Peshawar, the mere linking of their names on a transatlantic call from the Kremlin to the White House had been sufficient to wrench Taras out of his new American life and catapult him back to Moscow.

What would it take to finally slam the door on Marcus, as he thought he had done that last night in their bungalow at Dean's?

After slipping out through the garden, Taras had flagged a cab to the USIA office in Peshawar's University Town district, where his new CIA contact had been pacing the vestibule. He had been asked questions all that night and far into the next day, the first of countless interrogations. They uncoiled in his recollection as an endless series of monotonous rooms, inscrutable inquisitors and unspooling cassette machines—his tunnelway to freedom. There had been more debriefings the following week at the U.S. Embassy in Islamabad. And they came, one after another, week after stupefying week, when he was flown to Washington. Nor had they altogether ceased even after he'd gone to work at Langley. But he'd accepted the bargain for asylum, and gave full measure.

In all those years Taras had heard nothing from Marcus. And the KGB dossier had offered few revelations. It mentioned that Marcus had been commissioned a captain in July 1985, and returned forthwith to Moscow. What the dossier did not say, but which Taras knew, was that Rodion Marchenko had also left Afghanistan around July of 1985, removed as deputy commander by the new general secretary; the top Afghan spot had been given to General Mikhail Mitrofanovich Zaitsev, transferred to Kabul from a key command in East Germany with an ultimatum to crush the *mujahideen* rebellion within two years. Zaitsev, needless to say, had failed, as had his successor, Gromov.

But there was to be an intriguing postscript to Afghanistan, both for Marchenko and Marcus—an event not to be found in the dossier, yet oddly confirmed by it when overlaid with the rough chronology in Arensky's memory. In February 1986 Brigadier General Jalil Muhammad Raza had gone to Geneva to address an international conference on the plight of the Afghan refugees. But Raza never gave his speech. He was shot getting into a taxi at Cointrin Airport in broad daylight. He died two hours later at L'Hôpital Cantonal without regaining consciousness. Two bodyguards were badly wounded. All five recovered bullets were rimmed 7.62mms fired from a single Dragunov sniper rifle.

The omission of this affair from Marcus's dossier, and the absence of any notated visits to Switzerland, could not be taken as evidence either way. Documentation concerning a *mokroye dyelo,* a wet affair, was often mislaid. But the official record revealed another, more suspicious omission. In its blizzard of pages Arensky could find no explanation for the fact that—in March of 1986, only a month after the assassination— Captain Marcus Jolly, while ostensibly holding a GRU staff job, had been promoted to major. And it had been around the same time, Arensky thought, that Marchenko had made colonel general.

These coincidences were more than remarkable; to Arensky they were conclusive. If Marcus had not done the Geneva hit on Raza, why would the KGB claim he had never failed a wet operation? No, it had to be Marcus. It was like him, and Marchenko, to finally get their man.

But there had been no further career climbing for either. As a minor offshoot of the Kremlin cataclysms of the early '90s, both patron and protégé had been sent to Siberia by Alois Rybkin—officially, according to an article Taras had read at Langley in the military newspaper *Krasnaya Zvezda*—to "shore up" the Siberian Military District. The old rocket general had gone obediently enough, eager, no doubt, to lay the groundwork for his *Spetsnaz* mutiny at safe remove from Moscow. But, as Biryukov had mentioned at this morning's briefing, Major Marcus Jolly had never arrived in Novosibirsk. Instead, obviously at Marchenko's behest, he had vanished from Soviet soil on a GRU deepcover assignment.

Which closed the file on the Question of the Hour:

Where was Marcus now?

Taras shuffled up his notes—mainly concerning the surprising discrepancies in Marcus's U.S. background—and dialed Hank Kelleher, who had returned to the embassy.

"Hank, come and get me out of the Lubyanka—now!"

But the next afternoon he and Kelleher were back in Biryukov's office. The KGB chairman wanted to show them something. It was centered on his desk blotter as Starkov ushered them into the office, a small pen case covered in burgundy velour.

Not touching it, Biryukov framed the object with his plump, splayed palms, like a TV pitchman reverently displaying The Product. "It arrived this morning from Munich by your Federal Express, addressed to me. Most reliable service. Better than diplomatic courier."

"What is it?"

"I will let Lieutenant Colonel Starkov show you. It is best not to handle it. There are still some tests to be made."

They came close. Starkov, wearing white cotton gloves, prised open the case's hinged top. Inside, a plastic liner was grooved to fit a fancy calligraphy pen, which was pictured on the satin lid lining. At the moment, however, the groove was occupied by a human finger, its severed base congealed with dark, dried blood. Taras now caught the faint sweet smell of decaying flesh. Under matted black hairs atop the finger, the skin was white and waxen; the nail was deep bluish. Below the large joint was a paler, indented band of skin, such as a ring would leave.

"Oh, Christ Jesus!" Kelleher's oath was one of distaste.

"Not a pretty sight so early in the morning. I apologize," Biryukov said. "It was formerly attached to one of our agents. We just got confirmation on the print. You are looking at the index finger of Captain Walter Bauer of the *Bundeswehr,* the GRU, and, quite recently, the KGB. Coincidentally, we have just received word that the *Herr Kapitän*'s corpse was also discovered this morning, minus this finger. It all fits together, you see?" Biryukov smiled at his own small witticism.

"Where was it found?"

"In Bavaria. We'll address that in a moment."

"And Marcus, you think he was involved?"

"We know he was. Bauer phoned his handler in Directorate S late last night. Told him that he had been contacted by Jolly, spent much of the day with him, in fact. Bauer was one of several GRU agents who were led astray by Marchenko's cabal, but who fortunately realized the error of their ways and began cooperating with us. The idiot should have informed us immediately, and let us take care of Marcus. Instead, he tried to be a hero and assassinate the assassin. Not a good idea for amateurs, you will agree, Major Arensky."

Taras nodded. "How do you know it was Marcus?"

The KGB chairman opened his other hand like a magician, revealing a wadded handkerchief. He proceeded carefully to unwrap this and withdrew a bulky finger-ring of steel, set with a round black stone that looked like onyx. Taras observed the width of the band matched the marks on the severed finger.

"That was on the finger when you opened the box?"

Biryukov nodded. "But the ring was not Captain Bauer's. It belongs to Marcus Jolly."

"How can you be sure of that?" asked Kelleher.

"The Roman initials 'MJ' are engraved inside the band. Also, there was a note enclosed. It's being analyzed, but I have a copy." Biryukov put on half-glasses and read from a scrap of paper: " 'Comrade Biryukov, I'm returning your ring as it is now out of ammunition. —*Do svidanya,* Major Marcus Jolly. P.S. You will have noticed another gift enclosed. Perhaps you can get somebody to explain its significance in American slang.' "

Biryukov glanced up. "I see that you are both chuckling. Perhaps one of you will be so kind as to explain the last part. A little joke, I think."

"Marcus is 'giving you the finger.' " Kelleher demonstrated the gesture. "It's like an Italian flicking his thumbnail at you or pumping his forearm. It means—"

"Fuck you?"

"Precisely."

"Of course, I've seen the gesture many times in American films. I just didn't know the vulgar idiom. I suppose he thinks it quite subtle. He might have sent me the captain's genitalia, but then, that would have been crude, wouldn't it?"

"If it's got Marcus's initials on it, why does he call it 'your ring' in the note?" Taras wanted to know. "And what did he mean about ammunition?"

"Because he either got the ring here in this building, or was given it by someone else who got it here. It is one of the amusing little items from our Technical Research Directorate."

"Of course!" Kelleher said. "A flamethrower, right? I've seen pictures at Langley. Don't look surprised, Volodya. I know damn well you're up on most of the stuff from our spy-tech shop."

"I try." Biryukov smiled.

Taras was staring down at the bulky steel ring. He'd seen switchblade rings, rings with hidden cavities for microfilm or cyanide capsules, cuff links that fired birdshot, hairspray-and-Zippo flame-throwers, but this was a novelty. "Well, I can tell you one thing. Marcus didn't wear this in Afghanistan. We didn't have time to fool around with black-bag tricks over there. Can you show me how it works?"

"Pavel?" Biryukov gestured.

Lieutenant Colonel Starkov stepped forward, took the ring, and moved to the conference table.

"There are two tiny buttons, here and here. This one opens the chamber." The top of the ring mounting flipped open. "It fires one shot, manual reload." Starkov held up what looked like an ordinary gelatin capsule, then inserted it into the small chamber. "This is a kerosene-based, gelled-flame capsule. Another version of the ring fires a twenty-two-caliber long-rifle bullet, and there's another that uses, um, chemicals. They're not interchangeable."

Starkov closed the chamber. "The other button cocks the weapon." From one side of the bulky steel mounting a tiny barrel suddenly protruded. "You aim by merely turning your finger. We recommend the index finger, because to fire, you depress this same button with the thumb, which retracts the barrel and projects the capsule with a tiny powder charge. It bursts into flame only when it strikes the target. The gel tends to be very sticky, much like napalm, and burns at a high intensity. The range is from three to ten meters. I will demonstrate."

Starkov slipped the ring over his forefinger and fired a capsule into a nest of papers wadded in Biryukov's wastebasket, which he had placed in the center of the office. The resulting whoosh of flame triggered the chairman's smoke alarms, singed his ceiling plaster, and was extinguished only when a uniformed guard burst in from the corridor with a CO_2 canister.

When the guard exited, taking the blackened, smoking container with him, Biryukov chuckled. "You know, Pavel, we might bring this up at our next budget meeting. Think how much money we could save by doing away with burn bags."

The rest of the briefing was less flamboyant. Biryukov passed along what other little information he had. The German officer's body had been discovered early that morning by children in a caravan camp along the Isar River outside Bad Tölz, Bavaria. The sender's address on the Federal Express airbill turned out to be a seedy hotel in Munich;

none of its employees recognized photos of Marcus. The assassin had sprung the KGB's trap and escaped. Worse, he would be even warier next time.

"Nevertheless," Biryukov summed up, "if he pursues Marchenko's mad vendetta, he will inevitably fall into our hands. We have only to wait. In the meantime, I leave it up to you, Major Arensky. Is there, perhaps, some line of investigation you wish to pursue?"

Taras wanted to leave Moscow, but he phrased it more diplomatically: "I'd like to go to Bad Tölz, I guess. That's still the headquarters for our 10th Special Forces Group, isn't it, Hank?"

"There's a detachment there, yeah."

"I can't imagine what connection there might be with Marcus, but I'd like to poke around. Maybe talk to your KGB people there, and the federal police, try to reconstruct Marcus's movements, figure out what he might have been doing. I just can't see hanging around here. As long as President Rybkin stays in the Kremlin, or just goes back and forth in his motorcade to Kuntsevo, I think he's safe."

Starkov coughed, and Biryukov spoke: "I agree, Major. A minor point, but the President is currently not in either of these places."

"Where the hell is he?" Kelleher cut in. "I saw him last night on *Vremya*, addressing the Congress of People's Deputies."

"He left this morning for his summer house in Oreanda."

"He's in the Crimea?"

"Yes, Oreanda is just west of Yalta. A lovely place, but a fortress nonetheless, in some ways surpassing even the Kremlin. The compound perimeter is double-walled on the land side, with elite troops, machine guns, and so forth. And on the other side there are sheer cliffs rising more than a hundred meters from the Black Sea."

Taras looked askance. "With all due respect, Mr. Chairman, that's an incredibly naive thing to say. Marcus and I were trained in the *Spetsnaz* to attack impregnable fortresses. In Afghanistan we got so we could run up and down sheer cliffs in the dark, with full packs and no ropes. The *mujahideen* couldn't believe it at first. The survivors learned better."

"I am fully aware of the capabilities of *Spetsnaz*, Major. The KGB academies have introduced much of the same curriculum. It is you who are overestimating your old comrade. In the first place, he could have no idea that Rybkin was *not* in Moscow. Even the CIA"—he gestured at Kelleher—"was not aware of it until I told you. And in the second place, Marcus would never get within twenty kilometers of Oreanda, by air, land, or sea, without our pinpointing him."

"Really? You expect me to believe this, after the whole world has seen a tiny Cessna land in Red Square with a German teenager at the controls? Believe me, Marcus is a bit more skilled at penetrating defenses than this boy. In any case, it wouldn't hurt for your people to tighten their security at Oreanda."

Biryukov arched his Brezhnevian brows, assuming a clearly patronizing tone: "Mathias Rust was a fluke, Major, as you well know. We could have shot the hooligan down the moment he crossed the Finnish border; we simply chose not to. We are always on maximum alert. That's the way we operate."

Taras shrugged. It was pointless to argue. He was calculating elapsed time and distance. Marcus had mailed the severed finger from Munich the day before around noon. If he did have some secret pipeline to Rybkin's movements and wanted to surprise the Soviet leader at his summer house, how close could he be now? The numbers blurred in Taras's brain, the calculation collapsing under too many variables. But one thing was certain: striking when and where least expected was Marcus's preferred mode of operation. The only thing to do was go and have a look. He turned back to Biryukov:

"You asked me what I wanted to do next. Okay. I want to go to Oreanda. As soon as you can arrange it."

"Of course." Biryukov picked up the phone, spoke briefly, put it down. "They will call back in a moment."

"Taras, do you want me to go with you?" Kelleher said.

"No, thanks, Hank."

When the phone double-shrilled, Biryukov grabbed it, listened, grunted, hung up. "A car is being brought around to the courtyard in back to take you to Vnukovo. The flight to Simferopol Airport in the Crimea takes two hours. From there you can either drive to Yalta or take a helicopter—"

"Get me a helicopter."

"Of course. In that case, you might reach Oreanda in, oh, a little more than three and a half hours from now. Is this fast enough, Major?"

"Let's hope so."

Chapter

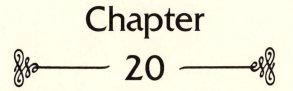

20

THE MADONNA-FACED, LIGHTLY MUSTACHED YOUNG WOMAN working passport control at Istanbul's Yeşilköy Airport looked from the photograph to the tall Canadian leaning nonchalantly against her counter, and hesitated. It was not because she was suspicious of the man. It was definitely he in the picture—with his boyish-rugged features, light blue eyes, sandy hair, shaggy mustache. Byron Landy; journalist; born Vancouver, October 28, 1957. *Let the bearer pass freely in the name of Her Majesty the Queen* . . .

No, she hesitated because this extremely attractive traveler was grinning at her in a way that dispelled her afternoon lethargy and made her feel suddenly and blushingly feminine. She held his gaze a long, teasing moment, then slid off it toward the anxious, arriving swarm from Lufthansa 1582 behind him.

Damn! Why were they all in such a ridiculous rush?

Her playful mood was broken. She closed the navy blue passport with the gold-stamped Canadian coat of arms and handed it back with her own best smile of the day: "Welcome to Istanbul, Mr. Landy. I hope you enjoy your stay."

"Thanks to you, it's off to a lovely start."

Marcus Jolly shouldered his single carryon and let his smile fade as he passed beyond the counter. He scolded himself for deliberately making an impression on the Turkish girl. It was spectacularly stupid behavior for an international fugitive, one down to his last two sets of false identity papers. But her eyes were languorous, dammit, like his image of a properly submissive harem girl, and he had wanted to bask in them a moment. If he was to be denied everything, then he might as well shoot himself—and spare his enemies the trouble.

The fact was, of course, Marcus enjoyed danger. It heightened the excitement of the game. Why else would he have gone to the extreme of taunting his pursuers—sending the severed digital message with attached fire-ring to Biryukov, whom he assessed to be the leading hound in the pack now baying at his heels? Well, let them catch him if they could.

Marcus pushed through the crowded concourse with his usual swagger and passed out into the humid late afternoon, angling for the taxi stand. He was still chuckling as he thought of Rybkin, Biryukov, all the rest of them. Those Politburo pragmatists would never be able to fathom what motivated a daredevil like himself. For there was no self-serving reason for him to be carrying out the assassination order of a commander who himself was dead, whose network was compromised, whose cause was lost. Even if Marcus succeeded in killing Rybkin, what then? All his bridges back were in flames. At this moment he was no longer *Spetsnaz,* no longer an adopted Soviet, could never again be American.

Riddle: Who or what am I?

I am Marchenko's weapon, fired into the night by a dying man. I am his samurai, his kamikaze.

Marcus recalled his last encounter with the old general. It had been three winters before in Moscow at the Yaroslav Station, Platform Two. Marchenko was departing for virtual exile as commandant of some shithole camp outside of Novosibirsk, thirty-three hundred kilometers to the east. Instead of the four-hour flight on Aeroflot, the old man had opted for the Trans-Siberian Railway and a marathon journey of three days.

"What's the fucking hurry?" he said to Marcus as they loitered alongside a bright-red carriage bearing the plaque MOSCOW–VLADIVOSTOK. "The tsars used to make poor bastards like me walk all the way to Siberia."

The old man waved the porter ahead with his baggage, then reached into his greatcoat, producing a half-liter of Ukrainian pepper vodka and his triumphant, steely smile.

"In the words of the great Shakespeare," Marchenko said, offering the first slug to Marcus. " 'Let a soldier drink!' "

They took turns infusing themselves with warmth against the bleak afternoon and a bleaker future. There wasn't much left to say between them in those last moments. Marcus had his two sets of orders—his official reassignment to Novosibirsk as aide-de-camp for Marchenko, and the old man's contradictory ultimatum for Marcus to get the hell out of the country and permanently alter his identity.

"Do your old trick, lad. You've got the documents. Fold your wings, crawl into a cocoon somewhere and turn back into a little caterpillar. At least for a while."

But how, in such case, was Marcus to contact the general again?

"Well, you can't," he had been told. "Anyway, I forbid it, so don't even try." Marchenko had left only one tenuous linkage—verbal instructions on how Marcus might check for messages along a secret *Spetsnaz* network the general was in process of setting up. "But if you ask my real advice, you'll forget about me. And if you're ever summoned, you won't respond."

"Rodion Igorovich," Marcus had shot back, "don't give me this bullshit! If you don't want me to respond, make sure you never call me!"

"I am just warning you, Marcus. Have it your way. If you wish always to be a glorious, suicidal idiot . . . well, then, I will take this under advisement."

The two men stood close together on the frozen platform, sharing a last bottle as grim-faced travelers flowed past—Tatars, Kazakhs, Buryats, even here and there a Russian. And it suddenly occurred to Marcus that he was looking—for the last time—at the only person on earth who really knew him and who, amazingly enough, accepted him whole. Though just what he was to this magnificent old dinosaur had never been quite clear in Marcus's mind. A formidable weapon, often enough, and a protégé certainly. But was he a friend as well, or perhaps something even more? Marchenko had no sons, Marcus knew, only a daughter, long estranged and married to some *apparatchik*.

The general put out his big bony hand. "Good-bye, Marcus. Do what I tell you now and get the fuck out of here. Fool the damn bastards on the *Stavka* and the KGB and find your sunshine again.

And sometime, when you are fucking some darling little cunt—Italian I hear is the best—you give her a good one just for me, okay? You do it right, and all the way in Siberia I will hear her screaming."

Marcus laughed and promised dutifully. Then Colonel General Rodion Marchenko turned and walked purposefully away, lifting his hand in a last wave before disappearing into the shiny red car. With a sudden hollowness in his chest and thickness in his throat, Marcus let himself be carried along with the crowd, down the platform and into the vast echoing gloom of the station.

The old man was gone. But his deadly legacy was far from over.

Marcus had never been to Istanbul, and, during the twenty-minute taxi ride, through the Topkapi Gate in the old Byzantine Walls and along Millet Caddesi into the Old City, he gawked at the passing picture-postcard views like any tourist—or like the world wanderer he had been in his carefree youth. But his was not a pleasure trip, and his current itinerary was extremely tight, with no margin for distractions or detours. Already Stamboul's fabled light was fading, its domes and minarets veiling for evening as the muezzins' tape-recorded calls went forth for sundown prayers; on the Asian shore across the Bosporus a scattered mosaic mirror of westward windows flashed the fires of sunset. Marcus had a great deal of deadly work to do in the hours of this coming darkness, and had managed to snatch less than an hour of sleep during the three-hour-forty-minute flight from Munich.

He had the taxi let him off on Kennedy Caddesi at the foot of the Second and Third Hills, by the entrance to the little fishing harbor of Kumkapi. Off to his left, a kilometer eastward along the ramparts facing the Sea of Marmara, was the cluster-domed magnificence of Sultan Ahmet, the Blue Mosque. Nearer to hand along the low seawall, brightly painted caïques and skiffs and smacks began to settle into their own dark liquid reflections, while quayside fishmongers iced their unsold wares and packed up their tables.

But Marcus's gaze was directed offshore, into the sunset haze of the Marmara roadstead, where perhaps twenty ships were anchored. They were mostly larger fishing craft and smaller merchant vessels, judging by their hull forms and upperworks. But moored farthest out, right where Marcus was told it would be, was a solitary military ship—a Soviet Polnocny-class LST. With binoculars from his shoulder bag, he scanned the elongated tank deck, picked out the white numbers painted on her gray bow—671. She was the *Gorodovikov* all right. And he'd cut it damn close—less than a half hour to spare.

After his betrayal in Bavaria, Marcus had been left with only two links to Marchenko's old European network. One was an electronic message drop in Helsinki. Accessing that required only basic hardware—a laptop with built-in modem, easily obtained in Munich—but Marcus had never really trusted E-mail security. The other contact was an emergency phone number in Budapest, again a relay point for coded instructions and information. Marcus had decided to risk it. He'd dialed the number from a pay phone in the Munich Hauptbahnhof, given his request, been called back two hours later with some startling information, directions for this rendezvous—and barely enough time to catch the Lufthansa flight to get here.

Would this turn out to be a setup too?

He didn't have a long wait to find out. Catching the pungent odor of Turkish tobacco behind him, Marcus turned around. A dozen paces down the quay a compact figure in jeans, windbreaker, and deck shoes was smoking and watching him. The man approached, gave him a level, dark-eyed stare and a flat cigarette, then proceeded to light it. They exchanged the correct sequence of trivialities. The man was Andrian Ivannenko, captain of the *Gorodovikov*. He was also naval *Spetsnaz*, Marcus knew, and once upon a time had worked closely with Marchenko.

Ivannenko gestured along the harbor wall. "The launch will be along in a few minutes. Let's walk. You can leave your bag. Kuzma will watch it."

A second man, also out of uniform—young-looking to be an officer, likely a seaman—was approaching. Marcus eased his shoulder bag to the cobblestones, moved off alongside the captain.

"Marcus, look out there, not far from the *Gorodovikov*. You know what happened there?"

"A lot, I'd guess. All kinds of naval battles—Greeks, Persians, Byzantines, Ottomans."

"I'm talking more recently. Like a couple of years ago."

"You mean that movie ship?"

"Yeah. Some Kurds jumped an old square-rigger, held about forty people hostage. Burned the ship to the waterline. It washed ashore not far from where we're standing. I saw it, ugly fucking sight.

Here's my question. What did those poor bastards get for their trouble?"

"They got dead?"

"That's right, Marcus. They got dead, and the Kurds still don't have a fucking country."

"What's your point, Andrian? Or is this just sort of interesting local color?"

"I'll tell you the point, Marcus, as if you didn't know. Number one. I'm going to help you, if you insist on it. I owe the Old Man that much. But I'm going to tell you something else. I don't like it. And the truth of it is, I resent being called on. No matter what happens, you're endangering me, what's left of my career, maybe some of my men. And you're doing it all for nothing."

"You're telling me to call it off, Andrian?"

"I'm saying think real hard about it, that's all. Rybkin's nothing. Just the latest asshole trying to ride the avalanche of history, trying to keep from being buried alive. The world's changed, Marcus. Marchenko's world is gone. The Old Russia is gone. Maybe that's bad, maybe it's good, but it sure is inevitable. They're carving us up into pieces, and what's left will probably end up reporting to Brussels or Berlin, just like the Brits, who lost their whole fucking empire. And you're not going to stop it all by yourself." Ivannenko halted and faced him. "So go home, why don't you, and take it easy?"

"I haven't got one."

"That could be arranged. That much we could do before we break up the Old Man's gang forever."

Nearby an old fisherman levered himself up from the cobblestones, started gathering the nets he had been mending. Even in the gloom, the red-dyed netting stood out. Marcus met Ivannenko's penetrating gaze with an easy smile.

"I'm sorry, Andrian. You're lecturing the wrong guy. I'm not a political animal. I'm not even a patriot like Marchenko. You know why I defected to your country? For the fun of it. And I'm probably attempting this for the same dumb reason. The truth is, I don't know for sure, because I don't always think things through. I'm an impulse guy."

"This is all bullshit, Marcus. You're doing it because the Old Man asked you to. At least admit this, or I swear I'll do nothing for you."

"Okay. I owe him, dead or alive, like you do. And also I want to see if I can pull it off, right under the twitching assholes of the KGB. And somewhere down there, in my adopted Russian soul, let's say, maybe I do think Rybkin's an evil bastard who'd sell his mother, let alone his Motherland, for whatever he can get on the open market. But don't worry, Captain. Nobody will know you guys were involved. Just get me out to the *Medtner.*"

The *Nikolai Medtner* was a Soviet Lentra-class converted trawler, or "survey ship," now patrolling somewhere in the Black Sea. According to the information Budapest had relayed back to Marcus, Black Sea Fleet headquarters in Sevastopol in the Crimea had been alerted that President Rybkin would be in their area for the next several days. Which meant he had gone to Kichkine, his clifftop estate in the Yalta suburb of Oreanda that had once belonged to Brezhnev. The "plan"— though nobody but Marcus gave it a chance—was to surprise Rybkin there, as Marcus had so often ambushed *mujahideen* in their strongholds. Getting out to the *Medtner* was the next critical phase of the operation, and that would require the considerable connivance of Ivannenko.

The captain stared at him a long moment, then started back toward his aide.

"Well?" Marcus asked, falling in step.

"I told you I'd help you, damn you. So let's do it."

Moments later Marcus and Ivannenko were settled in the sternsheets of a little motor launch as Kuzma slalomed out through the anchored shipping toward the shadowy bulk of the *Gorodovikov.* The Soviet LST, the captain explained, had just returned from landing operations— part of Trans-Caucasus Military District exercises—near Batumi, an Azerbaidjan enclave on the Georgian Black Sea coast. They were enjoying a three-day layover in Istanbul, and most of the officers and crew were on liberty.

As they drew nearer, Marcus was able to resolve the bargelike silhouette of the Polish-built landing craft into its components. The long forward sweep of the low-freeboard tank deck was designed to carry eight BTR-60PB amphibious personnel carriers, which were ramp-launched through bow doors. At both ends of the low-slung, raked superstructure he now discerned the stubby fingers of twin 30mm antiaircraft guns and SA-N-5 Grail launching posts.

But what directly concerned Marcus was the giant grasshopper shape squatting on the platform just forward of the bridge. This was a Ka-25 Hormone helicopter, its drooping, twin coaxial rotors extending several meters on each side of the deckwide platform. The Ka-25 was just visiting, Ivannenko said. Its home and hangar were on a larger Rogov-class landing ship, which was now steaming back to Sevastopol. During the landing exercises the Ka-25 had been used mainly for reconnaissance and utility transport, and so had been fitted with external fuel tanks. These gave it an effective range of over six hundred kilometers—enough to fly to the Crimea and back. Tonight's scheduled flight, however, was one way; they were delivering the chopper back to Sevastopol. With only the slightest deviation in course, they would be able to drop Marcus in the immediate vicinity of the *Medtner,* which, according to the last position Ivannenko had received, was about sixty kilometers south of the Crimean peninsula.

An hour later, as a jaundiced quarter moon rose over the neon-sprinkled Asian hills, the big Ka-25 was thrashing its contra-rotating rotors five hundred meters above the Bosporus. Only the pilot seat was occupied in the side-by-side cockpit. Senior Lieutenant Krikor Hovhannes had just finished talking to air-traffic control at Yeşilköy, which had routinely forwarded his flight plan to the Turkish NATO airbase at Izmir. The young Armenian flight officer had been vouched for by Ivannenko: "Krikor hates all Russians, and wishes you great success tonight."

Four meters behind Hovhannes, clad in black wet suit, with life jacket, web belt, face mask and fins, Marcus had the main cabin all to himself—except for the tiny inflatable raft in its carrying case beside him. The other eleven fold-down seats were unused. And so, officially, was his; Hovhannes was supposed to be ferrying an empty Ka-25 back to Sevastopol.

As they reached the entrance to the Black Sea, the pilot's voice crackled in Marcus's headset—the only way to communicate above the deafening racket of the twin turboshafts. With their cruising speed of two hundred kilometers per hour, Hovhannes estimated arrival at the drop zone in two and a half hours.

"Now, Major, put in your earplugs and try and get some sleep. Captain Ivannenko's orders. Don't worry. I'll wake you in plenty of time." And incredibly, despite the unholy din, Marcus did find a little sleep—his first in thirty-six hours, except for the brief nap in the Lufthansa 737.

* * *

"Major? Time for your evening swim."

The pilot's voice wrenched Marcus out of the uterine depths of unconsciousness, slamming him back into the cramped, shuddering cacophony of the helicopter.

"Are you awake, Major?"

"Yes, Lieutenant. Thanks."

Marcus shook the sleep from his mind. Hovhannes was explaining they were now only a couple of minutes from rendezvous with the *Nikolai Medtner*.

Marcus peered out the small, square window to his left, saw moon-flecked waves dimpling a vast blackness, Ursa Major twinkling icily above. He unbuckled, made his final equipment check, removed the spare headset. From then on he'd go by the pilot's hand signals.

They were dropping quickly, the swells looming larger in the lac-quering moonlight. On a signal from Hovhannes, Marcus slid the cabin door aft, sat down in the opening, legs dangling, arms braced against shrieking windblast. They were hovering at only five or six meters, their landing lights bathing a surface being whipped into a maelstrom by the downdraft. Marcus knew it was no easy matter for the pilot to gauge his height in these conditions, and waited for his "go" signal. An instant later it came: Hovhannes motioned violently downward with his palm.

Marcus tossed out the raft. As it cleared the helicopter, its attached static line disconnected, activating its CO_2 inflation cartridge. Looping his left forearm through his fins and mask, Marcus grabbed the di-agonal strut of the rear landing gear, slid out and hung suspended a flailing instant. Then he brought his legs together, swung forward and let go, clasping his fins blades-up, falling straight and slicing cleanly into the dark water. By the time he rose to the surface, he had his fins and mask on and stroked quickly to the welcome vinyl sheen of the inflatable, still hissing and unfolding to its two-meter length.

Spotlighted from above, Marcus slithered inboard and activated a tiny battery-powered RDF beacon to help the *Medtner* locate him. Then, as the Ka-25 lifted and went hammering off to the northwest, he settled himself in the raft, abruptly alone in the vast undulant darkness. By his watch it was only twenty minutes to nine. He was making excellent time . . . if he didn't spend too long bobbing around in this giant bathtub.

Five minutes passed. He broke out the raft's flare kit, swore in disgust. He'd expected a pistol and 26.5mm parachute-flare cartridges, or even 40mm hand-launched rocket flares. Instead, he got what looked like a toy—a pouch of nine tiny cylinders about the size of double-A batteries, and a ballpoint pen–sized launcher. Marcus sighed, fitted one together, fired it off. It went hissing up into the night, burst seconds later into red luminescence seventy meters overhead, staining the surrounding sea and sky scarlet.

Marcus reverted to the American version of a favorite Russian oath: "Motherfucker!"

In five seconds the flare was extinguished. But Marcus had already picked up the soft throb of diesels. He turned around, squinted, saw navigation lights, a curl of phosphorescent bow wave.

He reached for another flare. This one blossomed blinding-white, enveloping him in five seconds of stark daylight. Even before it faded, an approaching searchlight began stabbing the darkness around the raft. Marcus semaphored his arms till the beam finally foreshortened and skewered him.

"Forgive me, but I do not welcome you to my ship," said the rheumy-eyed, heavily bearded man as he thrust a steaming glass of tea into Marcus's hands. "The fact is, you know, you are not really here, and therefore I am addressing only an apparition, a product of this bottle of old vodka. This is understood?"

"If you say so," Marcus replied. He was more interested in a decidedly nonapparitional plate of salted mackerel now proffered by the bearded man.

Evgeny Chapayev was master of the "survey ship" *Nikolai Medtner,* whose two short masts and small aftercastle were bristling with electronics, indicative of its principal use as an AGI, an intelligence-gathering auxiliary. Chapayev explained he had scant previous connection with *Spetsnaz* operations. He was merely obliging his old friend Ivannenko on Marcus's behalf. Marcus took this to mean that like Ivannenko, the captain was a reluctant participant, but, unlike Ivannenko, chose not to belabor the point.

Chapayev took another deep pull from a quarter liter of *starka,* and began to speak of operational details. An hour's steaming would bring them twenty kilometers off Yalta, he said. It would be perfectly natural for the *Medtner* to be in those waters, as they were currently helping the Soviet marine science ship, *Keldish,* search for the wreck of the

Sanspareil, which, despite its French-sounding name, was an English warship sunk hereabouts in 1854 during the Crimean War. The *Keldish,* with its forty-million-dollar, high-tech minisubmarine, was working the deeper waters farther out, while the *Medtner* remained closer inshore with its smaller, more modestly endowed midget sub. However, Chapayev emphasized, this little submersible would be quite adequate for conveying Marcus unseen and undetected to the base of the Oreanda cliffs.

Marcus interrupted. "May I suggest, then, Captain, that I might better use the next hour in becoming familiar with its various systems—navigation, ballasting, sonar, and so forth?"

"Why? These are not your concern."

"They'd better be. I'm driving it!"

"Who told you this? Surely not Ivannenko? Warrant Officer Prilepko will be driving the *Flea.*"

"Excuse me, Captain. But I have a problem with that. You see, I don't really know how long this operation will take. If I find a good place to conceal myself, it could be two days before I get a good shot."

"Ha! I grant you this may be a problem. But it is not *my* problem. I told Ivannenko I would take you there, no more! In any case, my dear apparition, you will not need a way back from Oreanda. You will most certainly be killed."

Marcus exploded in laughter. "My God, you're serious!"

"Killed or captured. Ivannenko assures me you will not hesitate to use your cyanide capsule when appropriate. This is most essential. We understand each other?"

And finally they did. Marcus, after all, was in no position to argue. And the captain was absolutely correct, if one looked at things from his perspective. It *was* a suicidal mission, and would be so for any discovered accomplices as well as its perpetrator. Marcus could hardly expect anyone else to share his own maniacal self-confidence.

So, having agreed to everything, an hour later he followed Captain Chapayev up on deck. The wind had freshened, the night had cooled, and a silvered quarter-moon now drifted through scudding cloud overhead. Marcus was introduced to *Michman* (Warrant Officer) Yuri Prilepko, a small, long-armed sailor with a shaved head and a Popeye squint. The *Michman* was in the process of stripping the tarp off a bulky cylindrical shape amidships—the midget sub.

Fully exposed, it was about five meters of aqua-blue fiberglass, teardrop-shaped, with a searchlight in the blunt bow, a tiny, canopy-enclosed cabin, tapering in the stern to a fin and hydroplanes with a single propeller. Marcus had never seen anything quite like it, although at *Spetsnaz* "finishing school" on Wrangel Island, he'd ridden several times in an SDV, swimmer delivery vehicle, and once in a self-contained DSRV, deep submergence rescue vehicle. The fiberglass hull, he knew, would minimize the acoustic and magnetic signature, and Chapayev had already explained that its battery-powered electric propulsion allowed it to run silently.

It was the *Blokha,* the *Flea*—both the Cyrillic letters and a stylized cartoon appeared on its bow. At burst speed of fifteen knots, Captain Chapayev had said, it could cover the twenty kilometers to the Yalta coast in an hour and twenty minutes.

Michman Prilepko climbed down into the forward tandem seat, Marcus slipped in behind, and the laminated-glass canopy was lowered and locked. It was a tight squeeze, and Marcus's seat wasn't very comfortable, but, according to the instruction panel, when the cushion was peeled off, the seat doubled as a hand-pumped water closet. He grinned. It just might come to that, he thought.

Under a "dry" diving suit he was wearing light body armor. Beside him was a waterproof "warbag" that had been stowed in the inflatable. In it were various items generously provided by Ivannenko: climbing gear, dismantled sniper rifle, AKR submachine gun and Makarov pistol, with ammunition and silencers for all three.

At a thumbs-up from Prilepko, the *Flea* was hoisted by a derrick, swung outboard from the *Medtner,* and lowered into the water where—to Marcus's considerable discomfort and slight dismay—the little torpedo hull began to bounce around almost as violently as Azib's Peshawar taxi on a rocky road. But the turbulence ceased an instant later as they were released from the ship, and a liquid-black void closed around them. Marcus became aware of the steady pulse of the propeller, watched as Prilepko fiddled his joystick to get the proper trim. They were still sliding downward, but at thirty meters, Marcus knew, they would level off and be on their way.

It wasn't exactly the first oceanic mission Marcus had undertaken with no way out, no escape plan. There was, for instance, the time he had stripped to his shorts and jumped into the Sausalito marina and swum out to solicit his first sailboat ride. At that time, as he recalled, he had not the slightest thought of ever paddling back to the dock in defeat. However, he *could* have. Not so here. He was fully committed, unless he tapped Prilepko on the shoulder sometime in the next hour and called the whole thing off.

Which he would never do. Better a madman than a coward.

Yet oddly, Marcus felt no sense of dread, little foreboding. He was wondering, with lively curiosity, just *how* he was going to pull the damn thing off. For he knew somehow he would do it. One way or another, he always had.

Chapter

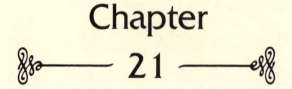 21

Taras didn't like chatty seatmates on airplanes. But Pavel Starkov, his KGB chaperon on the two-hour flight from Moscow to the Crimea, not only didn't speak; the young lieutenant colonel didn't smile, fidget, visit the toilet, or read. In fact, for the first hour he scarcely seemed to blink his blond-lashed eyes. Maybe the ramrod-stiff bastard *wasn't* human. Maybe the organs of security and the Academy of Sciences had somehow interwoven their fantasies and synthesized the perfect state-run automaton. But if that were so, Taras thought, why did they have to pattern him so blatantly after old Aryan stereotypes, housing his photo-sensors behind Alpine-blue glass beads, and his cranial circuitry in a crew cut, Gothic skull?

But finally, somewhere over the Ukraine, Starkov spoke, pitching his voice barely above the drone of the Aeroflot Tu-134's twin turbofans:

"Excuse me, Major."

Taras turned, saw a tiny cardboard box in Starkov's square pink palm. "What's that?"

"It's for you. From Chairman Biryukov."

Taras opened the lid, took out the fire-ring, looked an inquiry.

"Earlier today," Starkov continued, "we showed this ring to several of our resident psychics. People who are able, or claim they are able, to tune into 'vibrations' from crime scenes, murder weapons, and especially what they call 'familiar objects.' You know what I'm talking about?"

"Sure," Taras said. "Spoon-benders, card-readers, ball-gazers. I didn't know you guys were still giving office space to them."

"My exact sentiments, Major. Spoon-benders, I will remember this. In regard to this ring, all they came up with was psychological garbage. 'This man is running from himself.' 'He takes long walks and had an unhappy childhood.' Something of that sort. Not one dared to guess his current whereabouts."

"And Biryukov thought maybe I could do better?" Taras held the bulky steel ring to his forehead, closed his eyes. "Hello, Cowboy, where are you? Talk to me, old buddy. Are you running from yourself, like they say? Taking long walks? Why is it you never talked to me about your unhappy childhood? . . . Sorry, Colonel, he's not coming through. Maybe it's the altitude, too much cosmic ray interference or something."

Starkov showed his teeth; Taras took it for a smile. "In any case, you may keep the ring as a souvenir. We have no further use for it. Also these." From his coat pocket Starkov produced a packet of five gel-flame capsules. "However, I suggest you not load the incendiaries while we're in the air. We don't want to violate Ministry of Aviation rules."

"What about your Makarov?" Taras pointed to the checkered butt of a shoulder-holstered pistol momentarily visible under the flap of Starkov's suit coat. Taras's own .45 automatic was packed away in his luggage.

"Most observant, Major." The KGB officer tugged at his lapels, sealing the offending aperture.

"It's nothing. Thank your boss for the thoughtful gift. And assure him I'll use it with discretion." Taras pocketed the capsules, slid the ring onto his index finger, a tolerable fit. The only clear "vibration" he picked up from it was one of plain ugliness. He could imagine it on Marcus, but on his own hand it seemed a grotesquerie. But then, Taras didn't take to jewelry. He had once worn a paratrooper ring; he'd given it to a merchant in Peshawar the day he defected. He twisted the fire-ring, smiling at the idea of stodgy, bear-faced Biryukov consulting with psychic "sensitives."

It was full dark when they touched down at Simferopol, the principal Crimean airport. Rather than take the regular Aeroflot helicopter into Yalta, and then drive three kilometers west to Oreanda, Arensky and Starkov were shuttled with their bags to the military section of the airport, where an Mi-2 light helicopter was waiting to fly them directly to the presidential compound.

They had the eight-place cabin to themselves as the pilot lifted into the night for the twenty-minute flight over the coastal mountains. Presently, peering through the cockpit canopy, they got their first glimpse of the Black Sea—a velvety dark wall dead ahead. Moments later they were looking down on a necklace of sparkling lights—the port of Yalta, sheltered by an amphitheater of forested mountains.

The Mi-2 now swung southwestward along the Crimean shore, skimming over illuminated geometrical gardens and courtyards that surrounded an Italianate marble edifice, impressive even from the air.

"In case you're looking for the helipad, Major," the pilot's voice came over their headsets, "that's not where we're going. The presidential estate is a couple of hills ahead. That's the Livadia Palace down there, summer residence of Nicholas II and site of the 1945 Yalta Conference. I'd give you more of a spiel, but right now, if you'll both excuse me, I'd better get our final clearance to land before we get shot out of the sky."

Taras had toured the area as a Young Pioneer, and was familiar with many of the sanatoria scattered over the dark mountainsides. They were above Oreanda now, site of several more spas terracing the steep slopes, including the sprawling Nizhnaya Oreanda complex. Then, on a thrusting clifftop ahead, he picked out the lights of a small minaret. As they hovered nearer, the needling tower, tipped with a spotlighted Soviet flag, rose slowly above a palisade of dark cypresses to reveal itself situated atop the white gleam of a miniature Moorish palace, complete with minidomes and crenellated battlements. This, Taras knew, was their destination—Kichkine, which in Arabic meant "little one," though it was surrounded by several, much smaller guest dachas, also in Moorish style. Taras could see why Rybkin, and Brezhnev before him, had fancied the retreat; though an even more exotic structure lay farther along the rocky coast in Miskhor—the little fantasy castle known as the Swallow's Nest, *Lastochkino Gnezdo,* on Cape Ay-Todor.

In a moment they were down and taken in hand by a distinguished-looking, gray-haired colonel of the KGB Guards Directorate—the Ninth, the only branch permitted to carry guns in the proximity of Soviet leaders. A signal exception was being made in the case of Arensky and Starkov. "For as long as you're here," said the colonel, whose name was Pasholikov, "we have been instructed to regard you as officers of our personal protection squad."

Pasholikov conducted them on a brief tour of the compound, passing without comment the lovely Moorish guest pavilions, the floodlit gardens and grounds, edged with palms and pines, cypresses and magnolias, leading to lily ponds, a tennis court, a swimming pool. Rather, he directed their attention to the various intrusion-defense features.

Taras was suitably impressed with the perimeter security, at least on the landward side. The compound was massively yet discreetly fortified, with guard towers hidden among the tall, thick-trunked Crimean pines; tripwires, microwave "fences," seismic and magnetic sensors; radar, thermal-imaging and multicamera TV surveillance; and a series of vehicle barriers that Pasholikov boasted would stop anything short of a tank. All of this, he emphasized, was manned and monitored by an elite detachment of Ninth Directorate guards.

When the circuit was completed, Taras paused by the dark, splendid sweep of sea frontage, peered through a copse of junipers down a hundred meters of sheer bluffs to waves creaming in the faint moonlight. He savored the salt tang, the surf murmur. Taras had been eleven when he was chosen for his thirty-day summer "shift" at the Artek Young Pioneer Camp east of Yalta. He had not been back to the area since. But how, he wondered, could he have ever forgotten that caressive, velvet breeze of the Crimea—air so restorative that sanatoria patients were regularly taken outdoors to sleep?

But there was something else in the air besides southern balm. He had an eerie sense of Marcus—as though his old comrade were here tonight, or had been here recently, or would be soon. It was almost a voice, and very like the kind Taras had learned to listen to during their heliops against the *mujahideen* in Afghanistan. But that had been long years ago. This was probably just self-delusion, stimulated by all the nonsense about picking up "vibrations" from Marcus's ring. The most likely danger here was of Taras's turning into a spoon-bender himself. Still, the feeling wouldn't go away, and it bothered him.

He turned to Pasholikov, gesturing seaward. "Colonel, what about your southern flank, if I may call it that? It looks rather exposed."

The colonel chuckled, then pointed to a moving silhouette a few meters away. The shape came nearer, became a uniformed KGB guard speaking into a transceiver, his submachine gun unslung and in hand. He saluted Pasholikov as he passed. In addition to the manned observation posts and gateside sentries, armed men roamed throughout the grounds and along the cliffside pathways.

"I mean in addition to your small army," Taras said. "If you could just summarize."

"How comprehensive a summary do you wish, Major? For instance, shall I explain the operation of our Voyska PVO network?"

"No, leave out your air defenses. What about from the ocean?"

"You saw the coastal radar and sonar displays in the command post. We track every approaching vessel, every plane. The nearest ship, as I recall, was that Lectra-class trawler, which has been poking along the southern coast for some old sunken English man-of-war for the last couple weeks. But there's a Grisha-class patrol boat due along any moment. You have to keep your eye on them, because at thirty-two knots they go by pretty quickly. We have three that keep us company: two under naval command, from Sevastopol and Balaklava, and one KGB Grisha II based in Yalta. It seems tranquil, but as you see, Kichkine is a very busy place, especially when the Boss is in residence."

"Are you satisfied, Major?" This was from Starkov.

"Just one more thing. I'd like to see Rybkin's quarters, if I may."

"I'll show you the outside. We actually walked by it a few moments ago. But we have strict orders never to disturb Alois Maksimovich when he's in his workshop."

"Workshop? Is he some kind of hobbyist? I hadn't heard."

"Yes. He repairs things." Colonel Pasholikov smiled discreetly. "It's not generally known. But he's actually quite good. Fixed my mother's old sewing machine last month. And no charge."

Alois Maksimovich Rybkin was indeed fixing something. He had the entrails of a Viennese Biedermeier clock spread all over the big chest-high workbench—gear-wheels, weights, gathering pallets. There were other benches, other intricate surgeries in progress. Across the aisle a just-refinished wing chair was upended, a bolt of muslin propped between its feet. He needed to cut and tack pieces of the fabric to the inside of the frame so he could get on with the real upholstering. Close beside it a mahogany jewelry box lay in the implacable jaws of a wood clamp, its regrooved rabbet joints being glued. A jolly round doll's head lay in the lap of its sailor-suited trunk, awaiting recapitation. At the far end of the room a recently acquired Spanish bellows organ also waited, well into its second century of silence. Alas, its wounds were too grievous to merit inclusion in this quick triage; it would be, perhaps, next year's project.

But right now he was completely involved in the clockworks.

He was talking to himself, and lecturing the stubborn escape-wheel tooth he was trying to straighten with the needlenose pliers in his stubby fingers. It was exactly the way his father, Maksim, would converse with himself in the old converted stable workshop in Ulyanovsk, while the cats brushed past his legs or attacked the socks that slopped around the ankles of the unlaced shoes, or lightly followed his heavy footsteps as he rummaged angrily and profanely through shifting mounds of debris for a mislaid bolt or bushing.

In fact, this *was* his father's old workshop, removed and trucked down from Ulyanovsk, piece by piece—everything but the spiderwebs festooning the corners—and lovingly reassembled like a three-dimensional puzzle, to Rybkin's best recollection, inside the gutted interior of a little guest dacha. Oh, he had added some new hand tools, spruced things up a little; he could neither recreate nor tolerate the perfect chaos in which old Maksim had flourished. But otherwise, it was uncannily the same, minus the confounded cats. And when Alois worked in daylight, a turn of his head fetched him a shining square of blue ocean, near enough the angle at which his father, squinting around from his workbench, used to watch a windowful of the mighty Volga.

The President of the Union of Soviet Socialist Republics came here in times of duress, increasingly these past few years, abandoning his wife and any guests in the main palace across the reflecting pond to wrestle with far simpler problems than those of state. Crossing the threshold with a nod to his guards, he would shut out the clamoring world and enter the shadowed habitat of childhood. How vividly he could recall those endless hours he would sit by his father—just over there, say, on that backless chair—with a little hardwood block and whittle knife, and watch the old man work. The boy would imbibe the fumes of the workshop—the sweet burn of lathing wood, the dizzy-making vapors of solvents and resins, the smells of the old man himself, his powerful arms socketing from the undershirt under the battle-stained coveralls, as, with explosive breaths, he settled his favorite crosscut blade into a deep sawcut.

Well, little Aloysha had inevitably become his father. He, too, was a fat old man now, though as a child he'd never thought of his father as fat. He was even wearing a similar pair of coveralls, and the exact red tam-o'-shanter, bestowed on his father in 1945 by an officer of the Highland Scots in Berlin, where Junior Lieutenant Maksim Rybkin had ridden on a T-34 battle tank with Konev's First Ukrainian Army Group. The ancient tam's tassel was worn off now, the tartan quite threadbare. No matter. Madame Rybkina had run out of adjectives to describe her husband's workshop ensemble—*nyekulturny,* outrageous, farcical, even pathetic. Alois Maksimovich didn't care.

He looked down at the scattered movement of the clock. And, as too often happened, he found that the world's insidious problems had followed him inside his refuge. The truth was, of course, that despite the clever trappings of nostalgia, he wasn't his father. His trade was statecraft, not tinkering, and the badly broken thing that he confronted, and which it was his sworn business to put back together, was not a timepiece but a vast country, fragmented along ancient fault lines from the irresistible tremors of a new age. Its pieces, strewn like these ratchets and springs and pinions across his worktable, were peoples—Slavs, Nordics, Kazakhs, Semites, Tatars, Yakuts, Turks, dozens more, each further fractured into nations, tribes, languages, and faiths; and, in the case of the Moslems, threatening to unite again under the banner of Islamic fundamentalism. They had been assembled into the continent-straddling colossus of Russia, God knows how, by the great warrior czars, Orthodox crusaders, and Cossack adventurers, then forged and hammered together on the anvil of mythic "Soviet man" by Lenin and Stalin.

But it couldn't last indefinitely.

Rybkin fitted a pinion to a plate, checked the meshing of the teeth. At least this heirloom had a blueprint, a schematic for coherence. His country no longer had. The world thought he was only accepting the inevitable and helping to dismantle the colossus, divest himself of the parts that didn't fit, reorder those that did into a new, streamlined state. But the world was wrong.

Alois Maksimovich had a desperate plan for putting his vast land back together, a great deal of it anyway—exactly as the new Europe was being shaped out of ancient, rivalrous states.

Amazingly enough, he had gotten his plan out of a think tank—IMEMO, the Institute of World Economics and International Relations—the same one that had first formulated *glasnost* and *perestroika* and argued the wisdom of dismantling the Wall and letting Eastern Europe go its own way, long before those astounding events came to pass. In the last months Rybkin had spent considerable time in discussion with academicians from that gray nineteen-story building at 23 Trade Union Street in Moscow, looking at their equations and economic and geopolitical models. Finally they had persuaded him into a new direction, a direction almost as radical as that which had resulted from their earlier idea that the new revolution—the STR, or scientific-technological revolution—had made Bolshevism a dinosaur.

The USSR was engaged in global chess against several opponents at the same time, and faring badly. It was being rapidly encircled by the new European juggernaut and the exploding economies of the Pacific Rim, while experiencing its own energy crisis and customary stagnation, with no real replacement for the trading partners it had lost in the demise of Comecon and the retreat from Eastern Europe. Now the time had come for the Soviets to make their decisive move, just like the Americans were doing—scrambling frantically to link up with the Japanese while maintaining their dwindling ties to Europe.

Ironically, there seemed to be a consensus among Rybkin's domestic allies and enemies—like old General Marchenko—that their leader was getting ready to dilute Soviet sovereignty, or sell it out altogether, in exchange for inclusion in the new United Europe. What else did the "Common European Home" and "Greater Europe" initiative boil down to? they wondered. Wasn't Europeanization from the Atlantic to the Urals the real thrust of the upcoming Potsdam Conference? The only difference was that Rybkin's allies called it pragmatism and his enemies treason.

But the IMEMO academicians had convinced the Soviet President he didn't need to settle for being the last invitee at the feast of a New Europe, didn't need to go to Potsdam with his begging bowl in hand, lacking as he did the energy reserves to export for hard currency and consumer goods. If the European leaders weren't eager to give him absolutely everything he demanded—and he should demand a great deal more than equality, IMEMO said, and surrender nothing—then there was another very large card he could play—or at least show.

He could threaten to turn away from the West—and toward Mecca. By continuing the long mea culpa over the invasion of Afghanistan, and granting limited autonomy to the Central Asian republics, Rybkin could dramatically improve his standing with the fifty-five million Soviet Moslems. And he could go further yet. By expanding his already substantial economic and military aid to the Middle East, and his presence in Syria, Iraq, and Libya, he could make the Soviet Union the real champion of the Islamic world. To solidify that position, he could turn next to the Iranian fundamentalists, even help them launch a new jihad to finally destroy Israel and overthrow the Saudi regime.

The West would be outraged, of course. But if he moved swiftly enough—and did not hesitate, as had Saddam Hussein—they would be unable to stop him. And in the final analysis, the West—and especially energy-dependent Europe—didn't need Israel, it needed Middle Eastern oil—desperately, just as Russia did, and the Japanese as well. And that oil would be firmly in the control of Rybkin and his new pan-Islamic allies.

Europe would be at his mercy.

Chief Academician Churkin had expressed it more judiciously: "It was Bismarck, if you remember, who counseled Alexander II to turn away from the West, that Russia's true destiny lay eastward. Of course, Bismarck had his own designs on the West. In any case, it is far from an ideal solution that we propose, Alois Maksimovich. But it may very well be the optimum gambit, for again and again it is the only one that comes up. Without this sort of Middle Eastern strategy, we grow increasingly weak and Europe increasingly strong. With it, and with a little luck, the situation can be reversed."

How far he should go down this road would depend, to a great extent, on what happened at Potsdam. Ultimately, if Europe and the Islamic states alike spurned his overtures, he would be prepared to attack Iran and Iraq—in overwhelming force, without any pretense of a "limited military contingent" as in Afghanistan, and seize the oil he needed.

One way or another—unless Marchenko's madman stopped him—he would save this country yet, and restore its lost greatness—ironically the very thing Marchenko had most desired.

He finished assembling the movement, mounted it, closed the cherrywood and ebony case, wound the clock. Listened awhile as it ticked.

And heard a knock at the door.

Chapter

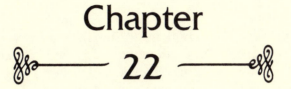 22

INCREDIBLY TO YURI PRILEPKO, SEATED AT THE HYDROPLANE AND steering controls of the midget sub *Flea*, his mysterious passenger slept through much of the hour-and-twenty-minute trip to the Yalta coast. Prilepko wasn't privy to the assassin's identity, but Captain Chapayev, sure of his *Michman*'s sympathies and loyalties, had hinted sufficiently at the objective; in any case, with Oreanda their destination, it was obvious. Think of it—to be able to sleep before such a business!

Prilepko, on the other hand, had never been so wide awake in his life, even during a four-man midget infiltration into NATO waters in the Baltic years before. He stared ahead into the spectral tunnel the searchlight drilled into liquid night, monitored every ambient sound, tracked every drop of condensation that trickled down the bulkheads, consulted his obstacle-avoidance sonar. Nor were his nerves steadied by the occasional pinging that resonated through his hull—transmissions, he assumed, from one of the Grishas patrolling the coast. It bothered him, even though he knew the *Flea* was too minuscule to be detected by them, and would also slip unheard through the coastal SOSUS chain—the Seabed Sound Surveillance System. But things could go wrong; systems could easily malfunction. Which reminded him to verify, once again, that his degaussing gear was properly activated to neutralize any magnetic and acoustic coastal defenses.

Then, having reduced speed from fifteen to five knots, Prilepko saw the sea floor shelving up. He gave a quick echo sounding; the bottom was twenty-five meters, then nineteen, rising sharply. He reduced speed to sixty revolutions—three knots—and came up to periscope depth. He allowed himself only a quick look, barely breaking the surface.

Khorosho! An easy swim, dead ahead in a faint wash of moonlight, the cliffs of Oreanda were right where his chart and gyrocompass said they'd be. Swiveling the lens around to port, the *Michman* picked up the small lighthouse on Cape Ay-Todor. Damn perfect! He'd stuck the *Flea* right up their impregnable asshole!

He slowed further, scraped bottom in ten meters of water, went slow astern, stopped, settled gently, nearly level. He blew out his breath as he took on more ballast. Then he turned to rouse his passenger.

Marcus hadn't really been asleep, though his body felt the acute need of rest. He had been in reverie, eyes closed, his sense of urgency merely suspended, not forgotten. At some level, if only kinesthetically, he remained aware of their steady movement through the water—and their destination.

At first he had tried to concentrate on the mind-clearing dicta of the *Hagakure,* which again and again counseled the samurai serenely to invoke his own death before embarking on mortal combat. But it wouldn't come. Marcus's mind kept deflecting from the astringent focal point of *ki,* into beguiling somatic images; it sought escape, not confrontation. He transported himself happily to the South Seas instead, flat on his back on the foredeck of the gaff-rigged ketch *Tusitalia,* watching the mainmast scribe endless arcs against a lurid Technicolor sky.

The languorous undulance of the boat next triggered a series of far more explicit images—of an afternoon orgy on a big schooner at anchor in Jokaj Harbor, Ponape. He could no longer recall the name of the vessel—she was a beauteous thing out of Auckland—nor of the two lissome Kiwi girls—their names were fatuous and indistinguishable, something like Dora and Dee-Dee, or Donna and Dodie. Memory dealt them back mostly in tandem flashes—lank, sunbleached hair;

nasal, singsong voices; freckled smiles; darting, pale eyes; light bikini stripes on well-tanned hides.

It had started innocently enough topside. Marcus, the luncheon guest from a neighboring boat, hunkered down to spread suntan lotion on their sleek brown backs. It had moved, then, with stunning suddenness below decks to a V-shaped, reflection-bathed cabin in the bows, where Marcus began heaving big sailbags off the bunks to make room for horizontal recreation. But the girls rapidly changed their minds, or couldn't wait. They had attacked him from behind, stripped him and then themselves, oiled him to rampant hardness. They took turns straddling him as he stood, his back braced against a bulkhead, gritting his teeth, pumping and posting like a carousel steed. Well, why not cooperate? Wasn't that the classic advice for the rapee? To his everlasting credit, Marcus had managed to endure till each transfixed and well-lubricated Kiwi had collapsed in his arms, before he groaned, shuddered, and slumped to the deck beside them.

The satiated sighs, he recalled, changed to giggles as the trio became aware of the stentorian snores that still emanated from the uncle's cabin amidships. Five minutes later Marcus and the girls had jumped overboard, raced each other twice around the seventy-footer, and climbed back up to nap and sun themselves on the fantail.

"How about I rub some more of that oil on your backs?" Marcus had deadpanned, and the girls had shrieked.

And in the midst of that stuporous contentment, there had come to him a small moment of self-awareness. He had thought: *This is what it feels like to be having the time of your life.*

It was true—there was never to be an afternoon quite like that again—and how odd that he had known it! But now the long corridors of memory were invaded by a sudden sensation of weightlessness. The sub was sinking—or, rather, settling down. He opened his eyes on the enveloping blackness, heard the distorted clinkings of fiberglass hullplates skidding along the bottom. Reluctantly, Marcus Jolly shook off the cloying fantasy of seventeen summers previous. It was twenty-one minutes after eleven; they'd made good time. He collected his gear and scooted ass-backward to the wet-and-dry chamber.

He huddled there in the tiny space, mask on, hugging his knees and adjusting the mini-regulator of his flashlight-sized air canister as *Michman* Prilepko flicked a switch and the watertight bulkhead doors banged shut. Then, through the tiny window, he got Prilepko's thumbs-up—the order to flood. Marcus hit the pump lever, and the tiny compartment began to fill with water—his second tepid bath in the Black Sea this night, with the summer ocean temperature at least seventy degrees Fahrenheit.

As the chamber slowly filled, Marcus felt a little like Harry Houdini preparing for one of his death-defying underwater escapes. But had the great magician ever attempted anything so perilous as that which Marcus was now embarked upon? Not likely. And just as he imagined Houdini might have done, Marcus began psyching himself for the great task ahead. He gave himself permission to slip out of control, for a more instinctive self to come forth and take possession. Social conditioning sloughed off, his body came alive, his senses more acute, his reflexes cocked and ready to fire. The lukewarm water was inching up his torso, the air venting into the adjoining cabin area, the increased pressure squeezing in on him. As the tide covered his face, he blew out his nostrils to clear his eardrums, bit down on the mouthpiece of the mini-tank's regulator and began to breathe normally.

Now he opened the vent in the upper hatch to equalize pressure, then opened the hatch itself and clambered out onto the *Flea*'s fiberglass casing. A minute later, having reclosed the hatch, he was arrowing up through thirty meters of lukewarm ink toward a graying ceiling, trailing his tethered warbag. He barely broke surface, and sank again before he could fill his buoyancy vest. The Black Sea, he knew, might in places equal the Mediterranean in warmth, but never in buoyancy. Its salinity was much lower, owing to the constant freshwater infusions of the Danube, the Dniester, the Dnieper, and the Don. With the vest inflated, Marcus switched to snorkel, saw he was a bit farther offshore than he would have liked. He estimated a thirty-meter swim to the foot of the cliffs.

He hoped to hell that was Cape Ay-Todor light over there and that these were the right cliffs, because if they weren't, there wasn't a damn thing he could do about it. His underwater taxi would be already on its way home.

Snorkeling in, he picked up a sound like an underwater tom-tom— distant, but growing perceptibly louder. Presently he ventured a surface peek, saw a dazzling white glow behind Cape Ay-Todor, caught a low turbine-diesel throb. An instant later a blinding searchlight stabbed the night, froze a green-breaking wave, then swept on as the high-raked bows of a patrol boat emerged behind the cape. Marcus recognized the Grisha II, one of the favorite craft, he knew, of the KGB's Maritime Border Guards Directorate. He hoped Prilepko had the *Flea* well out to sea, for if detected, the Grisha might give chase and—unless Prilepko convinced them he was prowling the coast in the middle of the night for an old sunken ship—it might lob one of the dozen World War II–type depth charges carried in its rails. But the patrol boat's searchlight instead swung around to rake the cliffsides, and Marcus quickly submerged.

He remained under snorkel till the vibrations had died away, and he judged the Grisha had vanished eastward toward Yalta. A couple of things were now clear. One, Marcus was definitely in the right vicinity; and two, Rybkin's security people weren't entirely ignoring the possibility of a hostile approach from the sea. Which led to the question: How long would he have before the Grisha returned to light up the cliffs?

He'd better hustle.

Towing the warbag, he paddled toward shore, carried along by a slight tidal surge, then held off by a backwash. Approaching steep cliffs with no shelf or shingle, he was glad he didn't have real surf to contend with. Fortunately, as he drew nearer, he saw the bulging bluffs weren't nearly as formidable as he'd been warned, and had prepared for. They were fissured, veined, and eroded. And the cliff base afforded a tiny ledge where he was able to strip and stow his skindiving gear, wedging and weighting the bundle with the ropes, climbing harness, and carabiners he wouldn't be needing. Unless he was fatally mistaken, he would be able to scale this rock wall with little trouble. He had done far more difficult free-climbs assaulting *mujahideen* strongholds, and carrying considerably more than the vastly lightened warbag—down to perhaps a dozen kilos—that he now slung on his back. Without further delay, he began moving swiftly up the cliffs, choosing a route, wherever possible, that traced the deepest shadows.

Twenty minutes later, soaked with perspiration, Marcus was crouched under an overhang just below the top. He could have reached this point in a quarter of the time had he not taken vast care to avoid dislodging even pebbles or clinking his backpack against the rocks. And despite the exertion, he had managed to keep his breathing nearly inaudible to himself. The brow of stone immediately above was cowled with thick shrubbery. Against the moon-grayed sky, the twisted silhouettes looked like holly oaks and juniper. He needed to get up there and hide in their cover. He planned his moves carefully, then froze.

Footfalls were approaching along a pathway above, and before they died away, the damn Grisha came back. Marcus burrowed deeper into shadow and bit off a blasphemous prayer as the laserlike searchlight scythed twice across the cliffs, the second pass only meters below his legs.

After the patrol boat vanished, it took him another fifteen minutes to worm his way over the brow, clinging to rocky knobs and exfoliated cracks, and to slither into the dark cave of shrubbery, feeling ahead for loose twigs or tripwires. He lay prone several minutes, listening, watching, gathering his mind. Thick vegetation extended to the edge of a stoneflagged path, gray-washed by a distant floodlight. Under the circumstances, Marcus wasn't worried about triggering any line-of-sight microwave systems. But anyone checking the cliffside perimeter with thermal imaging would spot him instantly. Which made him abandon the idea of trying to hide out anywhere in the compound with the Dragunov sniper rifle, hoping for an eventual shot. The chances of finding any cover secure for more than a few minutes were basically nil. He would have to rely on a quick strike, in and out.

A KGB guard walked by, kneeboots glossy in even the faint light, near enough to touch. Marcus had timed four sentry passes, averaging five minutes between. He'd better take out the next one.

The man showed up maybe twenty seconds early, solitary like the others. Marcus waited till he'd gone a stride past, then sprang and looped a guitar string around the neck and tightened as he kicked the knees out from under. In an instant the throttled guard was dragged back into the shadowed shrubbery, expecting instant death, hearing instead a fierce whisper in his ear:

"Stop thrashing, asshole, or I'll pull this fucking thing tight. Tell me where Rybkin is, and I just knock you out. I'm good at it, you'll live. Keep silent, you die now, like this." Marcus cinched the garrote, watched the eyes bug, arms and legs flail. "Nod your head, I let you breathe. Make a sound above a whisper, you're dead."

The guard nodded frantically. Marcus gave him air. The voice rasped, a strangled whisper: "If I tell you . . . you'll kill me anyway."

"Maybe. Maybe not. It's the only chance you got."

"He's in his quarters . . . main palace"—an arm gestured feebly—"on the third floor . . . you can't get in."

Marcus tightened the noose again. "You just pointed to the KGB barracks, asshole. I know the layout. One more lie does it. I hear Rybkin's an insomniac, likes to putter in a workshop. Is he there tonight?"

"I—don't know. . . . Sometimes."

"Where is it? Careful."

"Guest dacha . . . last one . . . down there . . . on left . . ." Another gesture, in the opposite direction. Marcus hoped it was accurate. He did have a layout, but it hadn't included that most crucial piece of information.

"If you're wrong, friend, I'll come back and make sure you never wake up. Nod your head." But before the guard could obey, Marcus jerked the noose tight, using his full body weight to pinion the now-thrashing legs while he completed the strangulation.

Several minutes later Marcus stepped onto the path in full KGB regalia. The visored cap and polished boots fit tolerably enough, but the green tunic with blue shoulder-straps—bearing a senior lieutenant's stars and a gold "GB" for State Security—was at least a size too large. On the belt was a walkie-talkie and an empty holster; Marcus carried the sidearm and submachine gun from his warbag. Actually, he would have preferred the guard's SBM—a German Heckler and Koch MP5—except it was not silenced like his AKR.

Marcus figured he looked damn good.

He also figured he had at most a minute before the next guard passed—unless he'd been hearing the same dude walking to and fro. He walked purposefully, not hurrying, in the direction of the workshop-dacha. A voice squawked over his radio. He ignored it. If the dead lieutenant was late for his next checkpoint, there was nothing to be done about it now.

He was getting ready for his big roll of the dice. He had to hope Marchenko's informants had been right—that the eccentric Soviet leader spent long hours every night at Kichkine alone in his fix-it shop, like Marie Antoinette playing milkmaid at Versailles. If not, Marcus didn't have much of an alternate plan. Now, if he were James Bond, he'd have maybe a nifty time-delayed nuclear satchel charge to take out the whole damn compound. He'd look back and see the little mushroom cloud after he'd swum the hell away, having rescued the girl. As it was, he had to stay lucky. And the *Hagakure* notwithstanding, suicide had never been part of the deal.

He moved along the path, his stony exterior belying the hammering adrenaline high within, just as the tranquil surroundings of this elegant formal garden belied the fact that he was crossing a prime killing zone. He heard his hollow footfalls on polished stones, caught his dark reflection gliding across a lily pond, looked up to see another uniformed sentry silhouetted at the end of a long radial pathway. The man gave a little wave. Marcus mirrored it and walked on.

The indicated dacha was set apart from the others, fronting the bluffs for an ocean view. A white-gloved, gold-braided sentry was posted in the well-lighted, Moorish-colonnaded entranceway. Marcus skirted it, doubling around to the back behind a line of cypresses. There was a colonnade in back, too, but no ceremonial sentry, thank God. Only potted geraniums, trellised flowering wisteria, marble benches, electric torches flickering in wrought-iron cressets along the stuccoed stone.

And a dim light inside.

In the middle of the rear colonnade were double French doors. Probably not alarmed, not here, inside the protected area, with all the bristling security systems directed outward. But it didn't matter. He was going in.

Marcus felt his own electricity lifting the hair on the back of his neck, shoulders, forearms. God, he loved this stuff! A hell of a night—hitchhiking on a chopper, a raft, a trawler, a midget sub, dogpaddling a little, climbing a piece-of-cake cliff, and now he was ready to walk in on one of the most powerful men on earth.

He readied the short AKR, its steel butt-stock folded forward but its muzzle considerably lengthened by a chubby, anodized-aluminum suppressor tube. Momentarily, he wished for a 12-gauge autoloader shotgun—an alley-sweeper, a real Technicolor splatter gun. But noise was a definite no-no, and dead was dead, after all. Deep in his Siberian grave, Old Man Marchenko could ready his stainless-steel choppers for a ghostly grin.

Now!

Marcus slid sideways along the back wall, touched the brass door handle. He held his breath as he turned it, ready to burst in at the first hinged squeal. But he was able to unlatch and open it outward silently, just enough for entry. He slipped inside, his night-adjusted vision quickly inventorying the jumbled darkness.

He'd hit the workshop, all right. The place was redolent with the resinous fumes he remembered from his high school woodshop class, along with the musty odors of old furniture, aisles of junk, stacked piece upon piece, blocking most of the ocean view. Beyond was an open workspace, a faint light, a section of pegboard with tools.

Marcus tiptoed down a middle aisle, the only sound the syncopated ticking of several clocks. Then he heard mumbling, saw, a moment later, against a side wall, the enlarged silhouette of a man—bowed shoulders, cap on head. The figure didn't move, apparently absorbed in its task. The mumbling continued.

Marcus inched ahead, moving sideways past an old bellows organ, its dual manuals a pale, ivoried gleam in the obscurity. Now only an old monstrosity of an armoire blocked his view around the corner, but the tile floor ahead was littered with organ parts. It was time to stop pussyfooting and go for it.

Marcus burst around the armoire, swinging the submachine-gun barrel toward the puttering figure hunched over a workbench in baggy overalls and faded red beret. Alois Maksimovich was dead meat!

Marcus stitched a deadly cross up and down, side to side, holding the silenced, kicking submachine gun as steady as he could—not an easy task with the enormous muzzle blast caused by the powerful rounds spitting out of the AKR's short barrel.

But he'd been suckered. It wasn't Rybkin, it wasn't even human. The head burst apart in a shower of splinters, the bullet-riddled body toppled woodenly forward onto the bench—and cold metal kissed Marcus's temple.

Into Marcus's peripheral vision slid the chromed-steel barrel of a .45 auto as a hand reached around, relieving him of the AKR. Marcus turned slowly—the .45 held steady, ending up between his eyebrows—till he was face-to-face with Taras Arensky.

"Hell of a stalk, Cowboy," Taras said, also removing the silenced Makarov tucked under Marcus's tunic belt, "but you just assassinated a dressmaker's dummy."

"Cossack!" Marcus was stunned. He forced a grin, but the .45 still didn't budge and Taras's eyes were implacable. "I guess I should be flattered, Cossack. You came all the way back here to stop me, didn't you?"

"Looks like it, doesn't it?"

"How'd you know I'd be coming here?"

"I didn't. Wild guess. Rybkin didn't like it much, but I was prepared to hang around the next five nights till he goes back to Moscow."

"So now what?" When Taras didn't answer, Marcus stretched his smile into a grinning appeal: "Christ, Cossack, what is this? I'm your friend."

"You were. Now it looks like you're a full-time assassin." Taras nodded at the KGB uniform. "You kill a guard? Anybody see you?"

"Yeah, it's what I do. And no, so far nobody knows I'm here. Only you, old buddy. You going to kill me—or turn me in, it's the same fucking thing as killing me—to protect an old fart who's giving away your old homeland?"

Still Taras didn't respond. Marcus saw the tightness in his friend's face, a muscular twitch in his jaw. Marcus spoke again, excruciatingly aware of the continuing silence from outside, the hollow ticking of the clocks within:

"Cossack, this sounds like I'm begging, but all I'm doing is reminding you, man—you owe me! I kind of lost count over the years. Maybe you can remember. How many times was it exactly I saved your ass?"

Taras nodded. "I kind of lost count too."

Marcus watched the indecision writhe on the face of his old friend, saw it resolve finally in his favor. Taras would not kill him. Marcus didn't know what tipped the scales, but he assumed it was simple friendship, and he was right.

To Taras it was inescapable. Somehow, from as far back as the White House, he had not really foreseen this moment, but it had come. He found himself staring over the gunsight at a man he had loved, whom he had missed, dammit, and whose grinning, cocky countenance all these years later still struck chords in his heart. *I missed you, Cowboy. Why didn't you defect with me?* He didn't say these things, but he felt them.

But there was something else. It wasn't the debt owed, and it wasn't mercy. Marcus had obviously become an assassin, but Taras had not, and would not. He had stopped Marcus; he could not kill him, or anyone else. Not for his new country or its President, not for world peace or even the liberty of his sister and her family. He would not become Marcus. That was why he had left Afghanistan.

Taras stepped back, set Marcus's AKR and Makarov on the workbench beside the splintered dummy, then put his own .45 beside them.

"Get out of here, Cowboy. Maybe you can make it. I never saw you. I can't do any more."

"It's Peshawar all over again, isn't it?" For Marcus saw the same look of loathing on his friend's face as he had when Taras had walked out of their bungalow in Dean's Hotel to defect. Only this time it was Marcus leaving. He turned to do so.

"Marcus. It was you in Geneva, you got Raza, didn't you?"

Marcus paused in the dark aisle by the armoire, grinned, tipped his KGB cap. "Yeah. And I'll be back for Rybkin too. How about you?"

"No. It's over for me. Get out."

Marcus was gone, a shadow gliding out the back door into the colonnade.

I'm through with this, Taras thought. *All of it.*

He put the gun down, safety on, removed the clip. He was through playing what Charlotte called his "dirty little games." Let Marcus be whatever he wanted to be. The fact remained, he had been a friend.

If there was no immediate hue and cry, Taras would sit tight for another couple of hours. He'd give the Cowboy a chance to exfiltrate the compound, climb down, and catch his midget *Spetsnaz* sub—Taras was positive that's how he'd gotten here. Starkov and Pasholikov would be along soon enough—either because they'd caught Marcus, or found the body of the guard he'd killed. And Taras would tell them exactly what happened. Let them throw a fucking tantrum. The KGB wouldn't touch him, not with Ackerman having sent him. Besides, Rybkin couldn't kick. Taras had saved the old man's life.

At least for a while.

Chapter

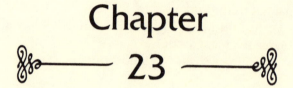 23

"HOW THE HELL DID HE GET OUT?" HANK KELLEHER WANTED TO know.

"Probably the same way he got in," Taras answered. It was the following day, and he was in the CIA station chief's office in the American Embassy compound back in Moscow.

"Okay, I'll bite. How did he get in?"

"Actually, nobody knows." Taras smiled and shrugged. "Marcus has had plenty of high-caliber *Spetsnaz* help all along, that's obvious. Biryukov didn't get the old man's whole network. Marchenko probably kept it locked up in tight little boxes."

"You know they're going apeshit over at the Lubyanka."

"Tell me. They can't figure it out. Within hours of the discovery they threw a net over everything that moved—in, on, or under the Black Sea, including a midget sub on a Lentra trawler that had been poking along the Crimean coast, supposedly looking for an old sunken warship. Marcus was not in the net."

"Your fault, I assume."

"You got it," Taras said.

The KGB, predictably, had protested Taras's negligence—and possible criminal complicity—in allowing, as Biryukov phrased it, a "world-class assassin" to escape with now less than two weeks remaining till Potsdam. There had been no gratitude for anticipating and forestalling Marcus's attack. In fact, for a wild moment there in Rybkin's compound, Taras had thought Pavel Starkov, the KGB Nazi, was even going to put a bullet into him. "Perhaps this Jolly was not a real defector," Starkov had said while awaiting Biryukov's telephonic orders, "but a CIA spy all along, and you were his confederate."

Taras's one-word response did not further endear him to Starkov, but fortunately the wooden-faced lieutenant colonel was empowered by Biryukov only to escort his American guest back to Moscow—an endurable torture for Taras, under the circumstances.

So Taras was alive, but decidedly off the case. In disgrace with the Kremlin, and perhaps the White House. And he couldn't care less. So long as nobody tried to force Luiza and her family back on a plane to Moscow.

"Maybe you made a mistake," Kelleher said. "Letting him go, I mean."

"I don't care, Hank. I never wanted this fucking job."

"Maybe you will care." Kelleher slid a nine-by-twelve manila envelope across the table. "Take a look at this."

"What is it?"

"Some faxes we got this morning from Washington. Answers to your query, actually. Remember those discrepancies you found in Marcus's dossier—what, only two days ago—on his American background? Well, the FBI ran them to ground. An interesting guy, Marcus Jolly. Only that isn't his name. It's Hofstatter, Eric Llewellyn Hofstatter. Jolly was the guy from Wichita, whose washed-out elementary school picture you saw at the Lubyanka. There's better pictures of both of 'em in here, and you'll recognize who's who. They were both born the same year—1957—both blond, blue-eyed, slim Midwestern kids. Hofstatter's the guy from Illinois who left home—"

"After his grandparents were killed in a fire."

"Yeah, a fire he was wanted for questioning about. A backyard kiln exploded, fire spread to the house, but the old couple never got out. The Hofstatter kid claimed the grandmother used to keep the burners real low during the drying-out phase, so the clay wouldn't crack, and the flame must have gone out and the grandmother relit it without letting the gas disperse. But the police in Rantoul—that's where he's from—kind of suspected the kid arranged it to happen just that way. He disappeared without a trace until you saw him in Siberia in 1977 calling himself Marcus Jolly. And the real Marcus, after he left home in 1974, he disappeared too. His aunt in Wichita got a postcard from Amarillo in '75, and then nothing. Who knows what happened to him? The FBI thinks he met up with your pal Eric, who decided to snatch his identity—and then made sure the real Marcus wasn't around anymore to confuse the issue."

Listening to the brief synopsis, Taras felt as if a series of stun grenades had just been tossed into the room. Half his life seemed to have been blown up. He reached for his coffee, rattled the cup in the saucer, set it back down on Kelleher's desk.

"Hank, do you mind if I take this somewhere and read it by myself for a few minutes?"

"Hell of a shock, isn't it? Make yourself comfortable. I'm going to go chat with some folks. Be back after a while."

So, numbly and for the second time, Taras found himself closeted with a dossier on his old comrade in arms, following the Cowboy's backtrail. Only it didn't take as long this time. He was able to wade through the sheaf of twenty or so faxes in a half hour, reading everything several times. It was pretty damn conclusive.

There were several teenage shots of Hofstatter. Two were class pictures. Another one showed him in a sweatshirt with sleeves hacked off, cigarette in mouth, Simonizing the front fender of an old two-tone Buick. The last one was a gag photo. He was grinning at the camera while holding a hammer and chisel up to a parking meter. There was a cardboard box below to catch any coins. They were all unmistakably a younger version of "Marcus," complete with cocky grin.

According to the police files, Hofstatter had been having frequent arguments with his grandparents. He'd hocked some family heirlooms, used their car without permission to joyride with an older crowd from the local Chanute Air Force Base. After the devastating fire, apparently caused by the kiln explosion, the boy had moved in with schoolmates, collected some insurance money. But when suspicion had gradually turned toward him, he had simply vanished.

The circumstances of the real Marcus Jolly's disappearance were just as Kelleher had synopsized, and as Taras himself had read in the official dossier at KGB headquarters—the dossier of an American defector turned *Spetsnaz* assassin. Whoever he was, by whatever name, he had worked out well for them. The covering fax, from the FBI to Kelleher and his bosses back at Langley, commented that the KGB First Directorate would have thoroughly researched the past of any American defector, and thus would have been well aware of "Marcus's" real identity as Eric Hofstatter, and the fact that he was wanted in Illinois for questioning in connection with a possible arson and homicide. Apparently, the FBI speculated, the KGB had decided for its own reasons to accept the impersonation.

Taras had another theory as he recalled the KGB case officer's notation on Marcus's dossier for further information—a request that seemed to have been ignored. Perhaps the First Directorate had been overruled by the GRU—in the formidable person of General Marchenko, who had taken such a liking to the arrogant young American.

Taras struggled to confront the specter of this strange new "Marcus"—he still couldn't think of him as Eric Hofstatter, the name simply didn't conjure up the Cowboy. Marcus's defection had always seemed capricious, but the younger Taras had simply accepted it, glad of the friendship. But was the happy-go-lucky vagabond Taras had known the kind of person who could have killed his grandparents, and perhaps a fellow drifter?

Or had he been a grinning sociopath all along?

Taras ransacked his memories of their time together, from Khabarovsk to Moscow, from Wrangel and Ryazan to Kabul and Peshawar. It was quite an assignment, sifting for evidences of sensitivity during years in which they were being turned into efficient killing machines and then sent off to exercise those hard-won lethal talents. Where did you look? The Cowboy had a pet rat for a while in Kabul, used to carry him around Bagram Airbase in his beret. And, of course, he had been Taras's truest friend in all the world, in battle and out. Not exactly the sort you could picture setting fire to his loved ones and running off into the night.

On the other hand, the Cowboy hadn't cared much about the plight of the wretched Afghans—the hundreds of thousands killed or crippled, the millions made homeless—but how many Soviet soldiers had? Their business was to kill, and stay alive doing it. Marcus was supremely good at both.

What else? The Cowboy had quickly acquired the Slavic knack of waxing sentimental—spiritual, if you will—over quantities of shared vodka. But probably so had Stalin, and he wasn't even a Slav.

Only one incident shone forth with any kind of special refulgence from the general murk of memory. That icy, leaden day in Khabarovsk when Taras had stood beside the Cowboy as they watched snow and fresh-thawed earth being shoveled onto the descending casket of Eva Sorokina, and both had wept uncontrollably in spite of mutual resolves.

It had been the tragic event that brought them together.

Two days later, after a final embassy debriefing in Moscow, Taras was on a plane back over the Atlantic—not *Air Force One* this time, but a British Airways 747 connecting from London to Washington.

He hadn't phoned ahead. He wanted to walk in on her, make his appeal face-to-face. But in his thoughts he beseeched Charlotte to be there, willing to listen and judge and finally be persuaded. Surely that was not too much to ask.

As Taras was crossing the Atlantic, "Marcus Jolly"—once again disguised and credentialed as Canadian journalist Byron Landy—was disembarking the M/S *Liapunov,* a Soviet Morflot steamer docked at the Karaköy Maritime Terminal in Istanbul.

Getting out of Yalta had been far more strenuous than getting in. He had slipped out of the compound, stripped off his KGB disguise, and descended the cliff without incident. But once in the water, having failed to get himself either killed or captured as Captain Chapayev had so confidently assured him would be the case, Marcus faced the further dilemma of having no getaway vehicle.

It had been a long, dark swim. He'd headed east, crawling and sidestroking a half kilometer offshore, and diving several times to avoid searchlight sweeps from a patrolling Grisha. By the time he was abreast of Yalta harbor—at least three klicks from Oreanda—he was exhausted, but struggled on, wary of the berms and beaches along the lamplighted embankment. A kilometer or two beyond in Massandra, having reached his last ebb and with dawn only a couple of hours off, Marcus angled toward a dark, deserted Intourist beach, dragging himself ashore along with his waterproof warbag—which also contained clothing, makeup kit, and identity papers, including faked entry visa into the Soviet Union.

He had spent the morning lounging in cafés along the Yalta waterfront, clad in blue jeans and sport shirt, and further concealed behind a shaggy mustache and a newspaper. The KGB Guards Directorate had undoubtedly been combing the area, but either they'd been damn inconspicuous or Marcus was just too fatigued to spot them. In fact, he was almost beyond caring whether he was caught or not, if they'd just show him to a comfy cell with a decent mattress.

In the afternoon he walked the gangway to the *Liapunov* and experienced vast relief as it churned away from the quayside and, with a basso profundo blast, nosed into the Black Sea. As the hills of Yalta faded astern, Marcus stumbled down a long alleyway to his private cabin, toppled fully clothed onto his bunk, and slept nineteen hours straight, not waking until they left Odessa at nine the next morning. In fact, he slumbered through much of the next day and their stay at Varna the following night. By the time they entered the Bosporus the afternoon of the third day, he was feeling fairly decent.

He'd escaped to fight another day.

He checked into a seedy hotel near Sirkeci Station. Not exactly his style, but the past weeks' adventurings had made serious inroads in his operational funds—and the GRU would not be funneling any more his way. And with the old pipeline sealed, he'd have to give some thought to the future.

Plenty of ex-SAS and Delta types, he knew, hired out as security experts to multinationals, or military consultants to third world nations. Some ex-KGB agents had even opened their own private detective bureau in Leningrad. Many special forces people, of course, went the straight mercenary route—out of idealism, or greed, or sheer ennui. A few got involved in low-level bodyguarding. Others turned their expertise to lucrative illegalities, like the smuggling of weapons or drugs.

But Marcus had his own daydream, something he'd thought about for several years, ever since the successful Geneva hit on Raza. He would hang out his own shingle, become a sort of traveling virtuoso—only his instrument of choice would be a *Snayperskaya Vintovka Dragunova,* an SVD sniper rifle, deadly in his hands from as far away as thirteen hundred meters. Like any new businessman, of course, he'd have to get the word out, attract the right sort of clients—powerful men who could both use and afford his services. But it could be done; he had contacts. The more he turned it over in his mind, the more he liked it. He could do very well as a Dragunov soloist.

But there was unfinished business.

Rybkin.

The Soviet President had to die. No longer because Marchenko had decreed it. But because Marcus had bungled his first attempt. Been beaten by Taras.

And that didn't sit very well.

He hadn't liked the ease with which he'd been outguessed, the cold, contemptuous touch of the gun against his head. And then let off, thrown back into the Black Sea like a small fish.

Taras had not been friendly. On reflection, that final look of loathing on the Cossack's face might not have been self-loathing, but meant for Marcus.

It was as if, all these years later, Taras had scored the final winning touch in their deadlocked and interrupted fencing match. Proved himself better than Marcus.

Question: What would it avail to take out Rybkin at the Potsdam Conference if Taras wasn't there to oppose him?

Answer: With apologies to Marchenko, it would avail absolutely nothing. It would be an empty victory.

No, he needed to get Taras back into the game, for one more showdown. They would never be friends again, that was finished. But they could remain rivals, deadly ones. And if that was all there was, so be it. Marcus wanted it.

He had to get him back. And he thought of a way to do it.

But did he dare?

Yes.

Before he could change his mind, he put down his sweet, tepid coffee, got up from the table in the dingy sitting room of the Otel Ali Pasha, and procured several sheets of hotel stationery. Then he settled himself again in the late afternoon light filtering through threadbare lace and no longer iridescent peacock feathers, and began to compose a letter.

Taras took a cab from Dulles International through five o'clock nightmare traffic to a Holiday Inn on Connecticut Avenue, checked in, shaved, showered, and changed, then took another cab to Cleveland Park and Charlotte's condo. It was dark when he pushed the doorbell. He'd rehearsed what he would say a thousand times, till the words were grooved into his brain and leached of meaning. And yet the apprehension still churned in his gut. Apprehension? No, call it what it was. Plain fear. More than he'd experienced before actual combat.

He pushed the bell again.

Why was he torturing himself over this one woman? He could find another—others by the dozen. There was no shortage; the District and environs boasted an embarrassment of available, attractive females. But of course Taras didn't want another woman. He wanted the one he'd walked out on. He wanted her back fiercely, more than he could remember wanting anything in his life.

She wasn't home.

He had willed her to be, but she wasn't. Jealousy swept over him. She was with another man. He imagined a tangle of sheets and bodies and the apricot glow of a bedside lamp, her elegant forefinger twining in his matted chest hair, whispered dinner plans. The vision left him eviscerated, his hand clutching the iron porch railing for support.

Somewhere in his suitcase he still had his key. But he had forfeited the right to use it.

He turned around. The cab was gone.

Maybe she was working late. Or off on sudden assignment. There were people he could call—including Charlie herself, if he had the courage. She would have left a message on her machine.

He walked a block, flagged a cab, went back to his hotel, dialed the paper.

The foreign editor had gone home hours before. One of the night guys on the desk said Charlie was in Europe. Taking a week of R & R before the runup to Potsdam.

"Do you know where?" Taras asked. "I'm an old friend, and it's absolutely critical. I have to talk to her."

"Sorry, I don't have it. Even if I did, you'd have to clear it with John." John Tully was the foreign editor.

"Can you give me his home number? He knows me."

"Hold on. The operator will patch you through if he's home."

Tully was home. He knew about the breakup. He commiserated with Taras, said it was a hell of a thing and that he'd be happy to help, but claimed he himself didn't know where Charlie was. "She's being secretive, Taras. I expect she'll let me know when she's ready. She's not planning to file till next week, a scene-setter for Potsdam. Any messages if she calls sooner?"

"Yeah. Tell her . . . Christ. Tell her I want her back. Tell her I have to talk to her. Ask her if you can give me her number."

"Can't she call you at the Agency?"

"No, don't even mention the damn Agency, John. If she asks, tell her I've quit. Tell her I sounded desperate."

Tully chuckled. "That won't be hard—you do. Look, Taras, I'll do what I can. Good luck."

Taras hung up, stared at the phone. Dialed her condo. Her breezy voice startled him:

"This is Charlotte Walsh. Sorry, my dears, I'm off on temporary assignment, working undercover as a B girl . . . in Punta Negra, I think it is, though I could be wrong. But I do call in regularly for messages. And I'd especially like to hear yours, right after the tone."

Taras hung up. God, she sounded wonderful! Funny and happy. It was as if he had never existed in her life, or been completely erased from it. He slumped in the hotel chair, then slowly straightened himself, took a deep breath. He wasn't going to pursue that pointless, self-pitying line of thought. He'd get her back.

He called mutual friends. Two sympathetic wives knew about the breakup, and knew Charlie had gone to the Continent. Both claimed she had been deliberately blithe about her destination, wanting to prowl around, so hadn't left a number. Were they holding out on him, perhaps under Charlie's direct orders? Taras couldn't tell.

Finally he phoned Brock Chalmers, who still sounded eager to have Taras join his institute, maybe as early as September, six weeks off. Chalmers proposed a luncheon later in the week. Taras told him he might be leaving town, promised to get back to him.

It was too late for any more calls, and Taras was undone. He watched an old war movie to escape flagellating thoughts, slept and dreamed badly, awoke at five with a feeling of hopelessness.

At eight-thirty he dialed Langley and was told a letter had come that morning. Federal Express. From Istanbul. From somebody called Hickok, William Hickok. Odd name, just like the famous cowboy, Wild Bill.

Taras went silent. It had to be the Cowboy.

"I'll be right over."

Chapter

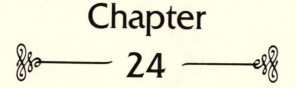 **24**

TARAS SAT BEHIND HIS OLD DESK AT LANGLEY, HIS ATTENTION riveted on the envelope before him. The Fed Ex return address was William Hickok, Otel Ali Pasha, Demirkapi Caddesi, Sirkeci, Istanbul. Of course, the Cowboy would now be long gone. One step ahead of the KGB, and still playing games. What had he sent this time, another finger? But there were no bulges in the envelope, no odor of decomposing flesh. And a date stamp indicated it had been checked for explosive content. It was, then, just a letter. He slit it, read in English:

Dear Cossack,

Dare I say it? I've missed you. And our recent meeting was hardly the reunion our long friendship deserves, was it? I don't want it to be our final encounter. Do you?

Let's do something about it.

Let's finish off our old duel, the one interrupted in Kirovograd so long ago. I'm willing to count the point you scored against me in Yalta, but it's my turn to riposte, or whatever you call it.

I'm going after Rybkin again at Potsdam. Why don't you try to stop me? What do you say? For old time's sake. Don't you like the historical settings, Yalta and Potsdam, for our private little showdown?

Oh, I know, Cossack. You beat me, and now you don't want any part of the Game anymore, do you? You're quitting a winner.

But I'm going to change your mind.

Remember the drunken oaths we swore on the Rossiya Express, somewhere around Sverdlovsk? Eternal friendship, Cossack, and we kept that pledge—until you walked out on me in Pakistan. The other pledge was eternal vengeance—on the murderer of Eva Sorokina.

But neither of us ever found old Kostya, did we?

Maybe you no longer care about the first oath, but what about the second one? I'm going to give you a chance to keep it. A second chance. Because, Cossack, only a few days ago you missed your first chance. You had Eva's murderer at your mercy, and you let him go.

Calm yourself. I feel your Slavic blood rising. Can it be true, you wonder? Yes, Cossack, it wasn't crazy Kostya. I'm the one who killed Eva. You won't believe me if I tell you how sorry I was then, and still am. It was an accident. I was blind drunk on Siberian White Dynamite, drunker than all of you, I think, though everybody but Eva and I passed out. I was out of my mind, but that doesn't bring her back, does it?

Why am I telling you this after all these years? Because it seems like the only way to get you back.

As an enemy, if not a friend.

You want the sordid details? I bet not. But maybe you can remember what happened when you were alone with her earlier? You attacked her, Cossack. When Kostya and I came back from pissing in the snow, she was on the floor screaming and you were on top of her, shaking her. I almost killed you myself.

Christ, she was lovely that night! And you saw the way she started hanging around me after what happened with you. Suddenly we were alone. What was I supposed to do? I did exactly what you tried to do.

But she fought me too. I wasn't expecting that. And she started screaming again. How she was engaged to you. All about her sacred virtue. She was hysterical. I was afraid she'd rouse you and Kostya.

I only wanted to stop her screaming, like you did. But she wouldn't stop. Until it was too late. I couldn't believe she was gone, Cossack. But she was. I think being betrayed by both of us was too much for Eva. She couldn't handle it. She preferred to die, that's what I really think.

I had no choice after that. You and Kostya would never have believed it was an accident. I had to strip all our clothes off and make it look like Kostya did it and then ran off with our stuff. I could barely get that fucking giant over my shoulder, but I did it. I managed to carry him through the snowstorm clear down to the river and chop open one of the holes left by some ice fishermen and stuff him in, along with most of our clothes and money.

Cossack, nothing I ever saw or did in Afghanistan came close to the nightmare of that night in Khabarovsk, running back through a blizzard in my shorts, then lying down on the freezing floor beside the naked corpse of poor Eva and you, with the damn stove out, shivering like a madman, waiting for you to wake up and find Eva, and then to wake me.

We both nearly died that night with Eva. Maybe we should have. Except for one thing.

We became friends. And our friendship was not a lie, even if I did not dare tell you the truth of what happened to Eva. You were the only true friend I have ever had, Cossack, far more than Old Man Marchenko. And I almost did tell you the truth one night in Kandahar, when we got roaring drunk. Do you remember? But I was afraid it would cost me your friendship. So now that I have lost that, I have told you. And only you.

I've got to get ready now for Potsdam. I hope you'll be there too. In fact, I just thought of one more enticement, to make sure you'll come. But I'll let you discover that.

Do svidanya,
The Jolly Cowboy

Taras threw down the letter, reeled back against his chair. The room seemed to be spinning and tilting like a carnival wheel, and he was clinging to this desk to keep from being hurled off.

Oh God! Evushka, forgive me!

He remembered how he had frightened her, how the terror had invaded her beautiful eyes, how she had spurned him and turned to Marcus. And he would never forget the frozen naked horror of the next morning.

An accident, Marcus said. He hadn't meant to strangle her. How sorry he was. But Taras had seen the ghastly empurpled marks on her neck. And he'd seen something else, too, before he'd covered her with the blanket. There had been tiny crystal droplets—frozen fluid—beading the golden fuzz between her thighs. The militia pathologist had later confirmed she'd been violated. The bastard! The fucking bastard!

Taras's rage now engulfed him till he nearly blacked out. It left him shaken and drained. Then it returned, unabated. The chrome-steeled .45 was in his bag. The one he was to have thrown away. He took it out, popped out the clip, saw the Cowboy's grinning face, pulled the trigger again and again, murder in his heart.

Marcus would get his wish. Taras would go to Potsdam. He would go not to save Rybkin. He would go to kill the Cowboy. For Eva. And for his own delectable pleasure, to end the duel and show once and for all who was the better assassin.

The phone rang. It was John Tully, the foreign editor.

"Taras, Charlie called in this morning before I got in. One of the interns took the call and didn't press her for details, dammit. All he got was the South of France, but also says he got the impression she's still on the move. Look, I'm sure she'll contact me as soon as she lands somewhere. Sorry I can't do better."

"I understand. Thanks, John."

Taras hung up. Fifteen minutes earlier he was going to throw away his gun and go after her, beg her to take him back. Now, after Marcus's letter, he wanted to hold on to it for one more kill. Kind of hard to explain that one to Charlie, if he could find her. There's this guy I gotta kill, a dear old friend who turns out to have been a sociopath. I'll be a much more loving husband after I put a couple bullets through his brain, and a few more through his heart.

But suppose he went after her, found her in the South of France, made his plea. If she said yes, that would be the end of it. But if she said no, he would be free to go after Marcus. It would be a way of keeping his options open, hedging his bet.

Only it wouldn't work, and he knew it. Emotionally. He had to choose. He could go hunting one or the other, not both.

Both courses of action beckoned him; two women—one alive, one dead—claimed him, paralyzing his will.

But he must decide. His secretary looked in and did not enter during the anguished half hour it took him to reach his verdict. It was: *Let the madman go. Eva is gone and mourned. Find Charlie and open your heart to her. Then let her choose. But leave your vengeance here, with the gun she despised.*

The decision made, a long struggle still remained, he knew, to fully accept it, to subdue the rage and turn away from Marcus's provocation. But he could do it, had to do it. For starters, he tossed the automatic into a desk drawer.

Fifteen minutes later the secretary popped back in, saw improvements. "I just made a fresh pot of coffee, Taras."

212

"Love some, thanks."

"Kind of a tough morning, huh?"

"You might say that." Taras made a chuckling sound, but there was no mirth in his eyes. "Charlie's somewhere in the South of France, and I'm going to find out where if I have to call everybody in this whole damn town. And when I do, I'm going to go to her as fast as I can."

About the same time, several thousand miles to the east, Marcus Jolly was pursuing the same objective in the same way. As Canadian journalist Byron Landy, he was making transatlantic phone calls. And ultimately he, too, reached Charlotte's foreign editor.

"The thing is, John, she asked me to get back to her on something, for a piece she was writing for you, I imagine. She wanted to quiz some of my contacts in North Sea oil, how all that affects European energy plans after 1992, and how it might impact the Potsdam Conference. Fairly obscure stuff, I'm not sure where she was going with it, but I've got some answers for her, and she promised me some sources in return."

"Mr. Landy, I'd like to help you."

"Call me Byron."

"Okay. The thing is, Byron, she asked me not to tell anybody."

"I understand. But I know she wants this stuff I got, and I'd sure hate to wait till Potsdam to give to her. It'll probably be too late then, and anyway, the place is going to be a fucking loony bin."

"Tell me about it. We're already buried alive in wire copy, and we got two weeks till play-ball. Okay, you can stop twisting my arm. Hang on a minute. She just called in, as a matter of fact. Cheryl, have you got that address Charlie just gave us? Thanks. Okay, Byron? Here it is. She's going to be there only a week. It's in the South of France. Place called Le Lavandou, just east of Toulon. L'Auberge de la Calanque. Here's the number."

Marcus took it down.

"I owe you one, John. Thanks."

"Do me a favor in return, Byron. When you talk to her, tell her to stay off those damn topless beaches. I don't want my star soothsayer sunburning her nipples."

"I'll do that."

213

Chapter

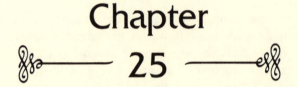

25

Charlotte Walsh lay supine on the beach of Le Lavandou, surrendering herself to the Mediterranean sun. She wanted it not only to bronze her body, but to cauterize certain emotional wounds and to burn the insidious Washington fog out of her brain. It was the Fourth of July, not a red letter day in the South of France, and certainly not here. She had deliberately bypassed her favorite spots along the Côte d'Azur—Villefranche, Nice, Antibes—and come farther west to this less than trendy resort unfrequented by American tourists.

But Le Lavandou was far from deserted. French holidaygoers flocked to the place, staking out early claims on its fine sand beach and staying past sundown. Windsurfers dashed back and forth across the sparkling bay. From the adjoining marina, boatloads of tourists were ferried out to the offshore islands, the Iles d'Hyères. And the beachfront boulevard teemed all day with a bright, motley parade. Little cars and motor scooters snarled endlessly around the corners from the perpendicular access streets, dueling for parking places. An open-sided tram snaked routinely through this melee, blatting its horn, flashing its red roof light, stopping at all the bayside hotels. Half a dozen tacky carnival booths along the harborside did a steady business, as did the sidewalk T-shirt, souvenir, and snack shops. Teens and preteens clattered by on skateboards, older townfolk in shorts and sandals were pulled past by straining poodles and shepherds.

Charlotte found it all refreshing. The erstwhile sleepy fishing village had turned itself into a bustling beach town devoid of glitzy pretense or cultural cachet. As far as she could glean from the tourist brochures, neither Picasso nor Matisse had ever loaded a brush in Le Lavandou, Maugham and Fitzgerald had neither one written a line, and Mick Jagger didn't have a villa in the vicinity. Further isolating the spot from the hordes of Eurailpassing wayfarers, the train entirely disregarded the Massif des Maures, this petite bulge in France's celebrated southern littoral. Charlotte had arrived on a bus from Toulon. She had preferred not to rent a car. Once here, everything was walkable.

She had settled in a white and pastel blue room whose private tiled terrace overlooked the marina and afforded a grand view of the beach and the circling Bay of Bormes all the way to Cape Bénet. On her second full day she still knew no one except the startlingly attractive young people who staffed her hotel. And so far, even John Tully was being *très sympathique* about not disturbing her.

The deluge would come soon enough, as she joined the legions of the fourth estate converging on Berlin and Potsdam, all in the earnest guise of Delphic oracles for their respective constituencies. In fact, the hype and handouts were already clogging Charlie's in basket and the mainframe's foreign wire queues the day she'd escaped her desk in D.C. Well, she'd survive Potsdam, and maybe even find something worth writing about it—and inflicting on the readers of her home paper and the eighty-three others which, her syndicate assured her, subscribed to her twice-weekly columns. But it was increasingly obvious that, like Super Bowls, these international conferences had become almost incidental to the surrounding media event, serving only to provide the initial spark for self-feeding firestorms of reportage and punditry. Of course, she knew she'd enjoy herself once she got in journalistic harness, but she wasn't eager to be off just yet. Another few days of sunshine, salt air, and tranquillity would do her just fine.

They would also give her a chance to shape up her psyche along with her physique, to unwind her nerves as she tanned her hide and toned her muscles with a daily seaside jog. The day after Taras left, Charlotte had gone back to the gym and repped herself ragged. She had chickened out on a further angry resolve—to spread the word among selected friends that she just might—deep breath—be back in the market for any available—and marriageable—males. There was no point in kidding herself. She was still hung up on her dark-eyed Slav. She wanted him back, dammit! But a week had passed without word from Taras, and now anger and frustration were building up again. She deserved a hell of a lot better, and if Taras couldn't see that, maybe she'd have to find somebody who could.

Her body, approaching forty, was still damn good. Tall, long-legged, and hyper, Charlotte had never succumbed to sedentary spread. And her intermittent exercise manias over the years had maintained her assets with a certain buoyancy. Not that she could compete with the *crème* of the *jeune filles* who habituated the Lavandou seaside, abundantly or boyishly topless, and some wearing only *le minimum* below. Charlotte had seen several girls who were breathtaking, and when one of these tawny young lionesses rose up from the sand to prance toward the water for a splash, all eyes followed—and not infrequently a zoom lens or two from the bordering sidewalk.

But Charlotte definitely held her own with the older ingenues. She had, for instance, bravely abandoned her trusty one piece in favor of a skimpy black bikini from a local shop suggestively called Kocaïne. She still hadn't summoned the nerve to unfasten the tiny halter while sunbathing, or to frequent the sidewalks without her extra-large T-shirt coverup. But she might yet. The resort atmospherics were definitely uninhibiting. Under no circumstances, however, could she see herself entering the pageant being advertised by a beachfront nightclub to select "*La Plus Grosse Poitrine de la Région*"—a title which Charlotte translated succinctly as "Biggest Tits in Town."

Of course, she wasn't really trying to draw the focus of local males. She was only on reconnaissance, not combat maneuvers. Anyway, she couldn't quite get used to European men in bikini briefs—what one woman friend, who did fancy them, playfully called "banana huggers" and "marble bags." However, Charlotte's morning jogs took her past a pair of appealing hunks—rugged-looking Swedish windsurfers day-camping out of an old VW microbus farther down the beachfront toward Port de Bormes-les Mimosas. Had she been seriously stalking, they would certainly have merited consideration. But so far her passages had elicited no signs of interest; the blue-eyed squints of both young men remained fixed seaward.

216

She turned onto her tummy, checking her watch to make sure she didn't overdo and burn her back, especially those tender derriere portions newly exposed by the bikini. She gave herself a half hour more, and picked up the paperback she'd bought that morning in a beachside *librairie*. It was an Agatha Christie in French, something to while away the sun-dazed minutes while refreshing her *grammaire* and *vocabulaire*. After fifteen minutes she made the vexing discovery that she'd read the damn thing in English under a title that bore not the slightest resemblance to the one on this French edition. She shut the book with an expletive, which she quickly emended to *merde;* there was no point in wading through pages of Gallicized British chitchat when she knew damn well who'd done it!

She'd just have to put up with her own thoughts for a while.

But *merde* squared! She didn't *want* to be stuck with them.

She snatched up her beach things, stuffed them into her tote bag, and hiked across the sand to the little card- and bookstore on the tamarisk-lined Avenue Général Bouvet. The proprietress would happily exchange it, and Charlotte could be back in her spot in five minutes with her nose in a fresh paperback.

As she was browsing, a tanned, fair-haired man was suddenly beside her at the paperback kiosk. For an instant, gathering a peripheral blur of rugged features, blue eyes, and muscular, blond-thatched forearms and legs, she thought it was one of the Scandinavian windsurfers—and was embarrassed how girlishly her pulse quickened. Then, as the kiosk squeaked around and they moved in opposition, she got a good look at him. He was older than the Swedes, but her heartbeat didn't diminish. On the contrary. He was terribly good to look at. She traced a sensual curve that repeated in the line of his jaw, in his cheekbones, at the corner of his mouth and feathered eyebrow. He seemed to emit a kind of constant, low-intensity masculine assurance even when, as now, he was obviously unaware of doing so. *He's always gotten whoever and whatever he wanted,* she thought. *The star athlete. No wonder he looks arrogant.*

What nationality? she mused further. In what language was he thinking behind those Arctic eyes? If not Scandinavian, perhaps German or Austrian? A Teutonic name would definitely fit him, something harsh like Horst or Gunther. The rotating book titles blurred as she browsed him further—his hands, tanned and veined and covered with golden hair like his forearms; strong legs swelling under mid-length khaki shorts; well-shaped feet in Mexican-style huaraches; a sculpted, pectoral slab visible through a half-buttoned Madras shirt. . . .

Let's stop right there, shall we, Charlotte? she told herself.

The man turned to the woman behind the counter, who was reading a Maigret. "Excuse me. Don't you have anything in English?"

"*Ah, dommage, mais non, monsieur.* Very sorry."

"They don't seem to get many English or American tourists here," Charlotte said.

"Thank God, a fellow American!"

They exchanged names. His was Jack Sanderson. And he, too, just wanted something to read on the beach. "They got plenty of American authors, I see, only in the wrong language. Judith Krantz, Jackie Collins. Harold Robbins is still big over here, I see."

Charlotte laughed. "What about *Martin Chuzzlewit?*"

"I'm kind of partial to thrillers and westerns. What's he write?"

"He doesn't. It's one of Dickens's novels. I've got a copy back at my hotel you could have. I finished it on the plane." *Christ, that just came out, didn't it? What adolescent subtlety was she going to blurt out next?*

"Thanks, but I'm kind of a hopeless lowbrow. Move my lips when I read, you know what I mean? Got any Alistair MacLean, Louis L'Amour, Mickey Spillane type of thing, about a hundred fifty pages, big type?"

Sanderson was grinning, enjoying his self-putdown.

She shook her head. "No, but I think there's a place on Avenue de Gaulle where you might find something."

"I don't know the layout yet. Could you, uh, maybe point me in the right direction?"

"Better let me show you. It's not far. Come on." She gestured toward the door, her Agatha Christie exchange utterly forgotten. *Dear Diary, am I imagining this or is something starting to happen here?*

Sanderson had fallen in beside her, and they followed the curving sea frontage past the little town hall with its tricolor flag and bunting, then turned up a narrow walkway to Avenue du Général de Gaulle, one of the main shopping streets. The bookstore had some British paperbacks, including a couple of old James Bonds that Sanderson hadn't read. Charlotte picked out a Delderfield saga. On the way back to the beach they detoured into a glass-enclosed brasserie with a view of the bay through palms and parked cars. Sanderson ordered a Beck's, then switched to join Charlotte in her choice of a local wine, a Côte de Provence.

"So what do we toast?" he asked.

"For starters," she suggested, "how about happy birthday, America?"

"Christ, it's the Fourth! I completely forgot!"

Their eyes met as they touched glasses, and Charlotte felt slightly flushed. Which was, of course, absurd. It had been a while, perhaps, but she'd had more than her share of affairs before Taras. She could certainly handle this without getting the schoolgirl wobbles. Be in control of it. She glanced deliberately away from Sanderson, watching the sunlight gloss the edges of the swishing palm fronds, the same sun that was bathing the bay beyond. The tension wouldn't go away.

"So, what do you do?" he asked. She told him, and he brightened. "I've seen your by-line. Doesn't the *Herald-Tribune* run you sometimes?"

"On occasion. Which one did you see?"

"I don't remember. Actually, like I said, I just remember the by-line. Over here I mostly just check out the baseball scores a day or so late. And lately I've been picking up *USA Today*. More my speed, I guess."

"Don't put yourself down, Jack. It makes me suspicious, since you strike me as a pretty bright guy. Which brings us to your turn. What do you do?"

"Lately I go to trade fairs. Not a bad deal, driving all around Europe, tax deductible. Actually, what I do, I look for products, things that these people I represent back home—I work out of an office in Chicago, the Merchandise Mart—can license and sell. Mail-order gadgets. Damnedest stuff you ever saw. Toy solar-power dirigibles. Floating sunglasses, don't ask me why. Underwater magnets, for picking up beer cans from docks, I guess, quarters from swimming pools. Backyard geodesic domes. Alpha-state stimulators. Personally, I like the toys best."

"Sounds like a perfectly wonderful way to make a living. Have you been doing it long?"

"Couple three years now."

"That explains your accent."

"What accent?"

"Your vowels are kind of roundish for a real American, if you know what I mean, especially a Middle Westerner. For instance, you just said '*ahk*-sent,' instead of '*axe*-sent.'"

"Did I? I guess I'm sort of a chameleon. They better send me home before I start putting my fork in the wrong hand. Anyway, the present deal is, I have a few weeks off and I'd never seen the Riviera, so I drove down from a trade fair at Nuremberg. I was heading for St. Tropez today, but I took a wrong turn, wound up here, and liked it. I like it even better now. I rented a room up on the hill. Hotel California, like the old Eagles song. Pretty nice."

She hesitated, but only a moment. "We're neighbors. I'm just below you. L'Auberge de la Calanque."

"Sounds sexy, the way you say it."

Yes, she'd meant it to. She wondered at herself, at the no-brakes speed with which she was allowing this to proceed. Did her boldness have something to do with Taras's not calling her? Or with the fact that this sleek, plausible fellow across the little table posed no emotional risk, and most definitely didn't fall into the category of potential mate? Whatever did or didn't happen between them, Charlotte knew, Jack Sanderson was a man who, in her old collegiate lingo, liked his space and would be moving on. But here and now he was looking awfully like dessert.

He reached over to shoo a noisy bottle fly, exposing a puckered ridge of scar across his right biceps.

"What's that?" She pointed. "Have you been knife-fighting in your spare time?"

"Nothing romantic. A .22 long rifle bullet did it. Fired by my cousin Donny when I was ten. He was demonstrating proper firearm safety procedures. Sorry to disappoint you. You thought maybe I was a hired assassin?"

"A girl keeps hoping." She laughed, and thought, *Mister, you don't know how glad I am you're not an assassin. I've already had one.*

Chapter

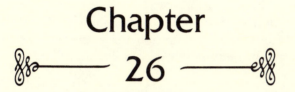

26

It was extraordinary that it had been Charlotte Walsh's column on Potsdam, which Marcus had read in Lugano back in April, that had first alerted him to the possibility of his current assignment. For Marcus had been aware for some time, from GRU contacts in America, that Ms. Walsh and Taras Arensky were "great and good friends." Marcus had, therefore, made a point of checking out the newswoman on several occasions when she had appeared on CNN's European feed.

His assessment of her had been favorable. Though by no means a classic beauty, she was definitely striking—dark-haired and stylish, with good cheekbones and brown eyes that flashed with intelligence and humor—and hinted strongly at sensuality. In fact, Marcus had been amused to see how closely she approximated one of his favorite types. Amused, because it seemed that again, as in the case of Eva Sorokina, he and Taras seemed to share a taste in females—an older woman this time, but equally appetizing.

And Charlotte Walsh was destined to play an even more crucial role in their lives than had poor Eva . . . if all went according to Marcus's plan.

After ascertaining Charlotte's whereabouts from her foreign editor, Marcus had cleaned out one of his safety accounts and assumed his final documented identity, an American mail-order sales representative, Jack Sanderson. He had flown to Marseille, rented a car, driven to Le Lavandou, verified again that she was still in residence at the three-star l'Auberge de la Calanque, then checked into the more modest hotel immediately above. In fact, his window overlooked the auberge's brick-arched Moorish entranceway.

Still, he'd nearly missed her the following morning. She must have exited on the opposite side, through a private garden of cypresses and second-growth plane trees. He'd been damn lucky to catch a glimpse of her on the pathway below, just as she turned onto a private staircase leading down to the marina and the beach.

He'd followed quickly, but loitered discreetly behind, frankly enjoying the rear view as she strode along, her bell of dark hair swinging metronomically. She was all in white—oversize T-shirt, jogging shorts and shoes. But the shorts were snug with side slits, showcasing long, shapely legs. Presently she ducked into a *boulangerie,* came out dispatching a croissant and licking her fingers. She was considerably taller than he'd imagined, perhaps only an inch or so shorter than he. Marcus found that provocative.

As she emerged onto the bright blue bayfront, she harnessed into her little tote bag like a backpack and set off on a beachside jog. Marcus admired her retreating figure a moment, then sat down on the low cement wall dividing the sidewalk from the sand, unfolding the newspaper he'd gotten at his hotel, a *Var Matin*.

Fifteen minutes later he picked up the peripheral swing of her hair, turned to watch her coming back to him, slowing to a walk, hands on hips, her chest rising and falling under the sweat-soaked T-shirt. Fifty meters away she veered off to stake her spot on the rapidly filling beach. Once settled, she stripped down to a black bikini—an extremely daring one, Marcus thought, for a woman nearly out of her thirties, as he assumed Charlotte to be. Would she eventually drop her top as well? He thought not, but was happily prepared to be proven wrong.

As she made her way down to the glassy bay, he further amused himself by wondering if she was going for a quick dip or a real swim. Marcus chose the latter and won his bet. She went breaststroking straight out until she had to pull up to avoid a little sloop exiting the marina on a port tack. She floated out there beside the breakwater several minutes before heading back. As she came dripping out of the sea with coltish strides, her dark wet hair sleeked back, Marcus felt the double barbs of desire and jealousy. He wanted this woman, wanted her to give herself to him exactly as she had to his rival.

But he decided against making any moves while she was on the beach. That would be too obvious. So he'd stayed put, stalking at a distance, though ready to intervene quickly if any local stud should plant himself beside her towel or exchange more than a *bonjour*. Marcus was prepared for a long vigil when, an hour later, Charlotte had packed up her things, covered up, and headed across the boulevard to the little book-and-card shop—an ideal location for them to meet, as things had turned out.

All along, Marcus had felt reasonably confident of his chances with the attractive woman journalist. But he hadn't been prepared for the directness of her response. It was there in her eyes, her voice, and body language. Suddenly it was as if his quarry were stalking him. And when, after only the briefest of exchanges, Charlotte had offered to escort him to another bookstore, he had the distinct feeling he had just been picked up.

Inwardly it had given him a chuckle. It wasn't, after all, an inopportune turn of events. In fact, his plan would work even better this way. Let the elegant lady reel him in at her own pace. All Marcus had to do was wait for his cues and brush up his rusty American accent. Certainly, after the first ten or fifteen minutes, he had little doubt that they were going to wind up in bed.

It turned out to be hers.

Charlie lay back against her headboard, sipping champagne. The door and curtains to the terrace were open, letting in an evening breeze and framing the solitary jewel of Venus suspended in a blue-velvet rectangle. But if she stretched her neck just a little, she could see the string of pearl lights of Port de Bormes-les Mimosas across the dark bay. But in order to see the tricolor dazzle of the Lavandou marina directly below her terrace, she would have to stir herself from her bed, and she was far too contented to do that.

Besides, she'd also have to shift the muscularly defined right arm that was draped across her left thigh, and she liked it just where it was, thank you. She didn't want to waken Jack from deep sleep—that blissful state from which she herself had only just emerged, and to which she intended very shortly to return. But for now she was enjoying surveying his subdued nakedness—this exciting beast she had lured back to her pastel cave—and listening to his slow, sibilant breathing, like a faint echo of the whispering Mediterranean beyond the terrace.

Their mating dance had proceeded with a languorous inevitability. After the wine they'd spent another hour or so on the beach, reading and chatting. Then they'd browsed their way back to the same *brasserie,* where they'd had an early and light supper of *salade niçoise,* pâté and cheese, watching through the shadowed palms as the beach thinned out and the afternoon tour boats returned from the Iles d'Hyères.

Afterward, since their hotels lay in the same easterly direction, they were able to prolong the delicious charade, setting out together, still not touching, yet both knowing their destination was shared. They'd stopped twice along the way, once to watch some teenagers playing *boule* under the plane trees across from the main beach, and again for Charlotte to buy a cold magnum of Veuve Clicquot, without so much as a word as to its purpose.

The first tactile intimacy had come at the foot of the *escalier privé* to the auberge. Charlotte, a step ahead, had paused. Obviously, this was not the way to the Hotel California; the sign said in simple French "for the usage of the Calanque" guests only. She'd half turned, offering Jack her hand. As he'd taken it, their eyes had raked briefly, with unmistakable import. She'd squeezed his hand a moment, then let it go, preceding him up the first few steps, the champagne bottle dangling from her other hand, her clenching and unclenching hips ascending at the level of his gaze.

He followed her on through the graveled garden of the auberge, then up a curving wrought-iron staircase past hanging bougainvillea, into the cool lobby, where she gathered her key, down a softly illumined corridor, and finally into her room.

They'd popped the cork and toasted wordlessly on the terrace, sipping, watching the lights come on all over the waterfront, hearing a drunken argument down in the marina, the isolated spiel of a dockside carnival barker, intermittent motorized flatulence from the street below.

Until the tension became unbearable.

Still he had sat there, as his rugged silhouette darkened and grew more defined against the sunset. Could this devastating guy, Charlotte wondered, be timid, pathologically shy? She resolved to make the first move.

Her voice carried a soft urgency in the evening air. "I'm going to take a shower, Jack. Wash all the sand off." Pause. "You're welcome to join me."

He'd turned his champagne flute, nodded slowly. "I'll be there. Go ahead."

She'd gone, peeling off her sticky things, turning the needling spray as hot as she could bear, luxuriating in the steamy barrage, all the while aware of her heart pounding. Several times she turned to peer through the steam and the curtain's translucence for a dark man-shape by the open bathroom door. *Get in here, you bastard,* she thought. *And right now!*

Suddenly the curtain was yanked aside and he was beside her, growing quickly and delightfully hard against her. She shuddered as she felt his lips nuzzling the back of her neck, his tongue lapping droplets of water. Then he turned her gently around, his eyes taking her in, his palms cradling her breasts as they finally pressed full-length together and kissed deeply. After so much anticipation, Charlie nearly passed out. And then she did slip, her foot skidding on the porcelain so that he had to catch her, then steady them both. They found themselves suddenly eyeball to eyeball and nose to nose, both giggling as water streamed between.

"What a way to die!" he said.

"I promise to do better next time. Kiss me again, Jack, and I'll show you."

He leaned in, then broke out laughing.

"What's so damn funny?"

"I was just thinking that this beats the hell out of reading Harold Robbins."

Now sipping her champagne, Charlotte recollected the implosive coupling that had followed that first kiss. They had climaxed together under the roaring shower, and again she had nearly lost her balance. Thinking about it now dizzied her with desire. Well, why not? That's what he was here for, wasn't it? She reached under his prone form, found and fondled his limpness until it responded of its own accord, even before his breathing quickened and his blue eyes opened with sly comprehension.

225

"Shh," she said, "you just keep sleeping. Don't mind me. I just wanted something to hold on to."

But he had rolled over, availing himself totally. So she slid deftly over and onto him, kneeling astride with a certain air of ownership. She began slowly, posting atop the saddle of his hips like the blue ribbon equestrienne she had been in her youth. Then gradually she increased the gait, putting them both through their paces till they had reached a full hell-for-leather gallop.

The first time with Charlotte, Marcus had felt little beyond vast glandular relief. But the second time he'd been flooded with contrary emotions, tasting both sweet vengeance and bitter betrayal. Taras, of course, was the object of both of these.

Odd, that this second coupling with his friend's sweetheart should somehow signify the breaking of the final bond of friendship.

Odd, considering he'd raped and strangled Taras's first fiancée. Of course, that had been in another country, many years before. And—ultimate irony—it had been the making, not the unmaking, of their friendship.

But only moments before—as Marcus had stared up at Charlotte hovering astride him, sheened in perspiration, eyes shut in communion with private lusts, launching herself again and again in pelvic shifts too wrenching for him actually to enjoy—he'd had an icy vision of that distant night with Eva.

How she had writhed beneath him like a terrified rabbit, as though she could shed her skin or flee her own pinioned body. But he was far too powerful. Marcus had seen that awful realization fill her gray eyes. It was almost the same moment he had realized that he had unleashed something within himself that he could no longer stop. It wasn't just the White Dynamite, though certainly he was drunk out of his mind. But there was another, stronger intoxication—a sense of sudden bestial power over this helpless she-creature, and the need to give that dominance primal expression.

Bringing his right knee up to pin her left arm, he had freed his hand to clamp her mouth and stifle her screams. Surely then Eva had glimpsed her fate, that he dare not let her live? She would have denounced him, he'd have been arrested, probably to spend years in a Russian prison. But Marcus had never killed a girl. Could he do it? He let his mind flood with a violent, seductive vision. He saw their eyes locking in the final, obscene intimacy of victim and predator, as both his hands crushed her tender neck.

Alas, the reality of her dying had been something less than the vision. To stop her screaming, he had already been forced to crush her windpipe. The horror in her eyes was already fading as he released his grip to tear at her sweater, frantic to have her naked and to penetrate her before she escaped him. Finally, frustrated by her layered clothing, he reached under her dress, yanked and ripped her underpants down. Then, in his panic, he had ejaculated almost at once.

Eva chose that moment to come back for a fleeting instant, as he was still in his final spasms. Her gray eyes, now horribly bloodshot, focused on him in puzzled anguish. *You've killed me,* her eyes seemed to say. *But why?*

Then she was gone.

Later he had stripped her, launching his desperate plan to kill Kostya and blame Eva's murder on him. By then her naked body meant nothing. Or if it did, Marcus had no time to think about it. Certainly he dare not feel cheated of his intimate moment. If Eva had died too quickly, nevertheless he had done what he wanted. So it could not be shame that he felt, staring down at the violated corpse at his feet, but unholy power. He had claimed that power now as his own, and it would never leave him.

The conjured face of Eva was replaced by Charlotte, whose increasingly abandoned struggles were not to escape Marcus, but to subdue him, make maximum use of him as a conveyance to her own completion. Marcus didn't mind being used in this way. He let his thoughts wander, deliberately holding off his own pleasure, till she finally shattered atop him and collapsed in diminuendos of delight.

Then he rolled them both over. As he began to thrust into her, she opened her eyes, but they were glazed and didn't focus properly. Which was fine; indeed, it was perfect. All Charlotte had to do was yield, lie there passively while he pounded her into a semblance of female putty. She might or might not like it, but she would feel it all day tomorrow, long after the residual glow of her self-inflicted orgasm.

On the fourth day of Jack Sanderson, Charlotte felt drugged. She had ignored several callback messages from John Tully. And it was getting so she didn't even glance at the daunting pile of reading matter she had brought along, including the latest issue of *Foreign Affairs,* entirely given over to advance analysis of the Potsdam Conference. Anyway, she could fake all that stuff when the time came. It would take her maybe an hour of prep to get current.

She had simply pushed as many things as possible off till the following week, as Jack had apparently abandoned his own plans to tour the Côte d'Azur east to Monaco. They hadn't discussed this, just done it—the same way he'd moved his big suitcase and carryall out of the Hotel California the second day and in with her. They couldn't stand being apart, what could be more obvious? And when they were apart—which probably hadn't amounted to more than a few hours in four days—Charlie's nerve endings still tingled with him, so that she felt constantly tethered to his body.

It was a little scary. She'd never experienced anything quite like it. Not even way back, during her wild sophomore summer in the Caribbean. And as devoted and energetic a lover as Taras had been, their early days together had been quite different. There had been so many other facets to their twoness. The long walks and endless conversation. Restaurants and movies. Sharing and comparing childhood memories. There'd been precious little of that with Jack. He didn't seem to have a large fund of conversation. If Charlotte had wanted a vacation from her mind, she was damn well getting it. He was more of, well, a blunt instrument, and a relentless one.

And they were insatiable. They'd done almost no sight-seeing. They hadn't visited Bormes, the offshore islands, or even the lovely neighboring coves of La Fossette. They ate, slept, and made love. No, that wasn't right. You couldn't call it love. They ate, slept, and fucked. Watched French-dubbed *Hawaii Five-O* reruns on TV. When they got tired of the pastel walls and ordering in, they'd venture out briefly, prowl a few shops, lie in the sun. He bought her a lavender sachet, a Lavandou trademark. They'd posed for a cartoon portrait on the beachfront and bought two color Xerox copies of it, one of which was taped to the dresser mirror. It showed them with huge heads, decent likenesses, and tiny cartoon bodies riding twin surfboards and holding hands. It should have shown them fastened in sexual combat, Charlie thought.

So how did she get over this? How should she go about purging the X-rated images from her mind and getting on with her life? Thank God, there was no emotional attachment. But the physical side had become addictive, and she knew it. She recognized the flaccid overtones of the unregenerate addict in her latest rationalization: *You're just not ready to give him up. Why not give it a few more days, and really get him out of your system?*

She waited till her last scheduled night at the auberge to decide. They were on the terrace, watching the sheen and shimmer of the marina lights on the water. The next day she was supposed to take the bus back to Toulon, the TGV to Paris, Air France to Berlin. She had a room reserved at the Kempinski. Jack had been trying all day to talk her into putting off her departure, since the conference didn't actually start for four more days. Charlotte had pretended to be adamant, but she was weakening, and they both knew it.

"Well?" he had said. "What's the verdict?"

"How can a girl make up her mind when she's being endlessly fondled?"

"All right. Look, no hands."

Charlie snorted. She wore only a cotton knit tank top, Jack was nude, and she was sitting on his lap facing him, with him deep inside her. They were being discreet about it, since there was a couple dining on an adjoining terrace, the candlelight flickering through the pebbled glass partition.

She whispered in his ear. "Hmm. Jack, I just had a thought."

"You keep doing that."

"Why don't you come with me?"

"I've been trying. Sometimes it works, sometimes it doesn't. That's why we have to keep practicing."

"Be serious. You know what I'm talking about. Come with me to Berlin."

"To the conference?"

"Just for the first few days. I have to check in and get credentialed, and so on. But I won't have to really start hustling till the main event on Friday."

"Well, what would I do there while you're out getting 'credentialed'?"

"You'd wait for me. Tied to the bedframe, maybe. Jesus, I don't know, we'll find something for your, um, peculiar talents. As often as I can get free. What do you think?"

"Well, what am I supposed to say? Hell yes, it sounds fine."

"But you have to understand, Jack, seriously, it would only be three more days at the most. When the real media circus starts, yours truly will be running her little ass ragged, and won't have any time for fun and games."

"Hey, I won't make trouble. Jack Sanderson takes what he can get on this deal, and not an hour more. Three days, and I'm history. However, I have a proposition of my own to make."

"Which is?"

"That we stop jiggling around out here wasting precious time, and get into some heavy action."

"I kind of like this, if you want to know the truth."

"But my ass is getting cold."

She sighed. "All right, if you must. Take me inside then, and have your way with me."

He rose carefully up from the chair, still wearing her. She was a big girl, but he managed to breathe normally as he carried her inside to the bed and toppled slowly sideways, holding her close and twisting so they landed on the mattress side by side, still locked together.

Then the telephone rang.

Chapter

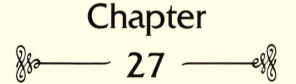

27

"CHARLIE?"

"Yes?"

"It's Taras."

"Taras, where are you? Are you all right?"

"I'm fine, Charlie. No. Actually I'm miserable. I want to come back to you. More than I've ever wanted anything in my life. You were right . . . about everything. . . ."

"Taras, listen, where are you calling from?"

"Did you hear what I just said?"

"Of course I did. Taras, I'm sorry, but you'll have to forgive me if I sound a little . . . confused." Jack was now on top of her, grinning playfully and refusing to disengage. Ignoring her gestured protests, he began to caress her breasts. "You disappear without telling me where, now you call me out of the blue telling me you want to come back, and I still don't know where you are."

"I'm in Washington. At the Holiday Inn on Connecticut Avenue."

"Oh."

"I'm quitting the Agency. I told John Tully to give you the message. Did you get it?"

"I've been away a couple days . . . visiting friends in St. Tropez. I got the slips that he called, but I haven't had the chance to get back to him. Did he give you my number?"

"After I threatened to burn down his building. Or maybe he finally took pity on me. Charlie, I've got to talk to you."

"And I want to talk to you, Taras. But right now I can't."

"Didn't you hear what I'm saying? Doesn't it mean anything to you?"

"Of course it does. But you can't expect me—"

"It's not too late, Charlie. We have the rest of our lives. There's still time for everything. Charlie? Are you alone? Is there somebody else?"

Jack had wrestled them sideways together, palming her ass cheeks as he moved slowly and rhythmically inside her. His mouth slid down to her right nipple. Christ, what if Taras heard the sucking sound! She tried to fend Jack off, but he wouldn't budge.

"No. I mean, yes, of course I'm alone, and no, there's nobody else. How could there be? It's a working vacation . . . I'm . . . I'm surrounded by books and magazines and newspapers in three languages, one of which I can't understand. I've got mountains of dull homework to get ready for Potsdam. . . . Which is why I just don't have time to get into all this with you now, Taras. When the conference wraps in a couple weeks, I'll be making a quick visit to Paris and London, then I'll be back, and we can—"

"You're talking about three weeks! Listen to me, please. I want to fly over there now, wherever you're going to be, and . . . we can talk. Have dinner. That's all. One evening is all I'm asking."

"I don't have one evening." Jack's grinning face popped back up, hovering over hers, his ice-blue eyes mocking. Then, still massaging her breasts, he began to lick her face like a cat—her chin, her cheek, the ear opposite the phone. "Taras . . . I want to see you . . . but this week and next are crazy . . . and the week after is worse. There's the usual nonsense . . . official receptions . . . dinners . . . editorial meetings, briefings . . . maybe a couple of TV guest shots, if it works out. You know how it gets . . . Taras?"

"Yes."

"I didn't walk out on you. You walked out on me, after I begged you to stay, because of your damn cloak-and-dagger games. I'm glad you've changed your mind, but . . . I . . . I just can't drop everything I'm doing and ignore my career . . . you understand?"

"I know, it's not fair."

"It's not!"

"Charlie, John Tully told me you may be leaving Le Lavandou tomorrow. That's why I had to call, even though I knew it wouldn't work over the phone. I'm getting bananas, Charlie—"

"*Going* bananas. You can *go* crazy or *get* crazy, but you only *go* bananas."

"You see, not only is my heart breaking, my idioms are going to shit without you—"

"*Going* to hell, you mean, or *full* of shit. Not—"

"I know, I did that on purpose. To hear you laugh. Please, Charlie, if you don't want me to jump on the next plane, please give me a phone number in Berlin, so I can at least reach you. Don't cut me off."

Jack, obviously gauging her mind's weakening resistance and her body's unmistakably growing response to his erotic offensive, had begun to accelerate his thrusting. Charlotte found herself straining to keep her breathing under control, her voice unaffected. She was desperate to get Taras off the phone. And even if she could, she no longer wanted to stop Jack. Incredibly, in spite of her stubborn resolve and mild outrage at his chauvinistic conduct, she was shuddering rapidly toward what felt like being a major seismic event.

"Look, Taras, please! I have to think about this. Give me a day or two. And let's leave it that I call you, okay?"

"Charlie, you know I love you."

"I believe you, Tarushka. And I'm glad you called. But . . . but . . . I'll call you. Take care. Bye." She replaced the phone quietly, then cursed the grinning face above her: "You bastard!"

They were the last coherent sounds she made for the next several minutes, though her abandoned cries continued to fill the little room.

Later, when she was able to speak and moderate her thoughts and feelings, she took a more restrained tone:

"That wasn't very nice, Jack."

"I thought it was fantastic."

"You know what I'm talking about. I asked you to stop, and you didn't. At the least, you owe me an apology. If it happens again, I'll ask you to leave."

"Okay, I'm sorry."

"Taras is an old friend. I had to take the call."

"So I gathered. Maybe I was jealous."

"Well, you don't—" she stopped herself from saying "need to be." She didn't need to say that; besides, she didn't know if it was true. She lightened her tone instead: "It was an embarrassing situation all around. I don't exactly know what the etiquette is, Jack, but it sure as hell wasn't what you were doing. It's damned difficult to carry on a coherent phone conversation when your brains are being turned to jelly."

The truth was, Charlotte wanted badly to call Taras back now, to reassure him, even agree to meet with him. But she dare not—not now, not with Jack Sanderson so prominently in the picture for the next several days. If having Taras on the phone and Jack in her bed just now had been awkward, imagine if Taras had been right outside, pounding on the door!

Suddenly she realized it would be impossible for her to take Jack with her to Berlin as she had agreed. For how could she keep Taras away? He'd pry the name of her hotel out of John Tully, just as he had the number of the auberge. Taras was a hotblooded Cossack, capable of anything, especially now, especially with that desperate edge in his voice.

What should she do? Bring Jack with her and thereby jeopardize any future with Taras? Or the obvious and rational course: Say good-bye to Jack tomorrow morning, go on to Berlin alone, immerse herself in work—and, if need be, cold showers? As she began to weigh these alternatives in the darkness, Jack's fingers announced his wakefulness upon her flank, then circled down to slowly trace the satin slopes of her inner thighs. She quite lost her train of thought, and when at some length she recovered it, she found the debate had been resolved in her mind's absence. She damn well wasn't ready to give him up.

For Marcus, the phone call had been an exquisite miniature of revenge—actually to hear the diminished and entreating voice of his rival in the earpiece, while Marcus was in the very act of possessing her. And nearly—oh, so nearly—forcing her to climax while she was still denying Taras's pleas! Come what might in the protracted duel between them, the Cossack would never be able to equal this. Twice now Marcus had brought it off, appropriating Taras's lovers for his own. And this time Marcus had done it with the breathless consent of the lady in question.

A thoroughly delicious encounter, that phone call, one he would savor again and again. And, he suspected, a disturbing one for the Cossack on the other end of the transatlantic connection. For Charlotte had sounded a surprisingly maladroit liar, certainly not up to the level of dissembling Marcus had expected from an experienced reporter and woman of the world. But, of course, she had been slightly distracted.

What must the Cossack be thinking now? And what would he think when the next little phase of Marcus's plan unfolded?

Taras had indeed sensed something peculiar in Charlie's reaction. Had she exploded in bitterness or feigned cold indifference, he would have understood and yet tried to plead his case. He had been prepared as well for righteous eloquence, or simply to have her hang up on him. He had even imagined, in a forgivable transport of euphoria, how her voice would sound delivering a tearful come-back-all-is-for-given speech.

But he had heard none of these. Instead, Charlotte had sounded hesitant, confused, uncertain—all emotions uncharacteristic of her. And in this odd metamorphosis Taras had felt the shadowy presence of a rival.

Certainly he couldn't sit by the phone, waiting "a day or two" for her to think it over and then to call him back. He could not endure it; he must act. If there was another man, Taras's pride demanded to know it as soon as possible and to force Charlie to choose between them. Perhaps, as he prayed, there was no one else. Then whatever the source of Charlie's uncertainty toward him, Taras would better be able to overcome it in person and, as his own ambassador, to convince her of his sincerity.

And he was still packed.

Two hours later, at six P.M., he was strapped into an Air France 747 nonstop from Dulles to De Gaulle. He dozed on and off over the Atlantic, through an exhaustive article about the leisure pursuits of Fortune 500 CEOs and a movie with no discernible plot but in which an astonishing number of police cars were crumpled. He was awakened from a final siege of pressurized stupor by the lilting French of a passing stewardess: *"Rebouclez vos ceintures, s'il vous plaît."* They were landing; it was 7:30 in the morning, Paris time.

By nine, after an airport croissant and coffee, he was strapped into another seat, a 737 this time, droning south by southeast toward the Mediterranean. An hour and a half later the city of Nice was rushing below the wing in a blur of red rooftops, followed by the long seaside runways of the Aeroport Nice-Côte d'Azur. With just a carryall, Taras managed to grab a taxi and reach the Gare Centrale by 10:45, but was dismayed to find he'd have to wait till noon for the next train to St. Raphaël or Toulon, from either of which he could rent a car and drive to Le Lavandou. Taras strode back and forth along the trackside, cursing himself. To hell with the cost, he should have tried to charter a small plane from the airport direct to Le Lavandou, or as close as he could get.

Instead, he pulled into Le Lavandou in a rental Ford Fiesta at two in the afternoon, then wasted fifteen priceless minutes driving in scenic circles before locating the Auberge de la Calanque terraced on a steep hillside overlooking the marina. A minute later he was standing in the cool, comfortable reception hall and being politely informed that Mademoiselle Walsh had just checked out.

How long, exactly? Might she still be in the area, on the beach, in a local restaurant, perhaps even in the hotel dining room?

The charming young thing behind the desk was certain mademoiselle was not in the hotel; beyond this she wouldn't venture a guess. When, now quite desperate, Taras produced his Agency credentials and voiced veiled concerns for Mademoiselle Walsh's safety, the girl located the manager. This dapper young man listened to Taras with a sympathetic gaze and slight inclinations of his head, then went off to make inquiries of his own. He returned ten minutes later with the information that Mademoiselle Walsh had departed around midday in the company of a young man with an American accent, in a small rental car that was not listed on her registration. The auberge had no record of her destination.

Would it be possible for Taras to see her room?

It would. A moment later he was ushered into a long, cool room with eggshell walls, teal blue carpet, streamlined white furnishings. The maid had already tidied up. Taras walked through, his pulse reacting predictably as he pictured Charlie lounging on the queen-size bed, holding that bedside phone to her cheek as she talked to him last night. What had she said? "You'll have to forgive me if I sound a little confused." But why confused?

Taras moved past the bed, opened the double glass terrace doors, and stepped into the panoramic dazzle of marina, bright bay, and encircling hills. The little balcony was a skillet now at two-thirty, but would be an idyllic spot for breakfast, an aperitif at sunset, or champagne under the stars.

Oh God, I hope she was alone here! But then, who the hell was this young American? Some journalist of her acquaintance, dropping by to give her a lift back to Toulon or Marseille? Taras couldn't bear to imagine otherwise, to visualize her in this romantic hideaway with any man but himself.

He went back inside, glanced briefly into the wardrobe and the tiled bathroom.

"*Ça suffit, monsieur?*"

"Yes, thank you. I appreciate your cooperation."

There was obviously nothing further to be found, lacking as he did either Sherlockian powers of observation or a portable crime lab. And Taras had sufficiently overstepped bounds, invoking professional credentials on behalf of personal jealousy.

The manager led him back down a narrow corridor. Halfway along, as Taras was squeezing by a maid's cart poking out of an open door, something caught his eye. He backed up a step, snatched a paper out of a plastic trash basket hooked to the cart. It was a colored drawing. Taras stared at it in horror.

"You have found something, *monsieur?*"

"Yes, I have. A picture of the man she was with."

There were two large cartoon faces on the drawing. One was Charlie. The other was Marcus Jolly. The artist had captured both of them with minimal exaggeration. Beneath their smiling faces he had drawn miniature cartoon bodies—in bathing suits, holding hands and riding surfboards.

Darkness descended on Taras's mind. A black screen on which he saw from floor level across a room the dead body of Eva Sorokina, ghastly white in the sepulchral light of a Siberian winter morning. Only it was no longer Eva's nightmare-empty face turned toward his eyes, but Charlie's.

Standing in that hushed corridor, he heard an anguished scream echoing from a dozen years earlier. Eva's screams—before the monster strangled her—surely Taras must have heard them that night echoing down the dark corridors of his alcoholic stupor. Because sometimes, like now, he thought he heard them echoing still.

It wasn't over. The Cowboy had come again to kill his girl.

What do you want with her, you bastard! Let her go! I'll kill you if you touch her, you know I will! But not only would Marcus know that, Taras realized, he would count on it. Hadn't he hinted, in his letter to Taras, of "one more enticement" to make Taras come after him again? Taras stared down at the picture of the two of them together, knew with terrible certainty that Charlie was that enticement and that Marcus was going to kill her.

The manager had returned, his elegant face only slightly marred with concern. "*Monsieur*, shall I call a doctor?"

Taras brought his eyes into focus, stilled the trembling paper in his hand. "I'm fine. This signature on the cartoon, a local artist?"

"Yes, Etienne. His studio is right along the beach, the Boulevard de Lattre de Tassigny. Between a *glacier*—you understand, ice cream?—and a *boîte à couture,* what I think you call a haberdashery."

Taras parked the Fiesta on a side street, two wheels up on the sidewalk like everybody else, then sprinted around a corner to the artist's closet-size studio.

The damn place was shuttered. Taras stared in the window. A hand-lettered sign advertised PORTRAITS, FROM 150 FR. PASTEL, BLACK & WHITE. There were samples taped all over the glass. Another sign in the door said Etienne would be back at two. But it was a quarter to three and the lazy bastard was still out to lunch.

Taras swore, stepped back, nearly lost his balance, and swore again as his shoe skidded in dog shit. Behind him someone giggled. Taras whirled angrily and a fat kid in a bathing suit backed away, licking an ice cream cone. Taras scraped his shoe on the low cement curb and felt despair sapping even his rage.

What the hell was he doing here, surrounded by somnolent, sun-blasted holidaymakers and blinding Kodachrome vistas? He was killing time—and perhaps killing Charlie—when he should be alerting the world and rushing off to Berlin. What did it matter what the sketch artist said about them? But Taras wanted to know. He hurried across the street to a *brasserie* telephone, deciding to call John Tully in Washington while he waited another few minutes for Etienne to show up.

But the fucking French phone wouldn't work. The barman gestured at him violently, then a nearby patron explained the telephone swallowed only *jetons*—tokens. Taras spilled out some change to buy some, when out of the corner of his eye he noticed a bent-over man in walking shorts poking a key into the portrait shop door.

Before Etienne had pocketed the key, Taras was beside him displaying the drawing.

"Yes, yes, of course I remember them. I have captured their essence."

"What were they like together?"

"Very much in love. Exactly as I show them here."

"But—but I found this in the trash. One of them threw it away. If they had been lovers—"

"That is only a color Xerox. They make around the corner. They bought several, I think. Perhaps this one was damaged. I am sure they have kept the original. She is older, but was like a very young girl with him. You know her?"

"Yes."

Etienne peered more closely at Taras, blinking rapidly as if from a nervous tic. "But I perceive, *monsieur*, that what I have said causes you great distress. I regret it."

Taras finally reached Tully from the PTT on Avenue de Gaulle. It was ten in the morning in Washington. "John, Charlie's in terrible danger." Taras gave the briefest explanation, promising to call back with more as quickly as possible. "Where is she going? You've got to tell me."

"Hold on, Taras." Tully was back in a few seconds. "Taras, who are you calling next?"

"The CIA."

"Christ! Okay, but get back to me damn fast. Where the hell are you?"

"In a *Postes* and *Télécommunications* in Le Lavandou. You can't reach me. I'll call you."

"You damn well better. You're giving me a fucking heart attack here. If there's anything we can do—"

"I promise, John. Give it to me."

"Charlie's due at the Kempinski tonight. It's right on the Ku-damm, in Berlin."

"I know it. Thanks. I'll call you right back."

When it took several maddening minutes for the PTT to place a simple call to Langley, which then got disconnected, Taras bolted out of the booth, drove back up the street to the auberge, buttonholed the manager, and exchanged a credit card for an hour in an empty room with a phone. He got through to the Agency's deputy director at once, spoke for twenty hectic minutes, then dialed John Tully back at the newspaper.

A half hour later Taras was squinting into the afternoon sun as he drove west on motorway A-50 to Marseille, racing to catch a direct flight to Berlin. His panic hadn't abated, his right foot squeezing every millimeter of speed out of the little Fiesta; but he had at least the comfort of knowing a contingent of CIA and plainclothes German federal police was en route to the Kempinski, ready to swoop down and save Charlotte, then take out Marcus.

Taras prayed they would show up.

He called the Kempinski from Marseille, again from the air, and finally from Berlin, only moments after his plane landed at the Tegel Airport.

His Agency contact prepared him for extremely bad news. Lufthansa had just confirmed that Charlotte had arrived in Berlin on a flight from Paris and had rented an Opel Omega at the airport, giving the Kempinski as her local address.

"So what's wrong?" Taras cut in.

"Unfortunately a few minutes ago a man with an American accent called the hotel to cancel Fräulein Walsh's reservation."

Chapter

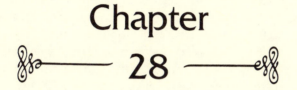 28

MARCUS DROVE THE LUXURIOUS OPEL SOUTH FROM BERLIN, PAST the dismantled Checkpoint Bravo at Kontrollpunkt Drewitz and onto the E6 Autobahn toward Leipzig and Nuremberg. Charlotte, close beside him in darkness pulsing with a Mozart divertimento, gestured ahead at the lighted sign for the Babelsberg-Potsdam turnoff.

"I see it," Marcus said.

"*Ciao,* Potsdam," she laughed as they flashed past. "I'll be back."

No, you won't, Marcus thought.

There would be, alas, one less scribe to chronicle the historic conclave four days hence, when the U.S. and Soviet leaders joined those of the major European countries a few kilometers off to their right, beyond the dark precincts of Babelsberg and the Potsdam woods, in the Cecilienhof Palace. In the meantime, at Charlotte's suggestion, she and Marcus were heading south, fleeing both duty and detection, sixty kilometers down the Autobahn to Coswig, where they would turn east onto a smaller road a few kilometers to Wittenberg. There Charlie had reserved a modest hotel room for them—under the name of Mr. and Mrs. Jack Sanderson.

An interesting charade, Marcus thought, and, again, mainly of Charlie's devising. Could he imagine such a union? No, he could not. Charlotte was attractive, amusing, and erotically imaginative. Their time together had not palled, as was so often the case when Marcus found himself in the uninterrupted company of a woman, no matter how lovely, beyond a day or so. Once the conquest was made, it was Marcus's experience, each frenzied repetition or coital variation counted for less, until he was merely going through the motions, while his eye wandered to fresh conquests. Worst of all were the tedious hours between sex, enduring all the ceaseless feminine prattle with its inevitable and pathetic romantic overtones.

But Marcus had not wearied of Charlotte. Thus far she had contrived to keep them both in a protracted state of light amusement and co-incidentally recurring horniness; and, of course, all this only further sweetened Marcus's ongoing triumph over his rival. His worry with Charlotte was rather the other way around—that she might tire too quickly of him.

To prevent this, he had exerted himself in several ways. Her sexual appetite must be gratified, yet constantly stimulated, so that he didn't cure the addiction he had created. His intellectual shortcomings—as compared to her sparkling erudition—must be minimized, concealed by his best insouciant manner and baritone chuckle. And never for an instant must she glimpse him without his mask of masculine charm.

He played upon her carefully, dismissing his own fictitious life with an occasional deprecatory anecdote, while plying her with questions about the political celebrities she had interviewed, the vagaries of her journalistic career, and the latest Washington party gossip. Charlie was a wonderful raconteur, and Marcus had little trouble maintaining a fascinated gaze and responding with loud and frequent laughter. In so doing, he saw in her eyes her reciprocal delight at the conquest she had made of him. So far, at least, his own general reticence hadn't seemed to bother her, beyond an occasional comment.

There were other ways in which Marcus had catered to Charlotte. He surfeited her with compliments, sometimes offhand, sometimes thoughtful, never formulaic. At times he had even flirted with servility, running her bathwater, enquiring about her favorite scent, the details of her toilette, makeup, and wardrobe, until she began to give him queer looks and accuse him of having quite lost his mind.

"Perhaps so," he had responded once. "But since I am obviously fascinated by your nakedness, and by you fully clothed and coifed . . . well then . . ."

"Well then, what?"

"Why not be fascinated by the magical transition from one state to the other?"

Marcus had his private reason for these intimate questions, and, having so thoroughly established his masculine credentials, he dared to pursue them, convinced they could only further endear himself to her.

He intended to continue this amorous performance for at least three more days until the opening ceremonies at Potsdam. Even under ideal conditions, Marcus thought, their affair could not last much longer than that. Even if his fascination somehow endured, Charlie would begin to tire of him and seek her freedom. But it would not have to come to that. Three days would do it.

Marcus felt now a sudden and unexpected pang, glancing over at her determined profile in the subdued glow of the dashboard lights, and knowing the unfortunate fate that awaited her at his hands. Charlotte had given him a great deal of pleasure, and, in many ways, he had come to cherish the creature.

Getting rid of her, however, if not an enjoyable task, would be an astringent and appropriate one for launching his new freelance career. For sentimentality or personal preference must play no part in the acceptability of his future victims. That was what professionalism was all about.

He reached over and found Charlotte's hand, enveloped its warmth, basked briefly in the soft gleam of her eyes.

The following morning Taras Arensky was standing beside the Holy Lake, the *Heiliger See,* in Potsdam's two-hundred-acre *Neue Garten,* watching a line of mallards peevishly abandon a thicket of reeds and take to the water in a series of splashlets, apparently upset by the approaching footsteps. A hundred meters down the waterside path the half-timbered bulk of the Cecilienhof Palace was just visible through the trees. A slight breeze riffled the glassy lake surface, which otherwise mirrored the hazy early sun with opaline serenity. It was a lovely vista, one laid out and landscaped expressly to tranquilize Prussian nobility, but Taras saw none of it. His eye was inward, and his spirit stretched taut on a rack of self-torture. He turned to the trim, bespectacled man beside him:

"Goddammit, Bob, she's here somewhere, and she's got to be found!"

The man, who had very hard eyes in a deceptively soft face, only shook his head. As the Berlin CIA station chief, Robert Strotkamp had just delivered to Taras all the news there was on the subject of Charlotte Walsh's disappearance and possible whereabouts. If there were any further developments, the pager on Strotkamp's belt would immediately announce the fact with an insistent vibration.

The federal police had checked every hotel in Berlin overnight without uncovering any trace of the journalist or the Opel Omega. Either she had registered under another name—perhaps whatever Marcus was using—or had simply driven beyond the radius of the search, which was, in consequence, being widened.

However, as the two men started back along the path to the Cecilienhof, Strotkamp had a further thought:

"You know, if it were still the 'bad old days' of Honecker and company, we could have eliminated the entire GDR by now. They were damn efficient, the *Stasi* and the *Vopos*. All tourists' passports were confiscated at their hotels and delivered overnight to the local *Volks Polizei* for checking. We would know exactly who is staying where and for how long. But with a new Germany and the state security apparatus all but dismantled, nobody is tracking random movement."

"What about the car? The Omega is a luxury model."

"Exactly. Before the Wall came down, a big Opel like that would have stuck out over here among all those midget Trabants and Wartburgs, like an honest man in Congress. Now, of course, people are used to seeing fancy cars in the east, even if they're still too expensive for most folks. But you're right. Sooner or later somebody's bound to spot it."

"Yeah, sooner or later," Taras echoed dismally.

"Don't worry. She'll either show up here today, or call in. She's a pro. She'll be in touch with someone."

That was precisely what was eating away at Taras. Charlie *would* get in touch—if she were still alive. Not knowing was the worst part. Taras had to keep fighting off nightmare images of her suffering at the Cowboy's hands.

Instead, Taras tried desperately to share Strotkamp's confidence that

Charlie would surface at the Cecilienhof Palace to pick up her press credentials. She had three full days to do so in order to be able to cover the conference on the fourth day; but, in Taras's opinion, after today the chances of her appearing would drastically diminish.

The other hope, of course, was that she would call John Tully, who was primed to alert her to her danger, unless he suspected Marcus might be eavesdropping, find out her location, and instantly relay the information to any of several numbers here or in Berlin. Taras had talked to Tully within the hour. The foreign editor had heard nothing from his correspondent, but hastened to explain that her actual filing deadline wasn't until the following day, for release the morning the conference opened.

Some earlybird journalists were already on the scene, their cars and vans crowding the asphalt car park in front of the Cecilienhof. But a negative headshake from a security man stationed near the entrance signified that Charlotte was not among them, so Taras and Strotkamp continued to stroll along the palace front.

The palace had been built before and during World War I by Kaiser Wilhelm as a pleasant hundred-and-seventy-odd-room country retreat. For some reason, he'd had it done all in Tudor style, with half-timbered gables, stone portals, and a profusion of tall, narrow chimneys. Locally it was overshadowed by Sans-Souci, the far grander palace of Frederick the Great on a hill overlooking all of Potsdam and the river Havel. But the Cecilienhof had won its surprising place in history during seventeen days in the summer of 1945 when Stalin, Truman, Churchill, and later Attlee had gathered there to decide the fate of the defeated Germany.

Taras paused to inspect the noisy queue of journalists outside the palace's hotel entrance. The Hotel Schloss Cecilienhof had been closed for the conference, and its reception hall set aside for the issuance of credentials. Everything so far was being handled with typical Teutonic efficiency, but Taras couldn't help wondering where in hell the Germans were planning to stick all the reporters when the event began. Some recent summits, he knew, had attracted an international press corps of more than two thousand. Potsdam invitations had apparently been restricted to half that. Even so, the conference rooms were extremely modest in size. Was the fourth estate to be relegated to bleachers on the back lawn? Or would they watch the proceedings via closed-circuit TV from the hotel dining room?

Actually, those ideas weren't in the least farfetched, as Taras found out an hour later, tagging along with Strotkamp on a Secret Service walkthrough of the arrival ceremony. The limousines would start pulling in at 9:45—on Friday, three days hence. There would be pooled television coverage at the entrance and in the large interior courtyard, which was emblazoned with a giant star formed of hundreds of red begonias, a blatant design originally planted by the Russians in 1945. The various delegations would proceed down a corridor and into the White Salon, a long, vanilla-rococo reception hall with red Turkish carpets, white-and-gilt Louis XVI decor, and neo-Corinthian pilasters.

There would be brief welcoming remarks made here, but only a select media coterie could be accommodated, roped off alongside the French doors. The bulk of the press corps would be outside on a garden terrace, just as they had been in 1945, and some farther away yet, massed on the lawns that sloped down to the *Jungfern See,* one of the lakes formed by the river Havel. And indeed, closed-circuit monitors would be mounted in various public rooms.

And although the first plenary session wouldn't be till Friday afternoon, the delegation would continue on into the main conference hall, a high-wainscoted, two-storied hammerbeamed space that reminded Taras of some of the larger Tudor rooms at Hampton Court. Again, only pool video would be allowed in, as the conferees and their aides settled into the red plush chairs and posed for the TV lights around the same red-baize-covered table used by the postwar Big Three.

Retracing his steps through the White Salon beside the Secret Service men, Taras had the sudden sense of being watched. He glanced through the lace-curtained French doors in time to catch the distinctive profile of Lieutenant Colonel Pavel Starkov moving away on the garden path. But later, outside, Starkov had come straight up to him.

"I am surprised to see you here, Major Arensky."

"Are you?"

"May I ask in what capacity you are here?"

"Unofficial."

"Good. Professional security officers, such as your escorts over there, don't usually tolerate amateurs who lack the nerve to pull the trigger on assassins. But perhaps you now regret that you allowed Marcus to escape?"

"Yes, I do." God, how he regretted it! And yet, on that fateful night on the Crimea, how could he have done other than he did?

"If you'll permit me a suggestion, Major?"

"Go ahead, Colonel."

"If there is an attempt made on President Rybkin on Friday, I suggest you stay out of my line of fire."

"Thanks. I'll try to remember that." Taras turned to leave, but turned back when he heard Starkov's chuckle.

"That ugly ring," the KGB officer said, "you're still wearing it."

Taras glanced down at the monstrosity on his index finger as if seeing it for the first time. The truth was, he wore it with a strange purpose. After getting Marcus's fiendish letter, Taras had sworn to rid himself of the cursed thing only by sliding it back on Marcus's lifeless finger.

At five o'clock Taras was pacing back and forth beside the ornate Gothic gateway to the *Neue Garten,* watching the passing traffic and incoming cars, repeatedly conjuring an Opel Omega, but to no effect. He had hiked the half kilometer of winding blacktop from the palace, needing to be in motion, unable to remain impotently rooted in one spot. Suddenly Bob Strotkamp drove up, pulled over to the curb, and got out.

He had an ashen expression.

"What happened?" Taras said, bracing for the worst.

"Charlie's credentials are gone. Her name's crossed off the fucking list! The idiot *Fräulein* at the T to Z table doesn't remember who picked them up, even after the goddamn briefing we gave!"

"I can't believe it! Jesus, Bob, Charlie couldn't have gotten by us."

"No. She must have sent somebody else in with her ID and a letter of authorization."

Taras swore again and again, and slammed his fist into his palm till it ached. So fucking close, then she'd slid through the net through a fluke of incompetence. He got in beside Strotkamp, who swung around and headed back through the park to the palace. As they pulled up, Strotkamp turned to him:

"You know, there's a good side to it."

"What?"

"At least it means she's alive and planning to attend."

"Yeah, I guess it does." That was a comfort, and he needed one desperately.

But where was she?

Chapter

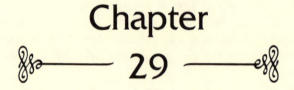 29

SEVENTY KILOMETERS SOUTH AND SLIGHTLY WEST OF POTSDAM, ON the river Elbe, is the little market town of Wittenberg, made famous by Martin Luther, who, one day in 1517, nailed his ninety-five theses to the door of the *Schlosskirche,* the Castle Church. Wittenberg's picturesque, cobblestoned Old Town, in fact, is today called Lutherstadt, and a bronze statue of the great reformer, ornamentally sheltered from pigeons, stands before the broad town hall in the market square. On all sides of the little square, cheek by jowl, are the dignified faces of Gothic buildings. And one of these along the south side, a four-story jade-green façade, is the Goldener Adler Hotel. It was here, in a second-story room overlooking the Marktplatz, that Charlotte Walsh had gone to ground with Jack Sanderson. But she was getting increasingly restless, surfeited with him and eager to return to her work and her world.

Jack was slumped in an armchair by the window, watching a televised tennis match, while Charlotte was reading an *International Herald-Tribune* that featured columns by several of her colleagues, when there came a knock at the door.

Christ, what if it's Taras? she thought as she hurried to open it. But it was only Frank, back from Potsdam. The spike-haired blond, leather-jacketed teenager grinned as he handed her the packet of press credentials. She foraged in her purse, handed him some deutschmarks, and smiled back.

"*Danke schön,* Frank."

"You need anything else, remember, I'm your dude," he said in his best Americanese.

"I'll do that."

She closed the door on the sound of his motorcycle boots crashing down the narrow hotel stairs.

"Cocky little bastard, isn't he?" Jack commented.

"Now, now, don't be jealous of a mere child, even if he is quite fetching. And if I remember correctly, you're the one who suggested I didn't need to pick these up in person."

"Only because you're so afraid your old boyfriend might be hanging around. Anyway, let's see them."

She perched on the wooden frame of the German-style double bed, opened the packet, dumped the credentials out on the eiderdown coverlet.

"You need two passes just to get in?" Sanderson said, moving beside her.

"Apparently." She looped one around her neck with the attached string. It looked like an elaborate baggage tag, with the conference dates imprinted below a holographic European Community logo that prismed in the light. "Pretty fancy. This seems to be a perimeter pass. Probably gets you into the grounds to park your car. Now this one, you see, even fancier. Because your little *Liebchen* happens to be one of the elite who gets right into the palace for the reception. They don't give these out to just anybody, only your way-above-average newshens."

"And that's it? Two pieces of paper and you're in?"

"I guess. After they x-ray my handbag and walk me through a metal detector."

"No strip searches?"

"No, but you're welcome to conduct one now if you'd like."

"In a minute." He smiled. "Honeymoon's winding down, huh?"

"Sort of." She glanced around the room. "I'm sorry our place is so little. The Kempinski would have been a hoot, and we could have gone strolling on the Ku-damm. But I just couldn't risk it. Forgive me?"

"It's not so bad. At least we have our own bath."

"It's damn intimate, and I guess that's what matters most for our last couple of days together. Jack, would you mind terribly switching channels for a while? CNN should have some background stuff on the conference, and it'll help me jump-start my poor lifeless brain. I'm supposed to hash out a column by tomorrow, telling my scads of devoted readers exactly what I think this big powwow will mean for the future of the world."

"Sure. I'll watch too. Maybe I'll learn something."

While he turned the dial, she unpacked and plugged in her laptop to charge the batteries, then sat down, keeping one eye on the little screen while she continued to scan the newspaper. Jack settled at her feet, his back propped against her shins, also watching the TV, where a map of Europe was gradually changing its colors to illustrate past and proposed changes in borders and strategic alliances.

So, Jack was aware of her distraction, her restlessness, she thought. It must be damned obvious, even though she'd tried to conceal it. She reached down absently and tousled his sandy hair as she watched the screen. He'd seemed a little sad just now, a little wistful. And he'd been such a wonderfully attentive lover. He deserved at least a good last couple of days—and her full romantic response. But surely he was under no illusions that there could be a future for them? No matter how fantastic the sex had been, there was more to life. And she couldn't even begin to picture Jack Sanderson as her husband or as the father of her children.

Much later, in the early morning hours, she found herself suddenly quite awake, staring up at coruscating darkness. To divert herself, she began to replay in her mind the most flagrantly erotic images of their last lovemaking. But an odd thing happened. After a few minutes her mind began to wander instead to issues of collective European security.

Charlotte Walsh, you are absolutely hopeless! she scolded herself. *But dammit, why not?* She threw back the coverlet, padded over to the desk, unplugged her recharged laptop, took it back to bed with her, flipped the screen up, and settled herself against the pillows. Then, while Jack snored softly beside her, she began to peck, watching a series of blue liquid crystal characters dance rapidly across the backlit screen. It was a column for John Tully, the one she'd file tomorrow:

FOR RELEASE FRIDAY, JULY 16

POTSDAM—The Schloss Cecilienhof seemed to many observers a peculiar choice for an international conference in 1945, and so it still seems to some of us all these dramatic decades later. But in a grand bit of diplomatic déjà vu, the world is once again turning its manic attention on this rambling mock-Tudor manor house built by Kaiser Bill for his brother on the watery outskirts of Berlin.

Here, Messrs. Ackerman, Rybkin et al. can deposit their respective backsides in the exact wickerwork garden chairs where Messrs. Stalin, Truman, and Churchill once sat surveying a quite different Europe, one still smoldering from the long firestorm of World War II. And, like those Big Three, our statesmen will also be overlooking, at somewhat nearer focus, the . . . ???

[Note to John Tully: Please have someone check the name of the body of water behind the palace; I can't recall it, and I don't have any maps handy. P.S. I don't mean the lake beside it.]

I mention this because, in one of those frequent ironies of history, sixteen years after the division of Germany was sketched on maps spread over the Cecilienhof conference table, the Berlin Wall began its obscene march across the city and countryside, following the Potsdamers careful tracings—and eventually marched right across the back lawn of the Cecilienhof itself, blocking that prized lakeside view that so delighted the diplomats.

Potsdam, you see, was placed on the frontier of the Eastern Zone, and just across the . . . [John, again, name of body of water, please.] lay the West, and freedom. If only the Big Three could have glanced out over the greensward and seen their monstrous handiwork-to-be before they adjourned—a twelve-foot-high concrete barrier complete with barbed wire and floodlights. Might it not have altered their minds a wee bit and saved us all a world of suffering?

In our time, of course, a great deal of the damage has been undone. That Wall has been torn down and the lovely view restored, not only to the back garden of the Schloss Cecilienhof, but clear across Eastern Europe. And the statesmen who glance up from their deliberations here this week and look out the garden windows will also be confronting a far more beckoning vista—that of a brave new, brand new Europe.

[Note to John: Please verify that the Germans have in fact torn down that awful eyesore behind the Cecilienhof. I assume they have, but, as you know, I'm still in the boondocks over here.]

Charlotte paused, coming up for air. Well, it was definitely what John Tully called her Radcliffe style, too full of collegiate conceits. But it wasn't bad for a backgrounder. And by the time she plugged in a few specifics, it would damn well run the right number of column inches and be filed on time. Which was, after all, the most critical thing.

Let John fiddle with it.

The next day, Wednesday, two days before the conference, Taras spent the morning making phone calls from his room in the Hotel Potsdam, a high-rise on the Havel near the *Lange Brucke,* the main bridge to Berlin.

There was, however, nothing new from any quarter. It was still predawn in Washington, and there was no need to disturb John Tully's sleep, but Taras had talked to the newspaper switchboard and the overnight attendant in the wire room, and neither one could find any trace of a recent communication from Charlie—no messages, computer downloads, telexes, faxes, or direct dictation. She was due to file, but thus far it didn't look like she had.

German police still had no leads to her or the rental Opel. The search radius had widened dramatically—to the northernmost suburbs of Berlin, east to the Polish border, south to Leipzig and Dresden, west to Magdeburg—but the net was wide-meshed, and a slippery fish like Marcus would not likely turn up in it. Taras was convinced Charlotte and Marcus were near to hand. What was needed was a task force to go from hotel to hotel and *gasthof* to *gasthof,* circulating photographs of them. Unfortunately, the manpower was not available; police and security forces were already stretched dangerously thin, meeting the imperatives of the Potsdam Conference.

Taras put down the phone, stared north along the riverside, his eye drawn to the burnished sunlight on an old copper church dome in Potsdam's Alten Markt. He was ready to do something decisive, dammit, but what? It was pointless to go rushing off, or even to proceed one step away from the phone, without some rationale. He sensed that the duel between himself and Marcus was reaching its finale, yet Taras was unable either to strike or properly defend. He could only wait for the Cowboy to make his final thrust—a thrust that could come at any instant, and from any direction.

At one-thirty John Tully called. A faxed column from Charlie had been on his desk when he'd arrived at 8:15; it had arrived in the newspaper wire room a few minutes before. The fax cover sheet indicated it had been sent from the post office in Dessau.

"That's just south of here!" Taras said.

"Yeah, about eighty kilometers southwest of you. I just looked it up. It's an industrial city on the river Mulde, a tributary of the Elbe."

"John, did she leave any number for you to call her back?"

"No. And she usually does, that's the damn thing. It's just not like her."

"What's the column say?"

"I'll fax you a copy at your hotel. It's one of her cotton-candy pieces, spun out of air. There are some nifty turns of phrase, but she's obviously not done any real homework or even been to Potsdam. She couldn't even think of the name of the Havel, or the *Jungfern See* behind the Cecilienhof, and she says she's out in the boondocks, whatever the hell that means. I'm worried, Taras. Find her for me, will you? And make sure nothing happens to my girl. I want to be able to give her a damn good scolding."

Taras swallowed hard, promised—and rang off. Then he immediately dialed Strotkamp, who was his liaison with various German security services, and passed along the information.

"I'll get right on it, Taras. Meanwhile, I suggest you hang right where you are. Who knows? Ten minutes from now she'll probably walk into some journalistic watering hole in Berlin and buy everybody a drink."

"I can't hang in any longer, Bob. I'm going crazy here, and Dessau's right off the Autobahn. I can be there in forty minutes."

Chapter
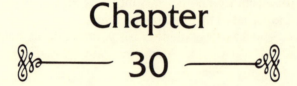
30

DESSAU STILL SEEMED TO BE STRUGGLING TO WAKE ITSELF FROM its decades-long Stalinist nightmare. Like Berlin, it had a bombed-out church, but this rubbled relic didn't seem to be a conscious memorial; it looked more like the downtrodden Dessauers just hadn't gotten around to repairing it. Amid the post-euphoric realities of reunification, the industrial city still lay under a gray pall of pollution. Old diesels and lawnmower-engined Trabants still grumbled through its streets, belching noxious fumes; superannuated trams that should have gone to the scrap heap instead went grinding and shrieking around the squares; and, driving in from the Autobahn, Taras had noticed a jaundiced froth clotting the margins of the river Mulde.

It had taken him several minutes to locate the main post office, which offered *Telefaxdienst*—fax service—and he was just in time to catch the clerk who'd transmitted Charlie's column to America over the *Fernkopierer* before he went off duty. But that was the extent of Taras's luck.

The young man recalled only that the copy had been brought in by a blond punker in a motorcycle jacket, obviously just a delivery person.

The postal clerk glanced over the pictures Taras showed him of Charlotte and Marcus without a flicker of recognition.

Taras thanked him, then went outside to ingest raw hydrocarbons while waiting for one of Strotkamp's federal police contacts to show up. Was the motorcycle punk a confederate of Marcus's? Taras didn't think so. More likely he was just a kid hired to do an errand. But hired by Charlie or Marcus? There was no way of knowing. All Taras could be sure of so far was that Charlotte had definitely written the column; he and John Tully agreed the style was hers. But that could have been days earlier. There was no internal evidence to date it more recently.

She could already be dead.

Or trussed up in a closet.

And there was another alternative, one he prayed for, though it was wretched enough—that she was just not ready to come out, still too enamored of the Cowboy, a devilishly handsome man who had not yet revealed himself as a homicidal maniac.

As Taras was forcing his mind to grapple with these grisly scenarios, an Audi sedan pulled to the curb. Taras jumped in and gave a quick briefing to the driver—a captain of GSG-9, the German hostage rescue unit—on the short ride to Dessau's main police station, where arrangements were made to duplicate the photographs of the missing pair and distribute them to the city's hotels. The police, Taras was assured, would also comb the streets and garages for the missing Opel.

Taras expected absolutely nothing to come of it, just like the ongoing stakeout at the Cecilienhof and the journalistic hangouts of Berlin. With an ever-increasing conviction of hopelessness, he got back in his own rental Escort and headed back to the Autobahn and Potsdam.

At five-thirty the following afternoon, the day before the conference, Marcus Jolly was shopping for a pair of shoes on Wittenberg's main thoroughfare, Schloss-strasse. He was looking for something plain, low-heeled, and very large.

After browsing several stores without success, he revised his plan and selected some white low-top Adidases in the *Modesalon* on the Marktplatz. He had them wrapped, then walked east on Collegien-strasse to the little bookstore where Charlotte had arranged to wait for him so he could pick out a present for her.

She wasn't there.

There were several other bookstores on the market square, but she wasn't in any of them. Marcus found this disturbing. He cut diagonally across the square, scattering pigeons and deranging a semicircle of Asian tourists who were pointing and clicking at Luther's statue.

In front of the Goldener Adler a young man with spiky hair was lounging indolently on his parked motorcycle, apparently watching the passing parade. It was, of course, Frank, the local hoodlum who had haunted this particular piece of sidewalk ever since he'd first laid eyes upon Charlie. The sophisticated charms of the older Western woman had apparently affected the primitive brain, as well as the heart, of the German youth. He now seemed to consider himself her knight errant, and viewed Marcus with open hostility. Infuriatingly, Charlotte not only tolerated but encouraged the adoration; Marcus considered it sickening.

"Frank, did you see Charlotte?"

"You mean like today, dude?"

"Yeah, dude, like today. Like in the last five or ten minutes?"

"Hey, I guess I don't remember." Frank snickered.

Marcus permitted himself a fleeting vision of the damage he could inflict on the cretinous cycle-Nazi, given about five seconds and no witnesses. Then he pushed past him under the little hotel marquee with its Golden Eagle plaque. Inside the low-vaulted lobby he nodded briefly to the desk clerk, then hurried up the dark stairs beside the two ground-floor restaurants. At the landing he turned sharply, then deliberately slowed his steps along the dingy corridor to their room, which he opened with his own key.

Hearing the clatter on the stairs, Charlotte thought it must be Frank. Earlier on the street she had bid the obviously enamored young tough good-bye, since she and Jack were due to check out quite early in the morning. Frank had immediately offered to take her to Potsdam on the back of his motorcycle.

"And what about Jack?" she had laughed. "What will we do with him?"

"Lose the dude, Charlie. He's a bad mother."

Again she'd laughed, then reached and brushed the spiky hair. The tender gesture had seemed to devastate Frank. His face had started to crumple. Then he'd turned and run off. She hoped he'd come back to say good-bye.

But the pounding footsteps abruptly ceased. Puzzled, she turned around to face the door just as it opened to reveal Jack Sanderson. He hesitated a second on the threshold, watching her replace the telephone receiver in its cradle, before coming in.

"You weren't at the bookstore. I got worried."

"I'm sorry, Jack. I had to make a call. You remember that man who called me in Le Lavandou?"

"Your old boyfriend Taras, sure. You been calling him?"

"I had to, Jack. I promised him I would. I'm sorry if it looks like I'm sneaking off, but I didn't want you to know about it. You've been so . . ."

"That's all right, I understand. I'm just not your soulmate. I've been told that before. So what did he have to say?"

"Nothing. He'd checked out of his hotel. I'm sorry if I've upset you. I . . . I wanted our last night to be special."

"Well, there's still time."

"Of course there is. And we'll make the most of every minute. Oh, Jack, I forgot you went shopping for me. Can I open it?"

"Later."

She went to him, kissed his cheek. "You're really a pussycat, you know? But I have one more favor to ask you. Would you mind terribly if I made a few more phone calls? Maybe you could prowl around awhile longer."

"Go ahead." He settled on the bed, clasping his hands behind his head. "Since you're not talking to Taras, you don't mind if I listen, do you?"

"No. That's fine." She picked up the phone, asked the hotel switchboard to dial another Washington number, hung up. "It'll take a few minutes. They'll ring me back."

She and Jack chatted about dinner plans. Since the afternoon remained pleasantly warm, they decided to try an outdoor café on the square in preference to either of the Adler's gloomy ground-floor restaurants. Perhaps they could find that Hungarian Riesling recommended by the desk clerk. Then the phone rang. Her American call was ready.

Jack asked: "Is that your editor, then?"

"No, I'm calling the CIA. The Deputy Director of Intelligence is a good friend of Taras's, as well as one of his bosses. I'm sure he'll know how to reach him."

"Oh."

Charlotte was just saying hello to the DDI's secretary, when out of the corner of her eye she noticed that Jack was no longer on the bed but moving swiftly toward her. She glanced up in surprise—just as his hand came down on the cradle, cutting her connection.

Her puzzlement flared into anger. And then, as she found herself staring into the blazing eyes of a man she did not know, anger was swept aside by sudden and savage fear.

At CIA headquarters in Langley, Virginia, Rhonda Hartnell, executive secretary to the DDI, stared at her phone. She wasn't accustomed to callers hanging up, especially from overseas. They must have been disconnected. She had been on her feet, ready to leave for lunch, when the phone rang. Now she sat down, pressed the intercom, and told her boss what had happened.

"From Germany, huh? But you didn't catch the name of the town, or who was calling?"

"No, but it'll be in the computer. There was something funny though. I heard her voice for only a second, no more than 'hello,' but I recognized it. I know I've heard it before."

"Did you hear anything odd before the cutoff?"

"No, nothing. What do you want me to do?"

"She'll call back, whoever she is, but it may take a while for her to get through, depending on where she's calling from. Don't worry about it, Ron. Leslie will put her through to me. You go on to lunch."

"Thanks."

Rhonda jotted the time on her pad, for reference in case she should need to check the computer logs. Then she gathered up her purse and a shopping bag with two blouses she wanted to exchange and headed off down the corridor with a wave to Leslie to cover her phone.

But darn it! She couldn't get her mind off the distinctive sound of that voice. Maybe it would come to her.

Chapter

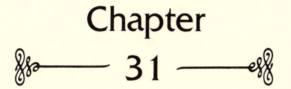 31

CHARLOTTE WALSH WAS HELPLESS, ON HER BACK, NAKED, HER
mouth sealed with wide duct tape, arms pulled painfully over her
head, wrists and ankles taped together and tied to the bedframe with
sashcord from the windows.

But she was alive, and she could see. Across the little room the
monster sat with his back to her at the dressing table, stripped to his
shorts, experimenting in the mirror with her makeup kit.

After he had disconnected her call to the CIA, it had taken Charlotte
a couple of bewildered seconds to realize she wasn't dealing with a
jealous and suddenly enraged lover, but something far more frightening. She had sought his eyes in desperate appeal—and found herself
confronting an alien predator.

"Jack Sanderson," the considerate and indefatigable lover, was gone,
discarded like a rubber mask by this other cruel man, who had been
there all along, hiding behind the easy grin, stalking and trapping her
for some terrifying purpose not yet revealed. What a vulnerable, pathetic fool she had been—from that first instant in the bookstore in
Le Lavandou!

And how easily he had reeled her in.

As the enormity of it had seized her, she had fought him with all her strength. But he had countered with an offhand skill that rendered her struggles childishly futile. One hand had moved swiftly from the telephone to stifle her screams, while the other circled her neck, his thumb finding and pressing the carotid artery.

She had blacked out.

And had come to on the bed like this—bound and gagged and flooded with terror. The sky out the window was evening blue, the shabby room illumined only by the tarnished brass lamp on the dresser, the cracked parchment shade tilted to throw light on the mirror where her captor worked. As Charlotte had moaned against the muzzling tape and thrashed against her restraints, his voice had floated back to her, calm and tinged with mockery:

"You know, if you keep groaning and bouncing around like that, the restaurant patrons downstairs will only think we're doing another one of our horizontal slam-dances. There, that's better.

"Now, I suppose you're beginning to suspect that I've lied to you. Women are always so suspicious, aren't they, especially newswomen? Well, of course you're right. I'm not really over here scouting European trade fairs for American mail-order firms. I'm an old friend of your lover's, actually. My name is Marcus. Surely he's mentioned me?"

The man who now called himself Marcus turned his head and flashed his Jack Sanderson smile. He had toweled off most of the makeup, apparently unsatisfied with the effect. Charlotte shook her head.

"He didn't mention me? I'm shocked. Taras and I were so close for so long. You know, Charlie, if only you hadn't tried so persistently to get in touch with the Cossack, as I call him, we'd be having a nice dinner right now. Still, that would only have bought you an extra hour or two. I'm afraid things were bound to end badly between us."

Then he had told her—as though it were some ingenious business coup he was plotting—of his plan to assassinate Alois Rybkin. The brutal inference drawn by Charlotte was that she had been scouted and selected by Marcus mainly for her journalistic credentials, which could give him access to the Cecilienhof, and her stature, which would allow him to fit into some of her clothing, including the wig she used when she didn't have time to fix her hair for impromptu TV appearances.

Marcus didn't mention why he wanted to kill the Soviet head of state. Not that Charlotte cared a damn about his motives, but after spending nearly a week with the man and then discovering him to be a total and terrifying stranger, she wanted desperately to find some clue as to what he might do next. Obviously he was crazy, even if he didn't act like a political fanatic. But was this just another demented game he was playing with her, or was he actually intending to go through with it? If so, surely he would be caught or killed. But then what would happen to her?

Her frail hope—which she repeated ceaselessly like a rosary in her mind—was that he would let her live. Why not? Why couldn't he just take her clothes and press pass, walk out the door, and leave her, tied up, to be discovered by the chambermaid next morning? By then, her knowing his identity and plans wouldn't matter. He'd have already made his attempt, succeeded or failed. And surely, despite the cruel mockery he now displayed, he must have some residue of feeling for her, or for the pleasures they had shared together. If he meant to kill her, wouldn't he already have done it?

Dear Lord, please let him be merciful.

The prayer brought a moment's respite from her surging adrenaline panic. Still, she wished he hadn't been so casual about giving her his real name, if that's what it was.

Heavy footsteps reverberated suddenly in the stairwell; floorboards creaked in the corridor. An insistent knock rattled the door.

Charlotte saw the muscles tighten across Marcus's bare back. Without getting up, he called out:

"Wer ist dort?"

"Frank," came the answer. "I got something special for Charlie. Come on, dude, I want to give it to her!"

"Charlie is sick. Leave it outside. I'll give it to her."

"Hey, dude, like I got to say good-bye to a foxy lady."

"I told you, Frank, she's sick. *Krank, verstehe?* Charlie is in the bathroom, *die Toilette*. Now, please, just go away."

"No, I wait till she's better. I be out here, dude."

"Christ!" Marcus whirled around, his striking features contorted by anger, obviously directed at her for having encouraged the young Wittenberger. "Hold on, Frank."

Marcus knelt beside the bed and whispered urgently: "Listen to me carefully. If you want that lovesick little Nazi to live, tell him you're too sick to come to the door. Tell him to leave whatever the hell he's brought outside. Thank him and tell him *auf Wiedersehen*. But no endearments. And if you try to cry out for help, or I even think you're about to, I'll strangle you, then kill loverboy. Got that? You may nod your head."

She nodded.

"I'm going to remove the tape, but I'm going to be right next to you." He turned to the door, called out: "Frank, here's Charlie. She wants to tell you something."

He tore the tape off painfully. She spoke hoarsely, with Marcus's menacing face hovering inches above her, yet her fear displaced by sudden tearfulness as she thought of the devoted young man just outside: "Frank, I'm very sick . . . I . . . I can't see you now. . . . Thank you for coming. . . . You're a dear." Then she winced as Marcus's hand vised around her upper arm. Oh, Christ, she'd forgotten; no endearments! "*Auf Wiedersehen,* Frank. Now please go away."

"Okay, sure, Charlie, but then I come here back again. I rev up *Das Vampir* and get my sister's husband, Rolf, he is a real out-of-sight *Doktor.* He fix you real good, Charlie. You wait!"

"No . . ." But her voice faltered.

They heard his bootsteps retreating down the corridor.

Marcus slapped the tape back on her mouth, charged to the door, threw it open, and shouted into the stairwell: "Frank, come back. Charlie wants to see you now, right away!"

No, Frank! Charlotte thought with all her might. *Don't come back!* But she heard the quick returning steps, leaping two stairs at a time.

Marcus stepped quickly back from the door as Frank burst into the room. A bouquet of yellow flowers dangled from his hand as he stood slack-jawed, registering painful confusion at what he saw—the woman he idolized, stripped naked, tied to the bed, mouth sealed with shiny gray tape. Charlotte tried to warn him with her eyes, but the leather-jacketed youth was far too slow in turning to confront Marcus.

Not that it would have made any difference, as Charlotte realized in the brutal ensuing seconds. For all his macho trappings, the German youth was no match for Marcus's lethal expertise. Frank dropped his bouquet and charged the older man. But Marcus simply stood there in his shorts, grinning. Then, with the insouciance of a matador, Marcus doubled his knee to the young man's groin and danced aside as his opponent toppled to the floor. Even before the youth had landed, Marcus's edged hand flashed down like a machete above the studded leather collar.

Charlotte heard the horrible sound of that blow and reacted viscerally, but the worst was to come. Marcus sprang astride his facedown victim, wrapped his right hand around the spike-haired skull, braced his left forearm against the back of Frank's neck, then wrenched upward violently. Charlotte heard that sound as well—the horrid crepitation of Frank's cervical vertebrae being whipsnapped. She saw the young man's body convulse on the threadbare carpet, then lie still beside the scattered flowers.

Nausea erupted from deep within her.

Marcus heard the glottal warning, leaped across the room and ripped her gag free barely in time to save her from strangulation. Racked and writhing, yet unable to rise up because of her restraints, Charlotte vomited all over the bedclothes and herself, again and again, till she fell back in wretched exhaustion. With her head hammering, she shut her eyes tight against the foulness that now slimed her face—and against the sight of the broken body of the boy who had come to give her flowers, and given his life instead.

The café bar of the Hotel Potsdam was awash in journalists, print and electronic, from all over the globe. Their faces were flushed, their voices commingled in a polyglot roar as glasses were refilled and *Gemütlichkeit* reigned supreme. They were warriors before the battle, mercenaries who had fought in many campaigns in many unlikely places, and now gathered five deep behind the long bar and around the little tables to compare wounds and swap war stories.

Taras only glanced in, then moved on toward the lobby, having recognized from a distance several Washington newsfolk he knew fairly well. He avoided the scene for a couple of reasons.

First, and mostly painfully, because it reminded him of Charlie. She belonged in that milieu, or in one of the more select collegial gatherings that would doubtless be taking place tonight along Berlin's Kurfürstendamm. Also, Taras didn't know how to respond to inevitable questions from any of Charlie's friends or colleagues who didn't know they'd broken up, and who might now be wondering where in hell she was.

But as he walked away, it also occurred to him that he felt like getting drunk himself. Not just pleasantly or raucously inebriated like this beer-bourbon-and-scotch crowd, but White Dynamite, falling-down-in-the-snowbank, Slavic drunk, like that night in Khabarovsk.

Taras was swamped with despair, or maybe just self-pity. It was hard to tell anymore. In the sick welter of his emotions, only his cherished hatred for the Cowboy and thirst for revenge stood out with any clarity.

There was still no break in the search for Marcus and Charlie. Only dead-ends, as Taras had feared. He had just come back from dinner with Bob Strotkamp, who was increasingly preoccupied with his security preparations for the next day's conference. In fact, as they had parted outside a Berlin rathskeller, Taras had come away with the definite impression that the CIA man was only persevering with the search in order to locate the GRU assassin, not out of any concern for Charlie's safety. Once during dinner Strotkamp had even commented that despite everything, Charlotte might still be enjoying her little fling, in no particular danger from Marcus, and would probably show up for work tomorrow at Potsdam.

Sure, Taras thought. And maybe Eva Sorokina would put in an appearance too. The Cowboy had a way with women.

Taras rode upstairs on an alcohol-fumed elevator with a former network anchorman recently put out to pasture for on-the-job intoxication. Taras had met the affable lout on several occasions, but was gratified that the famous face now couldn't recognize his, as the newsman leaned for support on a local *Fräulein*—indubitably, considering her catch, of mercenary bent herself.

Taras's floor came first, and he lost no time in stepping off. He had been ready to punch the ex-anchorman in the pink jowls, just out of frustration and the desperate need to have someone to punish.

Inside his room he went to the window, drew the drapes and tugged back the outer lace curtains, stared out at the floodlit copper dome of the church whose name he did not know. Then, after a blank moment, he began hammering his fist against the window frame.

Chapter
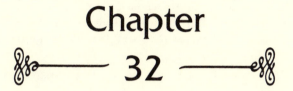
32

In her condominium in Rockville, Maryland, Rhonda Hartnell switched on her bedside lamp. It was only eleven. She had gone to bed early, but had been awakened by a circuit firing on and off in her brain. Charlotte Walsh, the circuit said. Okay. Why should the name of a columnist stick in her synapses? Rhonda shook her groggy head, unable to piece the thought together.

Then all at once she had it. She grabbed for the phone. *Jesus, Mary, and Joseph, of course!* Her boss and Taras Arensky and Bob Strotkamp in Berlin were all looking for Charlotte, had been for days. And that had been Charlotte—the voice on the phone from Germany—wanting to talk to the DDI, her boss! Rhonda had heard Charlotte often enough, in person at parties, and on Washington talking-heads TV—CNN, C-Span, Sunday morning punditry. How could she have failed to recognize even that hello? *Dear Lord, let it not be too late!*

She got hold of someone in the Office of Communications of the Deputy Directorate, Support, at Langley, told him who she was and what she wanted done and how urgently she wanted it. She had to check her temper as the man repeated her request nearly word for word:

"Now, let me be clear about this. You want me to go to your office, find the time you jotted on your deskpad, and cross-check the phone logs for any incoming calls at that exact time on the DDI's general line, and try and get a location?"

"Exactly."

"That's going to take a while."

"Why? Don't you have access to our phone system computer?"

"No, I can do that. If there was a call, then the information's in our daily ASCII logfiles. But I'm just telling you, Ms. Hartnell, they're humongous files, and I'll have to search it backward chronologically, or print it out . . ."

"No, don't print it! There's no time! Can't you narrow your search to a specific range of minutes?"

"Yeah, I can do that."

"Then do it! A life may depend on it. Make it fast and get right back to me. I'm calling the DDI at home right now."

The DDI's reaction was predictably vesuvian.

"I'm so sorry," Rhonda said, "I should have followed up immediately, and racked my brain until—"

"For God's sake, Ron, I'm not mad at you. You can't think of everything, though you come closer than anybody I know. Let's just pray she's still there. I want somebody else to back up that tekkie down there on that phonelog check. And let me know the instant you hear from him."

Five minutes later she had her answer and relayed it to the DDI: "The call originated in Wittenberg, Germany, from a hotel called the Goldener Adler."

"The Golden Eagle. Okay, great work, Ron. I'll take it from here. You get back to sleep if you can. Maybe say a prayer for Charlie first."

The call from Washington shrilled in Taras's room at five-thirty in the morning, rescuing him from an exhausting dream in which he had been trudging across frozen tundra and sinking to his hips in snowbanks, on some obscure quest.

It took several seconds to recall where he was, and the real urgency he confronted. Then the DDI's words exploded in his brain. *Charlotte was in Wittenberg.* Why hadn't Taras thought of it? It was within a seventy-five-kilometer radius of Potsdam and exactly the sort of quaint hideaway she would have chosen, over some toxic slum like Dessau.

"Taras, I'll leave you to contact Strotkamp and link up with GSG-9 or whoever's available. Godspeed. Our prayers are with you."

"No! Don't hang up. You call Bob yourself now, tell him I'm on my way to Wittenberg. If he can round up any GSG-9 guys, great, send 'em along. But tell him not to alert the local cops. Not against Marcus. They'd just walk in and get blown away. If they hit anybody, it'd be Charlie. I can't wait."

Four minutes later, barely buttoned, zippered, and shoelaced, with his .45 auto holstered under his windbreaker, Taras was gunning his rental Escort out of the hotel parking lot and swinging right onto the bridge over the Havel—and wishing to hell he'd rented a BMW or a Porsche.

Dawn was still an hour off, and gray fog banks shrouded the river. Taras switched on fog lights and wipers, and barreled straight down the Heinrich Mann Allee, slowing only at stoplights like an ambulance driver to scan quickly for cross traffic before accelerating through. In moments he had put the immense dark tract of the Potsdam Forest behind him and was flashing through the night-forsaken suburbs of Waldstadt and Bergholz-Rehbrücke. Just beyond lay the southbound onramp to the E6 Autobahn, where he could push the little Ford flat out, thanks to reunification, which had brought the Federal Republic's unlimited speed limits to the East.

It was the same route he'd taken the day before on the wild-goose chase to Dessau. But this time something told him the game was for real—the duel was on, sabers unblunted, masks off.

Keeping the speedometer hovering around 150 kph, Taras figured to reach Coswig in just over twenty minutes, maybe five or ten more to Wittenberg.

He prayed it would be quick enough.

Marcus sat on the edge of the bed, watching Charlie sleep. Earlier he had unpeeled the strip of duct tape from her mouth, tipped her head back and forced her to swallow four 100-milligram secobarbital capsules. When she had finally ceased her struggles and gone under, he went into the bathroom—his eyes avoiding the leather-jacketed corpse that now sprawled in the tub—for a basin of water and wash-cloth. With these he cleaned off all traces of the vomit from her face. Next he had tenderly bathed her long, elegant body, that lush and undulant countryside on which he had passed so many delightful hours. From time to time, as his cloth-mittened hand slowly traced the pale curves and hollows, she would moan or stir, like a child in troubled sleep.

Perhaps, he had thought, the prolonged overhead stretching of her arms was hurtful, impairing her circulation. He cut the tethering sash-cords, then removed the tape from her wrists, chafing them in his palms briefly to restore blood flow before lowering her arms beside her torso. As long as her ankles were taped and secured to the foot-board, Charlotte could not escape.

He had put off killing her for several hours then, while he continued to experiment with her makeup and wardrobe.

He selected a long black polyester skirt with elasticized waist, the only one he'd been able to fit into—and as it was, the pleats were drawn taut over his hips. The white angora tunic sweater was also considerably more form-fitting than intended. Marcus had ripped out the shoulder pads; his own deltoids provided a sufficiently mannish effect. A tissue-stuffed bra beneath falsified a modest bustline. He had not been able to squeeze into any of Charlotte's coats, but it should be warm enough to go without, yet not call attention to himself. The Adidases he had purchased the previous night completed the ensemble. More and more women wore athletic shoes, he knew, especially for occasions like today's, where there would be a good deal of walking and standing around.

The makeup was just passable, he thought, but the best he could do, based on trial and error and what he recalled from his kibitzing of Charlie's toilette over the past week. He'd shaved carefully, smoothed on foundation, and dusted each cheek with blusher.

He had labored nearly thirty minutes doing his eyes, twice having to wash everything off and start over. Christ, he thought, what a wretched nuisance! How did women suffer it daily? He had used an eyeliner pencil, brushed on eyeshadow, tipped and darkened his own lashes with mascara. The objective was not to make himself look feminine, but to mask his features as much as possible from Taras, if he was there, and the KGB bodyguards, who would have studied his photograph. Sunglasses would aid in that disguise.

Finally he was ready. It was essential that he make his exit from the hotel and the town before darkness bled off to dawn. And on the bed Charlotte was now beginning to stir more persistently. He wanted to do it while she slept. He took a pillow and stood over her a long moment, staring down at her delicate and well-remembered features, saying a silent and sentimental good-bye. Then he lowered the pillow, softly at first, then more and more firmly, and finally viciously, with all his strength, as she struggled up from unconsciousness to wage a brief, convulsive fight for her life. Then it was over, and she lay still.

Marcus turned and heaved a great sigh, but the straitjacketing tension did not lift from him. He looked down at his hands, usually rock steady, now fluttering with nerves. *Christ, don't tell me the bitch got to you that bad? Pull yourself together*. Yet he sensed within himself the sudden collapse of some inner structure. *It was not just another death*, a voice insisted. *This one did not have to die*.

"Yes, she did!" Marcus cried out. She had been Taras's woman. And he must find her like this, after the death of Rybkin, used and discarded by his once-loved, now-hated rival. That was to be the final exquisite point in their duel—Cowboy over Cossack.

Oddly, the adrenaline surge seemed to steady his nerves. He must move quickly and methodically. Gray light was already beginning to filter through the lace curtains overlooking the square. He must forget the thing on the bed, ignore its grotesque reflection in the mirror as he sat down at the dresser for the final touches.

Marcus placed the brunette wig carefully over his own hair, pulling and tugging, then using Charlie's teasing brush to flounce it. But on the left side a clump of curls stuck out at an odd angle, as if it had been slept on. He patted the curls down; they sprang right back. He rummaged through her travel vanity case, found a small hair spray canister, sprayed the entire wig, then combed and teased the offending curls into a semblance of order.

He gave himself a final inspection in the mirror. Dark-lashed, blue eyes; long, equine face; strong cheekbones; slightly cleft chin; full, lightly glossed lips. Marcus made a mouth, blinked his lashes in what he thought was a feminine way. Christ, he looked exactly like a goddamn transvestite, one of those desperate-eyed TVs who take out ads in the kinky contact magazines. Let's see, his could go:

International assassin, looking for a good time and a victim to share it with. No limits respected. Contact: The Cowboy. Box 9E.

No, not really.

He stood up, smoothed the skirt over his hips. There was sufficient resemblance to the photo on Charlie's press pass to get him through perimeter security. That's all that mattered. After that, no one who knew her and saw him would make the connection. They'd see just another mannish newswoman, a fairly common species, he imagined.

Next item. The little camera he'd picked up from a GRU contact in Munich, and which had already passed successfully through several airport metal detectors. Japanese logo, plastic case and interior mechanism. It could even take pictures—but not in its present configuration. It was fitted out so that with a touch of the shutter release it would go snickety-click like any SLR—except the lens would snap aside and a mousetrap fuse would fire a tiny dart through the lens opening. Marcus opened the back and made sure a dart was in place. Three millimeters long and a millimeter and a half in diameter, of platinum and iridium, the projectile was needle-pointed and, when fired from a range of five meters or less, could pierce several layers of clothing and skin, and release on impact its deadly poison—ricin, twice as toxic as cobra venom. Marcus would aim for groin, thigh, or buttock, depending on opportunity. Rybkin would feel a sharp sting and probably die within the hour, despite medical intervention. And Marcus would have a decent chance at escape.

Time to go. He found himself standing beside the bed, then, unable to stop himself, lifted the pillow for a last look.

Suddenly she sat up, eyes staring. "Taras!" she cried.

Marcus cried out too—a womanish scream—and slammed the pillow down, mashing her face as her arms and legs thrashed. *Fucking Christ, it was like crazy Kostya again!*—the way the unconscious trapper had suddenly revived in the freezing water of the Ussuri when Marcus had shoved him through the ice hole. Again and again Kostya had risen to the surface, a wild-eyed ghost in the moonlight, bellowing for help while Marcus kicked his face into bloody ruin. Still he wouldn't stay under—like Rasputin, whom he so resembled with his febrile gaze and scraggly locks. Finally, with Marcus screaming at him to die, the feeble-minded trapper sank and rose no more.

Now, as the body beneath him subsided into quiescence, Marcus slumped back. It was his own fault. Careless or squeamish, he had stopped too soon before, before she was really gone. He ought to have made damn sure. He lifted the pillow, saw the vacant, terror-glazed eyes. No carotid pulse. He pushed the jaw closed but left the eyes open, not wanting to touch her again.

He had to get out of there. He was breathing too rapidly, not thinking clearly. He made a tour of the room several times, afraid he was forgetting something. Credentials in the handbag, carryall and camera over the shoulder, wig on straight. Body in the bathtub and on the bed. *Okay, Christ, just get out!* Pearl-gray light was quickly filching the shadovs. He switched off the lamp, slipped into the corridor, eased the door closed, went down the dark stairs, his steps cushioned in the Adidases, a tall woman with a mannish build and a tricked-out hairdo.

Chapter

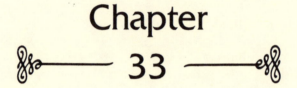 33

FEAR HURTLED AT TARAS IN WAVES, LIKE THE ONRUSHING AUTO-bahn and the unrolling farmlands alongside. He pushed it away, concentrating on the wet ribbon of asphalt, the muted hiss of the tires, the speedometer needling at one sixty. But the fear always came back, and it wore a face—Charlie's, dark-eyed and gaunt, hovering just outside the windshield.

As the road descended, silver mist swirled up from the emerald fields, veiling the road ahead. Taras cursed, lifting his foot from the gas and praying for a return of visibility. Of all the times to have to slow down! He clenched the wheel in impotent rage, squinting ahead, foot braced to floor the pedal the instant the vaporous curtain parted.

Still at reduced speed, he passed the first sign for Coswig, then a second one, which announced it as the exit for Lutherstadt Wittenberg. Ten more kilometers to the turnoff. He peered ahead, watching oncoming cars materialize suddenly out of the mist. A miniature tractor-trailer. A big red coach emblazoned MOTO-VIÀGGIO, full of Italian tourists. A battered, green and white ex-Vopo van with a young woman at the wheel and a Happy Holstein decal on the side.

Peeling off the Autobahn at Coswig, Marcus narrowly missed side-swiping a mustard-colored Trabant that ran a red light. Taras glanced angrily back at the woman driver—and, for a heartstopping second, saw Charlie. But it was only a trick of the hairdo; the profile was square-jawed and mannish.

Christ, you're losing it, Taras told himself. *Get a grip on yourself.* He was only five minutes from Wittenberg, as long as he stayed alert. The last thing he needed now was to dope off, miss a sign, and drive down the wrong fucking road.

Marcus scolded himself for running the red light—and nearly colliding with that Ford—as he headed up the Autobahn ramp. He had hot-wired the Trabant out of a parking lot behind the Goldener Adler rather than risk Charlotte's Opel Omega, in case it was being searched for. By the time the Trabi was reported missing, Marcus would have discarded it.

But even with the midget vehicle's twenty-six-horsepower two-stroke engine maxed out on the Autobahn, Marcus found he couldn't average much more than eighty-five kilometers an hour, which kept him in the right-hand lane. But that was good enough. He was ahead of schedule.

And now that he'd left Wittenberg and Charlotte in his wake, he felt his old confidence returning. When an overtaking businessman in a big BMW gave him a sidelong appraisal, Marcus smiled back and flounced his dark curls. *All right,* he thought. If he could fool that oaf, why couldn't he waltz through the Potsdam security checks just as easily, get off his shot, and slip away in the bedlam? There was only one area of apprehension—or perhaps concern would be a more accurate word. And that was the Cossack. Would he be at the Cecilien-hof, seeking the revenge with which Marcus had so carefully enticed him? And if he was, would he be able to spot Marcus in disguise? But that was the game, after all. And Marcus had already given Taras all the hints he could.

Wedged into the tiny car and tucked behind a poultry truck that was steadily molting feathers in his direction, Marcus schooled himself to relax, not to keep thinking ahead. He chuckled as he recalled a Trabi joke: *Question: Why is the Trabant the quietest car to drive? Answer: Because your knees cover your ears.* A little later, just past the turnoff to

Niemegk, the morning mist finally boiled off and allowed slanting sunlight to gild the summer fields. A fine day, Marcus thought, and wished for his old vagabond harmonica.

On the outskirts of Wittenberg, Taras slowed to ask a pigtailed girl on a bicycle the directions to the Goldener Adler. She smiled and pointed over her shoulder.

"You see down there, the entrance to Lutherstadt, that is the Schlosskirche. You turn left just there, then you go one long block straight down Schloss-strasse and there is your hotel, right on the Marktplatz."

It was just past nine o'clock, but Lutherstadt's cobblestone streets and sidewalks were surprisingly empty of traffic as Taras pulled to the curb by the market square. He jumped out and began loping along the sidewalk, looking for the Adler. Then he saw the small marquee ahead with HOTEL in black Gothic letters. A motorcycle was parked outside. Taras suppressed the urge to sprint, slowed to a walk.

Careful now.

Inside the small, dark lobby a family with several children was blockading the hotel desk, the father haranguing the elderly woman clerk, who was nodding her head but maintaining a steely glint in her eye. Taras shoved between them, ignored their sputtering Teutonic protests as he showed his credentials, and then the photos of Charlotte and Marcus.

The clerk's eyes narrowed further and her mouth tightened as her glance shifted from the pictures to the credentials and back to Taras. Finally she nodded, only once but emphatically, and gestured at the ceiling.

"Ja, Zimmer sieben."

They are both in?

"Ja, ja."

Chalky light filtered down the gloomy stairwell from a stained glass window on the landing above. Warped wooden treads groaned underfoot as he climbed, so Taras hugged the railing, placing his feet carefully along the edges. At the end of a narrow corridor on the first floor he found a black enameled door with a brass seven, slashed in the continental manner. *Zimmer sieben.*

Taras stood with his ear against this door, gun in hand. But the only sounds were stage whispers drifting up the stairwell from the lobby. Taras tried to imagine some acceptable condition under which Charlotte would still be inside with the Potsdam Conference due to start in less than forty-five minutes. He drew a blank. But he had to go in. If he waited out here any longer, a squad of GSG-9 commandos would show up with explosive charges, stun grenades, and H&K submachine guns. And this was not their show, but his.

He braced his arms on the balustrade behind, leaned back, cocked his right leg, kicked out explosively, aiming the sole of his shoe just above the door handle.

The door caved in, but only slightly. The latch was still caught in the splintered frame. So Taras flung himself forward, impacting with shoulder and hip and caroming inside, pointing and swinging his .45.

The room was empty except for Charlie.

And she was gone too. Leaving her body behind, naked, ankles tied to the bed.

Black rage exploded inside Taras. He stumbled away, smashed open the bathroom door, ready to empty his clip into anything that moved, preferably Marcus Jolly.

A leather-jacketed boy with spiked blond hair was lying dead in the bathtub, one arm draped over the side. A miniature Iron Cross dangled from one pierced pink ear. There was a fecal stench. Something clicked in Taras's memory: *The kid who'd faxed Charlie's column from the post office in Dessau. His motorcycle downstairs.*

But Marcus was gone.

Taras backed out, felt his knees buckle, sat down on the carpet, back propped against the bed. After a second or two he sucked air deep into his lungs and forced himself to look behind him. He avoided her eyes, saw the tape burns on her wrists and around her lips. His darling had been gagged and bound hand and foot. Then, with trembling fingers, he reached out and lowered her eyelids over the congealed horror of her last seconds.

He began to sob. He thought of the first time he had seen Charlie on the terrace at that party in Chevy Chase, of the time they had hiked out to her special place overlooking that woodsy Virginia valley and, instead of sharing poetic thoughts, had stripped and coupled like frenzied teenagers. He lay his cheek now against her arm, allowing himself to be cruelly deceived for an instant by her skin's residual warmth and plasticity. On another nightmare morning, Eva Sorokina had been far colder—but no more dead than Charlotte was now.

He held her lifeless hand in his.

Why did you go with him? Why didn't you wait for me to come back to you? You know I loved you, Charlie, I loved only you.

Realizing his grief could totally incapacitate him, Taras stood up and flung it away, embracing his rage. In two strides he reached the dresser, grabbed up a chair, and smashed it to kindling on the carpet. He looked around for something else to destroy and saw the desk clerk standing in the splintered doorway, holding a corner of her apron over her mouth, her eyes enormous.

"Polizei!" Taras yelled at her. "Go call the police." He motioned her violently away, and she went, stomping down the stairs in a panic. Now his gaze swept the room and fastened on the old armoire. He threw it open, pulled an extra blanket out, and draped Charlotte's corpse.

Then he stared down at the jars, vials, tubes, and makeup-smudged tissues spread over the dresser top. He remembered the tidy elegance of Charlie's taffeta-skirted vanity in the Cleveland Park condo. She hadn't left this litter. He scoured the dresser and armoire and even under the bed for her emergency wig. It was gone. So was her handbag—and with it, he knew, her press credentials.

The fucking twisted bastard was going to Potsdam in drag. To kill Rybkin.

Then Taras realized he had *seen* Marcus in drag—no more than fifteen minutes before—in Coswig, driving a mustard-colored Trabant and wearing Charlie's wig.

If he alerted Strotkamp immediately, they might still catch Marcus at the gate to the *Neue Garten,* or even on the Autobahn. But so what? Why should Taras do that? In order to save the life of Alois Rybkin? Or to preserve international stability?

At this moment Taras cared about only one thing. *He* wanted to be Marcus's executioner, exactly what he had told President Ackerman he did not want.

I just changed my mind.

When the desk clerk saw Taras hurrying downstairs she quickly hung up the telephone, eyeing him warily. But he ignored her, glancing into the restaurant where a TV showed a man with a microphone, fronting the Cecilienhof Palace.

Taras checked his watch. Nine-fifteen. The presidential motorcades wouldn't be showing up for another thirty minutes. There was still time.

He hurried outside and turned left, then froze. His car was gone. In fact, the street was empty of cars. He turned the other way, saw his little Ford just vanishing into an alley, upended behind a tow truck.

"Parken verboten!" explained a cheerful old man standing nearby. He waggled his cane helpfully at a large no-parking sign.

"Danke." Christ! Hell of a law-abiding hamlet they had here. Tow an illegally parked car after fifteen minutes, but let a murderer walk away. So why was the big motorcycle left alone?

Taras looked at the cycle a split-second longer—a big Yamaha sport-bike with red and white fairing—then dashed back into the Adler. Within a minute he had returned with a set of keys filched from the corpse in the bathtub. The second key he tried fit the ignition.

As a local police car pulled to the curb a moment later in response to the desk clerk's terrified summons, the crescendoing whine of the Yamaha's engine was still reverberating around the market square, but Taras was already out of sight.

"Guten Morgen, Fräulein."

The guard at the gate of Potsdam's *Neue Garten* smiled as he glanced at Charlotte's perimeter credential and waved the Trabant through. Marcus smiled back in genuine relief, and joined a slow-moving serpentine of cars and vans on a narrow asphalt road that wound through overhanging lindens and oaks to a large parking area.

Leaving their vehicles, the arriving journalists were herded by uniformed guards with walkie-talkies along several parallel paths toward a perimeter fence of crowd-control barriers, then funneled into a half-dozen queues to pick up their press handouts and have their credentials checked again before they passed through metal detectors. Marcus gave no more thought to his disguise, made no attempt to feminize his walk or mannerisms. Rather, he convinced himself—temporarily, as an actor—that he was simply what he seemed to be, a reporter, who happened to be a woman, on her way to cover a major event. If that subtly affected the way he walked and carried himself, so be it.

As a result, he was able to stroll through the security checkpoint and collect his camera at the end of the belted metal detector with hardly a quickening of his pulse. Next he found himself on a crowded footpath trailing a half-dozen voluble Middle Easterners, all of whom seemed to be feasting on Egg McMuffins from a big plastic sack. One fellow, catching sight of Marcus, made a gallant bow and offered him a Styrofoam container.

Marcus was grateful, having been running on adrenaline since yesterday's lunch. "I'm perfectly ravenous, thank you so much," he answered, surprising himself as he heard the tenor lilt that had replaced his customary baritone. But there was nothing remotely ladylike in the way he wolfed down the little breakfast sandwich.

The parkland now opened on the long, sweeping palace front, which was obviously modeled after a steep-gabled English manor house. But the idyllic setting was under full-scale media siege this morning, ringed with monster media trucks, smaller vans with hydraulic microwave masts, throbbing generator units, cables snaking across grass and blacktop toward the Tudor edifice. Federal police guards slung with submachine guns roamed everywhere, bolstered by sidearmed officers from several local jurisdictions and blue-blazered event security personnel—all talking into handheld radios. The police bandwidths must be nearly gridlocked, Marcus thought as he kept scanning the crowd. He was looking for plainclothesmen, KGB or GSG-9 types, blank-faced, shrewd-eyed men with no apparent function. These, he knew, would constitute his greatest danger.

Despite his private errand, Marcus was not immune to the contagion in the air, the media-induced euphoria of a headline political event. Camera crews were unlatching their custom aluminum cases, testing battery packs, fitting gargantuan tripod-mounted telescopic lenses to little camera bodies. A dark-suited Japanese network commentator, doing a sober standup against a tree trunk with the palace over his shoulder, had a horse chestnut bounce off his head, cracking up his crew and finally himself. Marcus hoped it was going out live.

Still, he thought, none of them could anticipate the morning's real shattering story. Not much more than an hour away now, if all went well.

It was 8:45, nearing the cutoff time for those journalists and invited guests with interior passes to present themselves. Marcus joined another queue, two or three people wide and twenty or thirty meters long, stretching from a projecting, half-timbered porte cochere to an arched gateway leading to the palace courtyard. Ahead of him in line he recognized several European television personalities chatting animatedly with colleagues. No one gave him a second glance. If any suspected his gender, perhaps they simply assumed him to be an accredited member of the transvestite press—and no doubt there was such an eccentric entity, Marcus thought.

They shuffled steadily forward, under a Tudor archway and around a courtyard whose centerpiece was a five-pointed red floral star planted on the grass. The square garden was enclosed by more half-timbered gables, ivy-draped walls, and little mullioned windows. At the opposite end they were ushered into an antechamber, where credentials were again scrutinized and handbags inspected.

They moved next double file along a hallway beside photographs and documentary exhibits from the original 1945 conference. Stalin was pictured in his tailored generalissimo's tunic with epaulets; the other leaders—Truman, Churchill, and Attlee—wore business suits. *Only one came dressed for battle,* Marcus thought wryly.

A left turn fetched them into the White Hall, a salon perhaps thirty meters long, whose only color contrasts were red Oriental carpets and the giltwork on the Louis something-or-other tables, settees, and armchairs. Here they were cordoned off and packed in like sardines five or six deep against the French windows, which opened onto a small garden terrace. As a television camera and lights were brought in and set up across the ropes, a white-haired spokesman in a gray morning coat walked the length of the hall to a podium, where he huffed into a microphone. He then proceeded to greet them in four languages, apologize for the crowded conditions, and go over the morning's agenda.

At about ten o'clock, he said, Presidents Ackerman and Rybkin and the European heads of state would all be coming through to this very podium, where brief opening remarks would be made. In the meantime, the spokesman suggested, they might wish to avail themselves of the coffee and rolls now available on the terrace. They need only turn and file out in an orderly fashion through the French doors.

Marcus decided to take advantage of the ensuing stampede to improve his position. It was essential that he gradually work himself into the front row along the ropes, for the best possible "photo opportunity" when Rybkin passed. With insistent elbows and lightly murmured apologies, he insinuated himself through the outbound tide toward the refreshments and quickly gained the red velvet ropes.

From here he could survey the entire salon. He picked out several plainclothes security types, but so far Taras Arensky wasn't among them. Marcus did note with satisfaction that many invited guests had brought their own cameras for the occasion. His single click would hardly be noticed.

He was in position, with a half hour to kill.

Chapter

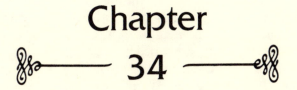 34

Just beyond Niemegk, for some diabolical reason, the two northbound lanes of the E6 Autobahn slowed, then ground to a complete stop. Taras, clamping the front calipers to brake the big Yamaha, saw flashing red and blue lights up ahead. It could be an accident, or maybe traffic was being temporarily halted for some security reason connected with the conference, or for the convenience of an official motorcade.

He could squeeze through on the Yamaha—if no doors were opened in his face. But what would that buy him? Instead, he swerved left off the highway, plowed through the grassy median, emerged onto the southbound lanes, and charged back to the off ramp he'd just passed.

Taras hadn't ridden a motorcycle in years, and then it had been only occasionally, on streetbikes. This speed-sculpted Yamaha was hard-saddled, its footpegs were too high, handlebars too low and too far forward, giving him the feeling his nose was on the gas tank. But it went like a bat out of hell, turning him into a projectile fleeing a nightmare and targeting on vengeance.

Five minutes later he was off the snarled Autobahn and roaring up alternate Route 2, through a succession of bleak postwar Gothic villages—Treuenbrietzen, Buchholz, Beelitz—the sort of somniferous places that had been seriously depopulated during the westward exodus of '89 and '90, but which were now slowly being reconstituted.

Now, if only someone would repave the old GDR roadbeds.

The Yamaha's suspension soaked up some of the minor jolts, but some stretches—where the asphalting wore thin or vanished altogether over bare brick or cobblestones—nearly bounced Taras out of the saddle. Still, he kept pushing as hard as he dared, laying it over on curves, winding it out on straightaways, accelerating through intersections, occasionally scattering pedestrians and bicyclists. He dashed over a railroad crossing an instant before the barrier came down. Approaching Buchholz, a tiny Wartburg sedan pulled out of a farm road, towing a sheep in a two-wheel wood-lathe cart. Taras swerved, nearly lost the bike in a slide, then straightened it out with horsepower. Near Beelitz he flashed past a roadside sign that wished him a GUTE FAHRT.

After fifteen minutes of tearing a hole in the wind with his unshielded face, he suddenly realized the green blur streaming by was the Potsdam Forest. Route 2 had turned into the familiar Michendorfer Chaussee. A moment later, off to the left, he caught the first sun flashes on the river Havel. He was damn close. He leaned into another dogleg and came out of it pointing toward the *Lange Brücke,* with the Hotel Potsdam now shouldering starkly over the trees.

At the bridge approach, traffic was backed up. It had to be from the conference, Taras decided, although the Cecilienhof site was clear across the city. Maybe all of Potsdam was gridlocked. If his rental car hadn't been towed, he could have used the mobile cellular phone Strotkamp had provided to radio ahead. As it was, he couldn't wait. He swung right and gunned along the graveled shoulder, then ducked back in to avoid some kids on bicycles. Once across the bridge and into the old Prussian city he split lanes, tailgated a streetcar through a jammed intersection, wove in and out of idling cars, and undoubtedly woke up a few patients in the big district hospital as he blasted past it and turned left onto Neue Garten Strasse.

It was backed up all the way to the royal park. But the oncoming lane was temporarily empty, and Taras used it at high speed, covering several blocks to the brick-walled Neue Garten gateway, where a federal policeman stepped out to greet him with a Heckler & Koch submachine gun. Taras flashed the honorary GSG-9 credentials Bob Strotkamp had provided, and the sentry moved back, opening the barrier as Taras shot through.

Inside along the meandering blacktop, police vans and motorcycles were parked at frequent intervals under the lacy trees. More police could be seen dotting the vast grassy expanses, carrying rifles and walkie-talkies. Three-quarters of the way through the long, narrow park, instead of following the road on to the main vehicle lot, Taras veered into a narrow, hedged lane, then nailed the front brake as three armed men appeared from the bushes.

Again his GSG-9 pass provided open sesame. Speaking into their radios, the policemen beckoned him through. Taras had to maneuver in low gear between red and white striped iron poles set into the asphalt before twisting the throttle to full snarl. He had gone only a short way before he glimpsed ahead, under the graceful canopy of oaks and lindens, the long, half-timbered façade of the Cecilienhof, perhaps three hundred meters away.

This gently curving lane, in fact, was aimed ultimately at the archway into the palace's main courtyard. That would make a dramatic entrance, Taras thought. Of course he'd probably be shot off his saddle if he tried it without benefit of credential check. In fact, as the palace front loomed closer, he saw a line of limousines already drawn up, with fender flags and swarming security personnel. The arrival ceremonies must already be under way. It could all be over in seconds—with Marcus fleeing in his disguise, or lying dead by another hand.

Emerging out of the lane, Taras skidded the big bike left beside an iron railing, jumped off, and hurried ahead on foot. As desperate as he was, he didn't dare sprint flat out for fear of activating the trigger finger of some overzealous policeman. He also decided to avoid the media and security-clogged courtyard and headed left instead to the hotel entrance under the porte cochere, where a half-dozen uniformed and plainclothes cops immediately converged on him.

In the White Salon, prolonged anticipation gave way to sudden, surging excitement as the first spirited notes of a military brass band filtered down the corridor from the courtyard. A moment later came the rippling applause and crowd murmurs generated by an approaching entourage. Marcus found himself pressed suddenly forward, and actually had to brace himself to keep from being shoved over the restraining ropes. An angry glance over his shoulder showed him the futility of protest; the throng behind had nearly doubled, jamming in from the garden through the open French doors. Marcus faced forward again, planting his feet as firmly as possible on the polished parquet and craning his neck along the packed gallery toward the corridor entrance.

According to the agenda printed on the media handout, the hosting German delegation would enter first, followed by the Soviet and American leaders side by side, then the other European statesmen, also paired off as diplomatically as possible.

An Adidas-shod, blue-jeaned technician passed by Marcus's position, mumbling into his headset; an instant later the long white-on-white salon was bathed by several 10K lights on tall stands and a quartz-halogen lamp mounted on the TV camera being used for pool coverage. Around Marcus many people now raised their own cameras. And in the throng behind him, more cameras were brandished aloft and angled hopefully downward over the sea of heads.

Outside the doorway the tumult crescendoed. The first person through was another cameraman, backing in and quickly out of the way. Then the first of several dark-suited bodyguards appeared, and immediately after came the German Chancellor, President, and foreign minister, all beaming broadly and directly into the video camera.

Marcus took a deep breath, let it out slowly, then finally raised his own customized camera. Rybkin and Ackerman would be next.

On the other side of the courtyard from the White Salon, in the palace wing normally used as the lobby and offices of the Hotel Schloss Cecilienhof, Taras had lost precious seconds trying to get past three large, stone-faced members of the *Bundesgrenzschutz*, all infuriatingly unknown to him despite the many introductions made by Bob Strotkamp in the past few days. When the plainclothesmen were finally persuaded, however, that this wild-eyed, out-of-breath and gesticulating man with the Slavic accent was who he said he was, and that there was a real possibility of a renegade GRU assassin on hand disguised as a reporter, an assassin whom Taras alone could recognize on sight, they agreed to escort him posthaste to the conference hall.

And they moved very fast indeed and provided invaluable interference. Someone thought of a shortcut, and all stormed up the lobby stairs to the next floor, then raced down a long corridor whose windows overlooked the red-starred courtyard. At the end of the corridor they halted before an unmarked door, pounding on it and shouting till it was thrown open. Rapid-fire German ensued between them and a uniformed policeman inside. Then they all swarmed into this small sitting room, past the penetrating gaze of Sir Winston Churchill from an oil portrait, through a connecting door—and found themselves suddenly in the small gallery overlooking the Cecilienhof's conference hall.

More than a dozen red-plush chairs were drawn up around the large baize table, on which microphones, carafes of mineral water, and neatly typed agendas had been carefully set out. But the large two-storied room was currently occupied only by five men on folding chairs watching a small video monitor—two technicians and three uniformed federal policemen. These latter now sprang from their chairs to point their weapons up at the gallery.

Fortunately there was immediate shouted recognition from above and below.

Taras led the charge down the carpeted stairs, ignoring the technicians who tried to hiss everybody to silence. Once down, Taras understood why they were upset at the clatter. The small color monitor showed the German delegation just now entering the adjoining White Salon. The ceremonies were under way, and doubtless being fed live around the world via satellite. Their view into the salon, however, was massively blocked by a wide-bodied TV cameraman wedged into the wainscoted doorway, his thick legs straddling a coiled nest of cables.

The German security men now gave Taras dubious glances, obviously hesitant to shove this indispensable giant aside and interrupt the historic proceedings—and quite possibly get themselves shot in the process by some lightning-reflexed bodyguard—all because of Taras's farfetched story.

But Taras did not intend to be trapped in there, staring stupidly at a monitor as Marcus made his kill next door and vanished in the ensuing melee. He dashed up to the big three-sided bay window facing the garden. It was really a large latticework of many small rectangular panes—one of which, on the bottom row, as Taras had seen from across the room, was now opened out on its hinges. It would be a close fit, but Taras saw no alternative. He dropped to his knees and began squirming through.

There were shouts behind, but at least nobody was shooting at him. A few frantic seconds later, with only minor abrasions, he was safely through and spilling headfirst nearly three meters onto a garden path below.

When he scrambled up, he saw he was one level below the long stone terrace that ran outside the White Salon. He also found himself conspicuously the center of vast attention, having landed unceremoniously in a no-man's land between a mob of roped-off media onlookers that stretched across the back lawn, and those more fortunate invitees whose massed backsides could be seen along the elevated terrace, many now jumping up and down in hopes of a glimpse inside.

In two steps Taras had vaulted onto the stone-flagged terrace—then turned around, attracted by the shouts of a stocky man who was sprinting forward from the cordoned crowd and pulling a gun from his suit jacket.

"Polizei!" Taras shouted back, then burrowed his way into the press of bodies. He continued to batter and shove a passage through the crush of humanity, ignoring all protests and beating off those outraged few who physically attempted to stop him.

By the time he had breached the French windows he was able to see into the room over the massed heads. The German delegation was now positioned against the opposite wall, and all heads swung left as William Ackerman and Alois Rybkin appeared in the far doorway.

As the two moved forward into a barrage of strobe lights, Taras picked out several familiar faces around them—Buck Jones, the bulky Secret Service man, Mike Usher, Volodya Biryukov, Ivo Kuzin, a swarthy Armenian translator whose name he couldn't place. And a blond, vulpine countenance, eyes shifting side to side—Lieutenant Colonel Pavel Starkov, KGB.

Then suddenly, a little way to Taras's left as the procession moved closer, Taras found himself focusing on a dark helmet of luxuriant curls—Charlie's!—and beneath it a white-sweatered, broad-shouldered man-shape leaning well out over the ropes to take a picture.

Marcus!

Taras manhandled the next three people ahead of him, removing one obstinate fellow with a knee in the groin. In the general commotion, the small disturbance Taras was causing seemed not to have caught the eyes of the security people. In any case, Taras had his gun out, as Alois Rybkin moved a little ahead of Ackerman and his own agitated bodyguards, smiling and waving at the crowd, his squat body an unmissable target.

Taras fixed on the glossy wig and began to push toward it, intending to yank Marcus around, stick the gun in his cocky face, wait for the instant of recognition, then smile and blow the bastard away.

But a crowd surge from behind blocked his way, then pushed him sideways. Meanwhile Rybkin and Ackerman had both halted momentarily halfway down the gallery to chat with someone, and now were walking forward again. Taras suddenly realized it was too late now to force his way through the crowd to Marcus. There was only one way he could possibly get the bastard—and, he realized, it would probably cost him his own life.

He decided to pay the price.

He leaped forward onto the back of a kneeling photographer and then dove up and over the ropes, landing heavily and awkwardly on the red carpet in front of the crowd, right between the TV camera and the oncoming Soviet and U.S. leaders.

The next instants tumbled at him in a series of frozen, horrific tableaux:

The astonished faces of Ackerman and Rybkin, their hands flying up like Oswald's had when he'd tried to ward off the bullets from Jack Ruby's revolver . . .

Then Taras's own gun sweeping past the two leaders to target the assassin leaning and pointing the little camera at the Soviet President . . .

"Cowboy!" Taras's voice, bellowing . . .

Marcus spinning around, his eyes suddenly agleam like a cornered animal as he saw Taras—and the leveled .45 automatic that would finally settle all scores between them.

Then someone stepped in front of Marcus, saving his life.

It was Pavel Starkov, his little Makarov pistol looming like a cannon, spitting fire. Taras was punched back and flung sideways like a puppet, hitting the carpet in a sliding heap.

He'd been shot in the neck, he knew, and somewhere high in the chest. He would surely die—but despair engulfed him now for another reason entirely. He'd been stopped, thwarted on the threshold of his vengeance.

Now he stared up at a swimming white ceiling, at silly stucco filigree-work encircling a crystal chandelier. There was a roaring cacophony all around him, echoing high off the white walls, men and women screaming in a babel of languages, stampeding and trampling one another.

"*Gott in Himmel!*"

"Rybkin is shot! My God, he's been shot!"

"*Slava Bogu!*"

Taras fought against a surging tide of pain, clung to consciousness, struggled to comprehend. Rybkin? Who had shot Rybkin? But, of course, Marcus had fired some damn projectile from his camera, probably some variation of the old Bulgarian umbrella poison. Except nobody had seen that. Rybkin must have felt the sting and faltered, and everyone assumed Taras had been the assassin. He'd not only failed to kill the Cowboy; he provided a perfect diversion for his escape.

Marcus would slip away. Game over.

Taras felt hands on him, not helping, but holding him down, making sure he didn't escape. Then his suit jacket was pulled back.

"Shoulder and neck. The bastard may live. Don't let him move. Hey, we need a doctor over here too. The bastard's alive."

The bedlam went on. But Taras tuned it out, closed his eyes, forgot even his hammering pain in the swamping bitterness of having failed.

Then he opened his eyes and saw Marcus.

The Cowboy was smiling down, his masculine features blatantly obvious under the grotesque makeup and elaborate hairpiece. Christ, what was he doing? Then Taras realized his old comrade must have stopped by to gloat before making his escape.

Taras tried to shout Marcus's name, but could produce no sound. Of course. He'd been shot in the throat. It must be gorily obvious, or the Cowboy wouldn't be standing there.

Marcus's victory, then, was complete. The assassin smiling behind his mask—a comic-opera travesty of Taras's last beloved, whom he had slain as he had slain Taras's first beloved. And any second now, having glutted himself on his triumph, Marcus would turn and walk away, leaving Taras bleeding to death and Eva and Charlie unavenged.

In a last ebb of rage, Taras tried to feel for his gun, realized the hand was now empty. Of course, they'd taken it away. But in doing so his thumb had brushed against another and forgotten weapon— the thick steel ring on his forefinger that had once been Marcus's.

One shot. A last chance.

Holding off the advancing tide of numbness, Taras moved his hand slightly, hoping no one would notice, trying to rotate his forefinger so the side of the ring would point upward. He'd have one shot, right into that face. Then someone blocked him. Christ, no! Pavel Starkov again. *He'd kill that bastard too.* But it had to be Marcus. Then Starkov stepped back. Taras shut his eyes, hit by a sharp wave of pain, opened them, praying Marcus would still be there. And he was. Looking down now with an odd expression—almost one of compassion. But Taras didn't care about that. He asked God for guidance and depressed the firing button.

The tiny capsule shot upward.

It missed. Taras saw only that, and, ready now for blackness, closed his eyes.

But an explosive whoosh opened them.

The flame gel had shot high, missing the Cowboy's face but striking and igniting the hairspray-lacquered wig, which promptly erupted into flames.

Marcus let out a high, piercing scream, both hands tearing at his flaming hair, finally ripping the wig off and hurling it away—revealing himself.

"Marcus Jolly!" It was Bob Strotkamp's voice. "Jesus, stop him, somebody."

Taras saw Marcus writhe out of his field of vision, heard him running, still screaming from his burns. Then he heard the thudding sound of bodies falling, chairs toppling. And still the screams went on.

Again Taras lost consciousness. Came around seconds later to find Pavel Starkov and Bob Strotkamp kneeling over him. Starkov was apologizing in Russian, or at least coming very near to an apology.

"I had to shoot, you understand? I could not hesitate. But you did it, Major. We got the *Spetsnaz* bastard. I think you burned half his forehead off. Good work."

"Taras?" Strotkamp was looking at him with a kind of fierce tenderness. "Listen to me. You're going to be all right and so is Rybkin. I'm not bullshitting you, man, you're both going to make it. Now, just hang in there."

Taras blinked in acknowledgment. Maybe he would live, since Strotkamp seemed so damn sure about it. But it didn't seem to matter. He couldn't think of anything particular left to live for.

Still, he thought as he finally yielded himself up to insensibility, he hadn't done too badly there at the end.

He wondered if the Cowboy had appreciated it.

Only a little ways from Taras the security personnel clearing the room herded people around a second body sprawled on the carpet. Marcus Jolly lay back, his chest heaving, his arms pinioned. He had just stopped screaming, clamping his teeth against the agony of his burns and shutting his eyes on the hovering faces of his enemies.

He realized now that he had been vanquished by his old rival, the Cossack. And yet, despite his fierce helmet of pain and the humiliation of that defeat, and the long ignominy to come, the Cowboy felt a strange relief. And after a moment he realized why.

The duel was over.